REBEL

CHERYL SAWYER

BANTAM BOOKS
SYDNEY • AUCKLAND • TORONTO • NEW YORK • LONDON

REBEL
A BANTAM BOOK

First published in Australia and New Zealand in 2000
by Bantam

National Library of Australia
Cataloguing-in-Publication Entry

Sawyer, Cheryl.
  Rebel.
  ISBN 1 86325 221 5.
  I. Title.
A823.3

Transworld Publishers,
a division of Random House Australia Pty Ltd
20 Alfred Street, Milsons Point, Nsw 2061

Random House New Zealand Limited
18 Poland Road, Glenfield, Auckland

Transworld Publishers (UK) Limited
61–63 Uxbridge Road, Ealing, London W5 5SA

Random House Inc
1540 Broadway, New York, New York 10036

Cover illustration by Evert Ploeg
Cover photograph by Eric Manukov
Typset in 10/11 sabon by Midland Typesetters,
Maryborough, Victoria
Printed and bound by Griffin Press, Netley, South Australia

10 9 8 7 6 5 4 3 2 1

To Bert, with love always

ACKNOWLEDGEMENTS

Countless authors have aided me in the research for this novel, and although I name but one I hereby express my gratitude to them all. Stanley J Idzerda's selection and editing of the Marquis de La Fayette's documents and correspondence, published by Cornell University Press, is a prodigious work of scholarship for which we all have compelling reason to be grateful.

Once again I offer heartfelt thanks to my family and friends for their wonderful support. In particular, I shall always be grateful for the advice of the late Cynthia Blanche, dear friend and perceptive critic. French friends unknowingly assisted me with the first scenes of this story: I took the liberty of giving the home of the Chercys the aspect of the beautiful Château de Breteuil (*and* of moving it to the Loire), and I borrowed from the Sainsaulieu family the lovely name of their castle in the Corrèze—my affectionate thanks to Séverine and Henri-François de Breteuil, and to Isabel and Gilles Sainsaulieu.

I would like to pay tribute to Al Hart, Philadelphian man of letters, who was the first to accept the challenge of guiding this book into the world. I thank Pat White in London for her unswerving encouragement. And my deepest thanks go to my publisher, Fiona Henderson, and to Maggie Hamilton and everyone at Transworld for their enthusiasm and professionalism.

CONTENTS

1

THE SUITOR

A young man rode up the avenue to the Château de Mirandol at a gallop, the August sun bouncing off his hair and the sleek haunches of his hunter. On this hot afternoon he and his mount seemed the only creatures moving in the woods and pastures that drowsed along a silver tributary of the Loire, as he shot like an arrow towards the seventeenth-century château standing with grave elegance amongst its formal gardens, ponds and fountains.

The great iron gates stood open, and the rider scarcely slackened speed when the horse's hooves bit into the main drive and sent gravel spinning into the parterres on each side. He was penetrating a classically ordered scene, for no creator of the picturesque had yet tried to wrench Mirandol into line with nature; in all this tranquillity, the only passion for change existed in the pounding heart of the man on horseback and in the mind of the young mistress of the château, who at that moment was walking briskly across the parquet floor of her salon on the upper storey.

Once over the bridge above the empty moat, the rider looked about with impatience but could see no one in the courtyard. He brought the hunter to a clashing stop on the cobbles, scanned the rows of windows above him, and tilted his face higher. All at once he made out a blue dress, and white hands stretched out to turn the latches.

'Viviane!'

His cry reached her as she pulled the wings of the window inwards and stepped out onto the narrow balcony. Her dark curls tumbled about her face as she bent to look at him, and her hands clenched on the railing. 'What is the matter? Is something wrong at Luny?'

'Not in the least! I bring you the best news possible— so tremendous I've been saying it over to myself the whole way.' He grinned up at her as the horse fidgeted, its shoes ringing on the cobbles.

She smiled back in relief. 'Let's hear it then.'

'The Americans have done it! They made up their minds last month and wrote a declaration. They've formed the United States!'

She gave a cry. 'So it was signed by them all? How do you know?'

'La Fayette—someone sent him a copy from London. He says the Congress—'

'Wait! I'm coming down.' She disappeared from the window and next moment was running down the two flights of the main staircase, her gown held high above her ankles. Fortunately the sole person qualified to comment on this lack of deportment was her Great-Aunt Honorine, who happened to be dozing in her chamber in the east wing.

At the foot of the stairs Viviane let her skirts fall and twitched the lace over the tips of her shoulders. She failed to do anything about her tumbled hair, however, which framed glowing cheeks and bright eyes as she paused in the hall.

When the major-domo swept open the grand glass doors, Victor de Luny handed over gloves and whip and strode forward with a hand outstretched to take Viviane's. He bowed over it. 'Mademoiselle de Chercy.'

'Monsieur de Luny,' she said breathlessly. 'An unexpected pleasure. My great-aunt is not able to receive you at the moment. But pray come into the salon.' As usual, she plunged from the formal to the familiar almost immediately. 'Heavens, you rushed here without a hat. What haste!'

'I couldn't wait to tell you.' He put a hand into the breast of his hunting jacket and pulled out two folded sheets of paper. 'I brought La Fayette's letter for you.'

'Thank you. Let's keep it for later.' She put it on an escritoire just inside the doorway, walked into the salon then turned to look at her friend. The light that spilled in at the tall windows brightened the spacious room and showed to advantage his lean, vigorous frame, the responsive sparkle in his deep brown eyes

2

and the healthy colour of his skin, heightened by the breakneck ride from his château to hers.

She said, 'I am so glad you came to me first! Have all thirteen colonies really agreed?'

'Yes. Now they're a nation, the United States of America. You see what it means: an undivided front in the war. If La Fayette joins them now, he knows exactly what he is in for. At last they have a common cause.'

'And who signed? All the great ones we hear of? Benjamin Franklin, Thomas Jefferson?'

'Yes. Jefferson drafted it, then it was a matter for Congress. The wording is remarkable. Wait until you hear it. I already have phrases off by heart!'

She sat down in a gilded chair near the windows and motioned for him to sit opposite. 'This is what they needed. It must have struck fear into the English troops. Now they are on American soil, with no right of occupation. They are invaders, and must expect to be swept into the sea.'

'The sooner the better, but the fight is so unequal.'

She said with energy, 'This declaration makes such a difference! It may not put one more musket in American hands, but it brings a new nation before the world. And who knows what others may decide to support the United States?' There was a pause as she looked out the window, across the narrow terrace towards the sunlit mirror pond. 'France,' she murmured, softly voicing their joint wish.

'It has made La Fayette more determined than ever. He says . . .' Catching sight of Viviane's face as she stared out the window, Victor let the comment fade.

Her mind was not as distant as he thought, however, for with a little laugh she turned to him and suddenly rose. 'It is too splendid a day to moulder indoors. Come for a walk with me.'

Victor opened the doors to the terrace himself since there were no servants by, and they went down three shallow steps onto the gravel. 'Where are all your people?'

She waved her hand: 'Everywhere—my great-aunt

3

and I have chivvied them into tidying up Mirandol for the Usurper. Too late, of course. I could have started days ago if only I'd known.'

'The who?'

She paused by the mirror pond, the great stone basin of water that stretched away to the beginning of the statue walk, and dipped her fingertips in the water. 'At least the gardens look lovely.' She raised her eyes to twin cedars that framed the view of sloping parkland, tree-lined river and broad valley beyond, and saw their dark, spreading branches begin to sway and dip with slow grace. 'There's a breeze coming up; it won't be too hot to walk. Let's go right down to the lake.'

'Very well. What's happening? Are you being invaded?'

Her skirts brushing the grass, she struck off across the lawn towards a path that opened from a chestnut grove on the eastern slope. Victor reflected that if he were anything like La Fayette he would be pestering her to see whether she needed a shawl, or a parasol, or more serviceable shoes; but Viviane had a delightful confidence in her own powers that often made her think so-called gentlemanly behaviour an interference with her rights.

Then she spoke. 'I must make the most of today and tomorrow. They may be my last hours of freedom on earth.'

Victor eyed her cautiously. He was tempted to remind her of some of her advantages: since her father's death she had run Mirandol, and her Great-Aunt Honorine, though strict, was not a gorgon. 'I don't see too many people curtailing your liberty at the moment, Vive!'

She turned to him, her large hazel eyes gleaming, one hand on her narrow waist and her fine shoulders set back a little as though it were himself that she defied. 'My uncle arrives this week—he did not even have the courtesy to specify the day. Not until Friday, I hope, since I only just received the letter. All these months after dear Papa died, he has got round to declaring himself Comte de Mirandol and is coming to snap up the estate.'

'How extraordinary. Now there's a man I thought we should never meet. Even when he was named the heir, somehow I couldn't imagine him actually returning. Anyway, he couldn't at first, could he? He was lying wounded in Canada.'

'Nonsense, he had months to recover. The siege of Quebec was way back at Christmas time. Lord knows what he has been doing since then—calculating the wealth of Mirandol, I suppose, to see if it is worth his while to come back to France.'

They reached the path, rather dusty now in the heat, which wound through the woods to the lake. The cool shade flowed over them, dappling his hunting jacket and her dress with patches of ultramarine and cobalt. For a few moments, as they made their way down, the only sound was that of the woodland birds.

'What exactly do you fear from him?' Victor said.

'The very worst—the end of my freedom. He cared little for my father, so he will care nothing for me. I shall be entirely in the power of a man who has not set foot here for nearly two decades.'

'But if he's come back to do his duty to the family, maybe you will find him a reasonable man, who knows?'

Viviane gave him a wry grimace and he smiled at her affectionately, realising he would hate it if their easy camaraderie, their intense exchanges of ideas, were interrupted. If she had cause to resent her uncle's invasion, he might turn out to have even more.

She said, 'I've a ghastly feeling I know him already: I've started reading his correspondence. It's all in the desk in the library, lovingly kept in order by my father. But there's no love in my uncle's letters. They say a great deal about Canada and Louisiana and his grand theatres of war, but nothing about him. And if he inquires about Mirandol or my parents, there's no warmth; he cannot squeeze out one intimate sentence.'

'It's true he is bound to be as different as possible from your father, but gentlemen like him are so rare. I have never known anyone more amiable. As for your uncle, I think you should see him before you make up

5

your mind. But if he is a veritable ogre, I'll do everything I can to protect you from him. I promise.'

She gave a grateful smile and put a hand on his sleeve, then brightened as they rounded a bend where low undergrowth spread amongst the tree roots. 'Look, strawberries.' She left the path and stepped across a mossy hollow.

'Watch out for vipers!'

She said over her shoulder, 'Oh, they'll have heard me coming by now.'

'Hefty as you are,' Victor murmured, then grinned at her look of mock outrage when she turned.

She gave him a handful of the tiny berries and they went on down the hill, where the trees grew thicker. Glinting through a birch grove at the bottom was the large duck pond the Chercys insisted on calling a lake.

Viviane was thoughtful. 'Think how we used to haunt these woods when we were small, and all the wild games we played—Indians and soldiers. And somehow we've never ceased to be obsessed about a land we've never seen. I wonder if we are unusual. I wonder if most people lose their dreams and imaginings when they get to eighteen or nineteen?'

'Perhaps, when they have nothing to sustain them. You're right, it is odd how important America is to us. I can't help it, I suppose, with La Fayette breathing fire every time I see him. But you—have you thought it's perhaps your uncle's fault, even though you've never set eyes on him? After all, you were for ever hearing about where he fought. Canada, the Indian wars.'

She shook her head. 'I'm not sure. My parents spoke of him so seldom. No, I think North America is in my blood; it matters to me in ways I can't explain. I remember an awful day, when we heard that the treaty had been signed and France had lost the war. I must have been five years old. We had visitors, a silly old woman and her husband, and after I was presented they kept up a cheerful conversation about a hundred other things and finally I said, very loudly, "How can you bear to smile when we have *lost Canada*?"'

Looking at her, Victor could see her again as a little

girl, with exactly that stricken expression on her face. 'What happened?'

'My mother took me aside and told me very quietly that their son had been killed at Louisburg, back in 1758. I have felt more wretched since, but never in quite that way.'

After a painful pause Victor said, 'And now the Americans have failed at the same attempt. They will never take Canada either.'

She roused herself. 'But they will keep their own country. I *see* them doing it, just as though I were marching with them. How wonderful it would be to go there and take part, to help make it happen. To watch them throw off King George and all his impositions, and found their republic on sovereign territory.'

'Just what La Fayette thinks. He'd take ship tomorrow if he could.'

'So would I! You know, if I could close my eyes and then open them and find myself in a city of my dreams, I'd be more thrilled to be in Philadelphia than Paris.'

They reached the edge of the lake, on the far side of which ducks and moorhens busied themselves amongst reeds and overarching willows.

Viviane scattered her handful of strawberry stalks and leaves on the water under the grassy bank where they stood, her forearms and the delicate skin of her throat and shoulders gleaming pale in the sunlight. 'I wish we were there right now.'

Victor, who had been observing her with admiration, said, 'Shouldn't you be afraid, with the English prowling about Pennsylvania?'

'Oh, not if we were together!' She looked at him and a faint blush appeared along her fine cheekbones. 'That is, of course I would much rather you had a handy regiment with you as well. Can your precious Marquis de La Fayette not contrive such a thing, with all his military connections?'

'And all his nineteen years,' Victor said with a sigh.

She bent to pick up a piece of silver-birch bark that lay at her feet. It had curled in the sun but the silky inner surface which she traced with one finger was still

7

soft and smooth. With a twinkling glance at him she said, 'We should have a ceremony, to mark this momentous day.' Turning, she went up the bank a little way to the trunk of a great tree that towered over the silver birches behind them but had tender young shoots growing at its base. When she came back she showed him a leaf on her palm. 'Linden leaves always make me think of green hearts.'

They always made Victor think of when he and she were children and used to climb trees together, but he just smiled in answer.

She crouched down, stretched out one smooth arm and lowered the piece of bark onto the pond; then, placing the leaf within it, gave the little boat a push so that it floated out into the sunlight.

'I hereby launch the French ship *Brotherly Love*. May she have fair winds to the United States.'

Victor said dubiously, 'What is her cargo?'

'Liberty.' She put a hand on his wrist. 'And this is the moment to let me hear those phrases you have learned. You may recite them now.'

His eyes on the fragile craft drifting before them, Victor said with a mock solemnity that irresistibly deepened to awe, '"We hold these truths to be self-evident: That all men are created equal; That they are endowed by their Creator with certain inalienable Rights; That among these are Life, Liberty and the Pursuit of Happiness; That to secure these Rights, Governments are instituted among Men, deriving their just powers from the consent of the Governed; That whenever any form of Government becomes destructive of these ends, it is the right of the People to alter or abolish it."'

'The consent of the governed,' Viviane murmured. 'All the Revolution is in those words alone.'

An inquisitive mallard left his companions and made a sudden surge across the water to see what they were offering. The glossy neck flexed, the beak darted out and there was a flurry of water where the curl of birch bark had been.

While the drake paddled away in disgust, Victor said

with a chuckle, 'I am sorry to announce, Mademoiselle, that your ship is sinking.'

She took his arm to go back to the path, and looked back over her shoulder at the leaf that bobbed, glistening, in the middle of the lake. 'But Liberty is afloat. And will remain so.'

On Thursday afternoon Viviane was in the hay loft of the stables scanning more of her uncle's letters, which he had sent with odious exactitude three times a year since his departure from France. There was only one missing—a message of condolence on the death of her mother, six years before. She wondered whether perhaps she should give him the benefit of the doubt: he might have written from abroad when he heard the news, his reply might have been lost, or perhaps her father had found the letter too painful to keep. Then she remembered the chilly formality of the condolences she herself had received in the spring, and the curt note he had written to announce his arrival, and her sense of foreboding returned.

She was, after all, about to confront not a true relative but a man who had been adopted by the Chercys as a boy. His upbringing under the gentle regime of her grandparents had been generous, but it had always been understood that eventually he was to make his own way in the world because the title, estate and all the Chercy fortune would pass intact to Robert, her father. Accordingly Jules Rollet de Chercy, choosing a military career, had trained as a cadet and left Mirandol to take up a captaincy in the army immediately after Robert's marriage. That was in 1758: the war against the English had called him to Canada at once and since then he had served overseas without paying a single visit back to those who had nurtured him, given him a noble name and launched him into a life of endeavour.

Viviane had not been frank with Victor when she denied Jules de Chercy's influence on her American dream. On the contrary, when she was little the picture

9

of her fearless uncle battling the English in the wild reaches of the Saint Lawrence and beyond the Appalachian Mountains had had a strong appeal, especially when she learned that his adventures had taken him far away to the Great Lakes and into the fierce company of the Indian warriors who allied themselves with the French. But it was many years now since she had relinquished that colourful image, for there was not a shred of evidence to show that high ideals or emotions inspired any of his actions. The little she knew about him pointed to total pragmatism and a complete lack of feeling, and as she grew out of her romantic notion she guessed with mortification that it would probably be ridiculed by the man himself if ever he knew of it. She had put such foolishness behind her, accepting the truth that Jules de Chercy was a man whose sole loyalty, if he had one at all, must be to his own career. He had clearly cared nothing for his adopted home, and he only came now when the rightful Comte de Mirandol was gone and he thought there was nothing but a young woman standing between him and fortune.

All at once she heard footsteps in the stable. Throwing straw over the letters, she went to the head of the ladder. A tall man stood by the coach doorway beneath, dressed in dark clothes and booted as though he had been riding. She began to descend, wondering how the stablehands could have let this stranger wander about—but they were tidying up the tackroom, according to her instructions.

She greeted him pleasantly as she went down, though he made her nervous. From above and with the light behind him, he looked absolutely black—the hair pulled back tight so that it shone like jet over the temples, the skin tanned, the eyes in shadow. He said not a word as she approached, and her polite smile faded: she might have been wearing her plainest dress and shoes for scrambling around the stables, but she hoped she never looked dowdy enough to be taken for a servant.

'I should be glad to know your name, Monsieur, and your business.'

She was now in the doorway. He turned, and the sunlight in his eyes made them shine a pale green. They looked at her without curiosity.

'My business is with Mademoiselle de Chercy.'

'Then why did you not call at the front entrance?'

'I did: the place was in disarray and so were the servants. I gather your mistress came this way an hour ago.' His voice was dark and severe, like his appearance, and the icy green eyes disturbed her.

'What makes you think she will want to speak to you?'

'She will be obliged to. I am her guardian.'

So there he was, come earlier than she expected to catch her out—and already he had insulted her and her housekeeping and strolled about the place without so much as a by-your-leave.

Before she could speak, he continued, 'You are my ward, I collect. I apologise—you look younger than your age and your appearance is not as I expected.'

She kept her voice steady as she replied at once, 'If you had not ignored this place over the past eighteen years, you would know how well it is run without you. And you would not make the mistake of thinking me a child.'

He smiled slightly. 'I take it you are ready to receive me in the drawing room, then, in due form?' He bowed, put on the hat he had been holding against his thigh, and began to turn away.

'Oh, I assume, Monsieur, that you have already spied in there as you were doing here.'

The half-smile disappeared. 'You forget yourself. I know every inch of this place. If you have a mind to be disagreeable, you must choose your subjects better.'

At this instant challenge, she gave herself no time for reflection. 'There is many a subject I shall be forced to discuss with you, Monsieur, but I have not finished with this one. I can see only one reason why we should happen to meet like this—you are already on a tour of inspection.' His hard profile did not change a whit, so she persevered, 'Are you astonished that I should object to such a beginning?'

The green eyes as they returned to her face were expressionless. 'I repeat, Mademoiselle, I came in search of you. By coincidence, I have found you in the stable yard.' He looked at her blank face and continued after a fractional pause, 'I say coincidence because it was here that I first met your father.'

If he had said the last word with even a hint of emotion it might have made a salutary difference to Viviane, but his cold tone wounded her as much as a direct slight to her father would have done.

There was a tremor in her voice as she replied, 'If you had cared to visit here at any time before April this year, you might have renewed his acquaintance.'

She thought for one bleak moment that he gave a start of displeasure at this, but he was only shifting his weight from one leg to the other, in a movement which revealed nothing more than impatience. 'Sarcasm from you, Mademoiselle, I must say does astonish me. However, I can see you think you have cause for resentment. Part of which I can remove: you need have no concerns about the management of Mirandol now that I am here.'

It was impossible for her not to flare up. '*I* resent managing Mirandol? That is the least of my worries! I have been a perfectly effective manager of our family property ever since ... for the last four months. I'll have you know there is not a neglected patch of ground in the whole estate, nor a single gap in the records.' The injured tone crept back as she forced out the words, 'If you had wished to be of use, Monsieur, you might have come when my father died.'

The deep voice was firm. 'I regret that it was not in my power.'

'Really? It is quite a wonder how nothing seems in your power. You are a high-ranking officer with thousands of men to command, but somehow you have not taken the time to visit France in two decades. You must forgive me for saying that your indifference to the Chercys is much too glaring for me to have any doubt why you come now. You are here to take over Mirandol without a shred of consideration for me or anyone else.'

These words came out very forcefully, for they summed up exactly what she had been thinking about all morning, but his expression merely became more obdurate. She suddenly felt rather ashamed and awkward about having read his letters; and they had given her no real preparation for this meeting, for her accusations dashed against him like water on stone.

He said coldly, 'I owe everything in my life to your grandfather. He taught me to honour this place and those in it. Your father named me your guardian and I shall respect his wish. I have returned to Mirandol to do my duty, and that is all I ask of you, Mademoiselle.'

Then he turned away, obviously expecting her to follow, and she realised her own worst fear was confirmed: her liberty was at an end and she had no right of appeal. He was there to stay and she was not to make a move in future without his sanction.

She walked beside him, out of the stable yard and along the bank of the stream under the avenue of poplars. Looking up at them miserably, she remembered how she and Victor as children used to climb to the slender tops and bend each one so that they could reach the next, and so make their way right down the line of trees without descending to the ground. If she let her uncle bring her to heel now, without a struggle, she would lose for ever the means to resist him. He was legally her guardian and this gave him rights over her home and her resources that he clearly intended to exercise.

Despite his athletic figure, he did not walk swiftly, and his grim silence gave her the chance to think. All at once a crucial section of her father's will stood clear and promising in her mind: the marriage clause. Her portion was untouchable until she reached the age of twenty-one, unless she chose a husband. At whatever age she married, her allowance from the estate ceased, but instead she received the portion of 50,000 livres. There was a dowry in addition, fixed at 20,000 livres. Both were payable in cash from the estate, at once and unconditionally.

On the footbridge she stopped and said in a low,

13

unemotional voice intended to match his own, 'What is my duty, according to you, Monsieur?'

'To accept my concern for your welfare. I have already given it some thought, and I suspect your present existence is unsatisfactory. We must make new arrangements.'

'I am perfectly happy as I am.'

'You are fortunate. I congratulate you.' He leaned on the railing and folded his arms. 'I do not speak of what you are, but of what you do. You associate with the same group of provincials you have known since infancy, you can have no knowledge of the world, and you obviously spend half the day running about the estate like a stableboy in skirts. You are my responsibility, and I have other plans for you.'

'Thank you, I prefer to make my own. Do not worry about your duty—you will be free of me soon enough.' She took a deep breath and said, 'I intend to marry Monsieur Victor de Luny. At once.'

He frowned. 'What is this?'

'He and I have been engaged for ever. Everyone knows we are to be married.'

'Excuse me, I do not know it. Has your hand been solicited?'

'Not as such, not yet. But my father always meant me to marry Monsieur de Luny.'

'Then I shall look to find that wish recorded in his papers, and reserve judgement until then.'

He turned away again but she said to his back: 'He will come tomorrow and demand my hand. We will be married, and you would be ill-advised to oppose it, for his father and everyone else in the district will approve the match. Then I shall have my allowance, and he will have my dowry and you will be relieved of any connection with me whatsoever.'

With that she left him and walked rapidly back to the stables.

Jules de Chercy hesitated only a second at this point before walking on. It was beyond him to go charging

14

after his ward, and it was better to give her time to rethink her outburst before they confronted each other again. He had imagined that sending her a note from Paris to announce his arrival would give her a chance to adjust her ideas, but evidently it had only afforded her the time to catalogue a fine list of resentments against him. She was right on one issue at least: he had never wished to return to France, and still less to Mirandol. The effects of the wounds he received at Christmas had for months made travel impossible, and when he did set sail from the east coast of America, the long journey across the Atlantic had been dismal. Once in Paris, renewing old acquaintances proved an empty affair and he had not particularly enjoyed hanging about the salons answering ill-informed questions about the American war. Then he had had to force himself to leave the capital and set out for the Loire.

Stifling a distinct feeling of dismay at the atrocious beginning he had just made with his ward, he tried to marshal his thoughts in readiness for discussing her with her great-aunt. But at the next fork in the path he came to a halt. One way led past the orangerie to the château, the other to a little knoll crowned by a copse of trees overlooking the family chapel. He felt the pull as though something had hooked itself under a rib and was tugging him uphill. Unable to prevent himself, he set off in that direction, gritting his teeth.

After the hot sun, the liquid shade under the plane trees flowed over him like a benison. The first grave he saw was that of Madame de Chercy, his adoptive mother. She was already frail when he first came to Mirandol at the age of ten, and she had died three years later. When he read the familiar inscription he found that the old man who had opened his heart to him and given him a home was buried alongside his mild, affectionate wife. The dreadful mixture of loss, guilt and remorse that the very name Chercy evoked in his consciousness hit him with a force that even he had not predicted. He took off his hat, bowed his head and said involuntarily, 'I have come back.' He would

15

have said, 'Forgive me,' but for the knowledge, chill around his heart, that no one was listening.

It was foolish to have imagined he could face the other graves in his present state. When he reached his brother's his knees gave way and he sat on the stone coping, shading his eyes. There were no tears, just the sensation of grief building like a tidal wave, on the edge of silence. Eventually he read the inscription, and with a forefinger slowly traced the name *Robert* in the warm stone. He could not ask forgiveness here: his brother had had a heart too wide to even consider the need for it.

He stood up and took a step towards where Violette de Chercy lay, then half closed his eyes as he made out the words on the headstone, turned away and put one hand against the smooth trunk of a tree. He felt as though she were hovering behind his shoulder, her soft mouth half smiling, her blue eyes misted with the secrets she had kept from him so long and now held locked with her in the earth. The stillness under the trees was somehow expectant, but not a word or a gesture of his could unravel what had happened between them. Instead a knell beat in his brain: *too late*. It had always been too late.

As he walked away down the hill, he stumbled for the first time. It would have been wiser to have a cane, a groom's shoulder, anything to aid him as he made his way back to the château. He had come on horseback over the last stage from Paris, thinking it might hurt less than the jolting of the carriage. Impossible to tell: the talons that tore through his muscles at every step had been at their work all day, and he could not imagine this blind and breathless exhaustion being any worse. God grant that he would meet none of the old retainers on the way back. It was hard enough to speak, let alone stand about reminiscing for hours: that would have to wait until tomorrow.

When he entered through the tall front doors of the château, Honorine de Chercy came at once from the principal drawing room to greet him. She had been upstairs when he arrived, and he had given instructions

16

for her not to be disturbed. Now she looked alert and eager to see him. The expression of interest and concern on her fine-boned face as he walked towards her brought memory flooding back. She had been in her late thirties when he last saw her—the handsome wife of the old Comte de Mirandol's unreliable younger brother, who had died, not heartily lamented by anyone except perhaps Honorine, when Jules was in Louisiana.

'Monsieur le Comte, welcome home.'

'Unless you call me Jules, Aunt, it can never seem like home.'

She put her hands on his shoulders and he could feel them shaking. Unaware of the shock his appearance gave her, he put this weakness down to age or infirmity. She drew his head down to hers and kissed him on both cheeks. He felt moisture on hers and was momentarily moved. How odd: they were neither related by blood, nor Chercys by birth, but invisible ties united them again in understanding, despite nearly two decades of separation.

'The journey has wearied you. I have a favour to beg: that before you take possession of Mirandol, you allow your niece and myself to play hostess for a day or two while you settle in.' Her grey eyes, which could grow flinty when she was severe, regarded him anxiously.

'With pleasure,' he said. 'Banish that phrase "take possession". My niece has it firmly in her head that I am about to ride roughshod over you all. Has she told you she met me only to quarrel on the most absurd grounds? You and I must talk. Tomorrow, if not tonight.'

'By all means. But now you will rest, I insist. Your room is ready, and your valet has been fidgeting about for an hour, predicting dire consequences from your wandering about the estate alone. He is city bred to the silliest degree: I had enormous difficulty persuading him you had not fallen down a well or been kicked unconscious by an enraged barnyard animal.'

He grinned and she smiled for the first time and led him to the foot of the staircase with one hand on his

17

wrist. He could see servants hovering in the main salon and, beyond them, near the tall windows that looked out over the mirror pond, was the figure of his headstrong and recalcitrant ward. But he was past caring about anything except the thought of lying down.

Honorine had regained the composure he remembered. She said briskly, 'There is no need to come down before supper. We eat at nine, country style. And pray do not let Mademoiselle de Chercy's attitude disturb you. She is an animated young woman, and is at her most biddable when one suffers her to talk. Only engage her mind, Nephew, and you will find her spirit less rebellious than you suppose.'

Viviane had left the house and was waiting in a copse of trees where the Mirandol land met that of Luny. Her bay mare cropped the grass at the edge of the clearing while she paced up and down waiting for Victor. She had sent a quick note by one of the grooms, in which she reported the altercation with her uncle, and the solution that had sprung so felicitously to her mind. She was confident that Victor would come, because she had insisted the groom wait for an assurance before returning, but she was not so confident about the phrasing of her note, for the words had poured out too fast. She reminded him that they had always known she would one day leave Mirandol and join him at Luny, so why should it not be now? She had no one to turn to but him; they had always helped each other, he was her best friend. She reassured him that she would not come to him empty-handed: her dowry was considerable, and to verify this he had only to ask his father, for he would have often discussed it with her own.

It was true that for years there had been a general expectation that she and Victor would get married, but oddly enough that very certainty meant that they had never actually discussed it themselves. Viviane walked about the clearing trying to stifle the embarrassment and unease she had felt ever since sending the note. It was unorthodox and indecorous to have written to him at all, of course, but Victor was used to her ways, and valued frankness as much as she did. With such a crisis upon her, this was no time to worry over breaking conventions. It was not so much the sending of the letter that bothered her, it was how Victor's face would look when he arrived at the secret meeting place. She felt a blush spread across her own cheeks at the thought.

When he did ride up, Victor spoke before she could utter a word, and such was their awkwardness that he could scarcely summon a friendly smile. 'My word, Vive, you've landed us in some pickles in the past, but this beats all!'

'What do you mean?' she said quickly as he dismounted.

'To send me such a letter! Both my parents were in the salon when it was brought in, but like a fool I opened it at once—the first few words gave me such a shock it must have been written all over my face. I had to leave the room to read the rest. And there was no hope of concealing who had sent it either, with your groom panting in the courtyard for an instant reply.'

Viviane watched him as he tethered his hunter to a sapling, and wondered whether he was avoiding her eye on purpose. She took a breath. 'Of course I know it was wrong for me to correspond with you, but this is an emergency, Toto. And I shan't do so again until we are betrothed.' For some reason it was hard for her to pronounce the last word, and she hurried on, 'And then it will be perfectly proper.'

Victor faced her again. The effort to command his own feelings and respond sympathetically to hers somehow gave his classic features a new dignity and strength. She was grateful that he managed to keep any reproach out of his voice as he replied, 'You do take things at speed, you know. If you're convinced this is an emergency, I'm afraid quarrelling with your uncle may have made it worse. He's not just a Chercy, he's the hero of Ticonderoga. The whole neighbourhood has been talking about him for months and everyone is itching to pay their respects. It's unthinkable for me

19

to barge into Mirandol and ask for your hand the very day he arrives.'

'Of course I shall secure a proper invitation for you.'

'I'm sorry, I can't turn up on your summons alone; it would set everyone against us from the start. And as for demanding your hand, may I beg you to think of it from my point of view for a moment? Imagine my father's fury if I did so without first consulting him. It is hard enough getting anything at all out of him lately—you know I have been asking to stay with La Fayette in Paris, and he's been as grudging as possible over it.'

'I do understand. I know that you have parents to please. And I have a guardian whom I shall *dis*please, whatever I do. Believe me, if I thought that my enduring him would improve his temper or his designs, I could smile and be tolerant, but I am sure he is a hopeless case. Tyranny is all I can look for in the future.' She tried to give this last sentence a humorous, ironical tone, but Victor did not smile.

After another pause she said quietly, 'I must hope that you can find a way to speak to my uncle directly. Unless you . . . don't care to.' Her voice caught a little, and she looked away into the trees.

Victor responded at once. 'Lord, of course I care about you. I'm your friend, I won't desert you. I'm not trying to find excuses, I just think we should go about this the right way.'

'So you will speak to my guardian?' A smile spread over her face and she felt like flinging her arms around his neck in gratitude. He had never looked so handsome to her as he did at that moment.

'If that's what you really want, yes, I'm equal to declaring I want to be engaged to you, but there is no need to rush things. Your guardian is committing no crime. You think of him as an intruder, but he has a right to be at Mirandol. He is your father's heir. If he is a brute into the bargain, of course I'll rescue you from him however you think best.'

'Very well, when do you think your father will call on my uncle? Can you encourage him to do so tomorrow?'

20

'I'll try. That will give me the excuse for a formal visit, and then I can broach the subject in the proper way. If your uncle is the villain you say, we do not want to look fools in front of him. Be brave and trust me.' He took her hand, as he had often done before in friendship, but this time a sudden sense that she needed a man's help, and that he had done a good deed in supplying it, made him carry it to his lips.

Viviane withdrew her hand and stood looking at him tenderly. 'I knew I could depend on you, Toto. I thank you from my heart.' They gazed at each other with a solemnity they had never felt before, but Viviane stepped back as though to shake off the mood and said, 'I'm afraid I must go. Great-Aunt Honorine will expect me to play the hostess to my guardian, and I cannot let her down.'

'I'll see you soon, then.'

'Yes. I do *hope* it will be tomorrow.'

THE CHERCYS OF MIRANDOL

Honorine de Chercy went up to her bedchamber after the conversation with Jules, and sat down at a writing desk under a window that looked out over the informal English garden at one side of the château. She was fond of this room, which she had used in the past, both before and since the demise of Aristide de Chercy, her second husband. After the death of Viviane's father she had installed herself in it for a visit—her sympathy had gone out to her grand-niece and she was prepared to put off her return to Paris for as long as she was needed. Now that Jules had returned, in theory she was free to go home, but Honorine shook her head as she sat looking out on the sunny garden, and wondered how peace and comfort could possibly come to Mirandol while Jules was in this state. She was upset by how much he appeared to have suffered—from his long illness and the rough voyage over sea and land that had brought him to this empty homecoming.

Honorine saw a strong contrast between Jules at thirty-six and the young man she had first met at Mirandol. When she married Aristide de Chercy, the brother of the then Comte de Mirandol, Jules and Robert were students. She grew to know them both in her visits to the country and in Paris, where Robert studied law and Jules had a cadetship at the royal military college.

She often thought that, as to learning, the two boys should have had the opposite pursuits: Robert was sunny, open-hearted and gregarious, could never apply himself to scholarship, and was ideally fitted to be the well-loved country gentleman he eventually became; but Jules was clever. It was a standing joke between them that when in doubt Robert always applied to Jules to decipher his lessons, and even on occasion to write parts of his essays. But they existed in perfect harmony which extended to all their activities, including the scrapes they got into in the country and in town, most of them inspired by Jules. Robert's eyes were often full of laughter and Jules's of mischief.

Looking back, Honorine felt that the happiest days at Mirandol were bright indeed. The last time she had seen the brothers together was at Christmas, eighteen years before, when the château had received the woman who was to become Madame Robert de Chercy. She came as a guest while Robert was away completing his law studies and Jules was finishing his cadetship. The Chercys always enjoyed having company at Mirandol and the district depended on them for the best dances, dinner and supper parties of the year. So the house was full of guests when Mademoiselle Violette d'Ollangier arrived.

One afternoon was enough to establish her as the most beautiful, accomplished and fascinating lady present, and as she went the rounds of the neighbours she charmed everyone. The Chercys were essentially rural people, while Mademoiselle d'Ollangier came straight from Paris, and Honorine had had a private idea that her visit had been timed so that she could assess the kind of existence she would lead in marriage to Robert. What she saw obviously pleased her: the family possessed considerably more fortune than her own, she stood to become Comtesse de Mirandol in time, and the life she would lead was inviting—the Chercys entertained lavishly, and the other families in the region contained many young people as lively and well bred as any Parisian demoiselle could desire.

Then, with three weeks to go before Robert's arrival, Jules obtained early leave from college and came home. There he met Mademoiselle d'Ollangier for the first time. The moment Honorine saw them together she was struck by their likeness to each other: they were both dark, intense, dedicated to the active life. With his brother absent, Jules seemed to think it his duty to entertain her. If Mademoiselle d'Ollangier considered she had already tasted all the rustic pleasures, he soon opened her eyes to more. They became inseparable. He took her riding, they visited new acquaintances together, and if they were at home they laughed over cards or games and indulged their joint passion for music, she playing while he sang. It seemed to Honorine that they were in love before they knew it, almost from the instant they met. She saw this with concern for them both, but said nothing to anyone: her own husband was never an easy man to confide in, and the count was too preoccupied with a houseful of guests to take note of who spent time with whom. Honorine was not on intimate terms with him, and since there was no wife to consult, for the count had been a widower for some years, it was not her place to speak.

The two young people could not stay away from each other. The lady's sentiments were hard to gauge, for she had a sparkling, seductive manner which concealed her thoughts, but Jules was clearly under a spell which he had no power to break. It made him blind—not to the notice of others, for as the days went by he tried to moderate his behaviour towards Violette in public—but to the inevitable arrival of Robert, when the lady would be obliged to confront a painful choice.

Honorine pitied and censured them, but she did so only in her heart, still finding no opportunity to express her misgivings. She hoped that others closer to the count would perceive the danger and warn him of it, but although there was a certain amount of gossip as time wore on, the gay atmosphere of Mirandol remained unchanged.

Robert duly returned. What had happened between Jules and the object of his passion before his arrival, Honorine did not know. She could not even tell whether they had seriously tried to talk things out, but in the first hour she noted a change in Jules. Perhaps his own conduct smote him, or perhaps the lady gave him sudden cause for pain; at any rate she could see he was miserable. Violette's manners were almost a pattern of what had gone before, except for a new brittleness in her conversation. She continued to shine, captivating with others, playful with Jules, and tender with Robert, who seemed unconscious of anything that might endanger his happiness. Except that at times he was quieter and more contemplative than before.

Honorine could feel a storm brewing, and it made her sick with apprehension. The only one who seemed to share her anxiety was Jules, who by this time did not know what to do with himself. He sometimes stayed away a full twenty-four hours from the château, but next day he would be back, hungry to know whether the lady had chafed under this separation as much as he.

On Christmas Eve the climax came. The Chercys indulged in all the old traditions of the season, and instead of there being a service in the chapel, the whole party rode to midnight mass in nearby Longfer, over a smooth frosting of snow. Mademoiselle d'Ollangier accompanied her fiancé in the beautiful sleigh which was Jules's present to them both, speeding to the church where in a few more days their wedding would be celebrated.

On their return everyone gathered around the fire in the great salon for the exchange of gifts. It was an hour of bustle, talk and laughter, and only Honorine seemed to notice that Jules stood aloof, in torment because since the church service Mademoiselle d'Ollangier had not addressed him by word or look.

Robert's gift to the lady was a ring—a very beautiful sapphire the colour of her eyes—which was a family heirloom. It was the custom for the future Comte de Mirandol to bestow this ring on the lady of his choice before their wedding. Whether Violette knew its significance or not, there was a deep consciousness in her expression as she allowed him to slip it on her finger and offered him her cheek to kiss amidst general congratulations and rejoicing. She did not raise her eyes towards Jules, but Robert glanced his way. Jules stood at the end of the hearth, and at that moment grasped the mantelpiece to steady himself. His sudden pallor was replaced next instant by a deep blush that reached his temples, then he turned and left the room.

The next few days were taken up with joyful preparations for the wedding, and the betrothed couple spent a great deal of time together, uninterrupted by Jules, who avoided company and usually appeared only at the evening meal, where he was silent and pre-occupied. Whenever the brothers were together their habitual affection shone forth, but no confidences could be exchanged: one topic, which they seemed to have tacitly agreed never to discuss, set a bar on their intimacy. As far as Honorine could tell, Mademoiselle d'Ollangier held only one conversation alone with Jules after this. It took place in the grounds on a chilly afternoon, and when Violette came indoors with a very uninventive excuse for having taken a stroll alone in the snow, the first and only sign of sadness crossed her fiancé's face.

The wedding day arrived; Jules attended the ceremony and left Mirandol that night. No one realised that he had in fact spent his last sojourn at home, but within a very short time everything was settled. Jules, who seemed only to want to quit France as soon as possible, said goodbye to his adoptive father in Paris. Honorine saw their farewell, which was very affecting, as their love for each other was sincere. Jules took his leave of Robert by letter. They never saw each other again.

When it was time to go downstairs, Honorine's mind was still charged with memory and distress, but she tried hard to rouse herself. It would not do to go down to supper in a melancholy mood: Jules was too exhausted, and Viviane too inexperienced, to ease the conversation into the right channels and ensure that they did not quarrel again. The civilising influence this evening, Honorine thought wryly to herself, would have to be all hers.

As the hour for supper approached, however, there was at least one other person in the house determined to adopt a civilised air. Viviane had decided that she would have the best chance of standing up to her uncle if she dressed and acted the lady. She had her maid arrange her curls so that they no longer looked wild, and she wore a dress which even the most prudish would have to pronounce maidenly. Looking at it in the mirror, she quite approved of it herself: the crisp white lace trim that ran over her shoulders and across the top of the tight straw-coloured bodice set off the translucent glow of her skin. She could never match the military tan of her uncle, but then who would wish to? And he could never equal her in elegance, when she put her mind to it.

She descended the stairs with one hand on the banister rail and the other on her skirts, instead of dashing down in her usual way, and saw with a start that her uncle was waiting severely at the bottom to escort her into the dining room.

She suddenly thought of the way her father used to meet her every evening at the foot of the stairs, and make her a gallant compliment—sometimes for a joke, and always in tenderness. She could not help tears prickling in her eyes at the contrast. But nor could she stay poised on the stairs all evening, so she blinked and walked down and they went in to supper without a syllable spoken.

She had spent a great deal of time with the cook and housekeeper in the afternoon, planning things so he should see how well she managed the kitchen and service, but his comments on the meal were no more than polite. She had decided not to argue with him again until Victor spoke, so she was not at all loquacious. Honorine put up with this uncharacteristic behaviour and filled the silences by asking questions about Paris society; since Jules had just left it, she considered the least he could do was keep her up with the latest gossip. Neither she nor Viviane broached the subject of the war in America or his journey home; Honorine because she felt it would make him even more grim than he already seemed, and Viviane because she was unwilling to show any interest in his concerns.

After supper, however, when they were in the drawing room, she unfroze enough to offer to play the piano for him. This was rather a sacrifice, since she had no heart for music just then, but even she felt that something should be found to fill the frequent silences.

Honorine gave her a grateful smile and she sat down and began a favourite piece of Mozart. Viviane had no idea whether she played at her best; in fact she never knew, because she always became caught up in the music.

When the piece was over Honorine felt it safe to excuse herself and go upstairs: the others seemed to have found a way to be polite, and perhaps if they were left alone together they would reach a better understanding. Both looked slightly taken aback when she abandoned them, but it was for their own good.

Alarmed at being left to entertain her guardian, Viviane could only think of offering to play him another piece. But he thanked her and declined, looking if anything more saturnine than before. So she got up from the pianoforte and sat down opposite him.

He spoke first. 'I have invited your great-aunt to stay on longer at Mirandol and give you the benefit of her advice. She is an ideal chaperone—she has the time and connections to take you into good society, and she will help you with your wardrobe and so on, and accompany you wherever she thinks fit.'

'I have the greatest respect for Great-Aunt Honorine, but she is far too old to advise me on clothes: she wears nothing but dark dresses. I have no desire to go trailing about the country with her, and I am sure she would much rather be in Paris at her old ladies' card parties. She is not my idea of a companion. Our characters do not suit: she is too gloomy.'

He said, 'Nonsense. The worst you can say of her is that she is over fifty-five and a widow. She is an astute and handsome woman, who survived fifteen years of miserable married life without sacrificing her self-respect or her reputation. Her wisdom will be an excellent guide for your youth—nothing educates a woman like an unhappy marriage.'

Viviane's lip curled. What could one think of the mind and heart of a man who could come out with that cynical remark? He seemed determined to make Mirandol her prison, and to turn Great-Aunt Honorine into a gaoler.

'I'm afraid I'm rather weary, Monsieur. You will forgive me if I follow my chaperone upstairs?'

He compressed his lips, quite well aware that she was making her escape, but rose and bowed silently to her as she left the room. As she mounted the stairs, Viviane wondered how long she would have to be lectured to and hemmed in by this intruder at Mirandol. Her only choices for the future were to be a prisoner or a wife. She clenched her hands, willing Victor's parents to pay their visit on the morrow.

Having retired to bed at such a sensible time, Honorine paid for it by lying awake in the early hours of the morning, unable to go to sleep again. The house was very still, and around three o'clock she caught the sound of soft footfalls as they passed her room and descended the stairs. She guessed at once that Viviane too was awake and restless, and thinking it might help to speak to her without Jules by, she took her candle downstairs, where she saw a light in the music room and went in.

It was Jules: she had forgotten how smoothly he always moved. He had come down the stairs like a cat and now stood in the middle of the room, holding a decanter of cognac in one hand and a glass in the other. He smiled ironically, then sat down at a table without a word and poured the cognac. His hand shook and the neck of the vessel clinked loudly against the glass.

Honorine sat down also and ventured the idea of rousing a servant to make some hot chocolate. He shuddered and pushed away the cognac untouched. She could see his face was pale and his skin quivered as though a cool breeze breathed over him. Abruptly she asked what ailed him.

He saw her glance towards the liquor, and said, 'Not that, thank heaven. I dosed myself up on something else. In Canada they kept me on the sick list so long I finally discharged myself. I managed to travel, but at night my body hit back with a vengeance. I had to take laudanum or go mad. Not long ago I decided it was

29

time to leave the stuff alone but I found I couldn't reduce the dose by a single drop: the only way was to throw the whole supply out when I left Paris.' He wiped a hand over his forehead. 'It's still playing hell with me: trying to surface in the mornings is like cutting my way out of a shroud. And at night I take the devil of a time to drop off. Every particle of my being lies there shrieking for one thing.' He looked at her again, his expanded pupils unnaturally dark. 'I don't suppose you—?'

Honorine replied that she never used laudanum, and at once resolved to get rid of all that she had. He gave a short laugh, recognising the lie, and clasped his hands together to stop them trembling.

Honorine said, 'You need an activity to turn your mind aside. Can you not read?'

He shook his head.

Honorine decided he looked too desperate for cards or conversation, and came up with the idea of playing for him. 'But perhaps your love of music has diminished—you showed no desire to listen to your niece tonight.'

He said quietly, 'I can't. Her touch is the same as her mother's.'

Not wanting to stray onto that subject, Honorine moved away, shut the door of the music room, and searched on the shelves by the pianoforte for her favourite pieces. She sat down on the stool and said, 'You cannot spend the rest of your existence fleeing from musical instruments, Nephew. I assure you that I play nothing like Mademoiselle de Chercy. But stop me if I irritate you beyond measure.'

He shifted to the sofa and stretched an arm along the back. 'I've always admired your style, Madame. This will be a pleasure.'

Honorine played for an hour, the notes falling very clearly into the still night. He submitted to it all without demur, and under the influence of the music Honorine too began to feel more at peace.

When she finished, she looked around to find he had risen and was standing at one end of the room, his hands clasped behind his back, looking at a full-length portrait of Robert and Violette, painted only a year before her death. He turned and came back to the sofa, and she took a chair opposite. She knew one topic could not now be avoided.

'I visited the graves today. On hers it said—' He stopped and chose the words carefully. 'On hers there was mention of a child.'

'Yes, her second baby is buried with her.'

His eyes narrowed as though she had struck him a blow and he was ready to fend off another. But there were no defences in his voice. 'She never . . . Robert never told me this. I was given to understand that she succumbed to a sudden illness.' But he saw in Honorine's eyes that this was not the whole truth and bowed his head. 'You must tell me. I can think of nothing else.'

She would have given a great deal not to have to tell him, for Violette de Chercy suffered atrociously during the birth, being already weak from a fever. Viviane was twelve at the time, and Honorine had been invited down to Mirandol some weeks before the expected confinement; it was possible that the baby would be born prematurely, like Viviane, and Honorine would be needed to run the household while Violette de Chercy was lying in. As it turned out, she, the servants and the physician were fully occupied trying to save Violette's life and the baby's.

As gently as possible Honorine described the progress of her illness, but when she got to the labour, which was prolonged and exhausting and which produced the child stillborn, she suddenly heard him begging her to stop.

She looked up. His elbows were on his knees and his hands screened his eyes. His hair, untied, hid the rest of his face. Then all at once he rose and left the room and she knew he was weeping.

She reproached herself for having been led into such an exchange, and hardly knew whether to go back to her chamber or remain in the room. After a time, however, he returned, hollow-eyed but composed, and sat down as before. Eventually he spoke.

31

'This is why I could not come back. Before, I should have cast a shadow on their happiness. Since . . . Every year I swore that I would return to France before winter, and every year I put it off to the next. Now there is nothing to face. I should be glad that my cowardice kept me away so long.'

She said, appalled by the self-hatred in his tone, 'Life goes on at Mirandol. You have their daughter to care for: concentrate on that.'

He rose and they left the room together. He took her elbow to go up the stairs, and as they ascended he said softly, 'Yes. Fate chose me, the least able, the least qualified, the least desirous of the task. I shall fulfil it, but God help me there is a curse on me in this place. Since that Christmas I can do no good here.'

Honorine squeezed his arm before she entered her chamber. 'This is a midnight fancy. Tomorrow it will be gone.'

He bowed and returned to his room.

Late next afternoon Viviane was walking slowly away from the château along the side of the mirror pond. Three swans were gliding in the same direction, eyeing her with a regal air which disguised their keen expectation that she was about to feed them. She looked at them sidelong and sighed. 'I forgot to bring you anything, dears. I'll come back later.' But only after Victor called; the Marquis de Luny had paid a visit to Mirandol in the morning, and she was confident that Victor must do the same before the day was out.

Viviane had received the marquis along with the count and her great-aunt, and hardly knew whether to be disappointed or relieved that nothing in the marquis' behaviour suggested that he knew of the marriage plans as yet. He was fond of her, and she had taken pleasure in talking to him again and imagining how well they would all get on when she snatched back her independence from her guardian and moved to Luny.

It would be a huge wrench to leave Mirandol,

however. She stopped on the path, turned and looked at the beautiful façade, with its double row of tall windows and the mansard roof, punctuated by bull's-eye windows and topped by the shapely central clock tower. Never before had she been obliged to look at this elegant, imposing building, the park and grounds, the farms around it, as property or wealth—they were simply home, especially dear over the last six years, when she and her father had been everything to each other.

She had attended a convent school in Paris, but once she was home her father did not wish to part with her again, and her visits to Paris were rare. Viviane did not mind in the least; she loved the life at Mirandol, and found equal enjoyment studying in the library or riding with Victor and their neighbours. Her father had had the benefit of a fine education, some of which he haphazardly passed on to her, and she filled in the gaps herself with reading. She obtained the latest books by mail from one of the best booksellers in Paris. She smiled to herself as she thought how astonished her uncle would be if he knew that most of them were about systems of government and republican theory, including a number of tracts from America and a few books containing notions that had only just escaped the condemnation of the Censor. It was unlikely that he would notice her own bold additions to the Mirandol library, but it gave her satirical amusement to think that she might even be better informed about current ideas in America than he was himself, despite his practical knowledge of that new and fascinating country.

Unhappiness coursed through her again as she thought of the power this man had been given over her life merely *because* he was a man. Her own father, though he loved her more than any other being, could not leave the château or its revenues to her while there was a Chercy male living. He had provided safeguards—her allowance, the future portion and her dowry—but one of those safeguards had been naming his adopted brother to look after her interests. She shook her head at this foolishness: she could see no sign that Jules de Chercy intended to serve any interests but his own. The relationship between him and her father was perplexing, for he had scarcely ever been mentioned, except when his letters arrived from abroad. When Viviane was a girl she had often tried to ask about her absent soldier uncle, but when she brought up his name it seemed only to make her mother silent and her father sad. Because she could read him so well, she knew that Robert felt a true brother's love for Jules de Chercy, but she could not press him to speak of it. Robert's lingering fondness, unshared by the hard man who had just returned, had caused him to sign a document that stripped his daughter of every liberty while she remained at Mirandol. She could not feel that it was wrong of her to question her father's will, for he had tragically mistaken the worthiness of his heir.

Indeed, her present plan did not stop at marriage to Victor. Her uncle might think himself rid of her once she moved to Luny, but he did not know how active she intended to be in pursuit of her rights. The crucial point in her father's will and her uncle's claim of possession was that he held the name Chercy de Mirandol. But by birth he held no such claim and, since he was adopted, it was just possible that legal objections could be raised to his inheritance of the estate. If it could be proved that in the distant past he had deceived or manipulated the old count, her grandfather, into stating that he was a member of their family, or if it could be proved that he had acted improperly since, was there not a slim chance of contesting Robert de Chercy's will?

This was one good reason for reading her uncle's letters. She had found nothing useful in them, so had returned them secretly to the desk in the library, but they were not the only papers on the premises. In the short time left to her at Mirandol, she would hunt out the rest.

Then she noticed Yves, the footman, step through the glass doors and gaze across the mirror pond. As soon as he saw her he ran down the stone steps and hurried across the gravel. She walked to meet him, praying that this meant action.

'Mademoiselle, Monsieur Victor de Luny has called. Monsieur le Comte is receiving him in the gold salon. Blaise tells me Madame de Chercy is upstairs. Blaise asks, should we——?'

'No, do not disturb Madame de Chercy.'

'Very well, Mademoiselle.'

Viviane entered the salon with an air of self-possession but, as the two men greeted her, she quivered with the sense of how important the next half-hour would be. It gave her a jolt to see a difference in her friend, who wore a well-cut green coat in figured brocade with spotless lace at the throat and cuffs, fawn breeches and stockings and silver-buckled shoes. For Victor he was positively overdressed, since he preferred to get about in short hacking jackets and boots. A burst of affection gave an added brilliance to her smile, and he responded by bowing very low over her hand.

It was intriguing to see how civil her uncle could be, for when the conversation resumed Viviane found that he and Victor had been talking quite frankly together, about the United States of America. She remained on the sidelines while they spoke, so that she could observe them both and watch for a chance to leave the salon and let Victor get to the point of his visit.

They made a striking contrast: the tall, dark man, dressed to her surprise in the latest Paris fashion; and Victor, shorter and more energetic looking, his brown curls scraped strenuously back, wearing an outfit his valet had most likely searched out and thrown together that day. Her guardian had clearly stayed in the capital long enough to order the services of some very expensive tailors. There was as much restraint in his clothing, however, as there was in his manner—the coat, finely cut, fitted smoothly across his broad shoulders, and the self-patterning in the russet brocade was subtly worked.

He did not smile as he spoke to Victor, but then she had not seen him smile once yet, except to be sarcastic.

He was ready enough in his replies, though, for Victor's enthusiasm about the American war was absolutely transparent.

The young man said firmly, 'There is no more glorious cause on earth, Monsieur, than the one you have already fought for: the cause of Liberty. When you were in Paris, I wonder if you met some of my friends who think the same way: the Marquis de La Fayette, for instance?'

'I have not had that pleasure. Though there were a number of young men who talked of glory as eagerly as yourself. I told them what I must tell you now—if that is what you are after, I'm afraid you have been born into the wrong nation, and the wrong half-century.'

Victor raised his eyebrows. 'Surely not, Monsieur! On what do you base such an idea?'

'My own career is a convincing example. When I left France as a soldier it was to serve in what we now know as the Seven Years' War. I was posted to North America: I was by the side of Montcalm when he died in the defeat at Quebec, and I managed to rejoin our army at Montreal a few months later, only to see it surrendered to the English by our commander the Marquis de Vaudreuil. You can see that French glory, by that stage, was a broken dream. I next threw in my lot with the French troops who joined the Indians in their frontier war against the colonists—fighting, you see, against the very armies you so admire today.'

'By heaven,' Viviane said before she could stop herself, 'then you might have been in the position of firing on George Washington! Did he not lead troops in that war?'

'He did. But I have never met General Washington, at either end of a rifle.' He turned again to Victor. 'The colonists were more successful there than they have been since: the Indian struggles were crushed when British regulars arrived.'

Victor said, 'Where did our army move after that?'

'I for one rejoined our forces in Louisiana. The province was surrendered to England after the Seven Years'

War, and she gave it to Spain; but no Spanish governor or troops cared to take possession. We waited until 1768 for that tragic and ridiculous situation to be resolved. Louisiana is no longer French; but if you walked down any street in New Orleans, you could scarcely credit that it belonged to any nation but ours.

'I served in Poland after that, but two years ago I resigned from the French army, returned to America and became a mercenary.' He saw a startled look on Victor's face, and the sarcastic smile made its reappearance. 'It is advisable to give occupations their real names. A gentleman seeking command in a foreign army is hiring himself out: however low he sets his fee, he must still be fed, clothed, armed and supported by that army. Incidentally, there are Frenchmen strutting about America today that Congress could very well do without.'

'What do you mean?'

'I mean gentlemen like Du Coudray, who is angling for the rank of major general and is set on demanding a salary of 36,000 livres for his services and a further 300,000 after the war. That is greed for glory on an outrageous scale.' He overrode an interjection by Victor to continue, 'So this time I fought alongside the colonists in their struggle against the British government. If . . . other duties had not called since, I should probably be there still. But not for glory. If the Americans win, the glory will be all theirs; as Frenchmen we are mere adjuncts. I suggest you promote this idea with your friends: it may keep their skins intact, and render them of more practical use to the cause you espouse.'

'As to that,' Victor said at once, 'my friend La Fayette would scorn to ask a sou of the Continental army. He is prepared to risk not only his life but his fortune. You know that he is a millionaire?'

'No pockets in Europe are deep enough for what the American army will need in the coming years. He must form his strategy with that in mind.' After a pause he said in a more conciliatory tone, 'But I honour his principles. Indeed, I am astonished to learn that they are so steadfast. The fate of the United States is the one subject on earth that holds any interest for me; but I should have thought young men like yourself and your friend would have a thousand more pressing things to occupy you.'

Viviane saw Victor open his mouth to deny this, then give her a conscious glance and close it again. What subject could be more vital or nearer home than their own betrothal! It was time for her to act, before their dearest plans were swamped by another flood of debate.

'Messieurs, you have so much in common that I shall not feel too guilty about leaving you. I believe my great-aunt requires me upstairs. You will excuse her if she does not come down?' she said to Victor.

Victor had a look of stern resolve on his face. He said, 'Certainly. Pray give her my greetings. There is something particular I wish to say to the Comte de Mirandol.'

Before she left the room, Viviane saw her uncle give Victor a sharp glance, and knew he had guessed at once what was to come. As she sped upstairs she willed Victor success in the struggle.

3

THE SUITOR BANISHED

Honorine de Chercy liked to spend an hour or two in her room on summer afternoons: it gave her a chance to read, take a nap, or keep up her correspondence, for she wrote regularly and at length to her closest friend in Paris. She was interrupted twice this afternoon, however. First she received a visit from her grand-niece, who spent half an hour chatting inconsequentially and fidgeting about then, noticing Victor de Luny go out into the garden, raced off to join him. Not long afterwards, Jules asked to be admitted.

He sat down and came to the point at once. 'My tiresome ward is walking about with young Luny outside. I dislike giving the appearance that we closet ourselves up to conspire against her, but there is something you should know at once.'

'My goodness, what?'

'Nothing alarming, only an inconvenience. An offer has been made for Mademoiselle de Chercy's hand. I had a little warning of it beforehand, but no confidence that it would be made: she flung it at me on first meeting and I had a strong notion it was more her idea than the young man's. He is Victor de Luny, of course. I would give a deal to know how she put him up to it—went down on one knee perhaps? I would have liked to ask the suitor himself, but he was quite embarrassed enough as it was.'

'He *spoke? Today?* Mademoiselle de Chercy gave me not an inkling!'

'We got onto military matters to begin with—I suppose you know he has a passion for them. He is a bright young fellow, is he not? I like his manners—frank but pleasing. At any rate we were well into conversation by the time he remembered his mission, drew himself up and announced that he intended to marry Mademoiselle de Chercy.

'I asked whether the lady had been consulted and he

said yes—not news to me, of course. I asked whether his father seconded the match, and he said yes again, with some hesitation. So I said that although I was reluctant to give my consent, I was prepared to discuss the matter with the Marquis de Luny. Our suitor began to look a little less ardent. It did not take me long to winkle out the truth: he has not really broached the affair at home. He must have thought I would leap at the offer and then talk his father round, but nothing could be further from my desire.'

'Oh dear. I had no idea he was fond of her in that way. Or she of him. They will both be wretchedly disappointed.'

'Do not fall into lamentation, Madame, until I have told you all. I encouraged him to express his views on the lady. He is fond of her, and admires her, but I could swear his admiration is not that of a lover. I see him as her friend, and a very loyal one at that. When he had finished I said that I considered my niece too young to marry. I conceded that the world is full of women who have become wives at a much earlier age, but then I pointed out to him how sheltered her life has been, and how inexperienced she is in many ways. Whoever might apply for her hand in the next year or so, I should think it my duty to reject.'

'And how did he react?'

'I'd take an oath that his main emotion was relief. In my view, he is just as unready as she is for marriage. After a moment he looked pretty downcast, mainly I think for her sake. I advised him not to relay any of my remarks, but simply to tell her I had refused.'

'Poor young man, it is very hard on him.'

'What, sending him out to face my niece unarmed? I heartily agree with you! So I gave him a little ammunition. I said, "You may say that you made your proposal very properly and persuasively, but I was adamant. You will be able to carry on the friendship as before—you are still welcome at Mirandol. And it will not be necessary to bring the subject up with your father." He shook my hand then, with scarcely less gratitude than if I had given my consent! He is walking about the grounds with her now, and I hope he is telling her the subject is closed.'

'To be sure,' Honorine said slowly, 'Mademoiselle de Chercy has had no one to compare with Victor de Luny whilst she lives at Mirandol. It is not surprising the young people have come to this point. And as for marriage, half the district has been predicting it for years.'

'Are you sure the Lunys feel the same? Look at it from Clarence de Luny's point of view: despite the friendly link between our houses, my niece is by no means the obvious match for his son. They are already the first family in the region. The young man would not obtain Mirandol by marrying, and she would bring him only her dowry, which is considerable but not grand. Our family offers no high-ranking connections: we have no voice at court or in any of the important Paris circles. If he were ambitious for his son, Luny would not necessarily promote the match. Have you ever heard a syllable of it from my late brother, or from the marquis and his wife?'

'No,' Honorine said, 'I must own I have not.'

He rose and said, 'I think we can leave it there. The issue is closed and need not be canvassed again unless the Marquis de Luny mentions it to me himself. I very much doubt that he will.' Honorine did not look up immediately, and after a pause he said with less firmness in his voice, 'What is your opinion?'

She considered him thoughtfully, wondering whether her approval meant anything to him at all, or whether she had now become a superfluous being at Mirandol, merely a buffer between him and Viviane. But his green eyes gave nothing away. 'I should tell you, Nephew, that I am extremely fond of your ward. If you come to any decisions that I consider are not in her best interests, you must expect me to tell you so.'

His expression changed at once and he took a step towards her. 'Madame, shower reproofs on me every day if you will, nothing could lessen my gratitude for having you here. You have seen how she reacts: without you I should have not the slightest idea how

41

to deal with her. You are a daily witness: her manners are deplorable and she has a response like a whiplash. She is not inclined to be managed by a male; with my brother Robert, I am sure it was all the other way.'

'That is true. She is used to directing, not taking direction. Yet she has been a kind and tolerant mistress in this house. The servants are too familiar with her, but take no undue advantage. The housekeeper and major-domo dote on her and so do all the rest, in their fashion.'

'Yes, I have noticed. I cannot tell you how much the likeness to Robert strikes me. The curls, the open nature, all the engaging qualities—the last of course invisible when I am around. I had prepared myself for quite another resemblance. Overprepared myself. But nothing is ever as we expect.' He turned and went to the window, looking out as though, like her, he could imagine the disconsolate young couple walking about the grounds. 'Scold as you like, but do not refuse your help. This place is desolate enough to me without having a rebel in petticoats to deal with.'

'Very well, Nephew, here is my view. You did right to refuse your consent. I never heard of such a madcap proposal. There are ways of forming an alliance between two titled families and this is certainly not one of them! If Victor de Luny is absolutely serious about this, we shall hear of it again from his parents. I shall then bring it up with my grand-niece. Otherwise I shall refrain from opening the subject. She is but too inclined to view my occasional comment on her behaviour as a lecture.'

He smiled grimly. 'I know what you mean. Thank you. You have given me the courage to face her at supper tonight without flinching. But I should warn you, it will not be a joyful meal.'

He bowed and left the room. Honorine took up her pen, but after a while she laid it down again and sighed. Writing letters could bring no solace while such conflict threatened on the horizon.

Viviane did not re-enter the château until sunset, when Victor took reluctant leave of her at the stables. They had fetched up there after wandering around the park, trying without success to decide what could be done to reverse his resounding defeat at the hands of her uncle. Even in her disappointment Viviane could not put it to Victor this way, however; she had felt her cheeks go cold when she had first approached him and he had given her a look which plainly said that all was lost, but she tried to conceal the depth of her despair.

She listened in silence as he reported on the exchange, and this restraint was so unlike her that it made Victor doubly distressed and anxious. She could tell that he was afraid she would burst into tears, which almost made her do so. She had no trouble guessing that Victor felt humiliated by the whole affair, for the only good thing he had to say about the count was that he had remained polite and gentlemanly throughout.

'Of course he did,' she said softly. 'He never loses his self-command, because he is never denied his own way. He is not like us, he has no feelings to be crushed or wounded. He acts by pure calculation. Have you thought why he does not wish me to marry? I suspect it has nothing to do with you or me and everything to do with the legacy. When I marry he must pay out the full sum of my dowry and my portion from the estate. And he does not care to part with so much cash, it is as simple as that.'

'Vive, are you sure that is just? You know him so little as yet. When we spoke of America today, it struck me that he has ideals, and the strength to live up to them.'

'He has had a military career, and tried hard to make it a successful one. I saw no altruism in what he said, and he was very quick to dismiss *yours*.'

'He was only trying to make me see the practical side of the war.'

'He is practical, yes, I give him that. Especially about Mirandol, now it is in his grasp. Victor, we must circumvent him. He will be obliged to listen when your

43

father speaks to him: he will not have the gall to insult the Marquis de Luny by telling him you are unworthy to receive my hand in marriage!'

On that subject she found Victor strangely lacking in confidence, and the more they spoke, the less sure she became about what had passed between father and son. Victor was an only child and had a great affection for his parents, which was returned in abundance. He always talked as though all three were the best of friends, and rarely complained that he was denied permission for anything. So it was a new idea to Viviane that he might be just as much under his father's thumb as she seemed to be under her uncle's.

When they reached the stables and Victor was about to depart, she stood playing with the reins of his hunter, looking down at her hands, unwilling to let him ride away.

Standing close beside her, he murmured, 'God knows I am sorry, Vive.'

She let the reins slip from her hands and turned to him. 'I know. That's just the thing—I know you have done your best. I feel so helpless. You have no idea how hard it is to have your independence stolen away. How can I bear it?' She bit her lip, closed her eyes, and fought against tears.

She felt one arm go about her, as with the other hand he laid her head on his shoulder. 'Don't,' he said, his breath warming her cheek, his hands gentle but protective. 'Lord, you never cry. I won't have it. I'll do what I can at Luny, you mustn't give up hope. I'll be back tomorrow. Keep your courage up until then and we'll find a way.'

After he had gone, that one fleeting embrace left an imprint in her mind that lasted all day. She even seemed to breathe and walk differently. The sensation of Victor's arms around her, and of hers wrapped around his lean, strong frame, heightened the feeling that they belonged together, but also told her how much there was to discover about this young man whom she thought she knew so well.

For most of her life she and Victor had acted as

though they were part of the same family; yet he had been somehow less than a brother and more than a friend. That first embrace caused a confusion inside her which she still felt as she walked down to supper that evening. Her guardian was waiting at the foot of the stairs as before; she met his gaze steadfastly, telling herself that she and Victor had secrets that even he, with his officious interference, would never spy out.

He had already escorted Honorine to the table, and the moment Viviane's eyes met hers she knew that her great-aunt was privy to what had happened that afternoon. She sat down with dignity, but she was bereft of words. They could hardly expect her to keep up polite conversation after dealing her such a blow.

It was painful to sit there in silence, however, while the others talked of what would be happening at Mirandol and in the district over the next few weeks. At last, when the servants had cleared away the platters of the main course, her stamina gave out. She said suddenly to her uncle, 'I am astonished, Monsieur, that you can converse so coolly before me when you have just blighted all my hopes.'

He started, then a flash of anger, such as she had never seen before, lit up the green eyes. He waited, put down his napkin on the tablecloth, and when he raised his eyes again their expression was more veiled. 'Tell me, why were you so keen to marry Victor de Luny?'

She was taken aback, but said at once, 'Because we are made for each other.'

'Explain.'

'We grew up together. We like all the same things.'

'Such as?'

Uncertain, she glanced at her great-aunt, who had the same inquisitive look in her eyes as her uncle. What was the point of interrogating her about the most obvious thing in the world? She said, 'Well, we both like hunting. At least, he hunts and so do I, quite often. We both like horses. And I read, and study music, and he enjoys hearing me play. We appreciate each other's company. When you have been here long enough to meet the neighbours, Monsieur, you will find it

45

generally known that Monsieur de Luny and I get on famously.'

Honorine said gently, 'We know you like each other, my dear.'

'Oh yes!'

'And?' persisted her uncle.

She was nonplussed. Then she felt herself blushing and said rapidly, 'Oh. You mean do we say silly things to each other and does he pick roses for me and cast himself at my feet? No, I should hate that, it's so stupid.'

'I don't mean anything of the sort, I am simply interested in your sentiments. And from what you say—or rather, what you have not said—I can see they are not deeply involved.'

Her lips quivered and she felt her eyes burning. Who was he: high judge and jury on her private feelings and conduct? 'You are not interested in my sentiments at all! You don't give a fig how I feel, you don't care if I am unhappy.'

'Let us say simply that as your guardian I cannot approve the match. I should prefer not to discuss this again.'

At that, Viviane surprised them and herself by bursting into tears. Mortified, she rose from the table with a sob, then, still unable to control herself, ran from the room.

Victor did not come the next day. Instead, half the gentlemen in the district turned up to pay their respects. In a week or two, once the Comte de Mirandol had returned their visits, they would be back again with their wives, and the invitations would begin to flow in. Viviane received the callers with her uncle; they spoke to each other only when necessary, but made sure that none of their awkwardness together was apparent to their guests. Viviane noticed that he was an effortless host and showed a perfect familiarity with the kind of conversation her neighbours were used to. This surprised her until she reluctantly admitted to herself that this was his home territory too, and of course some of the visitors were already known to him. She was also relieved that every exchange proved him a sensible man: if she was to be superseded at Mirandol before the eyes of the province, at least she would not be pitied for falling under the domination of a fool.

It seemed to Viviane that somehow all the interesting people made their appearance in the morning and the boring ones in the afternoon. Once, while the room was empty of everyone but themselves for a moment, she detected that he felt the same. He had just sunk with a muffled groan into a chair by the window, when the major-domo appeared at the door and said, 'Mademoiselle, Monsieur, the carriage of Monsieur de Trémin has pulled up. Should I show him straight in?'

She heard her uncle mutter what sounded rather like an oath, then he nodded curtly to the major-domo, who withdrew. 'Trémin: is he still with us? I remember him vividly, the prosy old—' He rose stiffly and gave her a rueful look, then said, 'If you find this as tedious as I do, pray do not feel obliged to stay. You have already done more than your duty. Perhaps you would prefer to join my aunt, she has some correspondence to share with you.'

'From Paris? Then I shall certainly join her.'

'Better take the servants' way, or you'll run against Trémin in the hall. And risk sending him spinning—I never met a man who looked so much like a *boule*.'

As she glided quickly from the room, Viviane smiled at this apt description and, speeding up the narrow stairs, came out onto the floor above, then walked at a more sedate pace around to the wing where the principal apartments were located. She was eager to hear from her friend Louise de Billancourt, who usually included a letter in the packets her mother sent to Honorine. The young women had been friends since convent school, and corresponded faithfully, which meant that Viviane had kept Louise up-to-date with every detail of what went on at Mirandol. She could not expect a reply to these confidences yet, but

47

any letter from Paris would make a bright spot in her otherwise gloomy day.

Honorine in fact had a letter in her hand when Viviane walked into the room, so the young woman spoke at once: 'I was tied up with the visitors and have not seen the mail. Is there anything for me, Madame?'

'There has been no mail today. Sit down, child, and let us talk. This message does not come from Paris, but from the Marquise de Luny.'

Viviane sat down slowly, her eyes on her great-aunt's face. Dismay came over her, but she said with outward composure, 'Will you tell me what it is about?'

'I should like to show it to you, so you could see how very kindly she speaks of you. But she has not authorised me to do so.' Honorine put the letter down on the desk and turned to face Viviane more directly. 'I am grateful to the marquise that she makes this an informal matter between women, instead of allowing the men to make a great fuss and bother. I am extremely glad that we are spared *that*, and so should you be. Her note tells me that she and the marquis have given their son leave to make an extended visit in Paris.' She ignored Viviane's start and continued, 'He will be staying in the home of the Marquis de La Fayette, that is, with the Duc and Duchesse de Noailles d'Ayen, the marquis's parents-in-law.'

Viviane said in a controlled voice, 'He is being sent away from me.'

'I am sure you are aware he has been pressing to visit Paris. His parents wished him to go only if he was prepared to take up a course of study: the law, for instance. But now—'

'Seriously, can you see him studying the law? All he has ever wanted is a military cadetship.'

'His mother does not wish that, and I cannot say I blame her. At any rate, they have given their permission without any such conditions, and he leaves tomorrow. He comes to bid us farewell in the morning.'

Viviane got up from her chair and began to pace about the room. 'What has happened at Luny? I suppose they are making his life as dismal as mine is here.'

'Don't exaggerate. There was a difference of opinion between him and his parents. Like your uncle, they consider it is too soon for either of you to marry. Stop walking about, and do me the courtesy of looking at me, Mademoiselle. I said *too soon*. That does not mean the matter can never be broached again. It simply means that at present you must make up your mind that a hasty alliance between Luny and Mirandol is unacceptable to both families. I cannot tell you what the thinking is at Luny—the marquise very properly does not go into that. And there is not an uncomplimentary syllable about you in her note, which is surprising when—'

'I should think not! This is intolerable, to have our lives decided upon between supper one night and breakfast on the morrow!'

'I say it is surprising, considering the letter you very indecorously sent to Monsieur de Luny the day before yesterday.' Viviane sat down again. 'I am afraid that did your cause little good, Mademoiselle. It is one thing to carry on a friendship with an unexceptionable young man. It is quite another to secretly send him what amounts to a proposal of marriage! Hear me out. If you intend his parents to consider you a mature woman who will make their son a wife to be proud of, you must mend your ways.'

Horrified, Viviane remained silent. She could not imagine Victor showing the note to his mother willingly: his father must have become suspicious since it was delivered under his nose, and demanded to see it. She was ashamed at being caught out in such a piece of immodesty, it made her look adolescent and conspiratorial. After a moment she said, 'Shall you show my uncle the marquise's note? Or give him the details of it?'

Her aunt kept her in suspense for a few seconds, then said, 'No. There has been enough said on this subject.' Viviane rose to go, but she forestalled her. 'I should like your assurance that you will comport yourself in a ladylike manner tomorrow, and at least pretend to accept this with dignity. May I count on that?'

49

Already at the door, Viviane turned and murmured, 'Yes, Madame.'

The steely glint in her great-aunt's eye disappeared, and her tone softened. 'Your feelings, of course, are your own affair. I respect your privacy, but if you ever wish to confide in me, my dear, please do so.'

'My feelings? It has been made very clear that I have none worth considering. Excuse me, Madame.' Viviane left the room.

Next morning saw the arrival of three splendid horses. The count had chosen them from a famous stables at Dourdan on his journey from Paris, and they had been brought south in gradual stages so as to arrive at Mirandol in the finest condition.

Viviane happened to be in the tack room when they arrived, and saw that her uncle had walked down to greet the handlers and take a look at his purchases. She did not approach, but waited in the doorway and observed the men and horses in the yard. Her uncle inspected each beast minutely, running his hands down over chest and legs, then standing in front of it, looking into its eyes with both hands on its neck, talking gently. For the first time, she saw him smile openly.

He knew she was there, but did not glance her way. She suspected that for once he was enjoying himself and wished to avoid conflict. It was too much to hope that she could ever make him as wretched as she was, but if her presence threatened to disturb his peace, she felt a certain mournful triumph.

Eventually she approached, and he was forced to turn and be polite. 'What is your opinion of these animals, Mademoiselle?'

'They look very handsome and capable. And unless my eyes deceive me, there are three of them. You intend to hunt every hour of your existence?'

He was not easily provoked in this mood, and replied smoothly, 'I grant you they are an extravagance; I never intended buying a third, but I could not decide between the roan and the grey as second string.

I did not know your tastes at the time, but it also occurred to me you might like to try the grey yourself. If so, she is available whenever you wish.'

She was taken aback, but after a moment said, 'Thank you,' in a tone that made the reply a negative.

Again he did not react, except with a slight smile that was hidden when he turned to the grooms who were standing about in admiration, and told them to take the horses into the stables. Patting the big black hunter on the rump as he followed the group, he disappeared into the building, leaving Viviane dissatisfied with him and herself.

Just then she saw another groom lead Victor's horse, Demon, into the yard, so at once she set off back towards the château. When she got to the avenue of poplars, she saw Victor coming in search of her, striding purposefully down the path and looking so much like his usual self that for a moment she believed he had found a way to end their troubles.

Not so. As soon as their hands met, he said, 'They told you? I have had no luck with my parents. They were even reluctant to let me wish you goodbye! But I put my foot down over that.'

'I shall never forgive them. Or my guardian.'

'You must not think my parents are against you, it is all me. They were furious at me for taking things into my own hands. They are hell-bent on choosing a wife for me themselves, but only when it suits them. We must wait until they come round. It is all we can do.' He looked at her with such tender apprehension that she felt sorry for him.

'It is my fault too, I should never have sent you that letter so openly. When you are in Paris we shall be more discreet.'

He started and dropped her hand as they began to walk back down the avenue towards the bridge. 'What do you mean?'

'Toto, I cannot bear to be left behind if I am to lose touch with you as well! I have a scheme: when you are in Paris, you must make the acquaintance of the Billancourts. Madame de Billancourt is great friends with my great-aunt, and her daughter Louise is the dearest friend I have in Paris. You will like her, she is the most delightful person. When we are in company I can never draw her into the discussions I like having with people, about politics at Versailles, or the war in America, but in private I can talk about them to *her* to my heart's content. She was my staunch friend at convent school, and would never let a soul attack me for my outrageous ideas. I know she will be our ally now. She and I write to each other all the time—nothing will be simpler for her than to pass on my notes to you, and receive yours in return. They can go back and forth in the packets we send each other, and no one will be any the wiser.'

He frowned and said dryly, 'You don't think it will look a little obvious if I sail up to the Billancourts and force myself on their notice?'

'Good heavens, we shall manage things more subtly than that! I have already asked my great-aunt to recommend you to Monsieur and Madame de Billancourt and gain permission for you to call on them. I pointed out how few people you know in Paris, and how lonely you will be there, and made my great-aunt quite sorry for you. And she does have some kindness for us in her heart; if I beg favours at the moment, they are likely to be granted.'

Victor thought for a moment, then his face brightened a little. When they reached the bridge he stopped and leaned on the rail, looking down at the stream. 'I should like to hear from you, and share with you what is happening in Paris. What does it matter if we flout convention? If my parents prevent me from seeing you, then it is their own fault if we are forced to write.' He turned to her and continued with his usual energy, 'I shall be able to tell you all about La Fayette's plans. And I intend to get in touch with the American commissioners. You will be the best informed woman in France on the most important subject in the world.'

He looked so pleased that she wondered momentarily whether he was more glad to go to Paris than he would admit. But there was no doubt of his affection, which shone brightly in his laughing brown eyes.

She looked into them with an answering smile. 'As long as you write, I shall not feel forlorn.'

He put reassuring hands on her upper arms, she swayed towards him, and he murmured, 'It's nonsense, their trying to part us. They'll never succeed.' His lips closed gently on hers and they stood locked together. The kiss was chaste for all its warmth, but it had the impact of shock on Viviane, and for an instant it was as though a bright light shone in her eyes and she could not see the face so close to hers. A kind of thrilling fear came over her and she felt as though they had stepped into a realm from which there was no return. Then, perhaps worried they might be caught in this first stolen kiss, Victor released her, and they broke apart. After a moment they met each other's glance with a shy smile, then walked slowly back to the château, arm in arm.

4

SECRETS

Shortly after Victor de Luny arrived in Paris, Jules received a letter from the Marquis de La Fayette, politely begging him to send any information he could in answer to some pressing questions about America. He replied briefly, knowing that he had now committed himself to a lengthy correspondence if all he heard about the young man was true.

He also replied to his friend Benjamin Franklin, who had sent him a letter from Philadelphia in late June. The courier to whom Franklin had entrusted it did not reach Paris until the end of August, and he took some time to ascertain where the count had gone and find a trusted messenger to deliver the letter to the Loire.

In his letter back to Franklin, Jules wrote:

I should like to show my gratitude for your kind inquiries by giving you the report you wanted of what is going forward in Paris. Alas, I am less confident than you that my letter would arrive unopened. I shall keep my remarks general and save the particulars for a meeting between ourselves—for I hope our government will recognise your country and that you will be appointed Ambassador to France.

Sir, America has need of you here. The very mention of your struggle raises a kind of fever that fires men in unpredictable ways. It makes tractable people contentious, dull men talkative, and languid youths suddenly bold and venturesome—and it frequently makes them ridiculous. You remember as well as I the French officers from Canada, the Sugar Islands and elsewhere who have drifted into the Continental army in expectation of reward solely because they strut amongst you—I regret to say that you must prepare yourself to see more.

Given the heady atmosphere that hangs about the

54

topic of your struggles against England, given the ignorance on the subject amongst the majority of Parisian leaders of opinion, given our King's youth and his caution over serious hostility towards Britain, we need a great deal more informed debate here before France's relationship with Congress changes. Such French government support as is already being offered, and which I shall not discuss here, is all that can be expected for some time. This is why I urge your coming to France: the respect, indeed the reverence for your genius which is so widespread here, the confidence in your wisdom, these ensure you a fair hearing.

Please remember me with respect and affection to Brigadier General Benedict Arnold. I am glad to hear that he is recovered since the time he and I spent in the field hospital after Quebec. You may thank him for making me out a cripple, and inform him that until I send to him for a stout hickory stick such as I have seen him use, he may assume me to be in the state of perfect fitness which I now enjoy and which I heartily hope he shares.

It remains only for me to urge you once again, Sir, to favour France with your presence. I have a selfish motive in this, for it would give me the opportunity of conversing once more with one of the wisest men it has been my pleasure to know. Until that day, and may it be soon,

I remain your faithful and respectful servant
Jules Rollet de Chercy de Mirandol

For Viviane, life at Mirandol showed no improvement, despite her great-aunt's efforts to be more kind and understanding. Honorine had developed a notion that Viviane and her guardian would get on with each other eventually if they were sent riding about the estate together. Neither of them shared her opinion.

One day when they were in the stables choosing their mounts, his eye fell on the sleigh that was kept in the coach-house, and he asked her if her parents had ever used it. Surprised, for it was the first time he had mentioned her family, she thought for a moment and then said she remembered being driven in it with her mother, when she was a little girl. But he made no comment.

Then suddenly the past rose up to confront them again. It happened almost half a league from the château, as they approached a steep slope below a rye field, where a bridle path descended to a brook crossed by a narrow wooden bridge. Instead of taking the path, Viviane immediately pulled the grey mare aside and began to skirt the field, moving towards the top of the hill. Her uncle called out to ask where she was going and she said reluctantly, 'I never ride down there since the accident.' He came to an abrupt halt and asked what she meant.

Viviane would have preferred to move on without explanation, for it hurt to see that he was unaware of details which he could easily have learned from the servants, if he had cared about the subject at all. It was her duty to give him the information, however, and she managed to summon the courage to do so, feeling a melancholy wish that, despite his coldness, the story might hit him with a fraction of the pain it caused her. In plain language she told him about the last few minutes of her father's life: how he had ridden down the hill, how his mare had been reluctant to cross the bridge, how he had forced her over and she had put one leg through a board of the bridge and pitched him into the brook, where he had broken his neck on the stones and died at once. With Viviane's last words, she saw him flinch.

She was about to resume her way uphill, but he said, 'Come with me,' and rode towards the brook. Despite herself she followed him. They stopped and he looked at the spot for so long she thought he would never speak. At last he said, 'Are you sure it was instantaneous?'

When she nodded he asked her how she knew, and in a rush she told him about the groom seeing the accident and going to her father's side, then riding back to the château to fetch her, and how most of the

56

household returned with her. At that point she found it impossible to continue talking about her father, and changed the subject by remarking that the mare had injured her leg in the accident. She suspected that he was relieved to have something else to talk about also, for he asked whether the mare was still in the stables, and she said no, her leg had been broken and she had had her shot.

As though held by some dire spell, they fell into silence, looking not at each other but at the spot where her father had died. Then all at once he wheeled his horse, sent it thundering downstream for some distance, took a run at the brook and flew over it, from one steep bank to the other. Startled, she remained where she was until he looked sternly back at her and called, 'You must do the same.' When she hesitated, outraged, he added, 'Unless you are afraid of not keeping your seat.'

Viviane forced every thought from her mind and did as he had done, but kept on past him, unable to stop and meet his eye, struggling for composure. Fortunately he took some time to come abreast of her, and as they entered the broader ride through the forest they resumed conversation in an almost normal tone. When he remarked calmly that he would have the bridge repaired, and made wider so that it would take the harvest waggons, she wished she could be angry with him, as she had been so many times before; instead she found herself trying to guess what was going on in his mind. But his reserve made this almost impossible, and on the rare occasions when she thought she could guess at his thoughts they were not at all flattering.

When they came to dismount in the yard he jumped to the ground and lifted her off the grey mare, but an instant later he released her, exclaimed, and sank down onto the rim of the old well. His face was pale, and she noticed he looked just as Victor had done the year before when he broke his arm during a hunt. The pain had made Victor ill, and then he had fainted, and had not really come to until they had got the physician to him. So she watched her uncle with interest, but after a while the colour began to come back into his face, and he rubbed his thigh and muttered something about it not happening often, and it depending on the cursed angle.

Viviane decided that he was one of those people who were always furious at themselves or someone else when they were hurt, and she could not help saying, 'Great-Aunt Honorine sometimes finds her rheumatism takes her in just that way, and I am always ready to run back to the hall for a walking stick. Though usually she won't let me because she declares it makes her feel old.'

Her uncle got to his feet and said very dryly that he knew just what her great-aunt meant.

To Mademoiselle de Chercy
From Mademoiselle de Billancourt

My dear Viviane
The meeting has taken place. You would have been proud of me, I was deliciously discreet. And I feared it would be complicated, for your V de L came with a friend. But this friend, the Marquis de La Fayette, proved a magnificent diversion for my mother, who was mouth agape at the visit of someone so illustrious (because of course he is a millionaire, and son-in-law of the Duc and Duchesse de Noailles d'Ayen, and connected by marriage to a marshal of France and so forth) and she could be counted on to miss the subtle messages I meant to pass between your Friend and myself.

When we had got a little acquainted, I proposed that we examine one of Papa's collection of travel folios, and they took the hint at once. We turned the big pages, and soon I said I had marked a very beautiful picture, and put my fingers into the gap and opened it up and there masquerading as a bookmark was your letter, folded in four lengthwise, and no more recognisable as a message from where Maman sat than a ribbon.

As we gazed at the scene—a snowstorm on Lake

Ontario—I pushed the paper gently towards him and at last he had the courage to slide it off the page and onto his lap, and then transfer it to his pocket. We continued very grave and appreciative over the pictures, and then I gave him the second cue by exclaiming, 'Now this is a very pretty scene, we must mark the place. Have you my bookmark, Monsieur de Luny?'

And he looked at me with a sparkle of approval— I do congratulate you on his brown eyes—and put his hand promptly in his pocket and laid the paper in the centre of the book with alacrity. And there was your letter all over again. .

On the instant he realised his blunder, plunged his hand in his pocket and felt there his letter to you, then froze, utterly nonplussed. And all our smooth naturalness dissolved. I did not dare catch his eye for fear of giggling, but he caught mine by mistake and that set him off, and the marquis leaned forward and innocently moved the letter to study a detail it was obscuring, and it fluttered onto the floor, whereupon V de L bent over and picked it up.

At that point the marquis guessed what was afoot, and looked at me with a bright glance that showed not an iota of the timidity he had displayed all afternoon, and I went hot with embarrassment, and at last with quick sleight of hand there was the right piece of paper lying on the page before me, and it was as much as I could do not to snap the covers to, rush from the room and howl outright with laughter behind the library door.

You see what agonies I go through for you. But Maman likes him and will ask him here again, and I am bound to meet him in other houses, so I shall carry your next letter about with me to be ready for an exchange.

Now, I promised to tell you about the only man in the world who occupies my thoughts, apart from your Friend. I dare not give you his name until I can whisper it in your ear: just for now it is A**** de R******. At first I only saw him at church, and all *he did was* look *when my mother did not. Then one day he joined us outside when we spoke to others. I came up to his shoulder, and I only dared glance up into his face once or twice, but I know it so well I see it clearly in my dreams. He has strong features, and always wears an elegant wig. He must be very fair, for he is known as the* Golden Boy *by his intimate circle, because of his hair and because he is lucky at cards* and *with women. Viviane, I fear I am pursued by a* libertine. *But he cannot be absolutely notorious, or Maman would not talk to him.*

The first time he spoke to me was once more outside the church, where someone said in an unpleasant way that they had never realised he was pious, and he replied, 'It is true I have neglected my devotions in the past,' and then said very soft, just to me, scarcely moving his lips, 'but I had not yet seen my good angel.'

I was so terrified someone might have heard that I trembled and dropped my reticule, and after bending to pick it up he rose to bring his face to the level of mine, his lips mere inches away and his eyes burning. It was strange—all around us people were talking, but he said more with his glance than they with their chatter. It is like being somewhere else when he is by, in another conversation, another world. He put my reticule back in my fingers, clasped both hands around mine, then released them and murmured, 'My mother's, next week. You must come, or I cannot answer for myself.'

A few minutes later, just before the group broke up, he said to Maman, 'I hope you and Mademoiselle de Billancourt are able to attend my mother's reception next Wednesday: she would be greatly honoured,' and I could not meet his eye when Maman nodded her consent.

Do I dare go to his mother's now that he has turned it from a polite visit into an assignation? If I go I shall seem to be agreeing to . . . whatever he has in mind. What has he in mind? I wish it were not impossible for me to have a reply from you before

60

then; I need your advice, for I cannot discuss a syllable of this with Maman. Remember once you and I had a grand scheme to establish a pigeon post between here and Mirandol? Why don't we ever do the clever, practical things we plan as girls? Why are we without resources once we are women?

My dear, I sense you and I are on the threshold of a new era. How men complicate one's life!

Ever your friend, Louise

Hidden within the folds of Louise's letter was the promised one from Victor. He had taken a great deal of trouble to compose it, for what went on in Paris made Viviane and the country seem very far away, yet he did not want to disappoint her by leaving out any details that might entertain her. He could scarcely do justice to the grandeur of the Noailles family home in the Rue du Faubourg Saint-Honoré, where he was staying with his friends the Marquis and Marquise de La Fayette; but he said everything to convince Viviane that they were the most welcoming and agreeable couple imaginable.

Victor could not help confiding in Adrienne de La Fayette, for though she was only sixteen she had been a wife for two years and was already a mother, and he was charmed by her seriousness and her sympathy when he told her about his unlucky suit. He wrote to Viviane: 'She very sweetly tells me we must learn to be patient. She and the marquis occupied separate wings of this house for years before her mother thought it proper for them to marry. It was an arranged match, but living close together they fell in love, and are so still. Just talking with her gives me hope.'

At first, though he did not admit this to Viviane, Victor found Paris something of a bore, for he was exasperated to discover how much time it seemed to take everyone to get ready to go out; and when they did, it was only for mindless activities like driving a carriage in the Bois de Boulogne. But La Fayette soon suggested remedies: he took Victor to his own fencing master and to the Epée de Bois, a cabaret on the way to the village of Montmartre where, amongst other company, they were sure to meet men who felt the same keen interest as they did in what was happening on the other side of the Atlantic in the new United States of America.

The second time they went there they had a bout with the foils in the long gallery originally built for a gaming room along the back of the cabaret. When their host had discovered that so many young gentlemen were prepared to make sorties from Paris into the country on fine afternoons and linger at his establishment, showing no tendency to frown on either his modest selection of ales and wines or the rough travellers and field labourers who also gathered at the tables, he had taken some pains to cater to their undemanding tastes and their keenness for sword practice.

The Vicomte de Coigny, a slight fair young gentleman dressed in a silver brocade coat that looked rather out of keeping with the place he was in and the scene he was observing, was lounging on a wooden bench, his eyes narrowed against the sparks of light that leapt up as the afternoon sun, shining through the row of windows behind him, flashed on the whipping blades.

He gave a sudden laugh when the Marquis de La Fayette, one soft shoe slipping briefly on the polished floor, had to duck and twist, and Victor, pressing the momentary advantage, gave a swift lunge that almost touched his opponent's shoulder. 'Too near for comfort, my friend?' the Vicomte called. 'Perhaps it is time you reported back to Metz for more training.'

'It is I who do the training, Coigny, and I should like to see you try drilling the men I am expected to—' he broke off as Victor's point flicked against his shirt sleeve, then had no breath to resume. His freckled face was creased in a frown and one thick lock of red hair, damp with sweat, clung to his forehead. Despite his grim concentration, however, there was a light in the alert blue eyes, intent on Victor's every move, that betrayed his confidence in the wiry strength of his own lean, supple body; indeed, trying a manoeuvre he had recently learned from the master at arms at the garrison, he took Victor off guard and forced him back several paces towards the dais at one end of the room.

The sword blades slipped and whined as Victor parried skilfully; he felt the relentless jarring in his wrist, but he was naturally the stronger of the two and enjoyed his ability to hold off the marquis, despite the other's superior knowledge of all things martial.

He said, 'That's a new trick. If Metz is where you picked it up, I shouldn't mind returning with you.'

'Metz is the back of beyond. And don't tell me you'd rather be anywhere but Paris just now, or what would happen to your amorous intrigue?'

Victor cursed as the marquis's point grazed his upper arm and growled, 'Touché.'

Coigny sat up. 'The little Billancourt?'

The marquis ignored the instant annoyance on Victor's face and said, 'Come now, yield and we'll have done.' Then, without daring to so much as glance at Coigny, he fought back furiously as Victor redoubled his attack. With a gasping laugh La Fayette said, 'Believe it or not, Coigny, there is *another* story behind our friend's impeccable friendship with the enchanting Mademoiselle de Billancourt.'

'But you are not authorised to tell it,' Victor said loudly, and with a strong thrust beat down the marquis's guard and had the satisfaction of pinking the padded waistcoat he wore over his shirt.

La Fayette tossed down his foil with an oath and stood grinning at Victor, his chest rising and falling rapidly as he tried to regain his breath.

Coigny said with mock resentment, 'I call that unfair. Up from the country a week and knee-deep in romantic conspiracy already.'

Holding Victor's eye calmly, La Fayette said at once, 'Enough said, Coigny. We are not here to discuss ladies.'

'Not even this year's Venus? Not even the incomparable Aglaë d'Hunolstein?'

The marquis blushed and it was his turn for discomfiture. D'Hunolstein, a recent arrival in select society, had scores of worshippers at court, and his own

63

admiration, which he had expressed far too rashly at Versailles on his last visit, had made no impression on her whatsoever.

Victor went over to the window, laid his foil on the bench beside Coigny and began to undo the fastenings of his fencing tunic. He was in no mood to join in the banter about Versailles beauties and was glad when La Fayette turned the subject at once to other things. He was not jealous of the freedom his friend was granted to attend the court, nor of the superior balls and entertainments held there, graced by the finest flowers of European aristocracy. On the contrary, the marquis's desire to shine in this milieu was the only thing that did not inspire Victor's friendly sympathy. If he was jealous of anything, it was of the devotion he had witnessed between the marquis and his wife, and it stood out in his mind, amongst his other somewhat vaguer aims, as the kind of goal one would not hesitate to do battle for.

Honorine de Chercy missed Paris. It was not only her comfortable home in the Rue Jacob, the card parties and her friends that she regretted, but the ordered and tranquil existence that had taken her almost a lifetime to achieve. Honorine was a woman to whom domestic happiness meant everything; but after her brief first marriage, she had been deprived of it. Her beloved husband and her baby daughter had both succumbed to the same illness, and in the long, dreary interval that followed, her only distractions were the many unwelcome offers for her hand that came from gentlemen who were tempted by her fortune. Hope had been revived when she had met Aristide de Chercy, and she had married him because she had believed him an amiable man, indifferent to her assets. She was speedily undeceived on both counts, and although she tried to create a peaceable and pleasant household for him, she was disappointed by his native ill-humour and his unresponsive company, and forced to realise that she could not regret their lack of children.

This did not stop her from being lonely when he died, but it did help her face up to some decisions: she would not marry again and there would be no children in her home, so the peace and comfort she craved must come from the absence of the ills her second marriage had brought her, and the cultivation of people who might bring warmth into her life.

In Paris, Honorine's closest friends were the Billancourt family, at whose hearth she saw all the unity and good cheer she had yearned for in her own home. And she was extremely fond of the Chercys in the Loire. They were not related to her by blood, but they could scarcely have been closer to her heart—even Jules, during his long absence, remained in her affectionate thoughts.

Thus it was that Honorine stayed on at Mirandol for as long as she felt of use. But she was discouraged to find that once Victor de Luny was banished to Paris the situation seemed to deteriorate, and her nephew was as much to blame for this as Viviane.

Jules was reputed to have had a black, savage temper as a boy, never directed towards his new family, but close to the surface nonetheless. Honorine had not seen much of it in his youth, and thought he might have grown out of it, until he decided to dismiss the steward at Mirandol, an old retainer who had been there more than twenty years. Jules took the decision as soon as he had finished going through the estate records. He refused to discuss it with either herself or Viviane, and wasted very few words on the man himself, Jean Lubain. All the women were told was that Lubain had failed to obtain the right prices for the wheat, rye and other crops over the previous few years, and that he had demonstrated his incompetence in too many ways to be retained in his post. Viviane tried to elicit more information from Jules, and when this failed seemed about to stage a formal protest, but she met with a stone wall. Lubain put on a self-pitying scene when he made his farewells, which moved Viviane and irritated Jules: Honorine could see he had difficulty restraining his anger.

As misfortune would have it, the matter came to a

head one day while the Chercys were all in Longfer, the principal market town near Mirandol. Over the previous weeks Jules had re-established acquaintance with most of the people in the region who had known him as a youth, and everywhere he was well received. He was looking after all the farm business himself, until his new steward learned the ropes of local commerce, and thus he had slipped quite easily back into rural life.

On the day he accompanied the women to town, he rode and they took the barouche. Viviane was very animated as they drove along. Honorine had been taking her out visiting lately, which lifted her spirits, and not having been into Longfer for some time, Viviane was looking forward to calling in at her favourite shops in the main street and seeing familiar faces.

Jules left them at a mercer's first and went to the market to transact some business, then rejoined them an hour later and, taking one on each arm, proceeded to walk up the street, stopping when they wished to shop or talk to an acquaintance.

They had dinner on the first floor of the best inn, where Viviane spent a great deal of her time gazing out the window at the street, leaving the count and Honorine to carry the conversation. They got onto opera, about which they disagreed in a friendly way, since he preferred the Italian and she the French, and the time passed pleasantly.

After that they strolled back along the street while the horses were put to the barouche, and Viviane entered a shop to look at some figured silks just down from Paris, which Honorine thought she might like to order for a dress. While she was there the count and Honorine fell into conversation with the Marquis de Luny, who was also in town. Honorine wondered how Viviane would react when she found them talking to the man who had sent her suitor away from her, but she saw no similar unease in Jules's expression. At awkward moments he always displayed a complete coolness, which she could well understand would annoy an ardent young woman.

Viviane burst out of the shop to tell Honorine about her purchase, stopped dead on seeing the marquis, blushed and looked crestfallen. Honorine was always surprised that none of Viviane's moods could dim her attractions; the marquis, who was really quite fond of her, greeted her warmly, and she was forced to look and say the right thing.

But they soon came to the subject of Jean Lubain, for the marquis said that Lubain had left the district while still making vague threats about retribution against the Chercys.

'Good riddance,' Jules said.

'I imagine you'll be glad to see the back of him. He certainly let his bitterness flow around here.'

Viviane said, 'Anyone banished overnight after serving more than twenty years is bound to be bitter, don't you think?'

The marquis, not knowing where to look, did not reply.

Jules lost no time, however. 'Lubain knew exactly why he had to leave, and his complaints are nonsense.'

'Oh, I don't know, there may be a few fair-minded people in Longfer who care to know the truth.' She lifted her gaze to his and held it. Her hazel eyes, flecked with gold, looked to Honorine like those of a half-tamed animal daring its keeper to come closer.

Honorine saw at once that Jules was angry—so angry he had to lower his voice to keep it steady. 'The discussion is over.'

'How very convenient—' Viviane said, but got no further, for the marquis prudently took his leave.

The others watched him walk away, then the count made a signal to the coachman and the barouche was brought along the street. He handed Honorine into the vehicle first, then Viviane, and with her hand still in his he said, 'You will never again stage such an exhibition. Our family business is not discussed in the street or with neighbours. When I get home I expect an apology.'

'You are not—' she began, and stopped. Honorine was sure she was about to say, 'You are not my

67

family.' Jules thought so too. His eyes flashed and he waited, poised for they knew not what, and for a moment even Honorine felt distinctly nervous.

When Viviane failed to continue, he said, 'I shall await your apology,' and turned on his heel.

On the way home Viviane scarcely opened her mouth. Honorine told her everything the count had mentioned about Lubain's failings, and remarked that anyone would be annoyed to have his actions criticised by a close relative in public, and that she would feel the same in a like situation. Honorine knew Lubain was not the real issue—there was a deeper enmity.

Jules was home before them, and as they arrived he appeared in the hall, facing Viviane immediately in full expectation of the excuses he had demanded. Honorine was irked to see him so implacable—she thought he might have waited until they were at least properly in the house.

Viviane obviously thought so too, for she went straight up to him and said in a low voice, 'You want me to be sorry for thinking you do wrong, and for saying so. But I am not afraid of the truth, and it is not my fault if *you* are.'

He reacted at once. 'The truth is you have allowed resentment to turn into insolence, Mademoiselle. I know what is best in this household, and you'll have to accept it.'

'I cannot say yes to injustice!'

He grabbed her wrist as though about to shake her. Honorine protested, he gave her a withering look, and pulled Viviane towards the library. She struggled, but he tightened his grip on her arm, and she exclaimed and then bit her lip. She said not a word more and Honorine realised that her grand-niece was frightened, which made her furious in her turn. As they reached the door Honorine sharply told him to let Viviane go, which he did.

He flung open the door and pointed at the desk on the far side of the room. 'In there I have spent the most tedious hours of my blighted existence. I have read, sorted and accounted for every fact and figure on this estate, for the last ten years and beyond. If you are so keen to express your opinions on how this place is run, you can gather a little information first.'

She raised her voice. 'I know all about Mirandol. I met every week with Jean Lubain—'

'And he told you what he wanted you to hear. He knew as well as I that a young woman cannot run an estate like this. But if you think differently, get in there, Mademoiselle, and give yourself a short education in management. Here is the key to the files. Occupy yourself until supper, then I shall listen to what you have to say.'

He spoke so harshly and looked so menacing that she backed into the library, whereupon he leaned forward, took the door handle and shut the door. For a moment Honorine thought he was going to lock it. She laid a hand on his arm and he shook it off and began to walk towards the stairs. Honorine followed. 'Nephew, I must protest. This is no way to treat your ward.'

'I'll treat her as she deserves.' Fury made his voice shake. 'I'll never have her liking, but by God I'll have her respect.'

Perhaps Honorine's eyes hinted that he risked losing hers, for with another baleful look at her he turned and went upstairs. Viviane remained in the library, where Honorine thought it best not to disturb her. Instead she went up to her room to reflect.

She decided that the only solution to the conflict at Mirandol was to invite Viviane to stay with her in Paris. She could not stand by and watch any more such scenes; in her view, the apology was as much due from him as Viviane, and she hoped he was not too pig-headed to realise it. She was disappointed in them both.

A few days later, Viviane rode alone to the top of the highest hill and looked down over Mirandol. Beyond the birch wood, smoke was rising from the long field where they were burning off the stubble, and she could hear the shouts and laughter of the field hands who tended the fires. The smoke drifted through the poplars by the river, where the milk cows were grazing in the sweet grass near the water. It was hot on the hilltop, and the green shade under the riverside trees invited her in just as it had when she was a child. When she was little she had thought the whole world must be heaven if it was like Mirandol. Now her guardian had turned it into hell. If she was in the library and he walked in, he made her feel that she interrupted the great business of the estate that he made such a fuss about. If she roamed about the stables she recalled his first assessment of her as uncultured and country bred. If she played music at any time of the day or night and he was in the vicinity, he walked off at once. Nowhere in her own home could she be comfortable and happy.

And now he had her great-aunt on his side. At first Viviane did not mind Honorine's reprimands about her hair, her clothes and her manners. She was aware that since her mother's death her father had spoiled her, so she was prepared to admit that her demeanour could do with a little Parisian polish, and that Honorine meant her strictures kindly. But in the large matters also her great-aunt was beginning to share his point of view. She supported him over Victor, and when Viviane tried to make her see how he might be twisting the family finances to his own purposes, she greeted every hint with disapproval or a change of subject. For a woman of such strong character, it was amazing what Great-Aunt Honorine seemed ready to ignore in order to preserve harmony in the house. Too late, too late; Viviane could never be easy with her uncle, he loathed her, and they had gone too far in their opposition to ever retrace their steps.

Looking back, she was filled with nostalgia for her old, cheerful existence at Mirandol. It hurt to be so at odds with her uncle, no matter what he had done to deserve it, for it was the first time in her life that she had ever had such a disastrous effect on another human being. It was time she gave up the struggle for a while and faced the idea of leaving home and conflict behind her. Aching to see some friendly faces, she had written again to Louise, enlisting her help in an attempt to be invited to Paris. She was even managing to appear docile with Honorine most of the time, so that her great-aunt would imagine her as a pleasant house guest rather than a termagant.

As Viviane rode down the hill again towards the château, she noticed that a line of waggons had pulled up at a side entrance, and large boxes were being carried across the footbridge over the moat. Curious to know what was being delivered, she put her mare into a trot. Then she reflected that the waggons had probably brought more of her uncle's belongings. With this came the memory of their altercation over Jean Lubain, and the aftermath.

In the library she had read the estate papers as best she could, crying with rage and frustration, and collected up all the ones relating to Jean Lubain. As she went through them she could make little of the lists of figures from the months before his dismissal, but she did find some comparisons of prices written in the new steward's hand, which showed better returns recently from some of the crops. And then she came across the copy of a letter sent by her uncle a week before, when Jean Lubain was still in Longfer. The new steward had written it out for the records, and scrawled the date in the corner.

The letter had perplexed her. It was in her guardian's usual unpleasant style and accused Lubain of far more than had ever been hinted to her. She was at a loss to know whether the accusation it contained was true, or whether this was just a threat from a so-called gentleman to a powerless man—Lubain was struggling to find a new place without a reference, for her uncle had refused him one.

She was so uncertain about the letter that she copied it out to send to Victor, so that she could seek his opinion. In her explanation, she would also have to be fair and mention that before supper on the night of the quarrel her uncle had begged her pardon for losing his temper. Viviane had been ready to apologise too, for

71

he was making efforts to be polite, but when she had started speaking about Jean Lubain he had closed his eyes and said for pity's sake to drop the subject. And they had gone in to supper, dissatisfied but civil.

The copy of this letter to Lubain was locked in the desk in her bedchamber.

Monsieur
It has come to my notice that since you left the post of steward to Mirandol you have complained of wrongful dismissal to a number of traders in the region. Those who over the last three years have bought grain from you at the advantageous prices you privately offered them, and who paid you the secret commission you demanded, will not be astonished to see you leave this estate, since they will correctly assume your dealings have been discovered by the owner. Others, however, may be taken in by your claims of injury. If you persist in them, I shall be obliged to make your shortcomings public. The reason I have not done so is that I have no desire to advertise the leniency of your late master, nor would I willingly show up the inexperience of my niece, whom you basely cheated. If pressed, however, I shall make the affair public, so hold your tongue or be damned.

At the stables, Viviane questioned her groom and learned that it was indeed her uncle's possessions that were being unloaded from the waggons.

'You would never believe the boxes of books, Mademoiselle. The carters are complaining—books are always the heaviest.'

'Books! Good heavens.'

'Yes, though I'd guess there are some additions to the gunroom as well.'

Viviane smiled and walked back to the château, taking the front doors so as to avoid the waggons, but heading for the boxroom where the luggage was being stacked.

Her uncle was there. He was bending over a wooden

72

crate with a crowbar in his hands, and he nodded rather than bowed when he caught sight of her, scarcely pausing before he bent to rip the box open and push the splintered boards onto the floor. Plunging his hand into the wood shavings, he came up with two long, polished pieces of wood decorated with tattered feathers.

'Ah, here they are.'

'Are those Indian bows?'

'Yes. Dakota.'

'Do you have that kind of thing in the other crates too?'

'No. The rifles are in the long flat one over there. The rest are books and pictures, except I can't tell which is which now they've put them down.'

The last of the boxes was carried in by one of the carters, and the count sent them all off to the kitchen for refreshments, then approached Viviane. 'Excuse me, I suspect this one has paintings.'

She moved out of the way and watched as he levered off the top, more carefully this time, then brushed away the shavings from a large object that reached almost to the sides of the container. Absorbed, he prised the parcel out and turned it over on another crate to peel apart the oilskin wrappings and padding. If this was a painting from Canada, he was about to uncover a relic of his own journeys, his battles, his past. She wondered what he had brought home.

When he propped the unframed canvas up against the wall she caught her breath. It was a landscape of overpowering beauty—a view through a mighty chasm between cliffs which revealed a tall waterfall scything down one side of a gorge and a sunlit valley beyond, widening into a tree-covered plain that misted into blue on the distant horizon. There were no figures—no explorers or picturesque Indians—just the grand and terrible contours of the land, cloaked in green, dappled with the gold light of summer.

'Oh.' She had to sit down to take it in.

They both looked at it for a long time. Viviane had nothing to say beyond the first subdued exclamation of delight. The painting itself seemed to speak, in some mysterious voice that blew towards her like fresh mountain air, carrying words in a language she would never understand.

'Do you know the place?'

'Yes, I could show you on one of the maps.' He still had not taken his eyes off it.

'And the artist?'

'No. I bought this from a dealer. Years ago.' He turned away and set himself to opening one of the square boxes. Viviane watched, fascinated now, and saw that it was full of books. He sat down sideways on a crate, one long leg stretched out, with his boot amongst the wood shavings and, turning over a few gold-edged pages, began to read. He was behaving exactly as she did when she received a book from Paris—perfectly happy to pause in the midst of whatever he was doing and relish a few lines, a tantalising paragraph, of the new work. Except that these books were all presumably old friends.

'Where will you put them?' He did not answer, but for once she was not affronted, knowing that he had not heard her. Running a practised eye over the square boxes in the room she gave a nod. 'About two hundred. Quite manageable, really. I know just the place in the library—a gap where I've been meaning to have shelves for years. I'll speak to Moulin.'

When she came back to the boxroom after consulting with the carpenter and showing him what was to be done, she helped her uncle with the rest of the things. The book crates were opened, dusted down, and then taken to the library where they were placed on large pieces of cloth on the parquet floor, ready to be unpacked later. Viviane volunteered to unwrap the rest of the pictures and he agreed with a smile, busying himself with the various weapons, American, British and European, that would be fixed to the walls in the gunroom.

As she freed each painting from its wrapping she stood it against the wall to admire it, and eventually the canvases surrounded the whole room. Most of them were unframed, and she wondered at his collecting so many when he had had nowhere to hang them, no fixed abode for months and years at a time.

With her head on one side she contemplated one of the smaller framed pictures—a landscape apparently from the same region as the first large one, but including people this time, in an Indian encampment. The scene was peaceful: a hunting party was returning, dogs circled the tents excitedly, the women looked out from the teepees or were walking back from the mountain stream as their children ran alongside. Their faces, clothing and stances were sketched with hasty, vivid brushstrokes, recorded with affection.

'This is my favourite,' she said. 'You could believe it was painted by one of these people themselves; there is love in it somehow.'

He glanced up. 'I see what you mean. They are Cherokee. The artist was not, however. I came across him out there and bought the painting on the spot. Lord knows where he went, or I'd have bought more.'

They worked together for more than an hour, and for the first time Viviane wished that such cooperation with her uncle were possible in the longer term.

Jules awoke next morning with two schemes in mind, for it was Mademoiselle de Chercy's birthday. Most of the families he knew acknowledged saints' days only, if at all, but this was Mirandol, where the Chercys had a firm tradition of making the most of every chance for celebration. He managed to confer at an early hour with Honorine, and actually took breakfast with the ladies, a dubious pleasure which he usually avoided.

He did so in order to observe his ward's face when she came to the table, and he was satisfied to see that she looked embarrassed but unmistakably pleased, and met his eye with what might have even been a spark of gratitude.

He rose and bowed, but before he could give her his good wishes she said, 'My aunt has just asked me to go and stay with her in Paris. I believe you know of this kind invitation?'

He nodded, bowed to Honorine de Chercy as she appeared, and they all sat down. His ward went on, 'This morning Madame de Chercy has given me a very pretty fan, and a lecture on how much more sophisticated I shall be now that I am nineteen. But best of all is the thought of Paris. I can hardly wait.'

'I hope you enjoy your stay. And if you find that you miss Mirandol, please return whenever you wish. Your aunt and I have discussed this: the choice is entirely yours.' He held her eye as he said it, knowing she would choose Paris and so put a temporary end to their intolerable conflict, but hoping also that she would not think he had conspired with Honorine to exile her from Mirandol. On the contrary, from a selfish point of view he dreaded the weary autumn months that he must spend in the château, without even her quarrels or Honorine's disapproval to distract him.

Her eyes were brightened by the surprise, and without a trace of her usual resentment and a fair pretence of interest she said, 'Do you plan to visit Paris yourself, Monsieur?'

'No. This month and October are the busiest months of the year on the estate. As you know.' Besides, he needed more time with the new steward. But he would not bring up that subject at the breakfast table, especially not while she was overcome with this sudden happiness.

She was so preoccupied it took her an instant or two to notice that on the table to the left of her plate was a large flat parcel done up in brown paper. He saw her start, colour slightly, and steal a look at him.

'Happy birthday. Open it.'

It was the framed painting she had so admired the day before. The colour in her cheeks grew more rosy as she stared at it, avoiding his eye, and murmured her thanks. She showed it to Honorine, and then had the courage to look him in the face and give him a genuine smile. 'I never expected you to remember my birthday.'

'Not remember it! I recall exactly where I was when

I received the announcement. My very surroundings when I read the letter, and rejoiced to know you were both safe ...' He stopped. It was an impossible moment. He knew there was no joy in his expression as he looked down at the table, and he could not make himself continue. Memory showed him tall cliffs, his mounted platoon strung out behind him patrolling a sunlit escarpment, the cruel beauty of the azure sky and the river crawling below. He had stood with one hand on the pommel of his saddle while the other held the letter, which a breeze tried to tug from his fingers. Violette was safe, home, enfolded with her child. He was a hollow figure in a landscape that the wind swept through.

Honorine came to the rescue and kept up the conversation, and he and his ward joined in as best they could, despite having very different things to occupy their minds.

Viviane often glanced towards the painting, and at one point said unguardedly, 'I look forward to showing this to Monsieur de Luny.' She caught Honorine's eye and said, 'If I am to have the privilege of seeing him, of course. And I should like to compare it with the books of travellers' sketches that Monsieur de Billancourt has collected. Mademoiselle de Billancourt has told me so much about them.'

5

PARIS

One of the great pleasures for Louise de Billancourt was a drive in the Bois de Boulogne at a fashionable hour, when the rest of Paris were driving about likewise, observing each other for signs of interest. On this sunny autumn day Louise was especially content because she expected to see the Baron de Ronseul go by in his barouche. Viviane was happy also, for she had at last persuaded Louise to accompany her on a visit to the Marquis and Marquise de La Fayette. Once they had done the tour of the Bois, Honorine de Chercy would drop them at the door of the great house in the Rue du Faubourg Saint-Honoré and collect them again after half an hour. Viviane hoped to achieve three things during this important call: to keep another rendezvous with Victor which they had arranged in a whispered exchange the week before, to discuss pressing matters to do with America, and to see whether the Marquis de La Fayette could achieve the revolution she hoped for in Louise's mind—namely, an interest in the future of the United States.

Viviane considered this a far less dangerous preoccupation than her friend's obsession with the Baron Alain de Ronseul. On being introduced to him Viviane was able to say that she found him perfectly the gentleman, and very good-looking, and she was not surprised to learn he had entry into every house in Paris. Privately, however, she could not like him. She suspected him of being a predator where women were concerned, and untrustworthy in other ways as well. He was not a flatterer, in fact quite the opposite: he gave the impression he rather expected women to try to interest *him*, and that he had a host of admirers waiting to fling themselves at him (some of the ladies on that first evening did their best to confirm this), and he had a style of delivery and a calculating glance that left room for too many double meanings.

78

Rather nervous for her friend, Viviane asked older women about him, but they tended either to laugh with a great deal of innuendo, or to frown and say that any woman who risked more than five minutes' conversation with him was a fool; but no one explained to her where the danger lay. She often felt frustrated by the oblique way people talked in Paris, and confided to Victor: 'No one seems to care about actual facts; I have met so many people who manage to *sound* very clever when they mention politics at court, or the latest news from London, but when you question them you find they are totally vague about what is really going on and look down on you for wanting to know yourself!'

The young women did indeed cross the baron's path that day. On one of the turns there was a press of carriages, and the traffic came to a standstill. By coincidence—or perhaps by the baron's arrangement—their vehicles stopped abreast of each other, facing in opposite directions. He leaned out and looked past the two young women, sweeping off his hat and greeting Honorine de Chercy with great ceremony, before allowing his gaze to linger over Louise and then Viviane.

'Mademoiselle de Billancourt, what a delightful surprise. Fate must be smiling on me: I seem to be always meeting you. I must have done something worthy, somewhere, to be so blessed. If only I could imagine what it was. And Mademoiselle de Chercy, I trust Paris is behaving well towards you? To my mind, in autumn Paris grows in beauty. In fact I have never felt the effect so strongly as I do today.' As he replaced his hat, his arm concealed his profile from Louise. Viviane, holding his gaze without replying, saw his eyes narrow in sly amusement, as though her silence somehow established a complicity between them. Next moment he looked ahead. 'We are untangled, I see. I had better move off and make way for the herd behind. Your servant, ladies, as ever.'

Viviane was not impressed by his arrogant glance or his indifference as to whether they had anything to say to him—their admiration, he implied, was all his anyway. It was no good discussing him with Louise: for one thing, they could not talk openly in front of her great-aunt, and for another she had already tried once, soon after reaching Paris, and had been rebuked. Louise had said indignantly, 'Here have I been taking unheard-of risks to help you, wearing myself out with your intrigues, and faithfully exchanging your scandalous letters, only to be told I am acting improperly by saying a few words to a gentleman! I do call that ungrateful, Viviane. And I scarcely speak to him anyway. I declare there are sometimes matrons of *thirty* pushing themselves in my way to get to him.'

The carriage reached the Rue du Faubourg Saint-Honoré sooner than they had expected, and Honorine de Chercy suggested they do some shopping before the visit. The young women agreed readily and, leaving the carriage at a convenient point, they began exploring the expensive shops at the western end of the street. As they wandered about they became separated from Madame de Chercy and were able to talk freely.

Louise said, 'Can you guess why I was so eager to stop? Because this is just where the Baron de Ronseul lodges. He does not live with his mother in their town house; he has a splendid apartment over the mercer's— there, across the way. I do so like shopping in this quarter, one never knows whom one may run across.' Viviane said nothing, and Louise continued, 'I suppose you noticed how he looked at me today?'

And how he looked at me, Viviane thought, knowing that she could never say it out loud.

'That's because he is so deliciously uncertain. Let's keep our distance from your aunt—I have been aching to mention this for days. You remember when I went to the Vauventins'? Now, I shall tell you exactly what happened and you are to imagine it as if you had been there yourself and tell me what you think. I promise to take notice.

'We were placed together during the meal, Maman was quite unsuspecting, and we were at the same table for cards. When our game broke up he asked me to go with him into the next room. I thought it was just another card room, and agreed. But it wasn't: we were all alone in a small space with other doors leading into the apartments.'

'Didn't that make you nervous?'

'Oh, I had no fear, for I knew if I raised my voice I would easily be heard by my friends. But I felt a bit awkward at being so readily alone with him, so I pretended to look at a pretty landscape on the wall. He lost no time in drawing close, and when I turned I found myself facing him with only an inch or two between us. His eyes glowed and he asked permission to kiss me! I had scarcely understood the question and opened my mouth for a denial when he acted as though I had given my consent. I should have struggled, I know, but I was overwhelmed. Wait until you know the power of a man's lips before you judge me. At first my mind was filled with a white flash, as though I had been struck by lightning.'

She caught Viviane's glance, opened her eyes wide and said, 'Scoff if you like, I am speaking the truth. You always say frankness is all, so if you are my friend you must listen to the rest. While he kissed me I was aware of such different impressions: his mouth grew hard and then soft by turns; he even allowed the tip of his tongue to slide between my lips.' She blushed and, putting her arm through Viviane's, drew her nearer to whisper, 'Bear with this wicked confession. If I describe everything to you, I may be able to see for myself whether I did right or wrong. At the time I could not think at all.

'He held me by my shoulders. Then I felt one hand slide lower so that his thumb was poised here.' She laid her free hand on the bare skin above one breast. 'At the same moment he withdrew his mouth from mine and I gasped. His fingers descended no further, and he murmured, "Never fear," and began to kiss my neck.

'One of my hands crept in under his coat so it rested on his chest. He said, "The readiest pupil! I'll warrant you were the quickest at every lesson." He said this looking into my eyes. Then he kissed me again and drew my hand down tightly over his body.'

Viviane said, 'Good heavens, Louise, are you proud of this? To be lurking in dark rooms with a man like that . . .' She withdrew her arm and walked more quickly, so that Louise had to almost run to catch her up.

'Do I shock you? I felt just the same, of course, and I drew back and began to protest. But he forestalled me: he let go my hand, gave me a clouded look and sighed, "You see how obedient I am—" and then he was gone! He walked straight off and disappeared into the apartments beyond. It was ages before I could bring myself to rejoin the company, but no one noticed a thing. He did not come back.'

'Today is the first time you have seen him since?'

'Yes. He left me in the deepest confusion. I could not work out whether he was annoyed with me, disappointed, alarmed, sorry . . . ? Please give me your opinion. I shan't be angry, whatever you say, for it gives me wicked pleasure just to talk about him. You see how far gone I am.'

They were inside a mercer's shop by this time, and Viviane halted to sort through some satins, wondering how not to offend Louise. It was the most difficult moment of their friendship, impossibly complicated by the fact of her own conspiracy with Victor. When she spoke, she tried to keep her tone light, and chose her words with care.

'I cannot set up as a moralist, since I know less of the world than you, after a lifetime buried at Mirandol. These are just my own ideas, and you must keep your promise not to resent them.' She took a breath. 'I think Monsieur de Ronseul speaks finely but acts coarsely.' She had the courage to look up and meet Louise's troubled gaze. 'This does not mean that you acted so, because he took you by surprise. Everything he did leaves me with a very bad impression, and oddly enough the way he sneaked off and hid himself away at the end is the worst. If I knew more of men I suppose I could tell you why.'

Louise said with the hint of a pout, 'Then what is there to accuse him of?'

82

'He does not seem to think of anything but his own desires. If he is so intent on those, can he ever really please you?' Louise looked unconvinced, so she pressed on: 'I do know what you mean about kissing. The first time Victor and I . . . it was exactly as you said. But we did not continue, and to tell you the truth we have not embraced since. We love each other, I think, but do not need to go off into corners to prove it. Oh dear, now I sound prim. But I am not trying to tell you how a pure young woman ought to behave, for I have never met a pure young woman, and do not consider myself one. I just . . . I do not believe Monsieur de Ronseul is fitted to be your friend, suitor or husband.'

Louise stiffened as she digested this speech, twisting the end of a length of lace in her fingers as she did so. Then she gave a muffled laugh. 'I know what you mean about the spotless and pure—the most dreadful little Saint Catherines at the convent were always the slyest creatures underneath. And I give you the benefit of the doubt over Monsieur de Ronseul. He does frighten me a bit, and I don't think he has the right to do that, do you? I shall have to be severe with him. And avoid him for a while—it will do him good.'

Viviane had to be content with this, for her great-aunt gathered them up just then and took them to the Duchesse d'Ayen's for the meeting with La Fayette.

There they were received with the kindness of friendship. Madame de La Fayette, a slender, fair woman who rather resembled Louise, took special care to welcome her, and with her sisters she soon created a circle around the new guest. This gave Viviane the opportunity to talk to Victor and La Fayette, at first under the watchful eye of the Duchesse d'Ayen, but later in a part of the room where they could not be overheard.

She said eagerly to the marquis, 'Has there been any further word from New York?'

La Fayette shook his head. 'Nothing since we last spoke.'

Viviane sighed. 'It is difficult to see how Washington can defend it. When you think that most of his men are militia, and they are faced with regulars on the other side—General William Howe has thousands of them on Staten Island.'

Victor said, 'And Admiral Lord Howe has reached Sandy Hook. The troops from England must bring the forces to more than 30,000.'

La Fayette said, 'My friend the Baron de Kalb has given me some figures on Britain's latest purchases of mercenaries. The Landgrave of Hesse-Kassel has personally sent 17,000 Hessians to the war, and Charles of Brunswick and other German princes will supply about 11,000 more.'

Viviane said thoughtfully, 'Imagine the money required for that! It is obvious that England has it to spend, and considers New York well worth it. What hope is there of sending funds like those to bolster up Washington?'

Victor said quietly, 'All the money available is being spent in Europe, to buy arms and supplies for shipment.' He looked up to see La Fayette's frown, and said, 'I have no hesitation mentioning such things to Mademoiselle de Chercy. She is our stoutest ally: has she told you what she is doing for Silas Deane, the American commissioner?'

When La Fayette looking inquiringly at her, Viviane explained. 'You know how Mr Deane chafes under the English surveillance of his premises: he can receive no one important there or the news is back to London in a trice. And of course he is spied on whenever he goes to other houses. I have found a solution for him. Did you know that my aunt's house is in the same street as Mr Deane's? The stables are enormous—there are two coach-houses, and the second one is empty and locked up. It has two doors, one onto the coach-yard and the other directly onto the lane at the corner.

'So, at a prearranged time, the outer door is left open for Mr Deane. He passes the lane when he sets out for his morning constitutional along the Seine. This is such a habit of his that the vigilance is relaxed then and he has no trouble slipping into the lane if we have arranged an appointment for him. The scheme is simple—the person he wishes to consult comes as a guest to us, makes the usual social call, and after saying farewell to my aunt and me is shown to his carriage. Once in the yard, he is taken aside by my groom, Edouard. I know Edouard is trustworthy, for he is . . . sometimes a messenger between Monsieur de Luny and myself.' She hurried on, 'Anyway, the guest is ushered into the coach-house where he can confer with Mr Deane in private. My aunt knows nothing of this; she has better things to do than notice how long it takes a guest's carriage to leave the yard. The other servants are aware of the meetings, but none of them can know who they are with, except Edouard, for he is the only person ever to see Mr Deane. They are all loyal, and well paid to remain so.'

The marquis smiled and said, 'This is ingenious. But what will you do if the meetings are discovered?'

'Nothing. Mr Deane would have to find another place of rendezvous, that is all. In the meantime I am glad to be of use to him.'

'Have you written to your guardian about this?' Victor said.

'No, my letters are dutiful but brief, which is all he deserves. I never discuss such things with him, for he is not forthcoming about America. I don't think he considers it a woman's subject, which infuriates me. At Mirandol he would sit a whole evening reading one of the books he brought back from Canada, but when I asked questions he just said that he spent his career fighting for territory that will never be French again, and he is not disposed to waste time talking about it. I expect it is natural for him to be bitter, but there is no need for him to act as though he were an old man and his life over. Mind you, my aunt told me just recently that he was in pain for months after Quebec, and still suffered when he first got to Mirandol.'

'But he is recovered now, or so he says,' La Fayette interjected. 'I greatly value his correspondence: there are a thousand things he can tell me that I would learn from no other man. I trust he is not concealing some illness?'

'Not at all. By the time I left home he was strong as he claims. In fact now that he is well again, and some of the frown lines have disappeared from his face, you would never think he is thirty-six, which is what I calculate him to be.' She smiled at Victor. 'I remember you were struck that his figure is that of a younger man. I suppose army life keeps men fit.'

'I wish I had the chance to find out,' he said in a low voice, then glanced meaningfully at La Fayette. '*You* certainly will. The English have raised a great fuss about your plans lately, but we shall circumvent them.'

The young marquis shifted his shoulders impatiently under his well-cut coat. 'This business of the mercenaries incenses me. When I think that there are men armed only with the muskets they use for hunting, hiding out in the woods around New York, forced to fight for their rights against fully equipped troops who are nothing but the toys of a distant German prince! After this, the English Foreign Office can surely have no justification for outrage if one lone Frenchman throws in his lot with their miserably persecuted enemy.'

Stimulated by the visit, and buoyed up by the anticipation of another rendezvous with Victor, Viviane was driven away from the Duchesse d'Ayen's in the liveliest spirits. She was a little disappointed, however, with Louise's answers when Madame de Chercy asked if she had enjoyed the visit.

'Oh, very. What a sumptuous house, I never saw the like. The drawing room is all lined in crimson damask and gilt panelling.'

'The duchess and her daughters received you well?'

'Indeed. I saw at once why they are known as "the nest of doves"! They all cooed over me while Viviane entertained the marquis.'

To prevent Louise from mentioning what she had talked about, Viviane said quickly, 'You seemed to get on well with Madame de La Fayette.'

'Well, she was very obliging, and I was polite back. But honestly I cannot imagine what you see in her—she is the most domesticated little creature I ever met and seems no good for anything but having babies.

And she talks of her husband in such an adoring way, it sets my teeth on edge. She told me she is frightened he really will try to take ship to America, against everyone's wishes, including that of her whole family. I must say I do pity her *that*.'

'So do I,' Honorine de Chercy put in. 'Monsieur de La Fayette would do better to concentrate on his wife and child in France than hatch these ridiculous plans. I cannot see why any sensible young Frenchman should bother himself about the United States of America. And the sooner you give up worrying about that sorry bunch of foreigners, my dear niece, the better I shall be pleased.'

'Madame, I am afraid I do not consider them as insignificant as you do. In fact I have decided to further my studies in their language. I have found a lady called Mrs Matthews who is the wife of an English merchant here in Paris, and she has offered to give me lessons.'

Honorine de Chercy looked at her in consternation. 'Really, Mademoiselle, you do waste your time on the strangest pursuits. Why on earth should you want to speak English?'

'So that I shall be able to converse with Benjamin Franklin when he arrives in Paris.'

Honorine de Chercy laughed, convinced she could not be serious, then said decidedly, 'If that man is coming here with his hand out to beg from the government and everyone else, the least he could do would be to learn French. Pray let us drop this subject, it exasperates me beyond reason.'

At that point they found themselves driving past the old Chercy town house in the Rue Dauphine, and Viviane looked fondly out the window of the carriage. 'Aunt, have we time to go in and have a look? I have not been inside since I came to Paris. The caretakers will open it for us.'

'I think not, my dear. Rest assured, it is in passable condition. But far too big now for anyone's purposes. I should not be surprised if your uncle thought of selling it.'

'Selling it! Our beautiful old house? What a

monstrous idea. Even he could not contemplate such heresy—all his childhood memories of Paris must be bound up with that house.' Then she stopped. 'But I forget, he is no Chercy.'

'He lived there with your father during his cadetship,' Honorine de Chercy said. 'But he tells me that he would find the house too gloomy to rattle around in alone. He will look for other premises when he arrives.'

Louise said in surprise, 'The count is coming to Paris? You said nothing of this, Viviane.'

'I received his letter only this morning,' Madame de Chercy said smoothly. Viviane, as startled as Louise, realised her aunt had chosen to reveal the news in company in order to prevent the worst of her protests. 'Things are in very good train at Mirandol, the harvests are all in, and I gather he has exhausted the attractions of country society and would welcome a change. I look forward to seeing him; he will stay with me while he looks for a place in town.'

'And when are we to enjoy this honour, Madame?' Viviane said in a calm voice that hid a surge of helpless anger.

'I expect him Friday fortnight. We shall spend all day at home and be ready to give him a welcome.'

That was the day of her planned meeting with Victor. Her uncle was already interfering in her life again, before he had even stepped over the threshold.

When the Comte de Mirandol duly arrived at the Rue Jacob, Viviane found that he looked fresh, vigorous and determined to be agreeable. He received an affectionate welcome from Honorine, and while his servants ran up and down stairs with his luggage he sat in the drawing room with the women, answering their questions about Mirandol.

He almost smiled as he said to Viviane, 'I must thank you for your last letter. It arrived on the very day Feray supervised the final picking of the fruit, and on his authority I can say the apples will be only "fair to middling lasters", but we have three bushels more of

88

them than last year. Feray and the others deal passably well with the new steward and the farms pose no problems.'

'You have had quiet months then, since we left?' Honorine said.

'Yes. Aside from the harvest, nothing of note has occurred. We did have trouble with a fox bothering the turkeys, and the best solution seemed to be to invite the neighbours in and let them and the hounds settle his business. A great time was had by all, except poor Renard, of course—he was neatly cornered at the shingle bend in the river on the far side of the estate.'

'Have you entertained at all?'

'Yes. In fact there was a late dinner at Mirandol after the hunt, and the staff carried things off handsomely. Some of the guests stayed to supper, and managed to look surprised that it was dark when they ordered their carriages.' He turned to Viviane again. 'I was glad that you wrote to say you are content with Paris; I was able to tell the household that you are doing splendidly, for they have all inquired after you.'

'Will you stay in Paris long, Monsieur?'

'I cannot say.' He glanced at Honorine. 'Of course I shall not trespass on your hospitality more than I can help. I shall inquire about lodgings tomorrow.'

'Madame de Billancourt has heard of a little house in the Rue Richelieu that may be to your taste. It used to be the residence of the emissaries from Rome, and she heard about it through Monseigneur the Archbishop of Paris. The Holy See is keen to sell.'

Before he could reply, Viviane said, 'I wonder you do not take up residence in the Chercy mansion.'

He turned to her, the green eyes intent. 'Do you? I thought Madame de Chercy had told you my plans. I have a buyer for the old place, and I shall use some of the proceeds to purchase another more suited to my needs.'

'And what about *my* needs?'

'Are you saying that you would like to live there yourself?' He raised his eyebrows at her, then when she did not immediately respond, he did so for her. 'No, thanks to the kindness of your great-aunt, you are much better situated here. The Chercy place is enormous—you would require an army of servants, where here you have only one. And you would need a companion. Generous though your great-aunt is, we can scarcely ask her to leave her home yet again for your convenience. I am sure you see all the difficulties as clearly as I do.'

'Thank you, Monsieur, I am only too well aware that I have not the funds to maintain the house. But it is part of the Chercy estate, and should not be alienated from us. Future generations may view its sale as dimly as I do.'

Honorine de Chercy looked as though she expected him to be irritated by this remark, but he gave her a smile and after a moment said to Viviane, 'You oblige me to explain my own reasons for wanting a different house, Mademoiselle. Of course I cannot expect you to share them. After a career living in bivouacs, I find a large residence rather daunting. That includes Mirandol, if you want to know, but I would never dream of making any changes there. The Paris house is different. Do you realise it is not ancient family property? It was bought by your grandfather in 1750. As for future generations, I must tell you I have no expectation of marrying. I understand your reluctance to see the old house go. But you have no use for it now, and will have none once you marry, so there is no point in its lying idle for the sake of sentiment.'

Viviane was about to reply, then hesitated. It would be shrewder to keep the rest of her arguments until she could lay them before Victor, which she would do that very evening, since he was invited to supper along with the Billancourt family and other guests. So she went on to sustain her part of the conversation with great fortitude, and by the time she left the room her uncle was looking quite content with her. Little did he know.

After Viviane had gone, Jules said to Honorine, 'It is kind of you to have my niece here for so long. I hope she is not a burden?'

'Not at all. Nor does she put me to any expense, thanks to you. I wish you would allow me to tell her that you pay her maid's wages as well; she was so grateful when I engaged her, I was embarrassed.'

'Do you think she would be happy to owe the favour to me? I very much doubt it. Let us leave things as they are. I must say either you or the maid or both have done wonders with her.'

'Oh, she is a delight to have in Paris, and Paris is delighted with her. One grows so used to her looks at Mirandol as not to notice them, but launched on society here, with the clothes and accessories she needed to set her off, she caused a sensation. She and my friend's daughter Mademoiselle de Billancourt make a superb picture together: the other young lady is fragile, with light hair, in such contrast to Mademoiselle de Chercy. They are both beautiful, but to my eye your ward is the more striking, with that clear complexion and bloom on her cheeks that always remind me ... of her mother. And she has no vanity, she is just as happy chattering away at the La Fayettes' salon, where there is more pretension to ideas than fashion, as she is being admired in the other grand houses.'

'What happens when Victor de Luny appears on the scene?'

'Nothing out of the ordinary. I must say she treats the gentlemen with complete naturalness and does not seem to know what it is to flirt. With her friend it is different, I am afraid, and my hints to Madame de Billancourt are in vain—her daughter twists her around her little finger. The demoiselle has a certain influence over your niece, too, but Mademoiselle de Chercy is the superior in intelligence, which balances things between them. They are both thoroughly good-hearted creatures, and it is a pleasure to see them together.'

On the whole, things went smoothly for Viviane's purposes that night. She had doubted her guardian's ability to turn from savage to socialite in one evening, and the supper party confirmed that he would never make a courtier. But she found that the company were scarcely expecting suave manners from him: they were all too dazzled in advance by his reputation as a man of action. The grand phrase 'the hero of Ticonderoga' seemed to precede him everywhere, along with the knowledge that he had been one of the leaders of the Americans' brilliant capture of this fort on Lake Champlain during the push for Canada the year before. It made no difference when he explained to people that it was but one attack amongst many, and that the campaign had ended in defeat before Quebec, nor did they listen when he laid the credit for Ticonderoga where he considered it belonged—with Ethan Allen and the famous Green Mountain Boys. Tonight, however, he coped with the situation very well; the supper passed off agreeably and the Chercys gave an adept impression of family unity for the occasion.

After the meal her uncle fortunately did not ask her to play to the guests, and he was so surrounded himself that she had no difficulty managing a confidential exchange with Victor in one corner of her aunt's vast salon. In a low vehement voice she talked to him about the Chercy town house.

'My uncle's excuse for the sale is that he has no plans to marry and does not want to live in the house, so he is looking for a more modest place. Victor, selling the mansion is like killing all my memories. Not his, of course, since he only became a Chercy when he was ten. Goodness knows where he lived before Grandpapa adopted him, probably some hole in the wall that he wants to replicate in Paris, while he spends the proceeds from our beautiful old house. You see what I meant about his first moves with the estate—he wants cash, not immovable assets, and he is determined to get it.'

Victor listened with an attentive look in his brown eyes that showed how closely he entered into her feelings. 'Have you spoken about this to Madame de Chercy?'

'Yes, but she just says he has the right to sell if he wishes. I see no point in making her miserable about it. No, I have decided to consult a lawyer. Will you be an angel and find a good one for me, and meet him with me so I can make a plan of attack? I don't care how much it costs—I have not spent anywhere near my allowance lately, and if the worst comes to the worst I have a little collection of jewels that were my mother's legacy to me, which I may do with as I please. I'm sure she would smile down on me as I sold them, if she knew that I was fighting the man who is out to devastate my heritage.'

'How can you do this without your aunt or uncle knowing?'

'Just arrange the meeting for me, and I shall go there on the pretext of shopping. Mademoiselle de Billancourt will accompany me but wait in the carriage—my aunt sometimes lets us go out together, with our maids. As long as we are not away for more than an hour, she does not play the duenna.'

His glance slid over to Louise, who was sitting with her mother and Madame de Chercy at the opposite end of the room. Louise caught his eye and smiled mysteriously back, and he said, 'Mademoiselle de Billancourt is a wonderful ally. I congratulate you on your choice of friends.'

Viviane went on hesitantly, 'I have something else to ask you. I don't do so for myself, you understand, so you must not be jealous, this is on behalf of . . . a third person. I think there is reason to distrust the Baron de Ronseul, but there is not a woman who will give me a direct opinion of him except to admit that he's handsome and rich and invited everywhere. You are so good at being frank, will you please give me the men's view of him? Then I can pass the information on, properly phrased of course, if . . . friendship requires it.'

Victor looked startled, then thoughtful: the inquiry piqued him unpleasantly. When pressed, however, he decided to give her the truth. 'Ronseul is generally considered one of the best fellows in Paris for company. He has vast estates in the Beaujolais that he never sees, and his income is well up to his expensive style. I don't care for him though. He's the idlest chap ever—follows not a single sport, not even hunting, and stares at you if you mention anything that requires more than a gentle stroll. As to his attractions, if you like a smooth face and eyes that look as though his valet has made them up for him, I suppose he's pretty enough.

'Aside from that . . . ' he paused, then went on, 'the man's an animal, since you want the truth, and boasts about his conquests. He's fond of saying he'll never marry, and then adding that if he did, for the wedding night he'd have a real charmer on hand who knew what she was doing, just to teach the wife her place.' Instantly regretting this last disclosure, he blushed and said, 'Do you want me to tell you more? I hate saying this, you shouldn't be hearing such things, especially from someone who thinks the world of you.'

Viviane, her eyes lowered, decided she had heard quite enough about the baron. She shook her head, and Victor continued in a warmer voice, 'I am not the only person who adores you. La Fayette is in awe of your beauty and cleverness, so much that I should be jealous if he were not in love with his wife. And she thinks you are wonderful. I am glad you like her too, for one day she will need her friends around her. La Fayette is doing his utmost to go to America and I am positive now that he will. Don't breathe a word elsewhere or let him know I told you. Of course I trust you with anything, you are more steadfast than most men I know, but La Fayette lives with a different kind of woman and does not recognise her strength as I do yours.'

'I hear that the King has a *lettre de cachet* signed and sealed and kept in a locked drawer at Versailles, ready to use against him if he attempts to go.'

'True. But our friend is cautious enough to avoid blatant opposition to His Majesty, and frequents Versailles without any unpleasantness.'

Viviane rejoined the company before her guardian could disapprove of her whispering in corners. But she could not prevent Louise from seeking her out and insisting on a private talk herself. They achieved this behind their fans, not far from the other guests, but on the opposite side of the room from the Comte de Mirandol.

Louise began in a teasing whisper. 'I've been dying to say this: in all your moaning about your guardian, how could you *possibly* have failed to mention how handsome he is? I was expecting the veriest monster to walk into the room, so when he was introduced I was lost in absolute confusion. Thank goodness he did not notice because he was too busy being polite—you never told me he was well-bred either! I can't see *one* of the horrendous deficiencies you have been cataloguing for months.' She caught Viviane's wrathful eye and said quickly, 'Oh, I am sure he is the devil you say, because I always believe you, but he looks like an angel.'

She could see that the cheeky smile on her lips was not enough to mollify Viviane, so she went on, 'Do not be cross with me, for I *have* found one or two things to disapprove. He is very cool, which would make it easy for him to be devious and deceitful. Also, he does not suffer fools gladly, for he gave the barest replies to Monsieur Fabre when he prattled on at supper. And I promise to find more things to dislike; you must bring him with you to our place constantly and I shall observe him and try to work up an active loathing.'

Viviane could not help smiling at this, and said, 'Dear Louise, you are not obliged to detest him, only to understand why I do. Let us not talk about him, I know you have much more interesting things to tell me. I saw to whom you spoke at the Marquise de Lavoile's last night.'

'Monsieur de R, of course. And I hope you noticed how seriously I take your advice. He told me himself that he has a shocking reputation, and when I asked him whether he is not ashamed of it, he said not until he had met me and seen the frown upon my pretty face; so I told him he was incorrigible and he needn't think I would bother trying to reform him. And he laughed and left me alone, so I doubt whether he will pester me again. While you were playing the pianoforte he was ready to approach me, but your friend sat beside me and looked proprietorial, so A de R was frightened off, and serve him right.'

She and Viviane looked involuntarily across at Victor, who was deep in conversation with the Comte de Mirandol. 'I do like your V de L, he always pays such charming attention to me. Of course I know for whose sake he does so, but that only makes me like him the more. Indeed he talked to me such a lot last night I reprimanded him for not listening to your playing, but he said he has heard you for ever and already knows you to be a capital performer, and kept on chattering with me. I hope A de R's nose was completely out of joint by the end of the evening.'

Viviane was preoccupied by the sight of the count and Victor talking earnestly together, and answered at random, 'Now that the season is in full swing, I daresay we shall have much more variety when we go into company from now on.'

'Yes, Paris is such fun in the cold weather, with everyone back in town, and balls being held. I have spent some time with the dressmaker looking at fabrics, and you should too, otherwise you will find every other lady in Paris has already ordered her cloaks and winter dresses, and all the seamstresses will be busy for other people until well into December. I do not know what it is like in the Loire, but December in Paris is killing. Let me know when you are going out to buy pelisses and muffs, and I'll come too. I have decided I want to look Russian this year—fair hair and black sable look splendid together. Or so someone whispered to me recently. Let us go shopping tomorrow. I have persuaded Papa that my winter wardrobe is long overdue.'

6

THE DUELLISTS

Viviane was at the house of the Duc and Duchesse de Brissac on the Ile Saint-Louis, playing quadrille in one of the duchess's vast upper rooms below a choir of angels upon the brightly painted caissoned ceiling, who beamed with Italianate benevolence at the somewhat dissipated scene beneath. Besides the innocuous games that Viviane and other young people were engaged in, there were, in the corners of the exquisitely gilded and panelled room, tables where older members of the aristocracy leaned with fell intent over the cards, scarcely speaking while serious fortunes hung in the balance, and contributing nothing to the general gaiety of the fashionable crowd.

Viviane's partner was a good-looking young man, the Chevalier du Buysson, whom she had met at once on coming to Paris, since he was a member of the circle around La Fayette. He had urbane manners, a charming smile and was always amusing company. Tonight they were having a run of luck, but since neither was a keen player, their conversation distracted them often from the game, which gave the two young gentlewomen opposing them some hope of turning the tables eventually. The stakes were not high, so the ups and downs of play had no effect on their mood, which was extremely merry.

The chevalier swept the cards towards him again and his grey eyes lightened with laughter. 'Our condolences, Mesdemoiselles; I am sorry to deprive you of your mite once more. I do wish I had had my partner with me when I played last week in the anteroom of the Queen. My talents have never given me an entrée to the grand table, but who knows what I might do with Mademoiselle de Chercy on my side.'

'You are much better off on the fringes, Monsieur le Chevalier,' Viviane said with a smile. 'The Queen's table is the likeliest place in the kingdom to be fleeced at—she took an Austrian château off one of her best friends only last month.'

The pretty young lady opposite the chevalier said with sly amusement, 'Can one wonder that they keep a *republican* at arm's length? Do you not reckon your chances of entry rather slim, whoever your partner may be?'

'All the more reason for them to take me on,' the chevalier said nonchalantly.

'And to match wits with Mademoiselle de Chercy,' said a voice behind them, 'for her views are as outrageous as your own.'

Viviane turned slightly and caught the gaze of Inigo Matthews, the merchant whose wife had agreed to be her English tutor. She had met him seldom, for he was very active about his own affairs, having established his business in Paris more than two years before. She was never sure how to take what he said, for he sometimes paid her adroit compliments and she often saw his pupils widen when his eyes rested on her, in sudden and involuntary interest. If this had ever happened while his wife was by, it would have been embarrassing, but he was devoted to Mrs Matthews in a gentlemanly way and she had never heard any rumours that he strayed.

She said, 'If my views are outrageous, I share them with the Congress in Pennsylvania, and I have not yet learned to be ashamed of them.'

'Is Congress the true voice of this rude collection that we are being asked to call the United States? It has usurped the lawful assemblies.'

'It had to,' Viviane said, 'once the British government was openly committed to exploiting the colonies. The union of the states was inevitable—the republicans had to hang together.'

'Or, as Benjamin Franklin remarked, they would all most certainly hang separately,' Matthews said, raising a laugh at both tables. Play did not resume, for everyone was enjoying the sparring match.

'No one could have been more peaceable or diplomatic in the approaches to King George than Benjamin

Franklin,' Viviane continued. 'Think of his years in your home country, Mr Matthews, and all his cogent petitions on behalf of his own. All ignored.'

'Oh, if we are to descend to personalities, I am not sure I value your Franklin too highly. Back in the mid-60s, when the colonies were railing against the Stamp Act, he named one of his closest friends as stampman in Philadelphia!'

'But then he agreed to his suspension, so long as the other states opposed the Act.'

'Was this Stamp Act so odious?' one of her former opponents asked in puzzlement.

Viviane smiled and put one finger on the pile of shiny new cards in front of her. 'Should you like it if there were a tax in France on the manufacture of every one of these?'

'Surely not!' said the lady, open-mouthed.

'Indeed yes,' du Buysson replied. 'Nothing could be printed in the colonies, not a hand bill, not a news-paper, not a legal document, not a playing card, unless official stamped paper was used. Do you wonder they would not let the paper land in the country?'

'The Bostonians had the same attitude towards tea, I believe,' the other young lady remarked dryly. 'Yet one can hardly hurl everything overboard just because it is taxed! I mean, everyone pays tax. Why were the Americans to be exceptions?'

Matthews said, 'Bravo: you have hit it. The fact is they would not contribute to the coffers because they were unwilling for American expenses to be paid for with American money.'

'Expenses such as?' the chevalier said quickly.

'The war in Canada and the Indian wars. They called on Britain for protection then, yet next thing they had the gall to object to garrisons that were there to main-tain their own safety.'

Viviane gave Matthews a challenging smile. 'Those were wars that the British were eager to win—against the French. But now, don't you think the Americans rather prefer us to the English? And what were those garrisons of redcoats used for at Boston, Lexington and

Concord? To fortify the customs houses and fire on civilians. To impose the rule of the gun on the people they were supposed to be protecting.'

'This has nothing to do with "the people", Mademoiselle, though I am sure they would be overwhelmed to see your eyes glow so when you speak of them. America is run by her merchants, who have grown mighty rich and are eager to get richer by shifting the balance of trade with England wholly in their own favour.'

Viviane shook her head. 'How can anyone speak of "balance" when effectively the States must trade *only* with Britain? They are forbidden to import from or export to anywhere else. The West Indies trade, any dealings with other countries—Holland, France, Africa—there is a virtual embargo on the lot.'

'They might continue to do very well if they had not this stiff-necked ingratitude to their home country.'

'Come now, Mr Matthews,' Viviane said pleasantly, 'should you like it if our King Louis forbade you to buy in your lace from Spain, or your bales of madras from India? Your wife showed me some of that beautiful Milanese silk last week. Should you not howl in protest if our sovereign ordered you to either send it all back to Italy, or pay twice its value again for the privilege of transporting it to Paris?'

'You exaggerate, Mademoiselle.'

'I never exaggerate about silk, it is a serious subject with me. And I can tell the company I never saw finer. I should be devastated if you were to be ruined simply because my king needed revenue and suddenly announced an arbitrary customs levy in order to raise it.'

'There now, Mr Matthews,' one of the young ladies said with a giggle, 'as I see it, you are forced to heed our friend, unless you wish to be declared a bankrupt!'

Everyone laughed and Matthews gave Viviane a wry grin. 'If anything of the sort threatens, I shall call on Mademoiselle de Chercy to defend my case. I believe she could hold off my creditors with eloquence alone. As to locking swords with her sovereign, I leave her to decide the wisdom of that.'

100

The others smiled and prepared to take up the game again but, looking into Matthews's eyes, Viviane saw that his last warning had been more than half in earnest. With a smile, she turned from him and picked up the cards to deal.

Jules settled into Paris with ease. Having seen and approved the house in the Rue Richelieu, he lost no time in putting a deposit on it and arranging a lease so that he could move in while the sale of the Chercy mansion went forward. He stayed at the Rue Jacob only long enough to renew his good relations with Honorine, meet her circle of friends, and learn that although his ward still cordially loathed him, she was too dignified to argue with him in polite company.

There was much to do in Paris, and with the new lease of strength he had gained at Mirandol, he went about his business with energy. He spent time with Silas Deane and caught up with what the commissioner was achieving and, less encouragingly, with what he was failing to do. One serious concern was the quality of the recruits Deane saw fit to send to the United States. From the description of some 'engineers' who had recently been chosen to join Washington, Jules suspected they had even less military knowledge than the eager young men like Luny and Coigny who seemed to be crowding around La Fayette. He kept up his correspondence with the marquis, who was in Metz, and visited the Epée de Bois cabaret, where the conspirators liked to discuss their plans. There he encountered the Baron de Kalb, who as a mature 'American' rather resented the respect with which the others listened to Jules about the war. On reflection Jules judged it wiser to leave the pistol-waving to Kalb; he preferred to deal with the people in Paris who were closer to what was really happening to the French and Spanish secret funds and on the fringe of Versailles diplomacy. What he discovered made him all the more eager for the arrival of Benjamin Franklin, who was expected before Christmas.

He frequented salons, including sometimes the political and intellectual one held by the Marquise du Deffand, and found himself invited to all the houses where he cared to call. He squired Honorine de Chercy to French operas at the Palais-Royal, but could not persuade her to accompany him to the Théâtre des Italiens. One evening he went there alone, and he caught himself wondering whether it might not have been more sensible to moulder a little longer in Mirandol.

The incident happened after the most enthralling performance he had ever heard. The talents of an Italian diva, Gina Farrucci, had been given a great deal of publicity before her arrival in Paris, and she had just begun a spectacular season in the role of Armida. Jules turned up to hear her as a sceptic, but walked out of the performance entranced. The audience loved her, and afterwards no one was in a hurry to leave the foyer of the theatre, which was crowded with people buying the lottery tickets that were being busily sold in one corner.

Jules found himself next to a group which contained Inigo Matthews, whom he had recently met, the young Vicomte de Coigny, and a few other gentlemen he knew but slightly, including the Baron de Ronseul.

It was Matthews who began it. 'What is your opinion of la Farrucci, Count?'

'She has a glorious voice.'

'We *are* in the realms of enthusiasm when the military wax lyrical.'

Recognising the sneer in the voice, Jules met the gaze of Ronseul. 'Being a soldier need not dim a man's admiration of excellence.' A flash of antagonism made him add, 'In fact it may give him the arms to back up his judgement.'

Ronseul replied in his coolest tones, 'Before we listen to any judgement we must ask ourselves who is the judge? If a man sets himself up as an *admirer*, he would do well to consider who might be there before him.'

'Who might be where, exactly?' Jules asked sharply.

'Why, in the lady's favours.'

Jules looked at him in angry surprise. At the same

moment he guessed that Ronseul must have made some advances towards the diva, or he would not be trying to put such a twist on the conversation. A shrewd look into Ronseul's resentful blue eyes gave him an answer to that: the lady's favours had been withheld, so far.

'I praise only the voice. The person, to my judgement, is beyond praise.' He held the baron's fixed, pale stare.

The others looked uncomfortable but Ronseul, misinterpreting Jules's remark as a point gained for himself, lifted his chin and said contemptuously, 'Yes, amongst connoisseurs you would do well to keep your admiration of la Farrucci to yourself.'

'You object to it?' Jules said softly, then before he could prevent himself he said more audibly, 'Not half as much as the lady would object to yours.'

'Really? Then I wonder why she should have bestowed this on me?' With a flourish Ronseul drew from his breast a rich blue scarf shot through with silver threads, which he crumpled in his hand and held an inch from his face, as though savouring its perfume.

Matthews, who found the gesture vulgar, intervened. 'I think this has gone far enough.'

The Vicomte de Coigny, even more alarmed than Matthews, said to Jules, 'If you are leaving, Count, may I beg a ride in your carriage—I believe you are heading my way.'

Jules said to Ronseul, 'You might have filched that from anywhere. Sporting like this with her reputation—'

'*Reputation?* La Farrucci? There is not much to be defended in that department. She is damned lucky to merit my attention.'

'Your sort of attention, to any woman, is an insult.' It was out before Jules could think, borne on a sudden wave of anger.

Ronseul flinched, then an expression of hatred marred the handsome lines of his face and he flicked the scarf very close to Jules's eyes, almost touching him, and said in a low voice heard only by the group: 'I demand satisfaction for that.'

Beside him Coigny gasped, and Matthews laid a hand on Jules's arm. He shook it off and said, 'That you shall have. Now.'

Matthews stood aside and glanced swiftly round the foyer. 'My advice is to drop this and go. Any more and you both face arrest.'

Ronseul had gone paler than ever, but he put a hand on the sleeve of the friend next to him and said, 'Bézères, you will act for me. Monsieur, name your second.'

Jules's anger still filled his head, but as he looked around the group he felt his isolation. His eyes instinctively met those of Coigny, and the young man drew himself up a little and looked back at him with a mixture of bravado and consternation which at any other moment would have been amusing. Coigny stammered, before Jules could speak, 'Monsieur, I should be honoured . . .'

Jules hesitated a split second longer, then said to the side of Ronseul's face, 'I name Monsieur de Coigny. He will call on Monsieur de Bézères in an hour. By issuing the challenge, you leave me the choice of weapons. I am told that you never held a sword in your life, so it's pistols.' With that he grabbed Coigny by the arm and marched him out of the theatre as though the young viscount were in disgrace.

The two men repaired to a coffee house, where Jules sat in silence. At last he looked up to see Coigny's dismayed expression and gave a rueful smile. 'Forgive me for the appalling example I've set you tonight. For no good reason I can think of, I have just agreed to fight a contemptible man over a woman I've never met.'

'If you wish to sue for peace, Monsieur, when I confer with Bézères—'

'Devil take it, when I say I'll fight, I fight. I just wish I had an opponent worth facing.'

Coigny looked desperately anxious. 'I should tell you that Ronseul is a rank coward. He must have lost his head: he has never challenged anyone like this before. But he is a dangerous man, with dangerous friends.'

Jules considered this and gave a smile that chilled

Coigny. He said: 'Anticipating the duel may twist our fine gentleman's vitals even more painfully than the meeting itself. Arrange for dawn with Bézères, if you can. Then we'll see how the baron stands up in the morning.' He rose, and the young man rose too.

'Where shall I report to you, Count?'

'At my house in the Rue Richelieu. I am going there directly.' He put out his hand. 'I am grateful to you, Coigny. I should be ashamed of asking so young a gentleman to be my second, but I understand your courage, and I know I can depend on you.' As Coigny blushed with pleasure, he added, 'And you are not to distress yourself about the outcome. Neither of the duellists would be much of a loss to mankind.' Over the instant protest Jules said coldly, 'Neither of us. Kindly remember that, if you please.'

At nine the next morning, while he was at table finishing a hearty breakfast, the Comte de Mirandol received a letter, written on a single square of light blue paper, folded and sealed, but with no insignia. He broke it open and read it over his coffee.

Monsieur

It has come to my attention that you hold an article of mine which you had the right neither to obtain nor to keep. I wish no correspondence with you, nor do I take any account of rumours and the petty claims that certain gentlemen presume to make concerning me. I scorn them, and you. I also demand your silence, and the return of what is mine. If you have any notion of honour you will satisfy me at once. You will not be received at my apartment, but my servants will accept what you send.

Yours in expectation

Mlle G Farrucci

of the Théâtre des Italiens

With a half-smile on his face, the count demanded pen, ink and paper, and shifting immediately to the other side of the table, wrote a reply, his pen moving swiftly as his servants cleared away the remains of his meal.

Signorina
I am not ignorant of what you mention in your note, but I am innocent of trifling with your name. You detest rumour: will you have the indulgence to hear the truth? I assure you that nothing I report will offend your delicacy or honour; on the contrary, it may have some appeal to your sense of the ridiculous, and let me say immediately that all the absurdities in the account were committed by gentlemen, or persons calling themselves such.

Last night I had the great pleasure of hearing you sing at the theatre. Under the first influence of your glorious voice I spoke your name with admiration in the company of some friends in the vestibule. A man standing nearby became instantly enraged at the sincere compliment I paid you, and seemed eager to cause a scene. This man, who does not deserve to have his name mentioned before you, claimed to be first in any homage towards yourself.

What follows I regret, for one reason alone—I am ashamed of allowing myself to be provoked by so unworthy an opponent. I have been twenty years a soldier, and am no stranger to sudden action, but it was inappropriate in public and in Paris. If my life had afforded me less of pain and misfortune, I might have been more tolerant of insolence; but who am I to justify losing my temper? If you judge that I injured you by it, I heartily beg your pardon. The challenge was given and accepted discreetly, and our seconds agreed that we should meet at dawn this morning, in the woods outside the city. In the meantime, I knew that my challenger had scarcely held a weapon in his life. From what occurred later last night, I realised he feared the opposite of me.

On the way to my house, my carriage was stopped by ruffians and my coachman attacked. The idea was to pull me from the vehicle and attack me too, but I reacted quickly, and the men ran. My coachman had suffered a broken head, so we reversed positions and I drove him home. Logic suggested an effort to keep me from the appointment, when my opponent would be able to boast that I had been too feeble to give him the meeting.

On the one hand, this made me all the more eager to face him; on the other, I already had scruples about firing upon a man with so little experience and such a keen wish for self-preservation. In short, I resolved to fire into the air when the signal was given. This decision was strengthened by the fact that my yearning to survive in no way equalled that of my opponent.

It is at this moment that we enter the ridiculous part of the narrative, and if I am permitted to make amends for whatever inconvenience I have caused you, Signorina, I hope I shall afford you a little amusement.

When I arrived on the scene this morning, my opponent betrayed chagrin and alarm, to which I was indifferent. We paced the clearing, turned, and the signal was given to fire. My opponent responded first, and missed me so effectively that I neither heard nor felt the passage of the ball. To put him out of his misery I fired well above his head. Signorina, I beg you to imagine something that I myself could scarcely credit: at that very moment a flock of wood pigeons darted over the clearing, my ball hit one, and it fell like a stone. It landed on the shoulder of my opponent, glancing off it and thence to the ground. Paralysed by the view he had of me, he did not see the bird; but he felt the blow, looked down to see the front of his shirt spattered with blood, and swooned.

Everyone rushed to his side, hardly clearer about what had occurred than he or I. I strolled over to inspect him, noted that he had had the impudence to carry a woman's silk neckerchief in his breast, and removed it. I went home directly, and heard over breakfast that he was conveyed to his house with great lamentation and put it about that he had been

107

*gravely wounded in an affair of honour. Like you, I
scorn rumours and what others may make of them.
I shall not deign to contradict this one. Except to the
one person who has the right to know the truth:
yourself, Signorina.*

*Before I return the neckerchief, I beg to assure you
that it is not besmirched by pigeon's blood. I shall
deliver it myself, this afternoon. If I have said anything in this letter to offend your sensibilities, as you
once thought my actions had, then I must accept
with regret that I shall be turned from your door.
But I hope I have said enough to convince you that
at no point did I wish to cause a scandal. I willingly
missed my opponent, for my aim was elsewhere.*

*I subscribe myself, with the deepest respect, your
true servant*
Jules de Chercy de Mirandol

As it happened, Jules did not call on Signorina Farrucci
that afternoon. Instead he made his way to the stage
door of the theatre after that evening's performance,
with her reply in his pocket. She had told him that if
he wished to mend his manners in public and in Paris,
he might begin that evening by making one of a supper
party to be held after the performance. The location
was to be given to him backstage at the theatre. The
sentence he particularly relished from her note read:
'Take care when you fence with me; a very diverting
document, but you took the foil off in the last line.'

He went to the theatre with a quite different feeling
of suspense from the one that had woken him that
morning. It was piquant to know that the singer would
resent his turning up as though he were a victor
viewing the spoils, while she would equally resent it if
he did not attend on her when she commanded it.

On admittance into her crowded dressing room he
was tense with the effort to greet her sensibly, but he
forgot everything when their hands met and he was
face to face with her. She was considerably shorter than
he, but looked up at him with a challenging gleam in
her dark brown eyes. Her hair was black, pulled up in

a glossy knot on the crown of her head, with curls falling at the sides to her high cheekbones. She wore deep red, and a ruby flashed from a black velvet ribbon around her throat. It bobbed softly in and out as she greeted him, with words that he could not afterwards remember. Then she turned away to the other guests.

A few minutes later they were again together in the crowd and he complimented her on the performance of the night before. She replied experimentally in Italian, and he answered in the same language. Seeing her surprise, he explained, 'When I was with the cavalry in Poland I recruited a young officer from Italy. He was virtually untrained, so I took him under my wing. He returned the favour by teaching me Italian.'

'He obviously found a ready pupil. And how did he progress?'

'He was killed in action a year later.'

She considered this dispassionate rejoinder, and said, 'Then you got more from his instruction than he did from yours!'

'You could say that. It was one of the few occasions when life has granted me more than I deserve.' Her answer to this was a mocking laugh, but he continued, 'Of course I treasure such moments, since they are so rare.'

She looked down to find that during the exchange her fingers had somehow been trapped within his. She lifted his hand with both her own, parted his fingers and examined them. As she let them go, she said, 'Strange for a soldier: one would call that a musician's hand.'

'I do not play, however.'

'Then you must sing,' she said with sharp confidence.

'I used to. In private.'

She nodded, satisfied. 'When you have conveyed me home after supper you shall sing for me.'

He had hardly digested this before the conversation became general, and it was time to go to the supper party, which was being given in an apartment in the Marais. Gina Farrucci somehow contrived to depart in

109

a carriage with three other ladies, so Jules offered to take some of the gentlemen with him to the party. None but he was aware that their host, Pierre Caron de Beaumarchais, was a secret agent for the crowns of France and Spain, commissioned to make clandestine purchases of arms and other military supplies, and transport them safely to the United States of America. For some months Beaumarchais had been the link between France's Foreign Minister, Charles Gravier de Vergennes, and the American commissioners in Paris. Beaumarchais had converted a former Dutch embassy on the Rue Vieille-du-Temple into the headquarters for a fake trading company called Roderique Hortalez. There he kept a dozen clerks busy on his accounts and shipping ventures, while he lived on the top floor with his mistress Marie-Thérèse de Willer-Mawlaz, who did the honours of his house.

Jules had discerned as soon as he met him that Beaumarchais revelled in a life of high drama and somewhat low comedy, so he valued him considerably more as an author than as a conspirator. Until Benjamin Franklin arrived in Paris, however, the count had decided to keep Beaumarchais's shortcomings to himself, and they were on cordial terms. Welcomed into the apartment by the charming Willer-Mawlaz, Jules contented himself with giving Beaumarchais a friendly grin and moving on into the main drawing room. Neither of them had the slightest inclination tonight to discuss the affairs of the United States, even if it had been safe to do so.

During the supper party Gina Farrucci spent no time with Jules, but contributed a great deal of gaiety to the evening. She sang twice, to her own expert accompaniment on the pianoforte, and in between circulated around the room, her witty remarks enlivening every group. Jules, who knew he was being tested, was pleasant to everyone and amused by the curiosity in their eyes as they tried to judge his reaction to la Farrucci's behaviour. No one had missed the implicit invitation she had offered him at the theatre, nor her patent indifference since. Every now and then they found themselves side by side, and at these moments she would make brief, mocking comments in Italian, to which he returned courteous replies that had an edge which only she was likely to understand.

At one point someone comprehended enough to say to Jules, in a pause, 'Your talents extend to singing, I believe?'

'Never in public.'

Laughter followed this, led by Gina Farrucci.

At last she decided it was time to go. She asked for her shawl and furs, and after taking her leave of the host and hostess, she stood by the door and looked serenely across at Jules, who went to her side and took his leave also. She went out on his arm and they descended to his carriage, where he handed her in, relayed her directions to the coachman and then sat opposite her. During the ride she entertained him with clever reflections on the company and he replied in kind, extracting a laugh from her more than once.

He hardly knew what he was saying, however; there was a giddiness in his head that he had not felt for years. Just before they reached the building where she had her apartment, he said, 'Signorina, tonight is the first time I have felt glad to be back in France.'

Her only reply was a beautiful smile, which was entirely without mockery.

When they got upstairs she threw her shawl and furs over a chair back and helped the maid to light all the candles in the salon, leaving Jules standing in the middle of the room. Then she dismissed the maid and turned to him, stretching a little as though this were the first time she had relaxed all evening.

'And now, Monsieur, it is time I heard you sing.'

He walked straight into her arms, as expected, and kissed her hard. Her hands came instantly around his neck and she clung to him in an embrace that surprised and aroused him with its strength. He drew his head back a little and looked into her dark eyes. 'Gina.'

She jerked her face away and the eyes challenged him. 'What gives you the right to call me so?'

'This.' His lips descended on hers again, but gently,

111

almost with tenderness. As he ran his hands smoothly over her neck and shoulders and down to her waist, he felt her pliant body soften and respond, and when neither he nor she could resist the impulse any longer, he lifted her and carried her into the dark bedroom.

7

BENJAMIN FRANKLIN

Viviane's next meeting with Victor was in secret, in the old coach-house. He arrived punctually and she let him through the door, scarcely waiting until she had bolted it behind him before saying, 'Well, have you found a lawyer who can help me?'

In the half dark of the old building it was difficult to see his expression clearly, but there was no doubt about the disappointment in his voice. 'I am sorry: I have talked to a notary and there is nothing you can do about your uncle's sale of the property.'

'But there is an old law against it—if a nobleman wants to sell part of his patrimony, it has to be offered within the family and be bought at whatever price the family buyer can afford. That means all Chercy property must continue to be owned by Chercys.'

Victor looked at her seriously. 'I'm afraid the notary disabused me of that. First, he said he was not sure the town house qualified as part of the ancestral heritage— your uncle said it was only purchased in 1750. And second,' he paused a moment, then continued, 'you will hate this: the law applies only to *men* of the Chercy name. If you wanted to buy the town house, the law would not recognise your first right of purchase. As there are no males in the family now apart from your uncle, not even distant cousins, there is no one to stop him doing as he likes with the estate.'

Viviane turned away from him to hide her reaction; then clasping her hands in front of her, walked up and down the dusty floor. 'Did you ask him whether it is possible to contest the will itself, then?'

'Of course. I went over every detail. I told him about your uncle's being adopted and he got quite excited and said you could inquire into his background. If it could be proved that he came from really dubious beginnings and coerced your father into willing the property his way, then you might have a case. He did say something else, however, that I did not like.'

'Tell me. I could scarcely feel worse than I do now.'

'Well, investigation might uncover more than you care to know, in terms of the family name. It would be highly embarrassing if it were discovered that your uncle were an illegitimate son of your grandfather and thus a Chercy after all.' Viviane looked at him open-mouthed with indignation, and he said swiftly, 'At that point I got a bit incensed and told the notary to keep such speculations to himself, and he became rather short with me and I left.' When Viviane remained silent he went on, 'I know the very idea is nonsense, for long ago your grandfather told me, in a most affecting way, of the day he found your guardian, who was a homeless orphan he met by chance and took under his wing. I never met a finer old gentleman than your grandfather and would stake my life on every word's being true. And imagine the kinds of things people might dare to say about the Chercys if you did start digging around in the past to try to injure your uncle.'

'Oh God, Victor, every way I turn I find he has the law on his side. I have no hope of ferreting around in his past anyway, short of asking him point-blank, and I can just imagine the reaction that would get! Aunt Honorine cannot give me any useful information, and I went through every record at Mirandol before I left, and found nothing.'

He was standing close, his head bent to hers, and his firm voice warmed her. 'Vive, I wish you were free of him and I shall help all I can. You always have my support. I would engage a lawyer for you myself if I thought it would do any good. But the notary I consulted is a very clever man, and he had nothing to offer you.'

She put her hand on his cuff and squeezed his wrist. 'What do I owe you for his fee?'

'Nothing, don't give it another thought.'

She was about to protest, then exclaimed instead with regret: 'Oh dear, I shall have to let you go. I am

114

expected at the Billancourts'. Louise is quite unwell, and has asked for me to tend her.'

'Really? Nothing serious, I hope?'

'I don't know, she wrote me the strangest note . . .' She undid the bolt of the big door as she spoke, and Victor stepped into the doorway, the light from the street making them both blink.

He turned and smiled at her, his brown eyes bright. 'Pray give her my best wishes for her recovery. Shall I see you at Deane's tomorrow?'

'Yes, you shall. And thank you. What should I ever do without you?'

Marie-Claire de Billancourt was a round, grey-haired, sociable woman who had once been extremely pretty. One of her habits in her maturer years was to fancy herself an invalid, and in this she was in marked contrast to her daughter, who hardly ever allowed indisposition to prevent her from pursuing entertainment wherever it might be met. Madame de Billancourt greeted her two visitors that afternoon with an anxious face that for once showed not a trace of concern about her own health.

'My dear friend,' she said plaintively to Honorine, 'Louise took to her bed yesterday and has not stirred since. And she refuses to tell me what ails her. I thought her a little feverish, but today, when Billancourt insisted we have the physician in, the man could not identify any symptoms. Should we call in your Monsieur Rémy? Though I do so *trust* our man, and Billancourt says . . .'

When Madame de Billancourt talked in this complaining way, Viviane often found herself wondering how her aunt, with all her good sense, could tolerate such behaviour in her closest friend. She said, 'Louise has sent for me, so perhaps if I see her alone she will tell me how she is feeling. Can she receive me? May I go to her?'

'Thank you, my dear, that is just what we should like. Bérénice will take you up.'

Bérénice, Louise's personal maid, was waiting by the door in expectation of this offer, and while the older women stayed in the salon to confer, Viviane went quickly to Louise's bedchamber.

Louise lay in bed in a cap and gown, looking flushed, but as soon as Bérénice had closed the door behind her she sat up and held her arms out to Viviane. 'Embrace me. I need your comfort, I am so wretched.' Then she burst into tears.

Viviane sat on the edge of the bed with her arms around Louise as she fought to control her sobs. Then she resettled the pillows and made her friend lean back. While Louise pressed a handkerchief to her face, Viviane said, 'Whatever has upset you? Are you in pain?'

Louise shook her head, still unable to speak.

'Thank goodness. Your mother is so concerned, she quite frightened us.'

'Oh! I could *never* tell Maman!'

Viviane made herself more comfortable on the bed and said softly, 'Then tell me. And we shall see what we can do.'

Louise took off her cap and began twisting it about in her hands. 'I think you must have half suspected that despite your kind advice I . . . have not been able to get the Baron de Ronseul out of my mind. I tried to distract myself but I failed; and the oftener he engineered it so that I was alone with him, the further I became entangled.' She looked at Viviane tragically. 'Do not tremble: my virtue is intact. But my life is in ruins.

'Two days ago I was talking at someone's house with people you would not like—I had only gone there in hopes of seeing him. They were so-called friends of his, and one of the ladies, a spiteful creature, whispered to me that the baron had fought a duel that morning over some woman, and lay wounded and expected to *die*.'

Viviane started, and Louise went on, 'I nearly fainted. She saw my reaction and laughed, but she would not say more. I left with what countenance I

116

could, but when Maman and I got into the carriage I gave way to a kind of fit, gasping and crying at the same time. Maman had no idea what was going on. By the time we got home I managed to look as though I had recovered, because all I could think of was that I had to see him.'

'You mean the duel was over *you*?'

'Oh no. The spiteful lady made quite sure I understood that he was mixed up with some opera girl and another gentleman had called him out over it. And still I longed to see him! I could not bear to think of him lying helpless with his life ebbing away.

'So I thought up a plan. I begged Maman to take me out again for some air. After we crossed the river I said I wanted to visit the big glover's, you know, opposite his apartment. Once Maman was occupied, I said I would slip next door and take Bérénice with me, to look at something in another shop. Maman agreed. I meant to spend only a little time away, and to be back before she began to search for me.

'Down the street near his place I told Bérénice to wait. I said I was going to visit a poor friend whom Maman did not approve of, to take her some money, and Bérénice was never to breathe a word and I should not be long. She was very understanding and admired my charity.' Her lip quivered. 'How easy some people are to deceive.'

'And no one saw you go in?'

'No, I put on a veil which I had in my pocket, and pulled my fur hood up over that. I found the kitchen entrance and paid my way with silver up to the door of his apartment. The servants were so willing you would think they had all done it many times before. Even the elegance of my clothes seemed not to surprise them, or prevent them from giving me some impudent looks. But they took my money.'

She broke off and seeing Viviane's anxious face she said, 'I can't imagine how I could have been so forward. By the time the footman opened the door I was half dead with fright. I would never do for a real intriguer—I was ready to fall at his feet. All I could

117

say was, "Monsieur de Ronseul," and he took one cool look at me and opened the door wide.'

'Were his personal servants as bad as the others?'

'I don't know, for I only saw the footman. I expected the place to be hushed, but as soon as I stepped through the door I could hear talking and laughter, all male. There was a room to the right of the vestibule with doors partly closed so you could not see in, but some of them sounded drunk. It was only the afternoon, too—I could not conceive how they could behave so when the baron lay wounded in the house. The footman frowned and ushered me to a little reception room and told me to wait. He did not even ask my name.'

'Which shows you the kind of house he works in,' Viviane said dryly.

'I peered out and watched him go into the large room, and all at once I lost my nerve and ran out into the hallway. Just at that moment there was more noise behind the doors, and I was afraid the men were surging out towards me, so I darted into another room next to the main one.

'Then I heard the baron's voice—and he was laughing! There was a servants' door next to me, set into the panelling, and I peered through the crack. I could see him, sprawled across a chaise longue with a glass in his hand, holding court to four or five others—I could not see them all—looking no different from the way he has looked a hundred times, when he is teasing me. His hair was loose, but apart from that he was beautifully dressed, and he looked fresh and full of health.

'Then the baron told the others to quieten down, and listened, and the footman said a woman had arrived and she was in the waiting room. And one of the others said something like: "You've done it after all—I'll wager it's the opera girl."

'The others all piped up then, but the baron leapt to his feet and told them to be quiet. He stood there uncertain for a moment, then he ripped off his jacket and dropped it on the floor, undid the lace at his throat

118

and kicked off his shoes. Then he leaned on the footman's shoulder and said to the others, "Not a syllable, from now to Kingdom come, unless I say so."'

'So he had sown the rumour about the duel! And he was about to greet you like that, thinking you were—'

'Yes,' Louise said bitterly, 'thinking I was a besotted little tart from the opera.'

'Why did you not leave, at once?'

'I was angry. I have never been so furious in my life. I had to confront him, so I quickly went back into the waiting room. I was standing at the far end when he entered; he was leaning heavily on the man and he moved very slowly. He transferred both hands to a chair back, and sent the man out, and said in this false, faint voice, "Mademoiselle, I cannot greet you as I ought. My friends tell me I am getting better, but I hardly yet have the strength to walk."'

'Louise, this is ghastly. You were in his power twice over, don't you see?'

'But he did not know it was me. He looked keenly at me, but I knew he did not recognise me through the veil. He said something about never dreaming I would respond to his suffering by doing him the honour of a visit. He said, "I thought my greatest privilege would be to kill or to die for you. I could not hope that the angel who inspired me would ever draw so near." He held out one hand towards me—but he said *angel*, which was his name for me! That was enough: I went to run out of the room.'

'Not before time!'

'He stepped in front of me and caught me around the waist with one arm; then he grabbed my veil and hood and flung them back from my face. He got such a shock he swore at me, he said, "Devil take it—you!" I struggled, but he pinned me more tightly against him and put a hand over my mouth. He asked me if anyone else knew I was there and I shook my head. He said, "You little idiot, do you want to get me killed in earnest?"'

'You frightened him. Excellent.'

'He hissed at me to keep my voice down, then he

wanted to know whether anyone had recognised me when I came up. I shook my head, which was all I could manage because I was choking with tears. He asked if I could leave the same way without being detected, and when I nodded he gave a sigh and leaned back against the chair. He still had my wrists behind my back, but his voice was less venomous. He told me to leave at once, and tell no one, and for pity's sake let him be the judge of where and how we meet.'

'Good Lord, even at that moment, after deceiving and abusing you, and treating you worse than a girl off the streets, he could talk to you of meeting again!'

'I said, from that moment I would forget he existed. He didn't give a fig for my anger, but he was cautious about seeing me out. He looked into the hallway, gestured to the footman to open the door, then when I had pulled on my veil and hood again he took me to the top of the stairs. He told me to go, and gave me a shove in the small of my back to send me on my way. He said, "A word about me to anyone, and the world will know how you behaved today, even if I have to dodge a duel to broadcast it."'

'And you got out safely and rejoined your mother.'

'Yes. She has been worried about me ever since. How could I possibly describe to her how sick I feel every time I *think*?'

'I don't understand why I have not heard about the duel. No one has mentioned it to me.'

'Oh, you and I are always the last to hear; no one ever tells us anything of the slightest interest. So I was determined to go out that evening, though I felt more dead than alive, just to find out what is being said. And someone did say that he is recovering, enough to hold parties for the intimates, in his bedroom.' She grimaced despairingly and threw her cap to the end of the counterpane. 'Perhaps the girl from the opera has been invited already, and received a softer welcome than mine. I declare I never want to go anywhere or see another creature again. Except you. You are the only person on earth who understands me.'

'Louise, you must not hide away like this,' Viviane

said. 'You cannot let him make you feel ashamed to hold your head up in society. He will never speak: you are safe from his malice.'

'That's true. He fears the men of my family too much to let anyone know how I compromised myself. But if he had struck me to the floor when I saw him, I could not feel more bruised.'

'My dear friend, you have had a lucky escape. Now you know him to be utterly worthless. You cannot blame yourself for anything that happened, for you were dealing with a devil who has much more cunning than you or I will ever have.' She took Louise's hand.

It upset Viviane to see her friend depressed, for she was used to relying on her verve and sparkle, in private and in public. She could never forget how Louise had transformed her first days of convent school from a lonely penance into a time of brightness and novelty. Later, when they went into Paris society together, the happy influence did not diminish. Thanks to Louise, Viviane had learned how to forget her provincial shyness and enter with ease into animated conversations of every kind. And she also gained an ally who never looked awkward or disapproving when her own ideas occasionally ran away with her, simply joined in with a laugh if an argument became vehement, and sprang to her defence if older women tried to quell the lively flow of spirits.

She tried a note of authority. 'Let's not talk about him any more, he disgusts me. Why don't you get dressed and come with me to the Hainaults'? I met the two daughters last week, and they are very lively company, with such wide interests. They like cards, and are ready to play for high stakes, so if we are minded to run some risks, we could take them on at quadrille.'

Louise disengaged her hand, gave a faint smile and drew her knees up under the coverlet, then crossed her arms over them and leaned her head sideways, looking earnestly at Viviane. 'What shall I tell Maman?'

'That you were overtired, but now you are quite rested.'

'And what shall I tell myself? I am so unhappy. Nothing can banish this pain.'

Viviane sighed, then said resolutely, 'No man has a right to make you so miserable. Help me bear up under my guardian's tyranny, and I shall soon make you believe there never was any such person as the baron.'

On 9 December Benjamin Franklin arrived at Quiberon in Britanny, bringing with him his grandson, William Temple. Behind him in America he had been forced to leave his son, imprisoned for pro-British sentiments. Meanwhile General Howe had taken Manhattan, and the rebels had lost 5,000 men. Tom Paine, an Englishman serving with them, was moved to write: 'These are the times that try men's souls. The summer soldier and the sunshine patriot will, in this crisis, shrink from the service of his country; but he that stands it *now* deserves the love and thanks of man and woman.'

While Franklin was making his leisurely way to Paris, Beaumarchais travelled by post in the other direction, to Le Havre, posing as a Monsieur Durand. His self-appointed task was to supervise the departure of four ships sailing for America via Santo Domingo, which were to carry sixty-three cannon, 20,160 cannonballs, 9,000 uncharged grenades, ten tons of ammunition, 6,132 muskets and forty-nine volunteers, including the twelve 'engineers' whose qualifications had already caused misgivings in the Comte de Mirandol.

Alerted to the illicit cargoes by his own spies, Lord Stormont, England's ambassador, raised an enormous protest in Paris and Versailles over the proposed voyage. The merchants of Le Havre, incensed with their port authorities for letting the ships load up, and terrified of retaliation by the English navy against their own vessels if they sailed, joined the outcry. The *Romain*, the *Andromède*, the *Anonime* and the *Amphitrite* raised anchor, but not for long. On 16 December they were recalled by royal decree, and three obeyed.

Only the *Amphitrite* continued on her risky voyage.

By the time Franklin appeared in Paris a few days before Christmas, the capital was buzzing with American plots. Viviane de Chercy shared the rage to meet Franklin, but had no expectation of seeing him soon. He had taken up residence downriver in Passy, had not yet been seen in society, and was no doubt busy with secret negotiations while the scandal of the rebel ships rocked Versailles.

Viviane was so eager to hear anything of Franklin that she even got caught up in an unguarded conversation with her uncle, the first since he had arrived in Paris. It happened after dinner one Thursday in the Rue Jacob, just before he left to visit the Marquise du Deffand, who held a famous salon on that same evening every week. They were all in the withdrawing room next to the dining room, and Honorine de Chercy happened to ask whether anyone of interest was expected at the salon.

'Why yes: Doctor Benjamin Franklin. I am conveying him there, at the marquise's request.'

'You *know* him, Monsieur?' Viviane cried.

'Yes.'

'Really, Nephew, I do think you might have told us. This is just like the first time I met the Marquis de La Fayette and found out that he had been exchanging letters with you for weeks. I stood there open-mouthed, feeling an absolute dunce for not knowing.'

'Well, this time you are suitably prepared.'

'Your niece even better than I,' Honorine said irritably, 'since she has been learning English especially for the occasion.'

'Really?' He looked at Viviane. 'You are aware, however, that Franklin speaks extremely good French?'

Registering her aunt's start of amusement, Viviane said, 'No, I was not. But I do not regret my lessons, they help me understand American writing. I am reading Thomas Paine at the moment.'

'I could not recommend a better choice, even though he's an Englishman.' He pulled out his watch and looked at it, then glanced towards Honorine de Chercy before saying to his ward, 'If you would care to accompany me, Mademoiselle, why not meet Doctor Franklin and spend an hour or two with us at the Marquise du Deffand's? I have no doubt that she will be pleased to receive you. I am collecting our guest from Silas Deane's. Is it convenient for you to come?'

Viviane leapt to her feet and exclaimed, 'Convenient? It will be the greatest thrill of my life!' To override any protests from her aunt she practically ran from the room, saying quickly to her uncle, 'I shall be ready in a moment, if you will be good enough to wait.' He rose and bowed slightly as she went out.

Honorine continued the conversation by asking him for more information about Franklin, which he was happy to give. At last she had to say what was on her mind. 'I consider your ward's interest in this man and all he stands for a waste of time.'

'You wish her to indulge in other occupations? But she does—there is her music, for instance.'

'In which you give her no encouragement whatsoever. Yet you are prepared to take her to meet this . . . this . . .'

'Wise old statesman,' he finished for her. 'There is no need to be anxious. The moment you meet Franklin you will be charmed by his manners and his intelligence—and his sense, an even rarer commodity than the other two. He is hardly a rabblerouser. Speaking of his country, he said to me yesterday: "A virgin state should preserve its virgin character, and not go about suitoring for alliances, but wait with decent dignity for the applications of others."'

'All very well, but he is here as a beggar for his country just the same. And I deplore the effect all this talk has on Mademoiselle de Chercy. She quite frightens people these days with her vehemence about the United States. Your support on that score is the last thing I could wish for.'

'What do you want me to do, withdraw the invitation?' He knew perfectly well she would not demand this, and Honorine remained in vexed silence until he surprised her by saying, 'I confess I am thankful to have stumbled upon the sole issue over which my niece and I are in agreement. If you can forget your objections today, I shall be grateful.'

Reflecting on this as Viviane re-entered the room, Honorine nodded and gave up the struggle.

Benjamin Franklin turned out to be a small, rounded man, who had a pleasant face with a long, thin-lipped mouth that often smiled, and who looked younger than his seventy years. He had greying hair which he took no trouble to conceal with a wig. To entertain Viviane while they all stood about talking at Silas Deane's, he implied that he had thrown his overboard in the teeth of an Atlantic gale on the way to France. Whatever the truth, since he lost it he had worn a big fur hat like a Russian's against the cold, and he had it on when the three of them got into the carriage and set off for the residence of the Marquise du Deffand, in the convent of Saint-Joseph.

Instead of speaking in English, and about America, Franklin came out with a series of questions about Paris in French, and amazed Viviane with the depth of his knowledge and the scope of what he intended to see. He asked her about a school for the deaf, the very first in the world, run by an abbé, and she felt ashamed of herself for not even knowing that it was nearby, in the heart of Paris.

Her guardian listened attentively to the conversation and made few remarks of his own. At one point he said to Franklin in English, 'You will oblige my niece greatly if you address her in your own tongue for a while. She has been taking lessons, and reading a quantity of American literature.'

Franklin raised his eyebrows at Viviane and, cursing her guardian inwardly, she ventured in English, 'I have read some of your work, but your writing is elegant and your vocabulary is very large. Sometimes I have great trouble.'

Franklin laughed. 'I should strive more for simplicity, which is the hardest thing, you know. But you have

125

made wonderful progress, and you have a London accent! From whom do you learn?'

'From an Englishwoman. Her name is Mrs Matthews.' She glanced at the count. 'I think you know her husband.'

He and Franklin exchanged a glance, and the count switched to French again as he said, 'I wonder what he is playing at, letting his wife give you lessons?'

'*Letting* his wife?' she repeated. 'It was her choice. She used to be a governess, but she is not the least ashamed of it, and I don't believe Mr Matthews is either.'

Her guardian said, 'So you pay for the lessons?'

'Oh no, she won't hear of it. She is a very keen horsewoman, and sometimes I ride with her in the Bois de Boulogne. As long as she enjoys the outings and the conversation, I feel I am giving her some return for her tuition.'

'Conversation,' Franklin said thoughtfully, and glanced at the count. 'What is your opinion of this Matthews?'

The count shrugged. 'He is clever, and francophile. Perhaps too heartily so to be credible, but it is hard to tell: he is a much subtler animal than Stormont.' Cautiously he said to Viviane, 'Does the wife often talk to you about your enthusiasm for America? About La Fayette perhaps?'

Knowing exactly what he and Franklin were guessing at, Viviane leaned back on the comfortable cushions of his carriage and gave them an ingenuous smile. 'Oh yes, often. She is always fascinated to hear about the talks I have with Mr Deane.'

This time the men avoided each other's gaze and kept their eyes riveted on her instead. She wondered which of the two would express his alarm first, then decided that Franklin would leave it to her uncle, and her uncle, despite his ruthlessness, would hesitate to interrogate her in front of Franklin.

'Yes, I enjoy prattling on to Mrs Matthews. I am always very forthcoming.' She smiled again, and put them out of their misery. 'But it is surprising how difficult it is to be accurate in every detail. I am afraid that if she relates the information to others, those others would be most atrociously misled.'

After a startled pause the gentlemen both laughed. Franklin threw her a glance of sparkling appreciation, then said to the count, 'I begin to think that all the lessons *I* need at the moment can be given by the Chercy family. I shall look no further!'

The count was still laughing, and Viviane realised it was the first time she had seen him do so.

At Madame du Deffand's, Viviane was well received by the hostess, whose energies were then immediately concentrated on welcoming Franklin and making the rest of the company known to him. Viviane, who had been nervous of the marquise, had time to become accustomed to her blindness and her formidable discourse without being asked to contribute very much herself. She had no chance to discuss America with Franklin or anyone else; the conversation was very wide-ranging, but it was all of France and the French. Everyone said how delighted they were that Turgot had been dropped as Minister of Finance; and the marquise, who hated him passionately, declared that only his dismissal and the appointment of Necker and Taboureau had saved the country from disaster. To all the talk about the court and the King's decision-making Franklin listened intently and interposed some acute but inoffensive comments. Viviane decided he would make a perfect courtier.

At some point another guest who was equally struck by his understanding of Versailles politics said, 'When we discuss such matters I imagine Monsieur Franklin may have Tom Paine's comment in the back of his mind: "In free countries the law is king; no other is needed."'

Franklin's eyes twinkled for a moment, then he said, 'One must first create a free country, an act we have not yet consummated.'

A lady who had been paying great attention to the Comte de Mirandol then said, possibly with the idea of pleasing him, 'Doctor Franklin, I hope you will remember there has been no dearth of Frenchmen to stand beside your brave Patriots in the struggle.'

Franklin bowed and murmured something but the marquise's voice cut in unpleasantly, 'They would do better to stay and fight despotism at home.' She turned her face towards Franklin. 'I do not begrudge you one or two professional soldiers, a few mercenaries from our ranks, Monsieur le Docteur. Men who are trained to kill are good for nothing else. But we must oppose the idea of our young nobles being recruited for another war. Too often have I seen the government falter in the face of internal difficulties and turn aside to seek conquests abroad. It is always easier to destroy than to build, to devastate an enemy rather than foster the good of one's countrymen at home.'

The lady beside the count exchanged a glance with him when the marquise spoke of men good for nothing but killing, but he just lifted an eyebrow ironically. By the end of the speech, however, she was sufficiently annoyed to say to the company at large, 'I for one cannot help admiring gentlemen who are prepared to give up comfort and safety and go to war in a just cause. Shouldering *that* responsibility is no light matter.'

'I only suggest,' the marquise said, aiming a pointed smile at Franklin, 'that any keen idealist who beats a path towards you has first the duty to ask himself what he may be running *from.*'

Victor and La Fayette were very much in Viviane's mind and she longed to utter something in their vindication, but she felt her guardian's gaze on her and decided to prove once again that she could be prudent. Then the talk turned to other matters and she was glad she had not spoken.

In the carriage afterwards, her uncle commended her restraint but said nothing more on the subject. He began talking to Franklin in English, while Viviane looked out the window at the darkening streets and pondered the Marquise du Deffand's remarks about the French military. She had never thought about her guardian quite like that before—as a trained killer—

but what else was he? As a youth he had put home and family behind him and chosen slaughter as his profession, so his greatest talent was for annihilating other human beings. To do this, she reasoned, a man must surely be deficient in all the gentle impulses, or take pains to stifle them early in his career. She thought that perhaps it was these heavy bars across his personality that made it impossible for her to get along with him.

She rejoiced at how different Victor was; she had complete faith in his affections, his generosity, and his love of France. La Fayette was the same: she felt that the impulse that took men like him and the volunteers to America would bring them home again, that whatever they did would be not at the expense of their fellow men but *for* them, especially for those they held dear. In that the marquise was right—if a man could not serve those he loved, he served no one.

When the carriage turned into the Rue Jacob to deposit Viviane at home, Benjamin Franklin gave her a kindly smile. 'The visit has made you pensive, Mademoiselle de Chercy. I trust that one day soon I shall share these solemn thoughts?'

She felt embarrassed at having ignored one of the most celebrated minds in Europe for most of the drive home, and afraid that she had just affronted her uncle's guest and displeased her uncle into the bargain. She began a reply, but the carriage came to a halt and the steps were let down without her finishing her awkward sentence. Neither of the gentlemen, however, seemed to be in the least discontented with her, and they bade her a courteous farewell before driving away to Passy.

8

DANGEROUS LIAISONS

On a cold day in late January, Jules was with Benjamin Franklin in Passy, discussing the diplomatic situation. Not for the first time, he wished that having served France for a lifetime might give him a voice at court. But more powerful people than he had failed to gain Franklin an audience at Versailles, and the only meetings that had been granted were in secret and in Paris.

The old man tried to dissipate the gloom by saying cheerfully, 'Vergennes takes quite an energetic line: if England lost her colonies—the Thirteen States and the Sugar Islands in the Caribbean—she would be diminished by the struggle and her trade crippled. He has it in mind to redress the balance of power in Europe by promoting the rise of France.'

'But I see no signs that he is about to carry the court along with his plans. The Patriot armies' fortunes and the attitude of His Majesty are both too shaky. And every moment I wonder whether Beaumarchais is about to do something to discredit the cause.'

Franklin ran a hand through his fine hair and frowned. 'I think it is time you explained your misgivings about Beaumarchais. He has been active for us since September 1775, and seems only too enthusiastic in all his dealings. What exactly do you fear from him?'

'Beaumarchais was in London that year because he was in virtual exile from France. Did you not know? He had bribed a magistrate in a civil court case in Paris, and then advertised his own criminal actions by trying to extort reparation when the case went against him! The man is a model of indiscretion. After London he went on to Vienna, where he trumped up a scandal concerning our queen. Her mother, the Empress Maria-Theresa of Austria, had no option but to imprison him on the spot.'

'Good Lord, I can see why you imagine he might be

an embarrassment to Versailles! How did he wriggle out of that?'

'The details are shrouded in mystery—mercifully. At any rate he came back to France and was still under a cloud when he began his negotiations with your agents. In September last year all charges against Beaumarchais were dropped and his civil status and duties at court were restored.'

'Ah. Then at least his respectability is not now in question.' Jules was silent, and Franklin went on resignedly, 'All right. Where are your doubts, on the money side?'

Jules gave a grim smile. 'The confusion is not exactly Beaumarchais' fault, because nothing can be discussed above board. You remember the ideas put forward that the money France sends to Congress could be considered as a loan, to be paid back at interest, or goods in lieu of interest? No firm conclusions have ever been reached over that.' He took a breath and chose his words carefully, knowing that whatever he said about Beaumarchais could also be taken to apply to Deane. 'The distinction between aid by way of arms and commercial ventures for profit has become somewhat blurred of late, and our ministry has done nothing to remove the confusion. Yet these are large sums: the Crown's aid, along with that of Spain, amounts so far to more than two million livres. Sir, Beaumarchais is the man appointed to deal with you, and you have little choice in the matter. But you should consider two things. First, his qualifications to select and supply what Congress most needs. Second, his ability to distinguish between funds supplied by one government to another, and moneys to be used for private profit.' He looked up and met Franklin's gaze. 'I must tell you that the top Paris bankers protested when they had to deal with him over the secret funds; they had no opinion of his head for finance.'

Franklin said with a hint of irritation, 'You are suggesting I ask for someone else to be chosen? It's true there are a number of candidates. The Comte de Broglie has already nominated himself to Deane as the true champion of the rebel cause in France. And I expect any day to be invited to meet your young friend, the redoubtable Marquis de La Fayette.'

'I should advise against that, Sir.'

'Why? Deane met him in December, and you see a lot of him yourself, I hear.'

'Because I like him personally. But his sympathies are disapproved of; he is far too public a figure, and has too little influence of his own. I share the latter disadvantage, which is why I can never serve you in the way Beaumarchais does.' He sighed. 'Don't mistake me: my opinion of Beaumarchais makes me cautious, but I only share it with you because you ask. I have given him every assistance: I have helped him assess the quality of his purchases, pointed him towards sources of supply, and advised him about the recruits. And I enjoy his company: his conversation is almost as witty as his plays.'

'Which is saying a great deal. You do not hesitate to recommend him to your family, either—I believe you intend taking him to sup with your aunt and your niece?'

'Yes. My aunt is a great admirer of his work, and my niece, I am happy to say, has grown conversible enough to hold her own with him on most subjects.'

'Of that I have no doubt. Mademoiselle de Chercy is a marvel of eloquence.'

While the Comte de Mirandol and Benjamin Franklin were conferring, two visitors were closeted with the Marquis de La Fayette in the Rue du Faubourg Saint-Honoré as he explained to them his latest idea for diverting suspicion about his activities.

'I am going to shut myself away and let the vigilance die down. I should like Stormont's spies to think I have things other than America on my mind. I am lending myself to a new experiment to find a prevention for smallpox.'

Viviane said, 'This is incredible! You don't mean you will have to expose yourself to infection?'

'Yes, but not to the disease itself. I am to have something called a "vaccination"—an injection of cowpox, a much lesser complaint.'

'Is not this dangerous just the same?' Victor asked.

'I believe not. I must wait six weeks for the effects to wear off—they are supposed to be very mild. I cannot be visited during this time, and my dear wife and one servant will be my only companions.' He smiled, and his eyes glowed. 'But my plans will be going forward just the same.'

'I see,' said Victor, and turned to Viviane. 'Our friend cannot charter a vessel to sail to America—recent experience proves how well all the ports are surveyed—so he has simply bought one that will carry legitimate cargo. It has been purchased under the name of Motier, and the Baron de Kalb is arranging everything for the voyage.'

'The ship will be prepared while you are lying low?' Viviane said to the marquis.

'Yes. You will all help greatly by giving the impression that I am discouraged about the fate of the United States.'

'That will not be difficult,' Viviane said with a sigh. 'London believes that Washington is finished. Think of it: New York occupied, a blockade by the British fleet down the whole seaboard, the Patriot forces on the run in the north.'

The marquis interrupted, 'But I believe absolutely that the Continental army is still a fighting force. It has not been disbanded or the cause given up; time and again it has been scattered and then reformed. The Patriots are never going to simply disappear, for the British must hunt them down to the last man. And Washington's tactics—think how far he has prolonged his campaign into the winter. It is too soon yet to know whether he has managed to protect Philadelphia, but everything I hear inspires my faith in him. How can I fail to do my utmost to join such a leader?'

'You are a strange case, Monsieur le Marquis,' Viviane said in friendly raillery. 'You have so many advantages: excellent health—aside from this self-induced illness!—a generous fortune, a promising military career, and a happy family life. Yet you would place all these second to an ideal. I am forced to think you must have the mind and spirit that will arm you for any danger.'

Victor said, 'These are strange times when a man contemplating battle chooses to contract a disease that only milkmaids suffer from! We shall have to converse by note for the next few weeks. Depend upon us if you need anything done while you are being nursed.'

The marquis took both their hands and his eyes gleamed. 'I shall.'

When Viviane was collected from this meeting by her great-aunt, Madame de Chercy had a request to make: 'My dear, I should like you to tell me this is the last visit you will pay to the marquis's household.'

Viviane smiled privately at her good timing, but prepared to stand up for herself, with the poise that was usually enough to tame everyone except her guardian. 'What are your reasons, Madame?'

'They are not far to seek. I have just learned that it has been declared a treasonable offence to mention the American war in the streets of Paris, and in the taverns and coffee houses.'

'But freedom of speech still lingers in the salons. Including your own.'

'As a guest under my roof you speak at your own discretion, my dear. I have never heard you say a questionable thing at home. But the talk that goes on in other houses seriously disturbs me, especially amongst the young people. There is a positive mania for volunteers in Paris at the moment; at the least it is unthinking, and at the worst it is extremely dangerous.' Viviane looked unconvinced and her great-aunt went on quietly, 'My dear, are you aware of the consequences of careless ranting on that subject?'

'Madame, you are not accusing me of ranting, I am sure.'

'No, but I sometimes feel that Louise de Billancourt

has a more sensible approach than you on this, and that is a rare judgement for me to make. She has no interest in the American war at all, and her mother and I are very glad of it.' She hesitated, then said in a more solemn tone, 'I ask you to think of the influence you have. As a woman—as a clever, beautiful and very persuasive woman—you invest your words with more power than you realise. We are talking about an appalling conflict that has only just begun; we are talking about men's lives. Think for a moment how you would feel if Victor de Luny became a volunteer and—'

'*Victor!*' This disbelieving exclamation broke from Viviane, then she held her tongue.

Madame de Chercy continued, 'These remarks are not the kind that can be made by your guardian, so I felt you should hear them from me before he speaks to you today.'

Viviane said with mild irony, 'I did not know he was expected. Is he to deliver me a homily?'

'Of course not. The sale of the Chercy house has at last gone through, and he is coming to ask my advice about refurbishing his own. But be prepared for him to raise this matter of the United States.'

The count was waiting for them when they returned to the house in the Rue Jacob. After they had greeted him, Madame de Chercy began asking at once about his proposed renovations in the Rue Richelieu, and Viviane was free to observe him. She was preoccupied at the thought of yet another stream of cash flowing his way from the Chercy estate, and at the same time she felt a new reaction: in a subtle way, he intimidated her. He did so not by his actions, his demeanour or what she could divine of his thoughts; oddly enough, it was his good looks that quelled her. Somehow during his time in Paris she had come to see him in a different light. The stern perfection of his features, his fine figure, gave him a masculine beauty that set him apart from other men. It was all the more powerful because he seemed completely unaware of it. Handsome men like the Baron de Ronseul could have no such influence over Viviane, for she saw straight through to the vanity beneath. But her guardian was without vanity; it was as though he had never properly looked into a mirror in his life. For Viviane, this unself-conscious beauty underlined his strength—and his remoteness. She could never sway him as she could other men. She was cursed with the fact that the head of her family was the most unconquerable male in the capital.

As soon as Madame de Chercy left the room he began the discussion she dreaded. His expression was distant, and it did not occur to her that he might be as unwilling as her to broach the subject.

He was surprisingly easy on her, to begin with. 'There is a lot of loose talk about the American war at the moment, all over town. I assume you do not join in it?'

'No, Monsieur.'

'I thought not. But Madame de Chercy asked me to speak to you, and I would like to reassure her you are using your good judgement in the case. By the way, I agree with her about curtailing your visits to La Fayette, for reasons you are aware of and she is not.'

It was a relief to Viviane that they understood each other about this at least. 'Domestic matters will unfortunately prevent my seeing Madame de La Fayette for some weeks.'

He did not respond to her half-smile; instead he changed the subject. 'Today I learned something from Doctor Franklin that surprised me. Your arrangements for Silas Deane, the meetings in the coach-house here.'

Viviane started, and sensing that he was about to say something disobliging, walked away from him a little.

He went on, 'I admire your inventiveness. The meetings are artfully managed. But I think there is one thing you have not considered enough.' He paused, tried to catch her eye, and failed. 'This is your great-aunt's house and you are here as her guest. How does it sit with your sense of right to be arranging such visits without her knowledge?'

She was annoyed with him for touching her conscience on this point, a sensitive one which she had never quite resolved in her own mind. But she had learned to control her emotions better in these confrontations. She turned to face him, half smiling again. 'While I am to be so cautious in my utterances in public, Monsieur, I rejoice that I can be active in private. But you would have me throw that away? Am I confined to playing the piano and embroidering screens?'

'I make no such recommendations, Mademoiselle. Your actions are up to you. I shall not mention this to Madame de Chercy, it is your decision alone.'

A grand concession: he knew quite well that if she confessed about the meetings, in her present mood her great-aunt would be appalled. And if she did not, he would henceforth have leave to consider her deceitful, as well as 'artful' and 'inventive'. He had boxed her into a corner. Again.

She could see he would have liked to continue the discussion, but she closed it with a quiet, 'Thank you.'

Her aunt, when she came back into the room, mistook the silence for one of agreement, and they began talking of their coming engagements. The count confirmed that he would be introducing Beaumarchais to them in the near future, then turned to Viviane and said, 'There is a musical soirée at the Duchesse de Brissac's tomorrow that promises to be interesting: her choice of performers is always excellent. Shall you attend?'

'Do you plan to be there, Monsieur?'

'Yes.'

'I am afraid I shall not be present. And now, Madame, Monsieur, with your leave I shall go upstairs to prepare for this evening.'

After she had gone, Honorine looked at Jules in dismay and he grimaced.

'I am sick of arguing with her. Please do not ask me to do so again unless the matter is grave. It drives her to pettiness, which is not in her nature.'

'Yes, I am sorry to see it.'

'I wish I had the luxury of avoiding her company, but I must lend her my advice, however firmly she sets herself against it.'

'She listened to you about not consorting with La Fayette?'

'Yes. But you can see how inadequate I am as a guardian. My influence may even be pernicious. This kind of antagonism is her only vestige of immaturity, for in everything else—her intelligence, her cultivation, her social acuity, her sympathetic influence on others— she is completely a woman. Perhaps if we had met first in Paris instead of Mirandol . . .'

'Nephew, you have her respect. You once told me that was all you required.'

He rose. 'True, Madame. I can always rely on you to set me straight.'

Thus it happened that, by not going to the Duchesse de Brissac's, Viviane missed a scandal that was to quite eclipse the American question. It was Louise de Billancourt who witnessed it, and her quick perceptions gave her an inkling of what was to occur almost the moment she walked into the duchess's beautifully appointed music room. The hostess always kept the musician a secret until everyone was gathered, but Louise overheard the name spoken in an undertone between two ladies, and determined at once to get into the first row with all the deaf, ancient dowagers, for the occasion promised much more than music.

The excited whisper went that the performer was to be the illustrious Farrucci of the Comédie Italienne. She hardly ever consented to give private concerts, and the patroness had to be most scrupulous not to injure her pride by openly hiring her. Instead she must be invited as a guest, and stay to supper afterwards. She herself did not discuss the fee or the venue—it was all done through an impresario—and she was treated exactly as the noble guests when she arrived.

Louise would have yawned over all these details, except for the fact that very early in the confidences the name of the Comte de Mirandol came up. To her astonishment she learned that he was the Farrucci's latest lover. And the duchess, in the spirit of the most scurrilous mischief, had made sure that he would be a guest that night, and intended to sit him opposite la Farrucci at the supper table. Louise shivered at the thought that they would both be exposed to the scrutiny, curiosity and high amusement of the whole company, who would be dying to see their faces when they realised what the hostess had arranged. She imagined la Farrucci sweeping in grandly and finding herself face to face with her current liaison, and every eye upon them. Then forced to perform in front of him while he lounged about as a guest, both of them unable to acknowledge the relationship or to pretend that she was not a mere stage performer and he an honoured member of Paris society.

Louise had never looked forward to a performance so much. She secured a seat in the front, depriving an old dame who looked very put-out. Soon after that she caught sight of the count, who entered from the card room and stood talking in a group at the back of the music chamber.

Then la Farrucci arrived. Louise had to crane to see them both, but she did not want to miss a flicker of an eyelid from either. Nor did anyone else, once they realised the singer and the count were in the same room.

La Farrucci was a splendid looking woman: dark, quick-moving but sinuously graceful, and with a presence that prevented one from noticing that she was short, and slight in build. Her eyes were magnificent— dark brown and penetrating—and Louise watched her so closely she saw every nuance of expression. She entered, caught the unusual attention everyone was paying her, threw one flashing glance around the room; then her eyes fell on the count for a split second and narrowed with fury. There was a tiny pause, then she swept towards the dais. She held her head high like an empress, and she looked like one, for her black hair was wound through with pearls and she wore a beautiful dress of dark red velvet sewn with gems. She had on a ruby pendant that flamed as her chest rose and fell.

Louise thought she saw the same anger in the Comte de Mirandol. He scarcely hesitated; by the time the singer was halfway across the room he had left the group of gentlemen and was approaching the pianoforte. He reached it just before her, and without the slightest embarrassment bowed, then handed her up onto the dais. Everyone had expected him to escape, or for her to find some excuse not to play, but clearly neither thought for one second of retreating.

They were so far in concert that their eyes did not even meet as she accepted his polite gesture. But they spoke, and only Louise, the closest to the platform, had the slightest chance of hearing what they said. For the first time in her life she was grateful for her Italian lessons, for without them she would have been unable to tell Viviane a syllable more about the scandal than anyone else. As it was, she was able to furnish her later with her very own translation from the Italian.

HE: I had no idea, I swear.

SHE: That we are *both* to entertain? I shall not forget this infernal duchess.

HE: Be angry later. Now we must give them more than they expect.

SHE: No one patronises me!

HE: We'll sing them—.

Here he gave the name of a piece that Louise did not recognise. But at once the lady's eyes glowed, she gave a tight smile and straightened her back, then in a thrilling voice she murmured, 'I adore you!'

The audience meanwhile had been muttering, but they fell silent the moment the singer turned and haughtily addressed them.

'When our hostess begged me to sing tonight, I did not realise there was an additional pleasure in store: Monsieur le Comte de Mirandol has agreed to sing my opening selection with me. We welcome you to this performance with a duet from my country, written last century.'

She began to play before anyone had recovered from the shock. Louise did not know the tune but she understood the words well enough, and so did most people in the room, including the hostess.

The theme was a subtle and delicious insult to everyone present, for the two lovers in the duet were guests at a depraved court in an Italian city ruled by despots. As Louise described it to Viviane next day: 'They alone were faithful and pure and steadfast, and all the rest—you know the kind of thing—and they lived amongst low minds and mean morals, and there was a lot in the song about the deceit and hypocrisy and triviality that surrounded them. It was a long diatribe, and it gave such a beautiful picture of the lovers' sentiments and such an ugly one of the world they suffered in.

'I was diverted by the words, but even more by the way they were performed. Have you never heard your guardian sing? I am no judge, but I cannot imagine you listening unmoved. He must be a baritone, I think—it is a dark voice, but warm, and the perfect foil to la Farrucci's, who must control her powers in a chamber or she would lift the roof. Her playing was very assured and her voice was like a spring that surged up effortlessly. I really cannot describe the effect they produced, but one saw it on every face. The disturbances in the room were all quelled and everyone seemed to breathe in unison. We were so rapt that when the song ceased no one moved or spoke, and your guardian took command of the silence, bowed deeply over la Farrucci's hand, and spoke so everyone could hear.

'He said he never thought when he arrived that he would have the privilege of singing with her. His time had already run out and he was wanted elsewhere, and he was desolate but he must take his leave.

'She inclined her head graciously without a word, then I saw the briefest look of triumph and hilarity dart between them, and he stood up and left the room, scarcely pausing to say goodnight to the hostess, and expressing no regrets to *her* about a thing, then he was gone!

'So there was the duchess paid back in ample

measure, and la Farrucci performed gloriously for the rest of the evening, and everyone said that she had never been in better voice. As for the ladies, I saw many a one looking pensive, and later when we sat down to supper I believe there were even more female minds busy about your guardian than there would have been if he had stayed and blandly played the gentleman.

'So do not you wish you had come after all and seen what a double-dyed villain you have for an uncle? And do you know what, I believe he was so intent on twisting the situation to his advantage that he stood within three feet of me during the whole performance and had not the least notion I was there. He was very cool, my Viviane, very cool indeed. Except that I saw his hand shake when he laid it on the piano and she struck up the tune, and I believe the emotion was anger, for I saw a wild glitter in his eye that makes me consider him a *dangerous man*.'

'I don't care what he is as a man,' Viviane said, 'but as a *gentleman* I wish he cared more for our family name.'

Louise looked surprised. 'Oh, I am sure he would never permit a breath of this to touch you or your aunt. You cannot feel insulted, dearest, that he looks beyond an old lady and his own niece for female company! As long as he is discreet from now on.'

Viviane chose to hide it from Louise, but this incident alienated her more than ever from her guardian. She felt ashamed of him, angry with him, and also somehow belittled by his liaison with the singer, though it would have been impossible for her to explain exactly why, to Louise or even to herself.

When Jules eventually turned up with Beaumarchais for the promised supper, he was preoccupied. He had just received a message from the Marquis de La Fayette, who even on his sickbed had come up with another idea to put the English off the scent: he planned a visit to London in March. The excuse was

142

a plausible one, since his uncle was France's representative at the court of George III. He would not be refused landfall on England's shores: the diplomatic situation was far too delicate for London to deliver that kind of snub to one of the most powerful families in France. Jules approved the scheme, but he wondered how far La Fayette would choose to extend his travels in enemy country. If he agreed to inspect the navy at Greenwich, for instance, it was inevitable that he would later be labelled as a spy. Jules wondered whether the marquis should risk his honour in such a fashion.

It was a successful meal, for his ward was on her best behaviour and clearly amused by Beaumarchais. Honorine de Chercy, too, looked delighted to have this great man of the theatre at her board. Not long afterwards, however, she began to feel unwell and announced she was retiring, leaving the count to look after the guest with Mademoiselle de Chercy.

After she had gone upstairs, Beaumarchais said he had often heard reports of Mademoiselle de Chercy's playing, and begged for some music. Jules instantly saw her direct a doubtful glance towards himself. To avoid awkwardness he said, 'You would oblige us greatly, Mademoiselle, if you would consent to play.'

Concealing her surprise, she led the way to the music room, where the count opened the pianoforte for her and then took a seat by the fireplace, opposite Beaumarchais. He could see his ward in profile as she paused with bent head, her hands on the keys, looking at the sheets of music placed before her between the candles.

The first peal of notes went through him with poignant sweetness, and he turned away and looked into the fire. She had chosen a piece he had never heard before, but he recognised the composer at once: Mozart. The notes of the sonata fell rapidly but clearly into his consciousness, as though he were a vessel being filled drop by drop with a potion that held him paralysed, intoxicated.

The effect on him was like nothing he had ever felt

before. After a time he had to turn his head again, and watch her as she played the slow movement. She was utterly lost in the music, her pale arms flexing gracefully and her hands drifting over the keys. There were no barriers between them here, none of her resentment or opposition to cloud the space that divided his body from hers. He saw her with the utmost clarity, as if for the first time. The crown of dark curls, with one tendril falling over her ear, through which a diamond sparkled like a tiny fire. Her bare shoulders, smooth and unadorned, bordered by lace as pale as her skin. Her slender waist, disappearing into the silk skirts of her dress that had billowed up around her when she sat down to play.

He gazed at her, disarmed, as though her soft, tapering fingers were playing not on the ivory keys but over his parted lips. It seemed impossible that neither she nor Beaumarchais registered what was flowing through him, leaving him so vulnerable that the reaction must surely be visible on his every feature. But they did not notice a thing. She continued to play and Beaumarchais leaned back, smiling in contentment, sipping from a glass of cognac. At last Jules was able to tear his eyes away from her and shade them with one hand, as if against the fire. After a lifetime of concealment, he ought to be good at this. All it meant was that he had to thrust this secret down into the wild places of his heart. It was the most beautiful secret of all, and the most terrible.

He could not move until she stopped. When they applauded she did not even look their way, but gave an absent smile and searched for another piece. She chose something that was suited to the background, intended as an accompaniment while the gentlemen talked; and Beaumarchais, accurately taking the cue, spoke when she was only a few tantalising minutes into the music. Jules felt like strangling him, or getting up and going home. Neither being possible, he was forced to converse.

All the while he was aware of her—her form on the edge of his vision, her graceful movements, her keen sensitivity—was she offended by his inattention, or totally oblivious of him? Beaumarchais meanwhile spoke not of the topics they had touched on at supper, but of America and the war. Obliged to give the appearance of interest in what he was saying, Jules summoned a few replies, then remembered a document which he had brought that evening specifically to give to him.

Under cover of a louder passage from the instrument, he took the letter of credit out of his pocket and handed it over. He motioned for the other to put it away at once but Beaumarchais opened it, read it, and just as the music slid once more into pianissimo exclaimed, 'Five thousand! This is generous indeed: twice what you promised me.'

Too late, Jules glanced towards the musician and motioned again for Beaumarchais to put up the paper. At that point her fingers froze on the keys.

She turned, got up and walked towards the hearth. Jules raised his head as she stopped in front of them. Her face quivered once, as though the heat from the logs touched her too closely, then she said with tolerable firmness, 'I should like to know what that money is for, Messieurs.'

Beaumarchais was utterly taken aback, and Jules hardly less so. He did not reply, so Beaumarchais ventured after a moment, 'This is between gentlemen, Mademoiselle. With respect, it is no concern of yours.'

Jules rose and found his voice. 'My niece disagrees.' With measured steps he walked to the door, closed it and came back to stand by Beaumarchais's chair. He touched the other man's shoulder to reassure him, and said to her, 'I do not object to your knowing where that money is going, as long as you swear the truth will not go beyond this room.' Beaumarchais looked up in astonishment, but Jules added, 'She will keep her word, I vouch for it.'

Poor Beaumarchais sat there in the greatest confusion and alarm, and meanwhile, with a kind of tender pain, Jules watched her thoughts flicker in her eyes. He knew why she hesitated: she did not want to pledge her word if the information he was about to give her could one day be used against him. She was too honourable to give her word only to break it later. And what if she wanted to discuss what he revealed with someone like Luny?

Sure enough, at last she said, 'I give my word. On condition that I am free to mention this to just one other person: Monsieur Victor de Luny.'

Jules winced, but said at once to Beaumarchais, 'You know him. And we know his loyalties.' There was a second's hesitation, then the other nodded.

After a pause, during which he realised he was being left to explain, Beaumarchais said, 'These funds, Mademoiselle, go to buy armaments for the American war.'

While she stared at them, amazed, Jules spoke again. 'Monsieur de Beaumarchais is responsible for purchasing consignments of arms, and shipping them to the United States.'

He had no need to tell her who Beaumarchais was responsible to, she knew it could only be the ministry. He watched the realisation penetrate her consciousness: she had just challenged an agent of His Majesty's government on diplomatic business.

At that point Beaumarchais, who had clearly had quite enough entertainment for the evening, rose to leave. He said his goodbyes in the usual way and asked for no guarantees of Mademoiselle de Chercy's silence, for which she was no doubt as grateful as Jules.

As Jules turned from the doorway, he saw she had sunk into one of the chairs by the fire, and was contemplating what she had done. She had interrogated him and his guest over a private transaction, without apology, explanation or even the semblance of respect. It was true she had just caught him giving away 5000 livres, but it was not to pay gambling debts or to fund some extravagance. His heart gave a great jolt as he thought of his other temptation to spend money—God grant she knew nothing of that affair. Now she realised that the sum was going to support the cause they both believed in.

Catching her eye, it shamed him to see that she fully

expected him to be flaming with anger at her rudeness.

When he reached the fire she rose and said, 'Uncle, I apologise.'

'The apology comes a little late for Monsieur de Beaumarchais. He was severely discomfited. The way he clutched that paper to his bosom, I think he expected you to rip it out of his hands. It was positively comical.' When she did not answer this wry remark he said, 'You have a habit of throwing public doubt on how I handle family business. I should appreciate it if you would make this the last outburst. I should also like to have this clear: there has been, and will be, no withdrawal of capital from the Mirandol estate whilst I run it.'

She nodded, but said quietly, 'The sale of the town house must have freed a considerable sum.'

'A portion of which will be spent to restore the east wing of the château. It has needed it for years, you know that yourself.'

'All the same, you had 5000 livres to give away tonight.'

His voice became more biting, despite himself. 'Has it never occurred to you, Mademoiselle, that in eighteen years with the army I might have amassed a fortune of my own? Without having to dip my tainted hands in the family coffers?'

She just stood there, staring into the fire, and he realised that she was aching for him to go. He could not do so without making another effort to reach her. 'Having always been a soldier, I am ill fitted for anything else. Duty has kept me in France these last months, and purchasing what Congress needs is the only support I can give. To be honest, I should like to do more.' He examined her. 'I know that even you feel the same where the United States are concerned.'

Her voice soft, she said again, 'Uncle, I am sorry.'

He sighed, turned, and she followed him into the hall, where the footman helped him on with his greatcoat.

She said, 'Of all things I would have expected tonight to make you most angry.'

He was pulling on his gloves. 'Tonight,' he said quietly, 'you spoke according to your sense of right. I honour you for that.'

She was so surprised she could not reply, so without another word he took his hat, bowed over her hand, and left.

9

PLOTTING WITH LA FAYETTE

Honorine de Chercy was visiting Marie-Claire de Billancourt in Saint-Germain. The two ladies were in the
salon, while in the music room at the other end of the
first floor, Louise was entertaining Viviane and Victor
de Luny. Honorine had spent a pleasant afternoon, but
she now had a matter to mention to Marie-Claire
which would not necessarily delight her friend.

'I must tell you something that concerns Louise. I
am as fond of her as I am of Viviane, so you will understand at once that this is not a criticism.' There was no
reply to this opening, so Honorine went on, 'You
remember that when I first returned to Paris from the
country, the Baron de Ronseul made Louise his object?'

'But of course—you mentioned it to me at the time,
we both took note, and eventually it came to nothing.'

'Yes. I must say I have had misgivings since, but I
never raised the subject; you are the most protective
mother, and I could have no serious fears for a daughter of yours. For a month or two now I have not heard
a word pass between them, but an incident at the ball
the other night made me wonder. You and I are of the
same opinion about the baron, so I must let you know
what I heard.

'Late in the evening I was annoyed to notice that
someone had opened glass doors onto the balcony—
very foolish in the dead of winter. There was no atten-
dant about, so I moved to close the doors myself, but
realised there were two people actually on the
balcony—Louise and the Baron de Ronseul. They did
not see me, and were speaking just loudly enough for
me to hear them as I approached. I did not conceal
myself to listen, I detest such behaviour; I simply
stepped forward after the briefest pause and suggested
they come inside, which they did. They both nodded
to me and moved off; he with the arrogant expression
he usually wears, and Louise looking a little nervous,

poor thing. I did not mean to startle her, and I certainly was not spying on her. But I overheard what they said.'

Marie-Claire shifted in her chair and said with a smile, 'Nothing of any importance, I am sure.'

Undaunted, Honorine went on, 'Your daughter was saying: "Why should I? You weren't so pleased to see me in the Rue du Faubourg Saint-Honoré."'

'He replied, "*One* of us had to show some discretion. You should be grateful."'

'Louise said something about having been deceived, and I distinctly heard him say, "Respected and honoured, you mean. How could I allow a woman I worship—?"'

'Marie-Claire, my arrival prevented his saying what he would not allow, but we both know there is nothing Monsieur de Ronseul would forbid a woman to do, provided it pleased him. He lodges in the Rue du Faubourg Saint-Honoré. Of course I do not suggest for a moment that she can have seen him in his apartment, but there are many shops in that street where a young lady might be waylaid by someone skilled at the kind of social trap Ronseul practises. Have you ever allowed Louise to go shopping with only her maid?'

'No, only when she and Viviane go out together. What an inconsequential conversation to be repeating to me!'

'It is not so much what they said as how they said it. They spoke in tones that suggested far more intimacy than you or I would ever permit between a mature man and a young gentlewoman, even if the two were affianced.' Marie-Claire looked at her with the most provoking serenity, but Honorine persevered, 'Your husband could give a hint to Ronseul without any unpleasantness, for the baron always backs off when the men of a family show their mettle. I have no need to explain why the baron avoids ever being in the same room with my nephew, and he shows the same caution with Viviane.'

At last Marie-Claire reacted, with a laugh that surprised Honorine. 'How alike you and I always think! When Louise told me about the baron following her tiresomely around, I suggested her father take a hand, but she protested that things were not so serious that she could not handle a clumsy suitor herself. So I gave her a few hints about discouraging him, which she was grateful for. Do not concern yourself. Recall: he spoke to her only of respect, honour and worship, though to be sure the last is daring, which I do disapprove. My mind is entirely at rest: he knows that familiarity between himself and my daughter is out of the question.'

It was Honorine's turn to look unconvinced, and Marie-Claire gave another laugh and said in a lower voice, 'My dear friend, the truth is that Louise is not the slightest bit interested in the Baron de Ronseul! She has formed an attachment for someone much younger. She confessed as much in our talk after the ball. She has begged me not to mention this, but after your frank and kind comments to me I feel it is the least I can do in return. She favours Victor de Luny.'

Honorine sat back in consternation and Marie-Claire went on, 'I don't imagine this will distress you, since the count still withholds his consent to a match with Viviane?'

Honorine nodded, wishing she had not bothered to bring up these thorny issues at all.

Her friend went on, 'And I am not so sure that there is much of a line to be drawn between the Baron de Ronseul and your nephew at the moment. If he were Louise's guardian I do not think I should be as tolerant as you about the liaison he has chosen to form. When he came up to Paris from the country, I thought him highly eligible—a fine career behind him, a good name and fortune, and one of the best-looking men in town—but while he is seen with la Farrucci so often in the demi-monde, no woman of good society is going to bring her daughters to his attention. You tell me he has no thoughts of marriage—I should say just as well!'

Honorine blanched under this onslaught, then rallied to say, 'I hope that affair has not been canvassed between you and Louise? I can assure you I have protected Viviane from even a whisper of it.'

'No, of course not. And Louise would have informed me if it had reached her ears. I am happy to say that as mother and daughter we exist in a state of complete harmony. She tells me everything.'

Louise was performing a very pretty piece on the harp, which she had actually taken the trouble to practise in anticipation of today's visit. She was piqued to find, however, that almost the moment she started playing, Viviane drew Victor away to the opposite end of the music room and began a murmured conversation which seemed to be getting livelier by the minute. Louise could not catch any of it, but after a time she began to suspect that they were quarrelling. With a sigh that was not entirely discontented, she concentrated on her music for a while.

'Victor, why on earth did you not tell me about Beaumarchais? I have never felt such a fool, it was ghastly.'

'There was no point: you were not directly involved with the shipments, so it was wiser for you not to know.'

'Are you suggesting I cannot keep a secret?'

'No, of course not. That is just the way effective conspiracy works—you know that by now, surely?'

She pounced: 'Then since *you* knew, I deduce you are connected with the shipments. In what way?'

'I . . . carried a message from La Fayette to Kalb, when he was on board one of Beaumarchais's ships at Le Havre. He failed to get away that time, of course. Since he has gone to Bordeaux I have had no personal contact with him. But there has been a lot to do with La Fayette's money—you have no idea how much of his fortune is going into this enterprise.'

'No, I begin to think I have not much idea about anything. And now I have had to give up my chance to be useful to Mr Deane.'

'He told me you advised him against the meetings. Why?'

She shrugged. 'I do not feel right about concealing

them from my aunt. So I asked him not to come.' She took a breath. 'I have made up my mind: I want to make a real, tangible contribution instead. I am selling some of my jewellery to provide funds.'

He took her hand quickly, squeezed it, then let it drop. 'This is too generous. But is it right to deprive yourself, in your situation?'

'You may well speak of my situation. If only I were a man, and could decide freely what to do with my life. I so envy the volunteers. How many are they now?'

'We are more than a dozen.'

'*We*?' She gasped, then stared at him, appalled.

He said in a rush, 'Yes, I shall go to America. You are the very first to know, for I have not yet told La Fayette that I accept his offer. He will have to advance money for the voyage—most of us are going without our families' knowledge or consent. Of course one day I shall be able to pay him back, with interest.'

'Oh God, why did I not realise?'

'Vive, I made sure you would understand—you have such a heart and mind for these great matters, unlike other women.' Avoiding her look of distress, he went on in some dejection, 'I hate to think how my mother will feel when I send her my letter of farewell, but I cannot allow such considerations to hold me back. She agreed with my father when he refused to get me a cadetship and tried to persuade me to study the law instead. They were both disappointed when I declined, but you know me, I am no student. So between them, all that my parents have done is fit me for an idle and purposeless life, which I hate. In truth, I suppose I am going to America less for the glory than for something to do, and so I shall tell them. At least you understand me.'

She was trembling. 'I don't believe this. You can talk to me about leaving, just like that. As though I shall be ecstatic that you are going away, perhaps never to return!'

'After all these months of talking and planning and sharing our dreams, I thought you would be glad.'

'Glad! What have I to rejoice about? Impoverished

by my uncle, deprived of my home and put under the
dominion of a man who until a few months ago was
a total stranger to me! My situation will change when
you go, I grant, for the worse, because I shall not have
you to turn to. You once promised to rescue me. Now
you want to rescue the Continentals. They are camped
in tatters in the wilderness, ground down by defeat.
They are about to be crushed entirely. Do you think
La Fayette and his tiny band can save them?'

'This is not like you. They are fighting for liberty. I
thought you above all would know why I want to fight
beside them. Why are you so angry?'

She half turned from him. 'I am too devastated to
be angry. But I am hurt. It does not comfort me to hear
that I am not like other women. I can tell you I am no
different from my sisters. But perhaps your emotions
have so changed that you would rather pretend mine
no longer exist.'

'Lord, is that all?' He took her hand again and said
in a deeper, more earnest tone, '*Of course* I shall miss
you. It hurts just to imagine it, especially if you think
I am abandoning you. Of course I want us to be
together—if only you could come to America too!
Vive, I am going alone, but that does not mean that
you and I are parted except by distance; in everything
else we are the same as we were. You are the closest
being to me in the world, whatever obstacles may come
between us for a while.'

She took her hand away and thought for a moment,
then said in a controlled voice, 'We have been so alike
in our dreams for the cause of liberty that I made the
mistake of seeing you as my partner already, the other
half of a soul that fought for justice and tried to rise
above the pettiness of our lives. But all the time you
have thought much less of me than I supposed, for you
spring this on me after thinking about it for ages, and
never sharing it with me. And you face our separation
without a single regret!' She looked him in the face. 'I
cannot reproach you for going to America, because
I understand the desire and share it. But I do reproach
you for thinking so little of me.'

He clutched his hair with both hands and said, 'Don't speak to me like this, you'll drive me mad. How could I bear to hurt you?' Then he said with quivering lips, 'I shall not leave if it will make you miserable. Serving in the war would be hell for me if I were sacrificing your happiness to do so. I cannot do without the support of the person who means most to me in the world.'

Her eyes filled with tears. 'I sound ungenerous. But I do not mean to be. It is just that I shall miss you so much.'

'And I you. I shall miss our talks, which are always about the important things in life. I could never feel about another woman as I do about you.'

She sat down on a sofa, and he sat beside her. They both knew that the crucial moment had passed and she had permitted him to leave. Neither knew quite what to feel; he could not gauge the depth of his joy and fear at the adventure before him, and she was unsure about the full extent of her sorrow to come.

He said gently, 'I did not realise how much you still hated the count. I thought that you could see his good qualities. They are not showy, but they are there. All he has done is ask us to wait. Cannot you agree to that, and give me time to do what I must?' Seized by unpredictable emotion, he said in a faltering undertone, 'Please tell me you are still mine.'

She whispered, 'Yes, Toto, I am yours.'

Before the end of March La Fayette was in London. His plan was to remain in the English capital until word arrived that his ship and the arrangements for the voyage were ready. He then intended to tell his hosts that he had been recalled home briefly on family matters. At that point he would travel back to France and go straight to the ship. No one would be looking for him in Paris, and those in London would be expecting him back any day, unaware that he was about to make a commitment which would thenceforth bar him from British soil for ever.

155

While in London he corresponded via a trusted courier with the Comte de Mirandol, saying in one of his letters:

You kindly ask whether there is anything you can do to help. Simply for you to put the most plausible construction on my actions will be of great service, for it will allay suspicions in Paris and elsewhere. Your record and your connection with America are such that people take what you say on these matters seriously. If you hint that I have been persuaded out of my rash schemes, you will be believed, and I shall breathe more easily.

Beyond this I have nothing to ask, knowing how generously you have already supported the cause. It has often occurred to me what a boon it would be if you too were travelling with the Baron de Kalb and the other brave men who will join us in this enterprise. There is no one whose experience I trust as I do yours.

During this time Viviane found that she could be of use to Madame de La Fayette, who had not accompanied her husband to London. Now that speculation about his activities had somewhat died down in Paris, Honorine de Chercy agreed with her niece that it would scarcely cause a scandal if she were to frequent the d'Ayen house once more. Viviane often kept the marquise company in the afternoon, and played games with her little daughter Henriette, whom her mother doted on.

Viviane found it awkward and distressing, however, when Adrienne de La Fayette spoke of her husband, for she was pregnant with her second child, missed the marquis greatly, and Viviane knew she had been told nothing of his latest plans. The marquise, though confused and worried about her husband's London visit, concealed her fears for him as best she could. Meanwhile Viviane herself began to wonder whether he was really in England, or had taken ship from Holland and set off for America in secret. She knew that regular cargoes of arms left Holland for North America, and it occurred to her that it would be easier for him to board a ship on the Dutch coast than to leave from France. She could not help wishing that he had already sailed, for that would mean Victor would not be going to America himself.

The next time she saw Victor, however, when they snatched a few words at a supper party, he assured her that the Bordeaux departure was still planned.

She sighed, then said, 'Well, at least it means I have time to hand over the money towards the voyage. I have a fancy to place the sum in the marquis's hands myself, if I possibly can. When I spoke to poor Madame de La Fayette yesterday, I felt the most terrible pang of rage and pity for her lot, and that of most women. All she can do is wait and hope and be useless at home. Victor, I must *act*!'

'How wonderful you are. I am sure there is not a woman in Paris with your spirit. I am sorrier than ever that we must part. I have heard from La Fayette in London. He goes to grand dinners and even grander balls, and has lulled the English into thinking he cares about nothing but showing a fine leg in the dance. When he slips back into France he has decided not to pass through Paris on his way; he will send me a message so I can join him.' He looked at her anxiously. 'If you insist on parting with your money, perhaps I can take it to La Fayette myself. But I think you should consider your own welfare. You already resent your guardian's power: having fewer resources will weaken your position further. America needs loyal soldiers even more than she needs funds—if I did not believe this, I would not go. If you were a man, you could bid Paris goodbye and stay at my side! But since you cannot fight, it is enough that you inspire men like me with courage. You have already done so much for the cause, it cannot be right for you to impoverish yourself as well.'

Viviane did not reply to this dissatisfying answer.

Benjamin Franklin's mind was also exercised about the Marquis de La Fayette. He said to the Comte de Mirandol one day, 'Like you I did not judge it prudent for your young friend to meet me before he went to England, and I am still uncertain whether he will do any good by going to Philadelphia. I work for the day when France and the United States form an alliance— and for that, we must be looked on more favourably at court.'

Jules nodded. 'At least the news from the States is heartening. The successes at Trenton and Prince Town, and Washington's great crossing of the Delaware to defend Philadelphia—these have raised international opinion of the Patriot army.'

'I should hate to antagonise His Majesty's Government by some contretemps, and I cannot guess how it may react to the departure of the marquis. Think what the reaction was in December when his brother-in-law and young Ségur openly asked the government's permission to sail to America.'

'Chancellor Maurepas scotched that. As he was bound to.'

'And there was an official outcry. I must tell you, we wrote to the marquis on that occasion to discourage him from his course of action, but he still went ahead and convinced Silas Deane that he should go on with his plans.'

'Have you corresponded with him since?'

'Only indirectly, through our secretary Mr Carmichael. I am every day tempted to send him a strong recommendation that he stay at home once he returns to France.' He leaned forward in his chair and looked at Jules over his spectacles. 'You have a better idea than I how your king will react when he realises the scion of such a prominent family has flouted a royal prohibition to join us. You can also judge how much anger will be directed towards us for turning a French gentleman into a blood-stained rebel! Tell me what you think.'

Jules was silent for a while then finally said, 'I am sorry, Franklin, I cannot advise you about La Fayette.

I would risk misleading you about the court's reaction. To be honest, I cannot predict what that will be. And it would be unfair of me to put obstacles in his way. Don't you think the man should be his own master? We were both nineteen once, and in love with liberty. One of our privileges was the freedom to make mistakes, and by God I took advantage of that!' He shook his head. 'Whatever the outcome, let the responsibility rest with the lad himself.'

Franklin decided to change the subject. 'How is your delightful niece? I see her so little lately.'

'I believe she is well.'

'I shall always be grateful for her services to Deane. Being "only a woman", she excites no suspicions amongst the English. Little do the spies know how effective women can be; they would change their minds if they understood your niece or her American counterparts. She is a perfect messenger and I trust her as I do you. And of course I vastly prefer her ravishing company.'

Jules smiled and found a change of subject himself.

It all happened in April. It began in the middle of the night after Viviane had returned from a supper party at the Vauventins'. She had dismissed her maid and was sitting in bed with a book, when there was a rattle against the window. It sounded like hail, but it did not continue, and she had seen no sign of bad weather in the moonlit sky on the way home. Another rattle, and she was sure: someone was throwing gravel against her windowpane. For a moment a stab of idiotic fear held her in the bed, then she flung off the covers and went to pull the curtains back.

Her bedroom overlooked the coach-yard. Below was the figure of a young man, looking up. She pushed open the window and her urgent whisper reached him: 'Toto! What on earth?'

'Come down. Please, at once, I have no time to lose.'

She hesitated only to throw on a wrap; then in bare feet, holding her bedside candle, she crept down the stairs, slipped along the back corridors towards the kitchen and emerged into the courtyard from a side door. The servants had all gone to bed, but she could not risk the noise of unbolting and opening the grand doors onto the yard.

She could see Victor quite clearly in the moonlight. She had never known him so upset: there was a deep line between his eyebrows and his face looked frozen and unnatural, as though he had difficulty holding in his emotions. She put a hand on his sleeve and whispered, 'The coach-house, quickly before someone sees us.'

They opened the heavy door and entered the cavernous place where they had already exchanged so many confidences. Leaving the door open so that there was some light from the moon, Viviane put the candle on a shelf and pulled Victor towards it by his sleeve, examining him by the flickering flame. 'What is wrong?'

'La Fayette is back. He is in Chaillot and leaves this morning. He goes to Bordeaux to join the ship with Kalb and the others. We are so dependent on secrecy and speed that he has not even said goodbye to his wife. But I had to say goodbye to you.'

She put her hands on his chest. 'Now it is happening, I cannot believe it.' Horrified, she found her mind racing, and seized on the only practical thought that occurred to her. 'If only I had the money down here, to give you.'

He shook his head. 'Oh Vive, I am not going to Bordeaux. I have just heard from my father: my mother is gravely ill and has asked for me. She caught a chill last week and it has reached her lungs. I am so afraid for her I can hardly think. Of course I am going to Luny.'

She clung to him. 'Darling Victor, how terrible.'

His arms came around her. 'I imagined so often, coming here to see your lovely face for the last time and ask your blessing. But now my heart is breaking. This is the worst day of my life.'

Her arms tightened. 'You must go to her quickly. Life is strange; we are ready to be brave, but when our courage is needed, the event can be so unexpected. I shall think of you. All the time.' She smiled into his eyes.

He said huskily, 'I promised myself I would claim another kiss from you on the day I left.'

She was still smiling at him with parted lips, and did not say no, so he kissed her swiftly, and as he did the tears welled into his eyes.

He let her go, turned away and brushed one hand across his face. 'The side door—it's safer.'

Together they pulled back the bolts and opened the door. The moonlight flooded over them and they stood looking at each other, pale and transfixed, their eyes shining with tears. Then he was gone, running around the corner to a cab that waited in the Rue Jacob.

The following days were a nightmare, during which Viviane spent most of her time with Madame de La Fayette. To her mind, the marquis, after all his lengthy and careful planning, had managed this last phase with a bewildering lack of judgement. He had not considered it safe or appropriate to take leave of his wife, but he had taken great pains to pen a letter to his father-in-law, outlining his whole project. This missive reached the Duc de Noailles d'Ayen before the marquis even looked like quitting the country.

Viviane was amazed that her friend had been rash enough to leave such a farewell letter. Granted he had made the nonstop journey to Bordeaux by post, in the impressively short time of three days, but she wondered why he could not have waited until embarkation to give his hand away so completely. As it was, on arrival he found there would be an indefinite delay before his ship's papers were complete.

Meanwhile in Paris the house in the Rue du Faubourg Saint-Honoré was like a building under siege, as every minute brought in more news of the marquis. Viviane watched the marquise maintain her dignity while she suffered, for as Viviane said feelingly to Louise, 'The world knows so much more than she was ever told!'

The uproar in Paris and Versailles eventually reached such a pitch that the young conspirators who were still left in the capital chose the Vicomte de Coigny as messenger to their friend. Coigny raced to Bordeaux to warn La Fayette to get away before the King could deliver a *lettre de cachet*, and at last the *Victoire* set sail.

At home one day, receiving a visit from Louise, Viviane unburdened herself a little, and on this occasion her friend was happy to listen, for La Fayette was just then the one and only subject in Paris.

Viviane said, 'We know for certain that the *Victoire* has got away, but I am afraid this will not be the end of the story. A royal command has gone south to stop the ship wherever it calls in Spain.'

'I declare it is quite thrilling. No one these days knows whether to applaud or curse the American cause. The "Franklin" wig has dropped right out of fashion, of course. I never did like it—too top-heavy. But the other day Mademoiselle de Gisors had on a very elegant creation, and when I asked her she told me it was the "Independence"! It was so bold of her to wear it.' Louise looked at Viviane more intently. 'The salons are ringing with the names of those who have gone as volunteers: Valfort, Fayolle, du Buysson, La Colombe . . . a dozen or more. Do reassure me: V de L is truly in the Loire with his family? And how is his mother?'

Viviane smiled. 'He will be touched by your concern. My aunt has received word that Madame de Luny is out of danger.'

'Thank heaven. I have an idea; may I go with you next time you visit Madame de La Fayette? I liked her so much, and I am sure she needs support.'

'How kind. Of course.' Viviane sighed. 'I do pity and admire her. She is carrying their second child, but she speaks of her husband's absence without a murmur of reproach. I could never be like her. When I marry I must live at my husband's side, wherever we are and whatever the danger. Otherwise I shall never wed.'

Honorine de Chercy was in confusion about the La Fayettes. She would have liked to reimpose her dictum

162

that Viviane cease visiting the marquise, but she suspected that an unpleasant argument would only ensue. She looked for no help in this regard from the Comte de Mirandol, who had hardly been near her for two months, and whose loyalties in any case were all firmly on the side of the volunteers.

Honorine tried to go about matters in her own way, by arranging for Viviane to be presented at court. But she was astounded to find that her grand-niece had no intention of appearing at Versailles. 'I can scarcely believe it, after all the trouble I have taken. The Duchesse de Brissac will be mortally affronted: she was about to give you her invitation in person! I never heard the like.'

'Madame, you know my thoughts on so many subjects; can it be that I have not explained myself on this? I am not going curtseying and scraping to Versailles at a time like the present.'

'This is ridiculous. Everyone you know, of any consequence, frequents the court. Your dubious friend the Marquis de La Fayette spent half his time there when he was in Paris. And so did the rest of his set—those with any standing in the world. I am sorry but I find your attitude absurd.'

Viviane shook her head. 'They are gentlemen. They are expected to take an interest in the government of France, to express their ideas at the seat of power, for one day some of them will be running the country. Young though they are, they can still hope to exert influence. It is different for us. No woman, even the Queen, has the vestige of a function at court. The *most* we can be is decoration. I decline to go anywhere on that basis.'

This conversation was taking place in Viviane's boudoir as she prepared to make yet another visit to Madame de La Fayette. Disappointed and annoyed, Honorine got up abruptly, causing a twinge in her rheumatic hip that made her even more uncomfortable, and began moving things around on the tall commode that stood by the window. With a jewel box under her hand, she looked over at the gold necklace the maid was placing around Viviane's neck, and said, 'That chain is too fine for what you are wearing. Why not put on the Italian one?'

She opened the box as she spoke, and found it half empty.

Viviane turned swiftly from her dressing table and said, 'Madame—'

But she got no further. Honorine had already opened the second case, which held nothing but a silver chain and an amber cross.

She turned to her grand-niece, and something in the demoiselle's eyes made her say sharply, 'At least three-quarters of your jewels are gone. Where are they?'

Viviane looked extremely conscious and the maid, who had stepped back from the dressing table at once, caught both the ladies' expressions and began to look uneasy herself.

Viviane said in a low voice, 'Mathilde, you may go.' She added kindly, as the maid gave a quick curtsey and prepared to escape, 'Do not concern yourself.'

Honorine lost no time once she and Viviane were alone. 'Your maid is obviously aware these pieces are missing. Should I call the servants?'

'No, Madame, I beg you. Nothing has been stolen. Mathilde only looked embarrassed because she disapproves of what I have done with my property.'

Honorine sat down. 'You have lent your jewellery to someone? Don't tell me you have *sold* it?'

'I have.'

'May I ask why? Is there anything you lack in your present position? If so, I think you might have consulted me before taking these extreme measures.'

Viviane sprang up. 'Good heavens, Aunt, you are the most generous hostess in the world. *Please* do not think—'

'Then what could induce you to throw away part of your heritage in this fashion? You have your allowance; if that is not enough, you may ask your guardian for more.'

Viviane gave an unpleasant laugh. 'Do you think I would stoop to beg a sou from him? Leave him out of this, if you please.'

'I am not sure that I can,' Honorine said. 'Some of those pieces were part of the Chercy legacy.' She rose. 'For the last time, may I know exactly why you have converted this very valuable property into cash?'

Viviane sat down again, turned to the mirror and said, 'To provide myself with some capital.'

'What for?'

Viviane remained silent, staring into the mirror with a face like marble. To prevent herself from another pointless outburst, Honorine turned on her heel, left the room, and went to the library to write a note to the Comte de Mirandol.

A few minutes later, Mathilde returned from below to help Viviane with her clothes. In her hand she held a message which in the interval had been passed to her by the groom Edouard, who acted as go-between whenever Viviane and Victor needed to correspond. Viviane tore it open.

Dearest Vive

I leave Luny today with the servant who brings you this letter. My mother is over the crisis, thank God, and recovering well. My parents believe I am returning to Paris, but I am going to Bordeaux after all.

La Fayette is there. A few days ago his ship put in at the Spanish port of Los Pasajes, where he received a barrage of angry letters from his family and a royal injunction to go to Marseilles. There he has been instructed to join his father-in-law and the Comtesse de Tessé and make a journey into Italy. It looks as though the King is not incensed enough to punish him severely, but neither does he want him in Paris. Anyway, my friend has returned as far as Bordeaux where he is staying with Monsieur de Fumel, the military commander. The other volunteers are waiting at Los Pasajes with Kalb.

I shall join La Fayette and persuade him to ignore the injunction. Half Versailles already admires him in secret, and the rest will soon forget about the venture until he proves himself in Philadelphia. I shall be able to contact him easily without alerting

the authorities, for he keeps open house at the
Chapeau Rouge Inn. In consideration for my parents
I shall not travel or enlist under my own name. I
shall be plain Victor Jacob—every time I hear the
name I shall think of the street where my heart lives.
We must go before the King orders La Fayette's
arrest. We cannot give up now.

    I wish I could embrace you one last time
    Yours for ever, Victor

When her guardian arrived that evening, Viviane was
fully prepared for him—mentally. To her distress,
however, she shrank from him physically, as though
there were something in his presence that oppressed
her. Thinking about this visit in advance diminished
her courage to face him, and when he walked into the
room all her carefully marshalled arguments flew
straight out of her head, for he was at his coldest and
most controlled.

After the polite greetings were over he said to her
aunt, 'Madame, I wonder if you would be kind enough
to allow me a few minutes in private with Mademoiselle de Chercy.' A moment later she was alone with
him.

He did not sit down or move from where he had
been standing. If he felt as nervous as she about what
was to come, he gave no sign of it. 'Your aunt with
her usual savoir faire has asked me here to supper, but
since the invitation is to give us the chance to talk, let
us do so now. Would you care to sit down?'

'No, Monsieur.'

'To business, then. I am told that you have sold some
jewellery to obtain funds. As your guardian I am
obliged to ask whether you need an increase in your
allowance. And secondly, which pieces you have disposed of.'

His voice was quite neutral, and she managed to
keep hers the same as she replied, 'The answer to the
first is no . . . thank you. As for the second, if my aunt
has given you all the details, surely you know the
answer.'

'How should I? Do you imagine she has been ferreting through your effects to see what has gone? She gave me a list of what she could remember—'

'A *list*?'

'And on it were several pieces belonging to the Chercy legacy. Minor ones, fortunately: two sets of garnet earrings, gold bracelets, a rather ugly necklace I saw your grandmother wear but once—I can't even name the stones.'

'Sardonyx.' For the first time, misgivings struck her. 'My grandmother cannot have worn it: nearly all my jewellery—apart from pieces I have bought myself— was bequeathed to me by my mother.'

He moved then, walking to the fireplace and back. Looking at the floor as he did so, he said with a little more animation, 'You are fond of talking about the family property—I wish you had a clearer idea of it. Some of your jewels were bequeathed to you in that way, but the rest came to you because you were born a Chercy and have the right to wear them. But only as long as you and the heir remain single: on either marriage those pieces return to the line, to be worn by the lady of Mirandol.'

'No one ever told me this. I see, so nothing of mine is really mine. At any moment it very conveniently becomes yours. I wonder you did not ask me to lay out everything I own before I left Mirandol, so you could label it accordingly.'

He grimaced. 'That was unwarranted. I am merely explaining to you, with all the patience at my command, that you held some items in trust. And I am afraid you have violated that trust; unwittingly, of course. Would you please tell me which pieces have been disposed of?'

His talk of patience, and his condescension, roused Viviane. 'Under your interpretation of our family inheritance, women do not figure very largely, do they? I am not to see my mother's jewellery as a gift to me, from one free being to another. I am not to exercise any rights over what she wished me to have, and to keep it, or to sell it, according to my choice. By this

167

definition I am merely a pawn in a man's game.' She strove to control her voice, which had begun to tremble.

He retorted more heatedly, 'That is sheer nonsense. The fact of the matter—and you are welcome to plough through the documents to see it—is that you have sold a number of pieces belonging to the estate. Kindly tell me what they are, before it is too late to recover them.'

'They were my mother's. If she were here, would you be trying to wrest them from her too?'

He took a step back. 'How dare you!' He walked back to the fireplace, saying through his teeth, 'This is intolerable.'

Viviane felt as though she had stepped over some boundary into the kind of anger that possessed him, and she said very clearly, 'I have no idea how much of my private property you consider yours; so I shall tell you exactly what I have sold, then you may state your claims if you wish. Besides the pieces you described, there are two diamond bracelets, a gold and emerald necklace and earrings, and some rings.'

He had been looking into the fire, but raised his head at this. He had changed colour; his cheeks were pale, which made his green eyes blaze in a way she did not like. 'Describe the rings.'

'A topaz, an emerald. And the largest: a sapphire solitaire.

He started, then lashed out. 'You can stand there and tell me you sold *that*! And I am supposed to believe you did not know what you were doing?' He was shaken with a fury that had something frightening behind it, but her voice was almost as loud as his as she replied.

'I know exactly what I am doing, Monsieur—leading my own life and disposing of my own affairs without reference to you. I must ask you not to interfere.'

'I shall interfere whenever it is my duty to do so. And I shall not be deflected by this ridiculous air of martyrdom.' He stopped and looked at her, as though a bitter realisation had only just come over him. 'I see it now: even my mildest remark over the last few months has been twisted to fit your private drama. You are convinced that you are a victim of persecution. Think what you like, Mademoiselle, I want nothing further to do with you.' He strode forward and she shrank, but he merely stood still a foot from her and said in a low voice, 'The name of the jeweller, if you please.'

Desperate to get rid of him, she said at once, 'I sold them to Lefévrier, in the place des Victoires.'

He bowed and turned away. At the door, he said, 'You must expect to hear from me when my duty requires it. Otherwise, in all your affairs please consult Madame de Chercy.' Then he was gone.

Viviane ran straight upstairs as though a demon were after her, dashed into her room and slammed the door. For a moment she stood with her back pressed to it, her eyes closed, then she walked across the room to a cheval glass that stood by the bed. She looked at the wild-eyed young woman in the glass, went closer and saw tears of self-pity gleaming in her eyes. She brushed them away and said to the mirror, 'He is not to be borne. *This* is not to be borne. I shall go, and leave tyranny behind me.' She compressed her lips and wrapped her arms across her chest, not seeing her image now, her mind already racing with what must be done. 'Victor, I am yours. We shall be married in Bordeaux. And sail to America—together.'

10

ELOPEMENT

Late next afternoon, Honorine de Chercy drove to her nephew's house in the Rue Richelieu and, on being told he was home, had herself announced. Surprised at the visit, he came striding into the downstairs drawing room at once to greet her. She gave him scarcely a moment to speak before she broke the news.

'I am sorry to tell you, your niece has gone.'

'What do you mean?'

'She left my house this morning with her maid, before I was up. In a cab, what is more. When I heard, I thought she was only trying to annoy me, visiting Madame de La Fayette or some such without informing me. I never dreamed . . . She did not come home for dinner, however, and I began to worry. I sent messages all over town but could not find where she visited today.'

'Why did you not contact me, for heaven's sake?'

'After yesterday? I am sure you can understand my reluctance there.'

He shrugged impatiently. 'Go on. Where did you find her? What has she done, moved in with the Billancourts?'

'My dear, she has eloped.'

He went white. It was a moment before he could speak. 'Luny. I'll kill the little—'

'Wait, listen. I have only just found out, at the Billancourts'. I was so upset I went over to consult my friend. Her daughter was there too. We all entered into the most distressing speculations, and at one point the demoiselle dropped a letter onto the floor. Something made me ask her what it was; she refused to say, then burst into tears and said she would die before she betrayed the confidence of a friend. I made short work of *that*, and I have the letter here.'

He held out his hand.

She said, 'It is not especially obliging, to either of us.'

170

'If you please.'
She handed it over.

Louise
Take care how you react to this letter if anyone is by, and destroy it afterwards. In three days you may tell my aunt what it contains, for by then I shall be on the way to America with my husband.

I cannot brook the tyranny of my guardian another moment. Yesterday he accused me of a crime, of despoiling the Chercy estate, merely because I obtained cash for some jewels that once belonged to my mother. If I had shouted back at him, I shudder to think what he might have been driven to, but I maintained my dignity whilst demonstrating my hatred of all his proceedings.

I never told you that I continued to correspond with Victor after you gave up exchanging our letters. We are as close as two people can be. We could not bear to be parted by this journey to America (yes, he is going, under the name of Monsieur Jacob, and even my uncle, even Franklin, do not know). I shall join him and share his fate—we shall be married in Bordeaux, travel to Spain, and board La Fayette's ship as man and wife.

I shall travel south as La Fayette did, by post, taking food and drink with me and not stopping by day or night. This part alone of my long journey will be hugely expensive, but I have money enough and to spare. I have persuaded my maid Mathilde to come with me, though she is terrified and cannot be forced to come to America. When she returns to Paris, tell my aunt to blame me, not Mathilde, for everything.

I have not left a letter for my aunt, and I am taking all my correspondence with me; I am not so rash as the marquis! While she is in a panic about me, no doubt she and my uncle will ask you where I might be. Keep my secret for at least three days. Then you may tell them I am married and they need have no dealings with me ever again. I am already remorseful over my aunt, but I have no choice.

Apart from her, the only person I regret in France is you, my dearest friend. I wish you all the joy and adventure in life that is before me. I wish I were not weeping; I can hardly see the paper.

Adieu

Viviane

He scanned the letter quickly but did not look up. Honorine remarked, 'I suspect Mademoiselle de Billancourt dropped that on purpose; she rather fancies Monsieur de Luny for herself.'

He folded the paper. 'Madame, I have not even offered you a chair. Pray sit down.' He went to the doorway and called one of his servants, who was sent off for some refreshments. He never used the bellpull: his all-male staff kept within hearing, military style, and sprang to their tasks with alacrity. Getting on well with him did not seem to affect their efficiency; on a less urgent occasion, Honorine would have asked him how he managed it.

'I am not here on a social call, Nephew, we must act, and quickly!'

He took a seat opposite her. 'First things first. Since the maid has gone too, your servants will know what's up. Can they be trusted to keep quiet?'

'Yes. And I shall tell all our acquaintances that Mademoiselle de Chercy is making an impromptu visit to friends in the country.'

'Your friend and her minx of a daughter will stick to the same story?'

'Absolutely.'

'Thank God, then her reputation is intact. As long as Luny's friends are not in the know.'

'That I cannot say. The letter is perplexing. I have no idea how they planned this; if they did so together, why are they not travelling together? I am furious with Mademoiselle de Billancourt, and so I told her: to be exchanging their letters in that shameless fashion, ever since last summer!' She clasped her hands together and beat them gently on her lap. 'What a child. I am so angry with her. An elopement, to *America*! The La Fayette scandal is *nothing* to this.'

'Rest assured, Madame, she will not get far.'

'But we are a day's travel behind her!'

'Reflect: it is no simple matter to arrange a secret marriage. Even supposing the bridegroom is willing, and God knows whether Luny is or not. There is time enough to prevent it. I shall have to find her before she compromises herself any further.' He rested his forearms across his thighs and stared at the floor. After a while he said, 'I must hope that she goes more out of hatred for me than love for him. Otherwise, have I the right to interfere?'

'Good heavens, Nephew, you are not going to split hairs in a case like this?'

When he looked up his eyes were bleak, but her indignant expression seemed to rouse him, and he went to a desk by the door and scrawled a hasty note, which he sent off to his banker's by another servant. He ordered a second man upstairs to do some packing, then sat down again in the same posture as before.

He said, 'To think of her travelling the highways alone, without sleep, comfort or protection. She expects to catch him in Bordeaux. But what if he does not know she is following, what if he goes on to Los Pasajes?'

'Where?'

'A seaport in Spain: La Fayette's ship is waiting there. Why is she doing this? If only I knew *exactly* why.' He put his head in his hands.

Honorine was not in much doubt about that—she guessed her grand-niece was driven as usual by her rebellious passions. Honorine had been unaware of quite how much Viviane loathed her present situation, and her guardian. But having read her frank and hurtful letter, she could see how an elopement might appear a wonderful means of escape.

She said, 'If it were a love match I could understand. But I have never seen anything but friendship between them. I can scarcely believe this is happening. She is mad to behave so. Lost to every sense of propriety. Do not distress yourself, my dear, she does not deserve it. If she could see you now—you could hardly be more concerned if you were her own father.'

'Her father? God!' he said through his fingers. He leaped to his feet and began pacing around the room. 'I shall travel post, non stop—it is the only way to catch her. She may meet with obstacles on the way that will slow her down. *Jésu*,' he said, striking his fist in his palm, 'how can I wish that on her? No, wherever she alights at Bordeaux, I shall find her. God grant I arrive before she makes contact with him.'

'You realise I am coming too?'

'Nonsense, Madame, you could not bear to travel in such a way, I cannot expect it of you.' Then he looked at her in despair. 'But how shall I persuade her to return? She will not bow to me, and I shall never use force.'

'I intend to follow behind you at a more sensible rate, by the diligence, and you will leave messages for me at the post inns. When you find your niece, ask her to remain where she is until I arrive, and I shall escort her home.'

'What if I have to pursue her right into Spain?'

'Then so be it. I shall travel as far as Los Pasajes if need be. Where she and I will have a full and sensible discussion and take care of this matter once and for all.' She rose and smiled at him for the first time. 'I knew I could depend on you to act. You have restored my confidence—we shall find her yet.' He bowed over her hand in silence and when he stood straight again she looked into his eyes, saying firmly, 'And while you are on the road you must promise me not to torment yourself. It is not your fault.'

'I beg to disagree, Madame. If I had treated her better from the start, this would not be happening.'

The only thing that kept Viviane going on her journey to Bordeaux was the thought of finding Victor at the end of it. Somehow she could not think beyond that meeting: she must see him standing before her, hold his hands in hers, before she could face the most momentous events of her life—marrying him, and escaping from France. Her decision was like an unwavering fire in the depth of her consciousness—Tyranny lay behind her, and Liberty ahead.

But the journey was tedious and exhausting. She quickly discovered that a young gentlewoman travelling with only her maid was a prey to suspicion, half-hearted service and, occasionally, downright insolence from the hirelings along the way and at the inns. Some of her fellow passengers looked as though they might prove conversible and even sympathetic, but she did not dare engage them in talk. At one of the inns in the Poitou, where she had been told she might alight and take rest and refreshment, the worst misfortune befell her—the post coach left without warning while she was in an upstairs room, and she and Mathilde had to wait several anxious hours before they could secure places in another. The staff of the inn were not of a respectable or respectful kind, and she found it hard to command their best service. But once on the road again, she adopted the queenly air that her aunt always wore when she swept into a hostelry. Such behaviour in a young woman was resented but taken seriously, and the last stages of her journey would have been more bearable as a consequence, if she had not been so bone-weary.

In Bordeaux she asked to be taken to the Chapeau Rouge. By now she could scarcely stand; if the innkeeper had not been able to provide a room at once, she would have lain down in the dirty straw of the courtyard and refused to move. The room was reasonably well appointed, looked out on the yard and had a small dining room attached. It was cold despite the spring sunshine outside, and she asked for a fire. While Mathilde unpacked her trunks she ordered a meal from the waiter, and before he left the room she came out with the all-important question.

'Do you know whether the Marquis de La Fayette is still in town?'

He was a short man with tight greasy curls and

round blackcurrant eyes that gleamed as he replied, 'He left yesterday, Mademoiselle, so I hear.'

Her heart sank. 'I am told he received some of his friends here. Are any in residence?'

'Not a one, Mademoiselle. They all left town not long since. There was only one stayed here, Monsieur de Mauroy. But he's gone, like I said. Very pleasant, was Monsieur de Mauroy, a very generous young gentleman.'

'Does . . . Does the name Jacob mean anything to you?'

'Why yes—left town the day before Monsieur de Mauroy. He was staying across the way, at the Croix d'Or, but he spent most of his time here. On account of our kitchen, Mademoiselle, which I beg to mention is superior to any you'll find in Bordeaux. If you'll excuse me I'll be off there now with your order.'

So that was that. She was too late. And still alone, with no one to turn to, no one to consult. She would have cried, but even tears required an effort. Bidding Mathilde to cease unpacking, postpone the meal and go to her room, Viviane flung herself on the bed and willed herself to oblivion.

Next morning her hopes miraculously returned. With the pale sunshine of a beautiful day slanting through an open window onto her breakfast table, she reviewed her finances, made sure Mathilde had arranged for the laundry and other necessities, and sent her off to talk to the inn servants and see whether they could say any more about Victor or his friend Mauroy.

She was seized once more by urgency. She knew her close relatives only too well: at the merest suspicion of what she had done, they would be heading for Bordeaux in hot pursuit. She was travelling under a false name, but neither this nor any kind of disguise would throw her guardian off the track.

The inquiries proved fruitful. Mathilde found a chambermaid who was even more convinced than the waiter about the generosity of Monsieur de Mauroy, and probably with more intimate reason. She was a self-confident girl who received Viviane's coin with satisfaction and answered her questions readily.

La Fayette's guests were a fine, cheerful group of gentlemen, and they usually met in the main room downstairs, then dined in a private room on the first floor. Monsieur de Mauroy was the most recent arrival, and it was because of him that Monsieur de La Fayette had at last quitted Bordeaux.

'What do you mean?' Viviane said. 'Monsieur de La Fayette was supposed to be leaving on a tour of Italy. Did Mauroy decide to go with him? Or did he persuade him to ... take another direction?' The girl hesitated and Viviane said, 'I am a close friend of the marquis. You may tell me exactly what has happened.' The girl considered this for a moment, and Viviane had time to realise what speculations might be running through her head. Never mind, the essential thing was to find out the truth. 'The marquis was staying with the military commander, wasn't he? Please tell me where he went after that.'

'It is as you say, Mademoiselle, the marquis was due to leave for Italy. But Monsieur de Mauroy came down in haste from Paris to warn him, to tell him to get away quickly. They held a conference in the room along the corridor, just here, and it was all decided. The marquis decided to drive out of town in a carriage with Monsieur de Mauroy—all proper like—then a few leagues out they planned to change places: Monsieur de Mauroy would sit up like jacky in the carriage and the marquis would dress different and ride postilion.'

'Ah! And they would turn and head south?'

'Yes, Mademoiselle.'

'Did anyone else travel with them?'

'No, it was just them two. The others took off along the highway. I suppose if you know so much, Mademoiselle, you know where they is headed?

'Thank you, that will be all.' Viviane would have liked to offer the girl more payment for her future silence, but she knew it would be money thrown away. She had her information, and she must act on it. She was only halfway to her goal, but she would get there

177

all the sooner for suspecting that even now her guardian was riding hard at her back.

Jules stopped only twice on the way to Los Pasajes. The first time, at Bordeaux, he went straight to Fumel, the military commander. When he was told that La Fayette had set out for Marseilles to undertake the prescribed visit to Italy, he drew his own conclusions. Verifying these at the Chapeau Rouge not long afterwards, and receiving unmistakable confirmation of his ward's passage, he left his usual note for Honorine and took to the road again. The second halt was at San Sebastian on the Spanish coast. He had no choice about pausing there, for he had lost the trail. A fruitless afternoon passed, and he was obliged to stay overnight in the town. His anxiety grew: if she had been held up in one of the villages in the hills on the way to San Sebastian, she might be in the hands of bandits. Or worse. He mastered the impulse to ride back along the road; it was more prudent to stay in town, for there were other inns at which he could inquire in the morning.

At one of them next day he found his answer—she had passed through, and he was still twelve hours behind her. As he walked out into the street, his heart gave a great thump in his chest and for a moment he could not breathe. In that instant he felt pure hatred for her—to have forced him into this, pursuing her like a demon down the length of France and across Spain. Hounding her through every hostelry, his body and mind aching.

He leaned against a shop window and looked blindly in at the wares. He was overcome by the temptation to give up, to turn back and leave her to the consequences of her own foolish decisions. He had a clear picture in his mind of what their meeting would be like, and of the frustration and fury it would unleash. He had no qualms about confronting Victor de Luny, for he had a strong suspicion he would be rescuing that young man from the most embarrassing fix of his life. Even if he was not, Luny's reaction could not dismay

178

him; it was her face that swam in his mind, the beautiful features contorted by defiance and contempt.

The shop was a gunsmith's. He tore his mind away from her and went in.

It was midday in the Spanish port of Los Pasajes. A brisk Atlantic breeze whistled up the seaside streets and around corners, carrying the scent of new tar from the docks and the voices of the stevedores who were unloading a shipment of wine that had come down the French coast from the Garonne. Further in, the lanes narrowed and the sounds from doorways and opened casements flowed out over the cobbles—servants chattering, the occasional voice raised in song. There were groups around the wells in the little plazas, and languid townspeople wandered past shopfronts where the tradesmen worked at their tables outside, under the gentle light of the spring sun. It was time to think about retreating indoors and sharing a tureen of mussel soup, a Los Pasajes specialty, and exchanging gossip to while away the early afternoon.

One of the more fascinating subjects lately was the vessel *La Victoire*, for the whole town knew where the ship was headed, and why. She had arrived, paid her port fees and, despite France's displeasure, the authorities had neither impounded the ship nor made things difficult for the captain or her owners. When the marquis was recalled to France, the young gentlemen who had arrived with him lounged about the dockside inns at first, but soon made themselves known to some of the best families. The fact that they insisted on giving inventive aliases instead of their own aristocratic names rather added to their attractions. The distant frowns of the King of France could not discompose the worthies of Los Pasajes—they welcomed the intrepid Frenchmen and admired their distinguished, though unidentified, family backgrounds, and their glorious mission. The marquis, rumour said, had not returned, and the *Victoire*'s captain was in a sad state of indecision about whether to sail without him. There was another rumour, however, which said that a servant in one of the inns had come upon a red-headed postilion stretched out asleep in the hay in the stables, and had recognised him at once. It was also said that the ship sailed at dawn on the morrow, and stores would be taken on board tonight under cover of darkness.

In the afternoon a young gentlewoman and her maid alighted from the mail coach and bespoke a room at the inn. The coach had met with delays on its route and all the passengers were atrociously tired, but to the inn-keeper's surprise the young lady refused to rest until she had ascertained where the French gentlemen were lodging. Armed with the location of a certain Monsieur Jacob, she at once set out on foot with her maid, accompanied by an ostler from the inn to show her the way.

At a hostelry called the Galicia she dismissed the ostler, summoned the landlord and, learning that Monsieur Jacob was alone in his rooms on the first floor, said abruptly, 'I am Madame Jacob. Kindly show me up.'

From his acquaintance with the young volunteers, the landlord was prepared for any announcement except this. He could not help exclaiming, 'You are his wife?'

'No, his mother,' she snapped. 'Must I wait all day?'

Abashed, he showed her upstairs himself, and hardly dared glance into the room as he announced her and admitted her and the maid. He closed the door with deferential haste and thus missed the expression on Monsieur Jacob's face as he rose from a chair near the window, turned and saw who had entered. After the first shock the young man stood absolutely frozen, unable to speak, and a look of horror congealed on his features, unmixed for the moment with any gentler emotion.

Less than an hour after this another visitor arrived at the post inn: a tall, black-haired gentleman with a look that fell little short of murderous. He had ridden for the last stage of his journey, presumably for the sake of speed, for he was in a mighty hurry to find out about the female passengers in the mail coach. He was dishevelled, spattered with dirt from a damp ride, and rough in his speech from tiredness, but he took no time to order a room or refreshment. Instead he gave curt instructions for the innkeeper to look out for the arrival of his luggage, then set off for the Galicia.

The landlord at this popular inn was surprised to be questioned again about Monsieur Jacob. Told that the young man was upstairs with his very beautiful wife, the gentleman closed his eyes in relief, but when he opened them again to ask where the room was, his expression was already changing into something else. It looked much more like fury that urged him up the stairs at a run.

When Jules threw open the door, Victor was standing by the mantelpiece and his ward was in a chair. Luny looked exasperated and Viviane tearful, but on seeing the count they both turned white. She tried to say something, but Jules ordered her from the room. She flinched but went on the instant, and through the chamber door he saw her maid on the other side, paralysed with nervousness.

Then he turned on Victor and asked harshly if they were married. Victor shook his head. More brutally still, he demanded to know if she were his mistress, and at this the young man said, 'What do you take me for, Monsieur?'

'I'll take you for an idiot if you think you can lie to me.'

'I resent that! I have always acted with honesty.'

That was nearly too much. Jules demanded to know what was *honest* about his correspondence with Mademoiselle de Chercy, and on what principle he could justify spiriting a young lady abroad against her family's wishes, and risking her life in the process—not only was he eloping with her, but he was dragging her across an ocean and into a war!

At that Victor's fragile dignity fell away. 'I understand you, Monsieur.' He took a breath. 'It is painful to say this, but I did not know Mademoiselle de Chercy would follow me here. I swear, I am at my wits' end over it.'

Jules sat down grimly to think. After a moment, he said, 'So none of your acquaintance could know she was leaving Paris?'

Victor shook his head.

Jules decided to keep the demoiselle de Billancourt's name to himself. 'Is it likely that she would have told anyone else?'

'No.' Victor added with feeling, 'Mademoiselle de Chercy is a very single-minded person.'

'Then there is some hope you have not compromised her in the eyes of society.'

Victor was outraged at that, but managed to calm himself when Jules went on, 'Do you think she could ever have brought herself to undertake this incredible pursuit of you if you had not been carrying on a romantic conspiracy for months? If you truly loved her, my young friend, you would have declared this to her and her family, and pledged to wait and receive her answer in due time. But no, your feelings were unclear, and instead of admitting this to her in good faith, you allowed the whole affair to slide into the morass where you both find yourselves.'

Victor had no choice but to apologise, which he did frankly and with feeling. Jules was not exactly soft-ened, but he knew he must take advantage of this mood of confession. He said in measured tones, 'Do you love her?' After an appalling moment of suspense, during which Victor did not answer, he said, 'Come now, you are talking to me, not her. It is not a question of hurt feelings, but of telling the truth. Do you have a passion for her, or no?'

Victor shook his head. Jules breathed a sigh, and got up. Victor looked alarmed, but Jules told him that he was satisfied, that the conversation was at an end, and he was to say not a word about the proceedings to anyone, ever. Mademoiselle de Chercy would be con-veyed back to Paris, her absence explained by a visit to friends in the Loire, and all correspondence between them was over.

Victor frowned and said with resolution, 'If you think to make Mademoiselle de Chercy miserable on my account, Monsieur, I shall consider it my duty to stay in France and be at hand, in case she wishes to call on me.'

Jules managed to hide the exasperation this caused him and say, 'Come now, I am not a tyrant, whatever she may make out. I shall offer her no recriminations, and she will continue under the care of Madame de Chercy. If you write from overseas, Madame de Chercy will answer you, and you will be permitted to make inquiries about my niece's welfare. We shall pass on her messages in reply.'

Victor still looked unhappy, but he was obviously yearning to end the conversation. Jules asked him to leave the inn for an hour so that he could hold a conference with Mademoiselle de Chercy and decide where she would lodge until her aunt arrived to fetch her. Victor requested to be allowed to say farewell to her, but Jules refused. They shook hands and Victor left.

Next came the difficult part. Jules went to the door of the chamber. There was silence within; it occurred to him that she might be standing with one ear to the panelling. But when he knocked, her footsteps approached from the other side of the room. She was too proud to listen at doors.

She certainly looked stiff-necked enough when she emerged. Showing her to a chair with his usual severity, Jules dreaded what he had to say. Her behaviour embarrassed and confused him; she was so steadfast in her inclinations that she never considered the consequences even of her most dramatic actions. So there was still a kind of purity about her: even in this impasse she was unaware of how much she had damaged her own modesty. He should have been ruthless and shown her the enormity of her misconduct; he should have made her an object of ridicule and shame in her own eyes. But he had not the courage.

He told her that marriage to Victor was impossible, and she was to return to Paris as soon as her aunt arrived to fetch her. She immediately came out with a characteristic phrase: she asked him why he was determined to ruin her life. He could not wound her by remarking how reluctant her bridegroom proved when she turned up to surprise him. Instead he talked about what would happen if the marriage were allowed to take place and they went to America. As a follower of the Continentals she would find life distressing and dangerous. She said that she would face any suffering for such a cause, and he told her none of the heroics she might imagine for herself were possible.

She would be the wife of a young man fighting in a poorly equipped and beleaguered army, constantly on the move. The living conditions would be uniformly uncomfortable and she would scarcely see her spouse. She would be an encumbrance and a worry to him, and as for advancing the cause, she could only be a drag on it, a foreigner, another mouth to feed. If she elected to stay in some town to await the end of the war, she would suffer constant anxiety about his whereabouts and his life, while she occupied an uncertain position in American society, where the language and the ways were not her own. If she cared about the cause, she would be of much more help back in Paris, using her eloquence and energy to rally support, keeping the lines of communication open between France and the Republican army, seconding Deane's recruitment efforts, raising funds. These she had already shown talent for; in these she could be of use.

She listened for once, but he did not think her convinced. At the end he said, 'You have a harder choice than La Fayette and Luny and the other young men: when they decide to fight, they have only to take up a sword. Your eagerness to go to America may be the same as theirs, and I believe your courage is just as great. But you are a woman, and cannot fight as they do. Mademoiselle, you must fight *your* way. Simply to follow them is meaningless. Indeed, I have tried to show that in America you would have fewer powers and less independence than you have now. Do you understand?'

She thought for a moment, then reluctantly nodded.

He saw the disappointment in her eyes, and wondered that she did not weep when she realised her dream was over. He could not bear to say more in case she did.

Eventually she said, 'How did you know I was here?'

He told her how Honorine had obtained her letter to Louise de Billancourt, but not about their suspicions concerning that young lady. In former days she would have been very preoccupied about such officiousness, but by now a sense of shame had begun to grow on her, for a blush spread over her cheeks at his mention of the letter, and she remained silent, her eyes cast down. Inwardly he cursed himself for a fool, but he pitied and longed to comfort her.

Then she burst out, 'I cannot let you think badly of Victor. I wanted us to be married and go to America, but when I saw him, when he spoke to me so—' She stopped and said with a moan, 'I have been very foolish. Somehow in his last letters, in the excitement of going away, he said much more than he really felt. Victor is fond of me, but he does not love me. You must not think he tried to seduce me. This dreadful mistake is not his fault.'

This seemed to be the end of her explanations, for she said no more. He could not be so restrained. 'My niece, despite how you feel about me, I have come to know you well. You have strong emotions, and you cannot help showing them. Your reactions to me, for instance, are so transparent that even from the way you walk out of a room I can tell the degree of animosity you feel against me at that moment.' She looked so disconcerted that he hurried on. 'The same goes for the way you treat others. Forgive me if I have guessed wrongly, but so far I have never seen anything to convince me that you are in love with Victor de Luny.'

She said in a faltering voice, 'Why do you say this to me?'

'You accused me of ruining your life. I have tried to prove that by preventing you from going to America I shall take nothing away from your happiness. But you would be right to resent me if I stood in the way of burning passion.'

She blushed more deeply. 'You are making fun of me.'

'Far from it!' He lowered his head into his hands and chose his words carefully. 'Tell me you love Victor de Luny, and I shall make what amends I can. Tell me you do not, and we can drop the subject.'

She kept him waiting for some time, then said, 'Very well, I do not. But what does that matter to you?'

'I would not have you marry a man you do not love.'

She looked incredulous. 'Few people would share that view. What about the arranged marriages and unions of convenience one hears announced every day?'

'In principle, I am against them.'

She was still quite disbelieving. 'On what grounds?'

He would have liked to get up from the table, walk away and spare her yet another lecture. And deprive her of another opportunity to despise him and his ideals. But her future was at stake, and her happiness. Looking at the tabletop, he began slowly, 'Mademoiselle, so far you have not known love. It is not my business to tell you what it is like, but I do have a duty to give you my particular views.' She sat back, perplexed, and he went on, 'Until love comes into your life, you can have no idea of its strength, or the way it eclipses all other emotions and preoccupations.'

He raised his eyes, and held her nervous gaze. 'If you were a milk-and-water demoiselle, we would not be having this conversation, but you have lately proved the power of your will and your desires. For a young woman of your temperament, to enter into marriage without love and then to encounter it too late in the company of another man would be torture. And the torture would be tenfold if your husband were fond of you and worthy of your respect—for I know you have principles and the strength of character to adhere to them.'

She said nothing, just sat with parted lips, her nervousness replaced by wonder.

He continued, determined to make her see. 'Mademoiselle, imagine if one day you found the man you could truly love. Imagine yourself on the brink of opening your heart to another, of tasting the greatest happiness we can know, and then realising that you had barred the way through your own thoughtlessness and haste. Believe me, you would then suffer far more misery than you now think possible.'

This was a revelation to her; she was stunned. She had never listened to him with such attention. He hurried on, saying again how transparent he had always found her feelings, and pointing out how quick others would be to see and condemn any illicit emotion; how, if she yearned for someone she should not love, she would be forced into concealment and deceit. 'I cannot contemplate such unhappiness for you. You must wait, observe people and find what draws you to others, and when love comes into your life you will be ready for it, and able to make a decision about the best partner for you. Think of the examples you have before you. How can you look at the union of Gilbert and Adrienne de La Fayette and fail to see that as husband and wife they possess the ideal? How can you, with all your aspirations, all your ... qualities ... deny yourself the chance to attain that ideal also?'

For a moment it seemed that there were no barriers between them, and he felt a rush of powerful admiration for her. Here she was at the end of a racking journey, she was exhausted, she had been scolded first by Luny and then by himself, she had been discouraged and hurt, but what a glow there was in her eyes! She had not looked so fresh and touching since the day he came across her in the stables at Mirandol, and with all his heart he wished he could go back to that moment and begin all over again.

As she looked at him he saw how beautiful her eyes were with some tenderness in them. She said, 'I never knew. How could I?'

'Why I opposed your marriage to Victor de Luny? But I made it clear from the start.'

'I did not know you cared about me.'

Another instant and he would have told her how

much. He rose and walked away from her. He heard voices below, looked out the window and saw several men in conversation in the yard. Amongst them was a redhead, more plainly dressed than usual, but recognisable just the same.

He turned to find her beside him.

She put a hand on his arm. 'I have offended you.'

'No, my dear.'

She said, 'Until now I have not known you.'

11

THE CROSSING

It was dark. Jules was still at the Galicia, where he had taken a room along the corridor from Victor de Luny. He had conveyed his ward back to the post inn, made every arrangement he could for her comfort, and recommended that she remain indoors until the arrival of Honorine. She had been acquiescent and embarrassed, and simply wanted to be left alone. He told her he would not disturb her again until Honorine arrived to take care of her, and tried not to be disappointed when she thanked him for his consideration.

So now he was alone himself, after conferring with Kalb and La Fayette about the ship and its departure on the morrow. He sat for a long time looking out on the obscure yard below, then took up a pen and began writing letters. To his major-domo and his agent in Paris, to the steward at Mirandol, to Honorine.

In the message to his aunt he described as briefly and as clearly as possible the meeting between himself and his ward. The closing paragraphs took longer to write.

So there is an end to it, thank God. She may travel back to Paris and live with you as before. My gratitude for your kindness I cannot begin to express, but at least the funds are available, as they have always been. I am sending instructions to my agent: apply to him for whatever you need.

Madame, I am going to America. I sail with the others tomorrow and I shall be back in a very short time, a matter of months. They are all too green and ill-prepared for this expedition, though I shall never say as much to La Fayette, for he's a fine boy and deserves the credit of leading them. I shall give them what advice I can during the voyage over, then leave them and let them make their own way with Kalb to Philadelphia. I hope to be available again when they

189

apply to the Congress, for they will need more than idealism to get them a place in the grand scheme.

The other reason is Victor de Luny himself; his friendship with La Fayette might have brought him to this alone, but I cannot help remembering our conversation at Mirandol when he first asked me about America and I put no discouragement in his way. If I were the boy's father, I might well detest me by now. He is an only son, much beloved, and with a temperament ill-fitted for that vicious war. I should like to think that when I return I may bring him with me. La Fayette, I imagine, will be for sticking it out.

So, I have prevented her from going to America but I go myself. If she hated me before, she will abominate me now. It seems to be my fate to do the right thing and be loathed for it. But I am convinced that at least I acted correctly over the young people. Her fondness for the lad has always been like that of a sister. His feelings in return are similar, and as you well know I am excellently qualified to judge which of a young man's impulses may be considered brotherly and which may not.

Perhaps she will seek to discuss me with you while I am gone. Say what you think fit, but for pity's sake I beg you never to talk to her of that Christmas I spent at home before going abroad. I cannot feel any less guilt and remorse when I look back, but over the last few months I have somehow learned to recall it without the deeper pain which lingered with me for many years.

Tell her I shall write to her but she is not obliged to reply (I enclose two addresses, in Chester and Philadelphia, for your use). I realise I have been hard and cold to her from the first, when I thought I was only protecting her. It is too late to mend all that now, I dare say. I leave her in your care, which has ever been more tender than mine. Bid her farewell from me, and until we meet again accept the grateful wishes of

Your affectionate nephew
Jules de Chercy

All night he lay awake, wishing he could find the words to write to her. But when he got up in the morning he picked up the pen and wrote to someone else instead. Then, entrusting all his post to the landlord and sending Honorine's letter to the inn where his ward was lodged, he went down to the docks.

His last message was directed to Paris.

My dear Gina,

As I write this I am overcome by the notion that you may never permit me to address you so intimately again. I remember once I said your only rival in my affections was America, and you shrewdly warned me to look nearer home. Be that as it may, I am afraid America has prevailed—for how long, I cannot tell. I should have liked the luxury of discussing this with you, but I had to leave Paris urgently on a family matter, and I find myself in Spain in the company of a few dedicated men going to the United States. I have decided to go with them.

I do not expect to be away long, but I know that my departure will displease you enough to render any apologies on my part in vain. I make them, however, because I am sorry, especially for myself: I now have to do without the delight of your company, and there will not be a soul about me half so worth listening to as you.

I can see you shrug and smile in your inimitable way and prepare to tear this up. Read on before you do, for I have a confession to make. I was dead when I met you, and had been so for many years. If I now have any human warmth in my veins it flows because of you. Our liaison has been totally unequal: I have had all the benefit, and in every skirmish you have been the conqueror and I the vanquished. I leave France to take up arms again, but I shall never encounter a more accomplished duellist than you. If you write to the address I enclose, even if it is to injure me, I shall receive your barbs with relish. From you, Gina, everything pleases.

But I have prepared myself for the fact that you

will not write. I wish I could prepare myself adequately for the blank that will follow your silence.

Adieu my siren
Jules

The lowest hold of a three-masted ship at sea was the most fetid, the most suffocating, the least habitable place on the globe; and its treated timbers, its bilge awash with rotting morsels of cargo and drowned rats, its formless baggage wrapped in damp cloth and festering leather, smelt all the worse because the only real escape from the stench was into the raging sea above.

Viviane, on this her first voyage, had no idea whether she suffered from seasickness or not—her permanent feeling of nausea could equally well have been caused by her surroundings. A stevedore from the docks of Los Pasajes, handsomely bribed two days before, had consented to carry two long canvas sacks aboard the *Victoire* and stow them behind the bulk of the cargo in the lowest hold. One contained all the possessions she had managed to bring from Paris. The other held herself, wearing several layers of clothing to guard against being bruised in the passage down into the hull.

Clambering out of the sack once the ship cast off, and finding herself squashed between an enormous bale of cotton goods and some tall wooden crates, she had made a platform with several planks laid across two upright barrels of wine, and covered it with her fur pelisse and cloak. Without this she would have been crouching directly in the filthy liquid that sloshed around the depths of the hold. In the heat of the day this horrible pool of unidentifiable matter evaporated slowly, surrounding her with a sickening miasma that made it almost impossible to swallow the dried fruit and nuts she had smuggled on board, and even seemed to taint the water in the large leather bottle she had had filled at a dockside shop.

She had meant to stay three days or more in this stifling hell, giving the ship time to sail south, to swoop closer to the trade winds that would impel it across the Atlantic. She knew La Fayette's steadfast nature, and believed that nothing short of catastrophe would compel him to turn back once the voyage was fairly under way at last. He had gone through too much, braved too many obstacles, to order a return just because he had one extra volunteer on board, even if that volunteer happened to be female. She would ask his permission to join them, beg him as her friend and the leader of the enterprise, and she believed he would give it. She was not throwing in her lot with a group of dubious adventurers; she knew nearly all the volunteers, and was confident of commanding their respect. Unlike most of them, she was also capable of paying her own way to Philadelphia. And they had with them an older, married man to offer advice and protection also: the Baron de Kalb.

All of this had stiffened her determination while she was at the inn, supposedly awaiting the arrival of her aunt. She had written a note for that ill-used lady, apologising for the anxiety she had already caused her, and would continue to cause. She had meant to write to her guardian also, but when she took up the pen her invention fled. It was impossible to ask his forgiveness for a step which made her elopement look pale by comparison. Yet she had to go. She could not expect him to understand—he was not a young woman thwarted by society, tricked by destiny, deprived of every chance of effective action while her life remained in the hands of others. She had digested his arguments against her marriage and departure, and given them all the justice that was their due. But in the end it was not for him to decide her fate. If she was making a mistake by going to America, so be it—she would discover her error and suffer the consequences.

But two days in the stinking hold of the *Victoire* had sapped her energy. Unwashed, unkempt and dispirited, she was the opposite of the bold young gentlewoman who had cunningly crept aboard at dawn the day before. And that was what impelled her up onto deck: not conviction about her mission, but the sense that she must make a stand before all her strength ebbed away.

The sun, low on the horizon, dazzled her as she came up the last companionway and faced forward. Above, the sails billowed silently, filled with a generous breeze that merely whispered in the rigging. On deck it was so tranquil in the sunset that it was as if the *Victoire* were sailed by ghosts. No one was in sight except for a long-legged man reclining on a roll of canvas, his boots crossed at the ankles and resting on a coil of rope, his head thrown back, with an open book across his face, shading his eyes.

As she approached he sat up, removed the book and gave her an inquiring glance which turned at once to shock.

He was her guardian.

Her heart stopped, and her ears rang. She took a step sideways and grasped at a ratline, swaying as the rope swung with her weight.

He leaped to his feet and took her by the upper arms. 'Sit down before you fall down. Here.' He lowered her onto the coil of rope. 'Christ. I don't believe it.'

She looked up at him. Everything was gently spinning. 'What are you doing here?'

'Need you ask? This is madness. Where the *devil* have you been hiding?'

She caught his expression and her back stiffened. Surely he could not think for a moment that this had anything to do with Victor? 'In the hold. I came on board in the dark . . . yesterday morning. God, was it only yesterday?'

'You've been in that disgusting hole without food or drink?'

'No, I brought things on board. But I have had no sleep. I never thought it would be like this.'

'But I *warned you*!'

'Yet you came yourself. Without telling me, or Madame de Chercy.'

'It was no plan: I made up my mind at the last hour.'

'So did I.'

There was a silence, during which Viviane registered

194

that people were gathering. In the last rays of the sun, the crew, alerted by the man at the helm, were heading aft to look at her. One or two officers had descended from the quarterdeck, and someone had gone below to summon the gentlemen. She said to her guardian, very low, 'Assist me if you can.'

He made a short sound, which might have been an oath, faced the group and took them all in with a sweeping glance. She made what figure she could in her demeaning position on the coil of rope; it helped that neither Victor nor the Marquis de La Fayette had yet appeared.

'Mademoiselle de Chercy has joined us unexpectedly. She will occupy my cabin and I shall move to share Monsieur de Kalb's. There will be a meeting tomorrow, at which we shall welcome her opinion as to our next step. Meanwhile, Mademoiselle, allow me to convey you below.'

She would have much preferred to stretch out on the deck and let the fresh breeze revive her. It was dreadful to think of descending into a close, dark cabin like a recaptured prisoner. But as he helped her to her feet she felt a weakness which was so obvious that he bent over her and said gently, 'Can you walk? Shall I—?'

'Thank you . . . if I may lean on you.'

He guided her to the main companionway behind the helmsman. She would have liked to speak to the men she knew, but the figures on the edge of her vision were all slightly blurred. She negotiated the steep descent without mishap and they soon reached the count's cabin, which she found more habitable than she had expected. It was in the stern, a narrow room fitted with tall leadlight windows that went almost from floor to ceiling, containing a single bunk, a desk, trunks and two chairs.

He pulled one of them forward. 'Can you put up with this for a moment?' She sank into it and he went to the door to call along the corridor for the captain's steward. The man came running, stripped the bunk and went away to fetch clean linen. Another man was sent to the hold to recover her baggage, and when he returned he was detailed to carry the count's trunk along to Monsieur de Kalb's cabin.

When it was all done, he said, 'You must get some sleep. I shall speak to the surgeon and when you wake you should consult with him.'

'I shall be well again after a rest. There is no need—'

'Mademoiselle, having a lady on board is the last thing anyone planned on. There will be difficulties to overcome, even on the short voyage back, and I'm sure you would like to minimise them. We cannot have you falling ill.'

Her eyes widened. 'You will not turn *back*! I demand to see Monsieur de La Fayette. I cannot believe he will make such a decision.'

'On the contrary, I do not see how we can do anything else.'

She tried to get to her feet. 'Where is he?'

'You are in no condition to argue with anyone. The bunk is made up, please rest.'

She held his eye. 'Only if you promise me that the ship will not change course whilst I sleep.'

He sighed. 'Very well.'

He remained before her, as though he had one further question that he could not voice. Through the fog in her head, she suddenly realised what it must be. Without looking at him, she said, 'I am undertaking this voyage for my own reasons. They have nothing to do with Monsieur de Luny or any other gentleman. Please make that clear to everyone.'

He bowed, and left her alone.

The meeting was held next morning in the captain's cabin. Seated around the table were the captain himself, the Marquis de La Fayette, the Comte de Mirandol, the Baron de Kalb and the other volunteers, including Victor. At the foot sat Viviane, beautifully dressed and coiffed, hiding her nervousness with Parisian poise. It was a relief to the young men to breathe the air of civilisation she brought with her. The only person with serious misgivings besides the captain was

196

Kalb, who jealously guarded every scheme La Fayette came up with, and was furious at this turn of events. Viviane noticed the frown on his heavy features and marked him at once for her enemy.

There was a third man who was unlikely to grant her a smooth voyage to America—her uncle. But when he entered he bowed politely, made no attempt to engage her in conversation, and chose a seat at the head of the table, next to Victor. He obviously had no intention of quarrelling with her in public—yet. As for Victor, her uncle had explained everything to him, and beyond exchanging a bright glance full of wonder and friendly admiration as he greeted her, he sought no private talk either.

After a swift look around the table, to catch the eyes of the friends she knew and the young men she hoped to know. soon, Viviane fixed her gaze on La Fayette. This was the man who mattered: the owner of the ship and cargo, the leader of the company, the person who had provided funds for most of his fellow travellers. He smiled at her, and she relaxed a little. But he let the captain, Le Boursier, open the proceedings.

'Mademoiselle, Messieurs, the Marquis de La Fayette has asked me to chair this meeting, to discuss the presence on board of Mademoiselle de Chercy. Two days ago she stowed away—'

'But I shall pay my fare. Indeed, I have already offered it to Monsieur de La Fayette.'

'Stowed away in order to sail to America. The question is, should we put her on land as soon as may be?'

'Where?' said one of the young men indignantly. 'On the Canaries? If Mademoiselle de Chercy is to be taken anywhere, it must be to where she embarked, surely.'

'This dilemma,' the captain said rather testily, 'is of the gentlewoman's own making. You must realise that there is no provision for a lady on board this ship.'

'I ask no favours, Monsieur le Capitaine. I shall eat what you eat, perform the same duties as the other passengers and look after my own effects.'

'You came aboard without servant or escort,' the captain continued.

'I shall engage servants as soon as I reach America.' She was about to tell him that the ship contained half a dozen young men who would be happy to be her escorts, and prevented herself just in time. Such a claim would have a rather improper ring to it, especially if they had heard of the thwarted elopement. She felt her cheeks go pink, and managed not to drop her gaze by staring fixedly at the top button on the captain's salt-stained coat.

To her amazement, it was her uncle's deep voice that broke the awkward silence. 'Mademoiselle de Chercy is my ward. Wherever she goes, she has my protection. So, she has both funds and escort. The question remains, shall she be given a passage on this voyage?'

The Baron de Kalb leaned forward and gazed solemnly down the table at the count. 'As her guardian, you may surely decide that yourself?'

'No, only this company can do that.'

When the Marquis de La Fayette spoke, it was with a smile that took in the whole table. 'True. You are determined to teach us democracy before we have even shaken the dust of Europe from our shoes, Monsieur le Comte! This assembly must conclude whether my friend Mademoiselle de Chercy should share our voyage or not. We must have a vote.'

She was grateful for the word 'friend', but he had not been looking at her as he said it.

La Colombe leaned forward and spoke eagerly, his blue eyes flicking to her face for a moment, then looking at the table. 'With respect, may we hear Mademoiselle de Chercy's reasons for going to America?'

'You may,' Viviane replied. 'They are similar to yours, I imagine. I take a great interest in the affairs of the United States. I should like to make some contribution to their struggle for independence. I have no idea whether that will be possible; if not, I go as a keen observer.'

'What sort of contribution, Mademoiselle?' Kalb intervened, his tone not far short of mockery.

'You mean do I go with arms, or a fortune? No. My funds are probably no greater than yours, Monsieur de

Kalb.' She waited a moment for this barb to penetrate, and was about to go on when Victor spoke up.

He too must have been annoyed by Kalb's question, for he said assertively, 'Mademoiselle de Chercy was of tremendous use to Silas Deane and Doctor Franklin in Paris. She has done her bit already. And I admire her for it.'

'Hear, hear!' said Fayolle.

The Chevalier du Buysson spoke next. He was the well-built, handsome young man who had partnered her sometimes at Paris card parties, and whom she had always considered a friend. Whenever they met in society, she found him open and amusing, very ready to laugh at himself. In this company, however, he was different, and looked at her resentfully.

'We must be practical. This expedition has no place for a woman. Excuse me,' he bowed slightly to Viviane, with not a hint of apology in his eyes, 'but your purpose is not the same as ours, and we shall have difficulties enough once we reach America, without having to worry about your welfare into the bargain.'

Crushed by this from a man she had thought of as an ally, Viviane for once was without a reply. La Fayette broke the silence with a rebuke. 'I think Mademoiselle de Chercy has the right to expect a little more chivalry than that, Chevalier.'

He was about to go on, but Viviane found her voice after all. 'I do not intend to be a burden to anyone. I shall pay all my travel expenses, and look after my own needs on board ship. When we reach America I shall engage servants as protection on the way to Philadelphia.' Her guardian looked up sharply. She held his eye, hoping he would keep his objections until later, when they could talk properly. In the past, she would have been quite prepared to argue with him in public; but now she felt it would be undignified. To her relief, he did not try to interrupt. She ended by saying, 'I shall be disappointed, Messieurs, if you decline my company on the grounds of my sex. I have the same hopes and ideals as you do.'

Silence followed this, and once more she examined

everyone at the table. Du Buysson was gazing into a corner of the cabin with a superior look that suggested the whole subject was beneath him. Victor did not meet her eye but she knew his opinion in advance and it was heartening to see that the expression on his face was mirrored on half a dozen others.

'If anyone has any more to say, speak now, please,' La Fayette said.

Viviane could see that Kalb had an urge to argue, and two of the company turned to him at once as he leaned forward. He simply grunted, however, and dropped his eyes to the tabletop. Viviane could not work out which gentleman's scrutiny had put him off: her uncle's, or La Fayette's.

After that it was over quite soon. The vote was taken and her passage to America was granted. The marquis said that henceforth she would be a guest of the company, which made Viviane smile as she thanked them.

Afterwards, taking the air on the quarterdeck with Victor and La Colombe, she said, 'We have yet to see how Monsieur le Marquis will fare as a commanding officer, but I begin to think he has the makings of a diplomat. He has admitted me into your company but he has not asked too much of you, only that you accord me hospitality.'

'Which we offer with the greatest pleasure,' La Colombe said at once.

'Should you have liked more?' Victor said.

'No! But I imagine in the new world that we are going to, more might have been *said*. American rhetoric is quite romantic, you know. A lady with my mission could well have heard herself described as a "sister in arms", for instance. Thank goodness, we French are pragmatic to a degree.'

Victor said earnestly, 'Do you see yourself as a sister in arms?'

'No. Unlike you, I am not going to war. I go to see what Doctor Franklin calls the virgin state. I go to see how a democratic nation is made.'

By comparison with her imprisonment in the hold, Viviane found life in the upper regions of the ship sheer luxury. After the surgeon held a discreet interview with her in her cabin, he pronounced her in the pink of health, and she was untroubled by the seasickness that laid low several of the volunteers. The cook came to her aid and supplied hot water whenever she asked for it, so she found washing herself and her clothes easy enough. The first time she strung her linen out across the cabin she smiled at her own satisfaction—it seemed a fitting and practical beginning to her American adventure, and she felt ridiculously proud of having managed her own laundry for the first time in her life. She locked the cabin door after her, though, to prevent the slightest chance of any of the men catching a glimpse within while her linen dried.

Shipboard life soon fell into a routine, and she managed to occupy herself agreeably, even when the novelty of being her own maid had begun to wear off. She soon found that she and the Marquis de La Fayette were the only serious students of English on board, so they pledged to read alone a certain number of pages of his books in the morning, then take turns to read aloud together in the afternoons. One of the volunteers, Edmund Brice, was an American, and he sometimes dropped in to give them some coaching.

There were some restrictions on their movement about the vessel: the crew remained forward of the mast and the business of sailing meant that they must often occupy the waist of the ship, so the captain constantly warned about the dangers of getting in their way when the important work was going on. Meanwhile the quarterdeck was reserved for himself and the officers. Being the owner of the *Victoire*, however, La Fayette could dictate to his captain to a certain extent, and Le Boursier was forced to give up the privacy of his quarterdeck at fixed times during the day, for this was the most convenient area for the passengers to stroll about and converse.

When she chose to walk on deck, Viviane was always sure of company. At the beginning she felt something of an intrusion, for the young men could not be easy when she was by. They were either over-polite or seeking to impress; one or two of them fell to boasting a little about what they would do in America, or pretending to a superior knowledge of the sea and ships. Vrigny, a fit young gentleman much admired for his horsemanship on land, decided to prove his agility on the ocean by climbing up to the peak of the main mast when the sailors were ordered up to reef the topsail; but he found on descending that Mademoiselle de Chercy had gone below to play a hand of cards with four of the officers in the wardroom. Before long, however, the atmosphere became easier, and even du Buysson became agreeable once more.

The weather was extremely favourable until the ship was off the Canaries, where they had to weather their first storm, but it was preceded by turbulence of another kind. It was only at this point that La Fayette realised how far his own ideas of the voyage diverged from those of the captain. The marquis had determined that the ship should make straight for the coast of the southern states and run the English blockade, so that the expedition could land as close as possible to their destination, Philadelphia. Le Boursier, however, was deeply wary of the English navy and fancied a landfall in the West Indies, where they could reconnoitre the situation in the United States and take advice about proceeding further. If the ship were challenged, she was neither sufficiently manoeuvrable nor well enough armed to withstand even the lowliest British vessel. A search would swiftly discover the weapons in the hold as well as the purpose of the French party; and they had with them a Dutchman, Bedaulx, who was con-vinced that on capture he would at once be strung from the yardarm, while the rest would be hauled off to prison in Halifax, the English navy's stronghold in North America.

Le Boursier's grey hairs were standing on end by the time he and La Fayette were fairly into their argument, but the marquis did not back down. The captain's caution was abhorrent to him and he was determined to talk him round. In the process, he forced out of him an awkward confession: Le Boursier had had a secret cargo of his own loaded in Los Pasajes—a vast assortment of goods stowed amongst the marquis's shipment of arms—and he counted on selling the lot at a handsome profit in the West Indies.

Victor, who was in the cabin when the quarrel took place, confided afterwards to Viviane, 'I was half afraid our friend was going to clap the captain in irons and try to sail the ship himself. A pretty time we should have had of it.'

She exclaimed, 'How dared Le Boursier frown at *me* for stowing away, when he had a vast deal more to conceal himself! But can he be forced to carry his goods all the way to America?'

Victor shrugged. 'La Fayette worked out a compromise in the end, once tempers had cooled. He has bought the cargo, with a promissory note. And since it is now legally his as well as the ship, the captain is obliged to land where he dictates. Which will be the Carolinas, come hell or high water.'

The real storm crept up in the dusk, after a clear day during which most of the passengers had spent many hours on deck, enjoying a steady breeze and smooth travelling under the azure arc of the sky. The wind was so fair and consistent that the men had hauled up the studding sails, which during the best conditions were set outside the other canvas, making the rather slow, ducklike *Victoire* feel as though she had suddenly grown swan's wings and was skimming across the wavetops.

Viviane went below with some of the volunteers for a meal with the captain in his cabin, and before it was over she was surprised that an officer came and entreated him to return to the deck, for the darkening view through the stern windows showed her merely the same cloudless sky and the same strong, regular swell running by them, with no hint of a change in the inclination of the vessel.

Half an hour later, however, when she was in her cabin trying to read by a swinging lantern, she realised that a constant tremor was coursing down the length of the hull, and their speed had increased. Shut in that narrow space, she soon had the unnerving impression of being driven into unknown depths, for the *Victoire* no longer skipped over the sea but crashed through it, pitching and shuddering, and the waves began to run high behind, flooding up the cabin windows, grey and seething. Putting a fine woollen shawl around her shoulders, she escaped into the open air.

At first she could not understand what caused the tension on the quarterdeck or the captain's agony of impatience as he barked orders at the first mate, for the sky, now a midnight blue, had a bell-like clarity and the wind had not veered from its favourable direction. But it was much stronger, and the full sails, taut and unmoving as drum skins, threw the *Victoire* into the waves with terrifying impetus. The only way to prevent this perilous advance was to take in sail as fast as possible. The studding sails that were set in the fine spell had long been removed, and the sailors of both watches had been ordered up to deal with the rest; but to reduce canvas drastically on a ship with a crew of average numbers like that of the *Victoire* was no swift matter.

The seamen who were out on the bowsprit struggling with the jib disappeared up to their necks in the sea every time the bow went down, and the water raged and boiled right over the forecastle, streaming out over the sides when the vessel rose again and revealing the pale, drenched figures of the sailors in their duck trousers and their summer shirts, clinging to their impossible perch. The jib was furled but only half secured when the mate ordered the men back in, frightened of losing them as the howling wind thrust the *Victoire* before it with ever greater power.

Then Viviane fully understood: for all his caution, the captain had been taken unawares by the strength of the gale. Hugging the rail and gazing the length of the decks, watching the waves surging relentlessly over the forecastle and the ship straining upwards to batter against the next roller, Viviane felt as though the wind that strove to tear the clothes from her body and keened through the rigging above her had been unleashed by some demon that howled for sacrifice over the waters of the deep.

The whole crew were working at desperate speed; and even the cook, carpenter and steward, the so-called 'idlers', were pressed into service to bring in the billowing canvas before it was lost. The topsails were taken in and secured around the yards, and others tackled the lower, larger sails. The mainsail held, but they were too late to save the foresail, which all at once split from top to bottom with a sound like a lightning strike. With dreadful rapidity it began to disintegrate: holes appeared in the tortured canvas and then it tore again and again, and streamed in ribbons along the wind.

The mate, directing the sailors from the deck, grew so anxious in this extremity that he accepted an offer of help from the three most able of the volunteers who had joined him on deck, and gave them permission to race up with some of the men from the larboard watch to take in the foresail. He had permitted them to scramble about the yards at the beginning of the voyage and had seen them keep their heads well enough in fair weather; but now, the moment after he had yielded to the crisis and let them aloft again, he frowned with unease as he watched them climb.

The rest of the French company stood grouped around the captain; but Kalb, La Fayette and the Comte de Mirandol were not on deck, for they had been holding a council of war in the marquis's cabin and so far had taken no account of the altered progress of the ship.

Viviane looked up at the long tatters of canvas snapping in the gale. Along the foresail yard, faint against the night sky, she spied the tiny figures of the men who must make it fast. Victor, Vrigny and Bedaulx were near the centre of the yard, which was the safest place to work, if anywhere could be called safe in such circumstances. The most experienced seamen were making their way out to the yardarms, where they hung over the deep on slender rope footholds as the

Victoire swung and dipped in the teeth of the gale.

Viviane clung to the quarterdeck rail, oblivious of the wind, straining to keep sight of the three figures far above. Then, as the ship gave a sudden roll, she found her guardian beside her.

'For God's sake,' he shouted against the wind, 'what is happening?'

'They must shorten sail. Victor has gone to help, with Vrigny and Bedaulx.'

'The devil they have!' He gave one swift look into the tops and turned to her again, his hand tight around her wrist.

'You should—'

Then it happened. The wheel rope snapped, whipped across the deck behind them and struck the bulwarks with a sound like a thunder crack; and the ship, instantly rudderless, lurched suicidally out of her course. The wheel rope was a heavy woven cord as thick as a man's wrist, yet it had parted like a twist of cotton under the gigantic strain of keeping the helm down. The mechanism below the now spinning helm connected it to the tiller, which directed the rudder: if the tiller and wheel could not be secured again, the ship, still top-heavy with canvas, would come broadside to the wind and capsize.

The count, fully aware of the danger, leaped towards the helm in the split second after the wild rope had smashed its way over the deck, and went to the officers' aid. He and two other men struggled to restore the tension on the wheel rope, while others went below to try to attach a holding cable to the tiller on the deck beneath. Viviane was torn between the crisis behind her and the terrifying scene above, as the distant men, flung out over the raging sea, fought to keep hold amongst a chaos of flapping canvas and twisting sheets.

The *Victoire* swung helplessly, lumbering foot by foot off her course, pitching wildly. The wind continued to howl out of the dark behind them, from a cloudless sky as smooth as black satin, oversewn with a million cold, crystal stars.

Viviane wrenched her gaze from the frantic men

above and turned towards the wheel. The quarter-master and her guardian were putting their full weight and strength into winding it back—at the last second, it seemed they had regained control of the tiller.

That was, if the wind permitted. She looked up once more and saw to her relief that most of the tattered foresail was now gathered in and held by gaskets to the yard. Meanwhile the other large sails on the mizzen and mainmast were steadily being reefed in. In a few minutes the ship would no longer be at the total mercy of the gale, and could run before it without risk of capsizing or losing a mast.

To her relief, she saw the three volunteers begin to descend. They could bring no more order to the tangled mess of what had once been the foresail, which must await calmer weather to be taken down and replaced. Instinctively she went to meet them, running quickly down from the quarterdeck into the waist of the ship. She was not afraid to do so, for she had already noted that, despite the turmoil, none of the tackle, cannon or other equipment had shaken loose, and there were no objects flying about the deck to cause injury. They were fortunate that Le Boursier kept a tight ship. His only error, so far, had been to let this gale catch him by surprise.

The *Victoire* was still plunging like a mad creature, however, and Viviane could only make her way across the deck as it bucked under her feet by darting from one support to another. Her hair whipped about her face and the shawl streamed in the wind. In a minute she was drenched by spray and breathless from the struggle to stay upright.

Victor looked at her in horror when he dropped to the deck and caught sight of her in the darkness. He said something, but the wind tore the words from his lips. Bedaulx and Vrigny followed and she beckoned them all after her, pointing to the companionway and imploring them with her face and gestures to follow her below. She could not bear them to expose themselves further, now that the *Victoire* was nearly under control.

She and Victor were moving aft and the others were

following when the ship rose high at the stern in a swift unexpected movement and the bow plunged deeper than ever. A great wave roared up and swamped the whole front part of the ship, flooding across the decks, knocking Bedaulx and Vrigny off their feet.

Hearing the cries behind them, Viviane and Victor turned just in time to see Bedaulx flung right across the deck, through a gap under the bulwark and over the scuppers on the port side. Vrigny followed, half taken by the wave, half under his own impetus as he rushed to catch Bedaulx. Too late: the Dutchman had been swept away and Vrigny fetched up inside the bulwark, his lower body held by the force of the water against a gun carriage, his upper body out of sight as Viviane waded through knee-high water towards him. Behind her, Victor lost his footing in the wet and was swept aft some way before he could recover himself and follow her.

The gun carriage supported a piece of artillery which had been set up on La Fayette's orders before the *Victoire* left France. Bedaulx had been flung through the bottom of the wide hole that had been cut in the bulwark for this carronade. When she reached the spot, Viviane gave a cry, which no one could hear. Bedaulx had indeed been washed overboard, but he was dangling against the side by one hand, grasping the raised edge of the scuppers, and Vrigny had a grip on his wrist. Bedaulx was a tall, raw-boned young man, and Vrigny, jammed against the gun carriage, could not move or shift his hold on his heavy burden without either letting him go or slipping overboard to join him in the sea.

Already Viviane could feel the *Victoire* swooping downward for the next plunge, which would certainly tear both young men into oblivion. But she had her shawl. Ripping it from around her shoulders, struggling as the fibres clung wetly to her, she managed to free it. With frantic haste she tied one end tightly around Bedaulx's wrist beneath Vrigny's white-knuckled hand, then twisted the other several times around a bolt on the gun carriage.

She tried to make Vrigny see that now he could release the other man's wrist and lean down to grab him more securely, but he was in such a state of exhaustion he did not seem to understand. Then two men appeared simultaneously beside her and with a sob of relief she made way for them, whereupon they lunged into the gap and seized Bedaulx by the collar of his jacket. Just in time: the *Victoire* plunged again, though not so steeply as before; a wave surged, cold and merciless, around the group, but when it had drained away Bedaulx lay prostrate and gasping on the deck, and the count and Victor were helping Vrigny to his feet.

They all struggled below, and safe at the bottom of the companionway, the young men all began to speak at once—except for Bedaulx, who leaned forward in silence to bring Viviane's fingers to his lips, his large hands trembling as he did so.

But the count interrupted them. 'Vrigny, you took a knock when you fell. There are no bones broken?'

'I don't think so.'

'Nonetheless, you'd best take Bedaulx with you to the sickbay. Let the surgeon look at you. And next time you fancy—' but with an effort that Viviane could plainly see, he made himself stop.

She considered him with interest. If she had not been by, if the event had turned out much worse, he might have given them the edge of his tongue for going aloft, for playing at heroes in a situation they knew nothing about, for behaving impulsively when they should have kept their heads, for endangering their own lives and others' too. Her old quarrels with him gave her an insight into his mind at this moment which the young men could not possess. But she was also better placed to see his restraint and sense of justice: Vrigny had saved Bedaulx's life in the midst of the storm, which was lesson enough for one night. The three of them, understanding something of his unspoken thoughts after all, wasted no time before saying goodnight and melting away. Even Victor, who might have liked to say something to the point, decided he had better not tonight.

When they had gone, she was alone with her

guardian outside her cabin, where he stood looking at her by the faint, intermittent light of a lantern further down the companionway.

'*Jésu*,' he said, 'how could I ever have let you do this?'

'I am unharmed, Monsieur. There are dry clothes in my cabin, I need nothing more.'

'To let you sail with this set of crackbrained— Do you realise whom you saved just now? Do you know that Bedaulx and La Fayette have a damned schoolboy pact for when the English board us? If we are to be taken off, Bedaulx has sworn to blow the ship to pieces.' He saw her shiver and continued helplessly, 'And here you are in this nightmare. With no escape except to America.'

She shook her head and wrapped her arms across her body, holding his gaze. A feeling of exhilaration flowed through her, despite the cold and exhaustion and despite—or perhaps because of—his agonised look. The first sharp danger had passed and the rest of her grand expedition was before her.

'Monsieur, I am inclined to think that the only real risk we run from now on is the overenthusiasm of our friend Bedaulx. And I am sure you already have *that* little matter under control.'

He said grimly, 'I have.'

'Then I shall sleep easy tonight.' She put a hand to the latch of her cabin door and smiled at him.

He could not speak for a moment. At last he said, 'Forgive me. I should never have let you come.'

'You forget: I gave you no choice. So there is nothing to forgive. Goodnight, Monsieur.' She went into her cabin and shut the door.

Jules was practising with one of the rifles he had bought in San Sebastian. A block of wood on a rope, tossed over the side, bobbed in the wake, and the rough square of tin nailed to the upright flashed tantalisingly in the bright sunlight. It made a satisfying thwang when his shots were true.

He was happy. The truce with his ward would probably collapse as soon as they reached America, but ever since they had weathered the storm off the Canaries, she had spoken to him without a trace of hostility. This time at sea had a charm which he would not destroy with concern about the future. He would tackle the dilemma of his emotions when they reached America; meanwhile he rejoiced in her nearness as an undeserved and fragile blessing.

Duty and his own will imposed barriers which meant that she was as safe from him as if she had stayed behind in Spain, and somehow he was able to approach her without constraint, to speak without having to consciously hide his impulses.

Shipboard life had settled back into a routine: she came up to the quarterdeck twice a day, at more or less the same hour, and the young gentlemen drifted up to converse, to walk about with her, to relish her presence as he did. He felt a kinship with them, and an ease with her, which would probably never be recaptured.

She surprised him this afternoon by coming early; at this time she was usually with La Fayette in his cabin.

'You and the marquis have run out of books?'

'Not in the least, we could read our way around the globe with what he has brought. He is writing; he has a long letter to his wife that he wants to finish.'

He double-checked that the rifle was empty and laid it on the deck at his feet. 'What on earth does he find to write about? Wind and waves? We are surrounded by feverish correspondents—I even caught Kalb writing to his wife today.'

'Monsieur de La Fayette has his wife and little Henriette, and a baby on the way. He misses them terribly. Writing is like talking to them, I suppose. I must admit I find a great deal to say in my letters to my aunt and Mademoiselle de Billancourt. It seems so odd, however, having to wait goodness knows how long before we can send them. But think how I should reproach myself if we met up with a French ship and I did not have my mail ready to hand over!' After a pause she said, 'Have you written a letter for my aunt?'

'Yes.' He began to haul in the target.

'Pray continue, if you like. Do not let me interrupt you. Or do I put you off your aim?'

He laughed. 'No, I should be a poor marksman if that were the case. The Virginia Riflemen would not have me at any price.'

She looked at him earnestly, holding stray curls out of her eyes with one hand as the breeze played around them. 'You think to join the Virginians? To command men you were with before?'

He shook his head. 'This time I shan't seek a command. I have had enough of sending men into battle and watching them ... ' He busied himself with coiling the wet rope that slid up over the side, and did not finish the sentence. 'Let's say I prefer to be responsible only for myself.'

She bent and picked up the rifle, running her fingers over the intricate chasing on the barrel, then the gleaming stock. 'What a beautiful piece of work. Yet I ought not to admire it, considering what it is to be used for.'

'Handsome is as handsome does: it is the only one of the three that has a fault. I shall get the regimental gunsmith to look at it when I join up, the sight needs adjusting.' It troubled him to see her holding it. He put out a hand to take it from her, and with a slight hesitation she let it go.

'You have *three*? Are they from the ship's armoury, or the weapons in the hold?'

'Neither. I picked these up in Spain; the armoury has nothing like them. All we have in the hold are Charleville muskets, French army surplus. There are plenty of them, and no doubt they'll be welcomed, for they're better than the English Brown Bess. But they are inferior to what the Americans make themselves—the Pennsylvanians excel at rifles.'

She leaned on the rail beside him, watching the wake spin out in smooth curls from the rudder. A yard away, he hauled the dripping target inboard. At last she said, 'What is your opinion of Monsieur de Kalb?'

He jammed the block and coil of rope under the

port-side gun carriage where he usually kept them. 'He does his best.'

She smiled. 'Just the sort of high praise I feared to hear. I suspect you think the same as I. So I must apologise for obliging you to share a cabin with him. No wonder you spend so much time on deck.'

'Don't give it a thought; I like the open air. And don't forget, I have seldom been able to choose with whom I share quarters.'

She considered him, a new light in the amber eyes. 'How could you bear it all that time, as a soldier? Never knowing quite where you were going, or what you would be asked to perform; forced to live day by day with men whom perhaps you could not stand?'

He shrugged. 'I compared it with the alternative.'

She frowned slightly. 'Which was?'

He leaned on the rail also, looking in the opposite direction, across the waist of the ship to the foredeck and the high bowsprit, which swooped gracefully between the two blues of sky and ocean. 'Returning to France and settling down in a modest way as a country gentleman. I could see that choice clear enough, but I could never see myself taking it.' After a moment he turned his head and caught her glance, confident that no secrets were revealed in his own. 'At any point in life, one has choices. Most people, for whatever reason, are not quite aware of that somehow. But the choices are there just the same. You made a crucial one in Los Pasajes: you compared a voyage to America with the alternative. And chose America.'

'Did your alternative have to be the country? What about Paris?'

He shook his head. 'Town life is idle unless one has a taste for influencing affairs. I should have no talent for government, so it would be pointless hanging about the seat of power.' He smiled at her. 'What about you? As a girl, did you ever dream of saving the world?'

She looked up, startled and mistrustful, then saw that he was not mocking her. The sun shone into her eyes and picked out flecks of gold around the pupils.

'Yes, but I have grown more realistic since. I take no

213

grand ambitions to America. Like you, I cannot see myself as a demagogue.'

He burst out laughing.

By the time they were six weeks out from Spain, there was a handsome collection of mail, for the young men who had been most affected by seasickness were all recovered and eager to give a good account of themselves to friends back in France. The *Victoire* saw no ships close enough to exchange signals with, however.

Viviane stood on deck one day watching the sails of a distant vessel fade onto the western horizon, while she and Victor speculated about the possibility of its being French and perhaps bound for the Caribbean.

She said, 'I am just beginning to think we shall really reach America. Up until now it has seemed a kind of dream.'

Victor grinned. 'I cannot think of another woman who would speak so of a voyage like this! It's been only too real as far as I'm concerned. But I know what you mean: we are running towards danger now, and pray God the next ship we meet is not English.'

'We cannot be sure that they are patrolling so far south. The captain is holding to La Fayette's course?'

'Yes, he expects to bring us to Carolina in the next two weeks. What will you do when we land—travel with us to Philadelphia?'

Viviane grimaced. 'I am not sure I can. I imagine American notions of propriety are not much different from our own; indeed, according to the Puritan tradition, I am probably a walking, or at least a *sailing*, scandal already. I can just imagine Great-Aunt Honorine if I wrote to tell her I had swept into Philadelphia with a private army of Frenchmen! No, I must travel differently. If I could find an older, married woman as companion—'

'Your uncle has offered you his escort, will you refuse him?'

She shook her head. 'He did so to back me up when I first came aboard, and I am grateful. But he goes to

America with his own aims, and it is not fair of me to get in his way.'

'I thought he would be coming with us!'

She shook her head again. 'I have a feeling that he will make his own way north. We get on much better now, but I still find it hard to guess what he intends. I do know that he is far different from what I imagined. You remember how I hated him for descending on Mirandol like a predator? From what he said to me not long ago, I realise he really had no desire at all to return to France. Ever.'

'So that is why he goes back to America now?'

'Perhaps. To escape, yes. From discontent, and from me.'

'Good Lord, what a shock he must have got when you turned up on deck!' Victor said, diverted. Then he glanced at her unhappy expression. 'You are not going to reproach yourself over that, surely? He's a strong man, with strong reasons for what he does. It's nonsense to suppose he would up stakes and flee France just because you were quarrelling with him.'

12

THE NEW WORLD

Before he had quite completed his Atlantic voyage, Capitaine le Boursier found himself one day in the unhappy situation of watching his worst predictions come true: a smart, swift-sailing ship appeared over the horizon and bore confidently down upon them. Putting the *Victoire* in readiness for attack, Le Boursier observed the other ship's approach, noting with alarm her rakish lines and ample armament. Then she hoisted her colours, whereupon she proved to be an American privateer, to the delight of the young Frenchmen.

At this auspicious and cheerful meeting everyone stayed on deck for hours while they kept the Americans company, until at last the sluggish *Victoire* was obliged to drop behind. Their own luck held once more for, as the privateer neared the horizon, two more vessels appeared, discernible through the captain's spyglass as frigates of the English navy. The privateer loaded on more sail to show them a clean pair of heels and soon disappeared, followed by the enemy in vain pursuit. To everyone's relief, they were not seen again.

The company aboard the *Victoire* first viewed the Carolinas on 12 June. Viviane was the only person on the quarterdeck apart from the captain when the lookout yelled from the crow's nest and pointed to what she had thought was a thin grey cloud on the horizon. She stared at it so hard her head swam, and her body tingled with impatience to fly nearer, to see the contours of the land she had held in her mind like a talisman for so long. At first it seemed low and featureless, but as they approached she made out rocky indentations in the coast, green islets, distant hills, and a mountain near the shore. By now the whole company was on deck, and when one of the young men questioned the captain, they were informed that the high point was Mount Pleasant, which meant that they were within reach of the port of Charles Town in South Carolina.

To Viviane's intense frustration, however, La Fayette and the captain could not decide whether to enter the vast bay below Mount Pleasant and sail in towards the harbour. They dallied many days in suspense. Le Boursier was still fearful of being seen by English ships on patrol, yet unsure about where to make landfall, and in his indecision he ended up sailing further north. The *Victoire* finally anchored in a sheltered bay which they believed to be level with a place inland called Georgetown, and La Fayette and Kalb went ashore to reconnoitre. Many hours later they returned to announce that the expedition would fare best if they all made their way back to Charles Town overland.

At this point the Comte de Mirandol broke his silence on the subject by pointing out that at least twenty-five leagues of unknown country lay between them and their destination, and there were the ship and its cargo to consider; but the young men were so eager that half of them elected to go with the marquis. Among them was Victor de Luny, who felt he could not refuse to follow his friend. The count elected to take his chances at sea with the rest and so did Viviane. She had not failed to notice that her uncle was the most sensible man on board; while the hotheads were on land, she had hopes that he would prevail on the captain to take a more rational course.

The shore party had not gone far through the woods and swamps of the area before they rather wished they had heeded the count's warning. Days later, when at last they happened upon farmland, most of their shoes had given out, and their feet and legs were painfully swollen. All except La Fayette were exhausted and discouraged when they came upon some black slaves working in the fields. These people took pity on them and led them to the farmhouse of a Major Huger, who eventually helped them to Charles Town. There, to the consternation of the young marquis, they were not received like gentlemen. Nobody had heard of them or wished to know them. The townspeople and the army were too familiar with the French military to find them a novelty, and in their bedraggled state they looked more like a set of adventurers. To their great joy, however, the *Victoire* soon arrived, as bold as you please, and the town suddenly saw the true picture. Everyone began talking about the Marquis de La Fayette, who had slipped by the blockade to sail into the harbour with his own ship and a determined band of volunteers. The gentry of Charles Town learned with approval that he was immensely wealthy, and ready to pay his way to Philadelphia and put his resources and men at the disposal of Congress and General Washington.

Things began to look more cheerful. They were fêted and dined, and the garrison went so far as to fire a fifteen-gun salute to the company. La Fayette began purchasing provisions, carts and horses for the trip north, and meanwhile the count led the others on an inspection of the fortresses that guarded the harbour, to see the gun batteries that had prevented three English frigates from bombarding the town the year before. On the following day a great party was given for them at the fort, during which La Fayette was much celebrated.

When he first came ashore, the Comte de Mirandol lodged at Pike's Tavern in Church Street, and persuaded Mademoiselle de Chercy to stay aboard the ship until he could find suitable accommodation for her. He was determined to place her with a family, but did not expect this to be easy, since he had never been to Charles Town before, and no one he met amongst the militia had a quick solution to offer. He had one contact in town, however: a prominent citizen called Thomas Henry Wilkinson, who corresponded with John Adams in Philadelphia. Wilkinson proved to have a grand house on Tradd Street, and a great curiosity about the count's plans and the intrepid young French lady who had chosen this extraordinary time to accompany her guardian to America. He already had one guest in the house, for his sister-in-law had come down from Philadelphia to look after his wife during her lying-in a month before; but this did not prevent the Wilkinsons from issuing an immediate invitation to

Mademoiselle de Chercy to stay with them while she prepared for the journey north. They made the same offer to the count, but he declined. He did not want a flicker of doubt in any person's mind concerning his relationship with his ward, and the best way to secure her reputation was for her to be accepted in her own right by the women of a family such as the Wilkinsons.

Thus it was that, one week after Viviane's arrival in the house, she was sitting in the grand front parlour in the company of Mrs Wilkinson; her older sister Mrs Christie; Mrs Pringle, the wife of a judge; a Mr and Mrs Gibbes; and Colonel John Stuart, superintendent of Indian affairs, who had walked across from his splendid house on the other side of the street to view the beautiful and accomplished Frenchwoman whom the Wilkinsons had welcomed into their midst.

Viviane found her hosts friendly, endlessly hospitable and very admiring of her clothes, her travels and her English. She also found that they rather expected compliments in return, so she was enthusiastic about the charming features of Charles Town and circumspect when she might have mentioned others, such as the muddy unpaved streets, or the knots of miserable poor crowded around the Church of Saint Philips.

Mr Gibbes, a portly gentleman buttoned into a coat of fine brocade, said, 'This is your first landfall in our country, I believe. I should like to hear what our city looks like to such a visitor.'

Viviane smiled. 'The view from the sea was overwhelming, sir. As soon as we entered the harbour, I exclaimed to my companions how ordered and beautiful the city looked. I was amazed to see the bastions, the sea walls, and the elegant buildings within.'

'The *Victoire* had no trouble crossing the bar?' asked Colonel Stuart.

'We touched the sand three times. But the *Victoire* does not reach more than seventeen feet. The captain was very relieved.'

'If your ship had sailed further up into the Ashley, you would have seen our estate,' Mrs Gibbes said. Though shorter than her husband, she was built on the same lines and just as richly dressed. She had a note of pride in her voice, so Viviane looked inquiringly at her until she explained. 'We live in South Bay; and to make business more practical, William had a wharf flung out from the mansion to the river, right across eight hundred feet of marsh. Few visitors fail to remark on it.'

'Indeed, I admire greatly the engineering and architecture of Charles Town. My preferred edifice is the beautiful Exchange on the waterfront.'

'The town is rationally set out, I think you will agree,' said Mrs Pringle. 'And the modern style of the houses is pleasing. Though you would not be used to so many timber dwellings in Paris, would you, Mademoiselle?'

'True, but your best wood is very handsome. Black cypress, I believe.'

Mrs Wilkinson, who had sketched in a number of such details for Viviane's benefit, gave her a warm smile. 'You will find the domestic architecture much more familiar when you reach Philadelphia, Mademoiselle. But I confess I have a great affection for our Charles Town houses.' She turned towards Colonel Stuart. 'Yours is built of cypress and heart pine, is it not, Colonel?' He was talking to Mrs Gibbes and did not hear her, so she leaned over and murmured to Viviane instead: 'Nothing but the best: over two thousand three hundred pounds it cost him!'

'You play delightfully on the pianoforte, I am told,' Mrs Pringle said. 'When you come to see us tomorrow evening, I do hope you will oblige us with something from France.'

'I shall be glad. It is charming to find your town is fond of music. All the ladies are so very clever.'

'Needs must,' said Mrs Gibbes. 'There will be no public performances of music, drama, *anything* until independence, so we must do what we can in our own homes. Gone are the days when the Douglass company used to offer us theatre—we have not seen them here these three years.'

'But you have your St Cecilia,' said Mrs Christie, 'the

first musical society in the country, so you have Philadelphia beat on that score!'

Viviane was relieved when the guests finished their inspection and left her alone with Mrs Wilkinson and her sister. She was still not used to summoning up so much English, and the Charlestonians' accent, so different from that of her English tutor in Paris, sometimes confused her.

Shortly afterwards the Comte de Mirandol was announced, and she greeted him gladly, for now she could speak French. Not immediately, however: Mrs Wilkinson soon left the room to visit the nursery, but Mrs Christie, who was always most affable to the count, stayed with them. Viviane was obliged to be polite and continue speaking in English.

'How goes Monsieur de La Fayette in his preparations?'

'He has assembled a veritable caravan of vehicles, but good horses to haul them are hard to come by.'

'Yet the Charles Town cavalry have excellent mounts,' Mrs Christie remarked.

'Precisely. All the fine horseflesh has been commandeered by the military. The marquis has made some purchases, but they look a sorry pack of nags to me.'

'Will you travel with him when he leaves?'

Mrs Christie's question seemed aimed at them both, but for a moment neither answered. Finally the count said, 'Our plans are not settled. I should like to visit friends in Virginia on the way, while La Fayette will probably take a more direct route. Whichever way we choose, Mademoiselle de Chercy's safety is the priority.'

Mrs Christie saw an opportunity. She was in no hurry to lose contact with the Chercys, as she found Viviane interesting and the count deeply attractive. At first she could not help her emotion being purely selfish, despite her mature years, but she soon chided herself and began to think instead of the two marriageable daughters who awaited her at home.

'I have a suggestion. I leave in a week for Philadelphia. I came down with just two servants, and I have

221

no mind to trail over two hundred leagues in solitude again. It would please me mightily to have good company on my road home. What do you say to travelling with me, Mademoiselle? The count may escort us as far as the Virginia border, then catch up with you later, when you are installed in comfort with me and my girls. I should like nothing better than to have you as a guest, for however long it suits you.'

Viviane said at once, 'Madame, that is a very kind offer,' but she was looking at her guardian. She still found his face hard to read, and all she gained from his silence was a conviction that he was leaving the decision to her. It did not take her long to make up her mind. Surely it was the solution that would fit in best with his own wishes, as it gave him a last chance to travel at his own whim before joining up with the Riflemen. 'I accept, most gratefully. As long as you are agreeable, Monsieur?'

He bowed and said something which was lost in Mrs Christie's exclamations of delight.

Having gained her desire, the lady did not waste more time in conversation, and soon went off to give her sister the news, leaving the count and his ward to return to their native French.

'It looks as though I shall be luckier than the poor marquis,' Viviane said. 'Mrs Christie is a great lover of luxury and is sure to travel in style. So I shall reach Philadelphia before you all!'

'We shall see. If anything dangerous is afoot in Virginia, I may accompany you the whole way.'

'Thank you. You are very good. But tell me, how is Monsieur de Luny? I have not seen him in days.'

'He is devoting himself to La Fayette. Matters are not going well for the company at the moment. There has been trouble with the *Victoire*. The captain refuses to land the merchandise and sell it in Charles Town—not that I blame him, for the tax is crippling and the Liberty Boys may well oppose it anyway. So our friend is drastically short of cash.'

'Surely the arms are ashore, though.'

'Indeed yes, but you will remember, there was also

a great quantity of dry goods, fabrics, wine ... all intended to fetch a profit in Atlantic ports. La Fayette owns it now, as you know. But unfortunately he signed an agreement back in France without reading it properly: it's up to the captain whether he offers goods for sale here or elsewhere. He's ready to leave harbour with everything still on board, and there is not a thing the marquis can do to stop him.'

'What a setback. He must be mortified.'

The count rose from his chair and straightened his jacket. Gone were the long brocaded coats he had worn in Paris, for in America his dress was altogether more sober and simple. It should have made him look stern but somehow, whenever he was with her, the old severity seemed to have disappeared.

He caught her examining him and smiled, the green eyes lighting up with amusement. 'Don't fret. It was easily fixed. I just lent him some funds.'

'Oh, how generous.'

'Not at all. What could be more secure than a loan to a millionnaire?'

The humorous glint was still there, and she realised with acute embarrassment that this was the first time she had shown approval for a single one of his financial transactions. She was immensely grateful when he took his leave without further comment.

Considering the lamentable jades on offer in Charles Town, Jules had a stroke of luck finding a horse for the trip. He had decided he would have to persuade some citizen to part with a good mount, but in the end he won a fine gelding off a cavalry officer. He was showing him the Spanish rifles, and when he praised their accuracy the lieutenant proposed a contest, putting up the gelding on his side. Jules's target practice at sea stood him in good stead, and desire for the prize lent him concentration. When the lieutenant lost, he parted with the animal gracefully and Jules was much pleased with it.

La Fayette and the volunteers arranged to make their

own journey with two waggons, each drawn by four horses, and they would be assisted by four domestics. The marquis had many vexations to overcome, but remained cheerful and determined. Watching him cope with the fuss and admiration that surrounded him in Charles Town, Jules found him a remarkable young man. There was certainly a bent for heroics in his nature, but he was modest and sincere, and his consideration for others was always evident. He expressed his belief in the Patriot cause most ardently, and Jules suspected that certain of his listeners, reeling under the onslaught, felt some shame about their own mixed conceptions of what was good for America. The young man's integrity was so obvious that he was forgiven his impetuosity, his lack of information and his uncertain English, and was respected in Charles Town by Loyalist and Republican alike.

The Chercys set off for Philadelphia only a day before La Fayette, and the young Frenchmen turned out to bid them farewell. Victor de Luny spent longer than most talking to Mademoiselle de Chercy at the carriage door, but the other volunteers looked just as regretful about saying goodbye. Every one of them was present, including the Chevalier du Buysson, and Jules noted with amusement that the young man was now, too late, thoroughly in love with her and could scarcely imagine a more wonderful prospect than squiring her the length of the United States. It was fortunate, he thought wryly, that the duty fell to himself.

Mrs Christie allowed him to stow his weapons and gear in the box of her carriage, while he rode alongside. If he parted from them in Virginia, he would buy a packhorse for the rest of the trip. The lady herself gave no sign of being a red-handed Patriot, and he discouraged the young men from seeing her house in Philadelphia as a rendezvous. Instead he gave them the address of one of his good friends in Vine Street, where he intended to stay on arrival.

It was a fine, hot day when they left, and the spirits of the whole company were high. They had at last found a French vessel to take their mail home—a munitions ship had just put in to port and its captain, Foligné, offered to convey all their letters back to France. In his latest to Honorine, Jules had detailed their plans without dramatising the conflicts they might run into further north. In fact, the news from there was not too alarming. Washington was not presently engaged with Cornwallis, Philadelphia was secure, and there was no sign as yet of any troop ships prowling down the coast from New York. If the reports had been unfavourable, he would have tried to persuade his ward to stay in Charles Town, but he was glad this was unnecessary, for he was not fond of the place: the gentry talked of nothing but slaves, land and rice-growing; it seemed that smallpox and fevers were ever-present threats, and she would end up with a poor view of American sophistication if she remained trapped here between the Cooper and the Ashley rivers. And he would miss her.

They had not long waved Victor and the company goodbye before Viviane discovered that Mrs Christie was also happy to be leaving Charles Town. As they swept through the town gate, that lady settled herself back on her cushions and sighed.

'I may have been born here, and I was glad to come to aid my sister this bout, but I always feel a lift when I leave. My health is never good here. Has anyone told you the saying: "Charles Town in spring is a paradise, in summer a hell, and in the autumn a hospital"?'

'No, Madame. Why does one say this?'

'Because of the damp and the heat. The air that comes off the swamps is a promoter of disease, you will never persuade me otherwise. And besides that, I cannot feel safe. You will have observed the rabble in the streets, I am sure.'

'I noticed many poor people begging in the centre of town.'

'Not to mention the crowds at the tippling houses. It is distressing to see so many opening up, all along King Street and Meeting Street—most vulgar. And I am ashamed to say that more than half the licensees are women!'

'I also see that most of the slaves are ill-fed and they wear rags. There are a lot of them in the streets.'

'Oh, not all those you see are slaves. There is a vast proportion of free Negroes, and a bad lot they are. There is a great deal to fear in a town of 12,000 where 6000 are black. Gadsden and the rest think it a fine thing to harangue the populace and have them running to the Liberty Tree to pledge our independence, but they may be risking their very necks in the process. Preaching insurrection in a town like ours is like a spark to tinder—the whole place could well burn without the English coming within a hundred leagues.'

So began the long journey to Philadelphia, through the rice fields of the South Carolina lowlands, over dusty roads past the cattle farms of the high country, along the rough trails through North Carolina forests where Viviane learned to recognise white ash and sycamore and the majestic conifers that flung deep chasms of shade across their path. Her questions about the land and its creatures were answered by her guardian, who often drew his horse alongside and rode within talking distance for a mile or two where the way permitted. On the other hand, her impressions of the towns they passed through were coloured by the trenchant comments of Mrs Christie and her comparison of every feature with what Mademoiselle de Chercy must expect to see at journey's end.

It was seldom that Viviane had the chance to balance this information against her uncle's, so she was glad one evening when the good lady retired to her room in a hotel in Raleigh, and they were able to talk freely.

'I must confess I fell into every kind of naïveté before coming to America. For one thing, I fully expected these to be the most liberal-minded people in the world. Yet they are such a mixture.'

'You looked forward to a nation of Franklins and I cannot quarrel with such a dream. As you say, though, the reality is different. You rub along all right with Mrs Christie?'

'To be sure; she is very well-meaning. But she is a case in point. The way she talks of the slaves, or the Nigras, as she calls them, you would think she was describing bands of marauding warriors instead of the miserable victims of oppression. That led to another of my misunderstandings. She was telling me that the Assembly of Charles Town has forbidden the importation of slaves, and I exclaimed how admirable that was, and then she said that it is because the citizens are afraid that the black people will all rise up and cut their throats!'

'The Charlestonians are afraid of mobs. And with good reason when they are led by vocal whites like the local Liberty Boys. They can amass hundreds when they boycott English goods at the docks, and all the big merchants go in great fear of looting.'

'But they are quite unashamed of having built Charles Town's wealth by trading in other human beings.'

'There are plenty of slaves in Paris,' he said mildly.

'And I hate it there just as much as I hate it here.' She leaned on the little table where she was sitting and looked across at him, over the larger table that held the lamp. He was lounging in a low-backed chair and showed no sign of wanting to be up and off to bed.

'Is there no one in this country who sees this as I do?'

'Of course. Pennsylvania has banned the import of slaves. And Thomas Jefferson put an abolition clause in the Declaration of Independence. But the others took it out.'

'Oh.' She was silent for a while, then brightened. 'I must ask you about those men selling horses in the square in that last little town we went through. Were they Indians?'

He nodded, and she saw the amusement on his face at the reverent way she had said 'Indians'.

'Could you tell what tribe they belong to?'

'I should say Cherokee.'

She was struck. 'To think they might have fought alongside you once.'

He shook his head. 'Most of the men I knew would be long dead.'

'They were not all youths, at the market. Some of them were quite old.'

He gave a soft laugh at this, and she realised too late what her words implied. On the contrary, though, as she examined his strong figure, the smooth skin and ironical green gaze, she could scarcely believe that he was already a veteran soldier, or that it was so many years since he used to write to Mirandol about the Indian wars.

He pulled his long legs under him, about to rise to his feet. She must ask the question now, for the opportunity might never recur.

'Do you remember—?' He obligingly sat back again, and she took a deep breath. 'There was a time when you used to put a lot in your letters about Indians. I was just a child, and Papa always faithfully read out those passages to me. Victor de Luny and I used them for our games together in the woods; we even made up tribal names for each other. You wrote of a great chief called Pontiac, who has always been my idea of the ultimate hero. Of course there was no one I could possibly share such notions with, except Victor!'

He looked uneasy but she persevered. 'I have been thinking how you wrote so faithfully. I suppose the first Indian story arrived when I was about five, and they continued for some years. It has taken me all this time to guess: were they intended for me?'

He hesitated so long she thought he was somehow offended. Then he said, 'Yes. I had not the knack of writing directly to a child I had never met. But your father wrote to say how you reacted to the stories, so I kept up the game. For a while.'

'I knew it! I used to beg for those passages to be read aloud to me, and Papa made a great play of searching though each letter and shaking his head as though there were no Redskins in it anywhere, but they never failed to appear. After all this time, may I say that I am grateful?'

He smiled and rose as she said contemplatively, 'It

is odd to be thanking you so late for such kindness. You possess much more talent as an uncle than you would have me believe.'

The smile held a hint of self-mockery. 'I shall take that as a compliment. Goodnight, my dear.' He bowed and left the room.

They reached Virginia in the second week of July, and Jules insisted on staying with the women until they got to Richmond, where he expected to get the most reliable news about what was happening in the Chesapeake and Delaware bays. It was also a pleasure to see his ward's reaction to the glorious landscape of Virginia in midsummer, and her admiration for the grace and richness of the towns. He wished there were time to show her the best of civilisation that the state could afford, to introduce her to the Virginian planters he knew. He caught himself imagining visits to their mansions, walking into splendid drawing rooms with her arm in his, watching the men's faces kindle and the wives gaze at him in deep speculation. His fantasies, with a mighty effort of will, went no further, but in all their innocence they still disturbed him. It was time to part.

The news in Richmond was encouraging: the English were clearly a great deal further from Philadelphia than they were themselves, and Congress was firmly in residence. Mademoiselle de Chercy and Mrs Christie were safe to go directly onward, cross the North Pamunkey River and make their way on passable roads to the port of Annapolis on the Chesapeake, where Mrs Christie had relatives. From there it was less than fifty leagues to Philadelphia. Jules, meanwhile, would go up-country to see friends in Charlottesville and then travel northeast again to visit the Ogilvy family in Chester.

Alone with his ward before departure, he wondered whether she felt the same dread of separation. It was too much to hope that she would regret his absence, but he was after all the only member of her family on this vast continent.

She said, 'Do you know, I am more eager to reach Philadelphia for the post than for its own sake? It torments me to go so long without letters. I shall go straight to your address in Vine Street and find out if there are any from Great-Aunt Honorine. And on our way, Mrs Christie says if we are lucky there will be ships in Annapolis that can pass through the blockade and carry our mail across the Atlantic. Shall I take yours?'

'Thank you, I had not thought of that.'

'No amount of writing will make up for what I have done to my dear aunt. Even if her first letters are full of reproaches, how I shall fall upon them!'

'I am sure she has forgiven you already. You must have noticed, Madame de Chercy has strong family loyalties. Perhaps all the greater because she has no children of her own. I have never done a thing to deserve her affection, but she bestows it on me without a second thought, as though I were her own flesh and blood.'

Her face grew grave and she was silent for a while. At last she said, 'I have been thinking of something that shames me. I have known you almost a year, yet I have never once asked what it was like at Mirandol when you were growing up, how you first came there, what my father and grandparents were like then. You might have derived pleasure from telling me. And I should be fascinated to know.'

He remained silent and she went on with uncharacteristic shyness, 'While we are waiting for Mrs Christie to get ready, perhaps you could tell me a little about what brought you to Mirandol. I shall understand if you refuse, since I ask so late.'

'Nonsense. I only hesitate because I must warn you, the story is not edifying. When I arrived at Mirandol I was as desperate a character as a boy of ten can well be: a vicious, penniless vagabond with a temper like a volcano relieved only by periods of sullenness.'

She looked up, startled by his sarcastic tone, but then the expression in his eyes must have reassured her, for she said softly, 'I long to hear your story. If you say

230

so, perhaps that was how you appeared on the outside. But within?'

He shifted in his chair, uncomfortable now that he was faced by a task he had never attempted: describing his childhood to another. He began in a detached voice: 'I find it hard to recall my early life, it is just as though a door slammed shut somewhere, dividing me from the boy I used to be.' He stopped, but she still had her eyes fixed on his face, expectant. He took a breath and began again. 'I was born in Rouen. My father had a drapery business, and our family name was Rollet, which as you know I still bear, along with the surname your grandfather gave me.'

'You had brothers and sisters?'

'No. And at the age of ten, no parents. There was an outbreak of typhus in Rouen, and my father and mother were among the first to succumb, within a few days of each other. I did not see them at the end: to isolate me, I was sent to the house of Madame Roseline Archambaud, my mother's sister. I stayed with her and her lawyer husband after that.'

Her gaze had softened unbearably, so he looked away. He could hear in her voice the knowledge of what his answer would be as she asked gently, 'Did they look after you well?'

'Not exactly. I used to try to find motives for what they did, and wonder what the ins and outs of the family finances might have been.' He shrugged. 'Now I have no desire to find out whether their tale about my father's affairs was true or false. The town was led to believe that the family business had been on the edge of ruin when he died, so there was little left even to feed me, and my uncle and aunt kept me out of charity. The town was obliged to accept this view, since my uncle was executor of the estate. I had no way of judging, and anyway I did not care. I cannot recall the first weeks in their house.'

He paused, but she chose not to speak, so he slowly went on. 'I was soon told that I was a burden to my kind protectors, who were appalled at my gloomy behaviour and perverse character. All I remember is that I cried a

231

lot.' He looked up and gave her a wry smile. 'Not the best way to recommend myself to my relatives, I suppose, since they considered that by housing me they afforded me all a reasonable boy could require. My aunt declared I was intractable and left the discipline to her husband, who favoured the belt over a scold, and a scold over any other form of communication. They cut short my education and planned to send me out to work, but local respect for my parents was such that they did not like to advertise this shabby procedure. I think I could have borne all this, and the charge of being idle and pernicious, if they had not also tormented me by running down my parents.'

'How disgusting. How terrible.'

'The crisis came one evening at supper when my aunt made a remark about my mother which I have neither forgotten nor forgiven; something snapped and I threw my plate of food in her face. My uncle grabbed me, marched me to the stables and declared that I was too far gone even for him to discipline: I was in for a beating with a horse-whip, by the head groom. Actually the man used to work for my parents, he was the only friend I had left. My uncle watched, then walked off when it was over. I stayed with the groom, who wept at what he had been forced to do on pain of losing his position.' He caught her eye. 'I did not. I was planning my escape.

'I was tempted to take a horse, since it would get me furthest away, but I knew if I ran off with their belongings my uncle and aunt would pursue me, whereas if I left on my own they might be glad to get rid of me. It's odd, I was young but I guessed rightly—they had my inheritance, which was all they wanted. I went up to my bedroom, gathered a few things and slipped down the back stairs. I left through the coach-yard, and I saw the groom waiting in the doorway of the tack room.'

'He did not give you away?'

'No. It was his last act of friendship. By morning I was out of Rouen and on the high road to Paris. I met up with all sorts of travellers, some disposed to talk and others not. I inquired what work I might find in the towns ahead, but they all laughed at me. Except one man, the owner of a travelling menagerie. I was fascinated by the poor creatures in their cages, and the shaggy little ponies that trotted behind the cart. When they made camp that night I helped to forage and feed the animals. I hoped that I might be offered some food myself.'

'This is ghastly. And you were *ten*!'

'But growing up very fast, I assure you. The boss wasn't averse to having free labour, so I worked for a few months in return for my keep. On the road I often drove the cart, which was painted up like a gypsy caravan—you would have approved of it, I think. In the towns I helped set up the boards around the grounds; then I collected entrance money, and told the audiences tall stories about the animals.'

'What animals did you have?' she could not help asking, and they both smiled at the childish question.

'We had a pair of ancient camels, and some Barbary apes. And there was a lion that my boss always referred to as a man-eater, and a dusty old eagle with clipped wings. I was allowed to help with the animals, but there was an older boy as well. Unlike me, he was paid, and he saw me as a rival. His first idea was to beat me into submission, but I'm afraid I was pretty fierce in reply and he was forced to back off.'

'Didn't the man protect you?'

'No, he left us to shift for ourselves. He was always promising me a real job of some sort, but he never granted it. He was not a cruel man, but he was ruthless. He treated us more or less on the same level as the animals, for which he had no sympathy whatsoever. When the eagle moulted itself into a decline, he acted as though it had died to spite him.'

He relaxed a little, stretching out in the chair, forgetting her for a moment and looking back with greater clarity. 'I suppose it is not surprising that I grew as savage as the beasts I tended, but I think my outbursts of rage really came from the time at my aunt's. I did not know what to do when my parents died;

I suppose grief turned into anger. At the time I had no idea what was happening to me; I just thought the world a black place where I must fight to stay alive.

'I had some bright moments, though, with the animals, especially the ponies. They were the most spirited, and they worked hard when we reached the towns, giving rides to children. One day the boss decided to try hitching two of the little devils to a cart he had made; it was supposed to carry an adult and child around the menagerie. All the ponies shied at that except two, but one of them was a bit lame, and I did not think it right to harness her. He ignored me, of course, and that's how we came to blows, right in the middle of a town. The pony kept on baulking, some bystanders started making fun of the whole show, the maid in the cart took her little charge out of it and demanded her money back, and then the boss lost his head. He took a whip to the ponies' backs, and when they still refused to move he lashed the lame one over the face. Maybe it was the sight of the whip, I don't know, but I went for him, swearing out loud to kill him. There was an uproar from the bystanders but I flung myself at him, catching him off balance so that he dropped his whip. He tried to fend me off but I was too slippery for him. I had a tent peg in my hand that I snatched up from somewhere, and I drew blood from his arm. When they pulled me off him someone had already gone for the guards and I was being called a murderer.'

He looked up to see her open-mouthed, and gave a quick laugh. 'It cannot astonish you to hear I have a temper! Goodness knows where it might have led me. But that was when your grandfather, Eustache de Chercy, stepped in from nowhere and took over. All I knew was that two men were hauling me off when a gentleman moved in, took me by one hand, removed my weapon from the other and said to the people at large, "I shall deal with this boy." Then he led me away sobbing and swearing towards the inn. He must have been watching from the balcony; it turned out he was pausing there between stages.'

'What did he say to you? Do you remember?'

'Yes, very clearly. He said, "You did well to protect the pony, dear boy—I doubt whether it will be used so again. Have you ever been in trouble with the law?" I shook my head, and he asked me if I had relatives in the town. When I shook my head again he thought for a bit and then he said, "To avoid any embarrassment with the guard, I think you should ride with me for a while."

'So we both got into his carriage, the steps were taken up and the door banged to, and we rode off towards Mirandol, for that was where he was going. I was always so terrified of being sent back to my aunt's, I had never told anyone my name or history, but I am sure you remember the way your grandfather had with children. I poured everything out and he listened with the greatest attention. I answered all his questions, never doubting that I had found a protector. He gave me his assurance I should not be sent back to Rouen. That was a singular promise, when you consider he knew nothing of the legal details and was going on the story of a wild and incoherent boy. He talked about my future, and painted a dire picture of what my life would be if I stayed with such men as the menagerie keeper. When I asked him in despair what I should do next, he paused for a while in contemplation and finally said, "You shall come home with me."'

He looked up at her. 'At last I have come to the part that will interest you: Mirandol. Your grandmother was living at the time, but she was frail, suffering from the illness that eventually claimed her. She was a mild woman, not very active or assertive. She was kind to me in her quiet way, and her gentleness never ceased to amaze me when I contrasted her with my aunt.

'Your father—' he stopped for an instant. She was right, it was pitiful that they had never spoken of this before. She longed to hear it now: he could feel her breathless expectation.

'Again, I recall the scene perfectly. Your father was out riding with a groom, and I did not see him until I was washed, tidied and arrayed in a suit of his own old clothes. The announcement that I was to meet the young master filled me with misgivings and antagonism—I knew what older boys were like, and I hated him in advance. Your grandfather led me down to the stables, and our first encounter took place in the yard, as your father dismounted from a fine Arab pony.'

He tried to smile at her. 'He looked at me very much as you are looking at me now. You may picture him: slim, straight-limbed, with an open gaze and a ready smile. He had long, unruly curls and a good-natured look that should have disarmed me at once. But I stood scowling at him without a word, waiting for the moment when his father would send me packing, and release me from having to be polite to aristocrats.

'Your grandfather said, "I have asked Jules to stay with us for a while." It was the first I had heard of it! Then he went on, "He's fond of horses—he'll need a mount."

'I still remember your father's expression. He glanced around—you'll recall we were in the yard—and the half-doors in the stable wall were behind him. There were several hacks and hunters hanging their heads out and observing us curiously. He grinned; I remember it showed the dimples on his cheeks. And he said, "Which one would you like?"

'Needless to say, I resented his condescension. I said at once, "That one," and pointed to the grey Arab he held by the reins.'

'What did he do?' she whispered.

'You can guess. With an expression of sympathy I don't have the words to describe, he stepped forward and pressed the reins into my hand. I tell you, the crowd of black thoughts that oppressed me flew away at once. I can also tell you, from then on he never once took back his generosity towards me. And I never fought with him, in word or deed.'

She was crying. Large tears rolled down her cheeks, and he could not tell her to stop, for the tears were for her father. He waited painfully until she wiped them away.

'I think at some point your grandfather made

inquiries about my unworthy relatives in Rouen. At any rate, it was about six months after I arrived at Mirandol that he decided I should be one of his family. Your father already thought me so, and called me "Brother".' Halted by the way his breath failed on the last word, he paused a moment. 'My dear, you have always known what a true gentleman your grandfather was. And I have no need to praise your father to you. I only wish I could have repaid my debt of gratitude and devotion while he lived.'

'Thank you. Thank you for telling me.'

There was silence for a moment, then suddenly he said, 'When I think of the day I arrived at Mirandol last year! You know, if you had been a child of ten instead of a young woman, I might have made some connections that I totally missed at the time. Imagine, I might so easily have entered into your feelings. I might have encouraged you to talk of your parents. For you lost them young, like me. But I did nothing of the kind.'

'But think how I received you. Think how little consideration I gave you.'

He shook his head. 'I never took into account your grief over your father. I should hate to see again the letter of condolence I sent you from Canada. I dictated it to an orderly in the hospital; if it expressed one tenth of what I felt, I should be astonished. I daresay it was just like the note I sent to announce my arrival at Mirandol. I have not been in the habit of describing my feelings—you must bear with a lifetime's abstinence on that score.' She looked up at him, clear-eyed and grave, as he rose to his feet. 'But at least I realise I treated you abominably when I first met you. Forgive me if you can; the apology comes a year late, and is the more abject for that.'

She rose too. 'Forgive? I was set against you before I even laid eyes on you. When we met, all you did was react to my outburst. Our first quarrel was all my fault, and I am ashamed I did not realise it ages ago.' He said nothing, just shook his head; then she said quietly, 'I shall be honoured, Monsieur, if you tell me it is not too late for us to understand each other.'

237

He took her hand. 'And I shall be honoured if you will only trust me.'

'I do.'

Mrs Christie entered at this point, announcing that she was packed and ready to depart. She could wait only long enough to extract a firm promise that he would call at her house the day he arrived in Philadelphia, then she clamoured to be gone.

The farewells with his ward were brief and subdued; no observer could possibly have guessed the emotions aroused by their long conversation alone. But afterwards, he could never recall that moment when their hands touched, without a flood of feeling that swept through all his defences.

13

PHILADELPHIA

For Viviane, Philadelphia meant the company of lively, stimulating, open-hearted young women. The Shippens, the Norrises, the Willings and the Whartons all had daughters, and they welcomed her into their midst the very first day she set foot in Mrs Christie's house on Chestnut Street. From that lady's descriptions of the town, Viviane had expected to be met by a stiff and formal Puritanism in keeping with the regular grid of streets and the wide, level thoroughfares lined with imposing public buildings. Instead she fell in love with the place at once. The young American women could not hear enough about Paris, and Viviane could not get enough of Philadelphia. Between visits during the day she often persuaded someone to take a stroll with her along the broad sidewalks; no one could quite believe her when she said the only equivalent in Paris was the raised paving that the d'Antins had put down for convenience outside their own town house.

The city was at war. The Delaware and its islands bristled with fortifications; the town bells were muffled; the curfew was strictly enforced; and everywhere there were signs of the nearness of the militia and the Continentals, who were camped out towards Germantown; but it was also pulsing with activity, for Philadelphia society was rich, extravagant and fashionable. And at the same time the Friends moved amongst it, men and women who had no admiration for the brocades, laces and canary-coloured coaches of the ostentatiously wealthy, and instead set an example of sober religion and honest commerce. They, too, proved different from Viviane's expectations, for their concerned Quaker interests had often led them to travel widely in the pursuit of education or trade and she met men who were formidable for their learning, their wit and their political power.

Her American dream was beginning to come true,

for wherever she went in the city, she saw the benevolent influence of Benjamin Franklin. She soon learned
from her new friends that one of the Philadelphians'
great fears was fire, and to combat it they had an effi-
cient fire brigade, formed by Franklin. His practical
genius had given Philadelphia the lanterns that lit the
streets at night, its library housed in Carpenters' Hall,
and a philosophical club called the Junto, whose
members met every Friday at Robert Grace's house in
Jones' Alley, and corresponded with thinkers in North
America and Europe.

True to her purpose, she called at the house on Vine
Street to ask for letters, and found to her joy that there
were two awaiting her from Honorine de Chercy,
alongside others addressed to her uncle, which she left
for him to collect. The first letter held scarcely a word
of hurt or anger, but there was reproach in every line.
The second was in more characteristic style.

*If you have had the fair voyage I have fervently
prayed for, I calculate you have now reached American soil. Doctor Benjamin Franklin has been good
enough to include this in a packet going to Philadelphia. He continues well, as does Mr Deane. You
will be impressed to learn that I have had both to
dinner—thus I risk being classed amongst the ranks
of the Republicans here.*

*I shall endeavour to make this Paris bulletin more
informative than my last—I spent more time wiping
away tears than I did writing, and I am sure you
would prefer a bright letter from me, since you must
imagine me very cheerful, ensconced in comfort and
warmth whilst you and your companions suffer
privation.*

*The chestnut candles have fallen from the trees,
the Seine sparkles while it waits for June, the town
is still buzzing with stories of his Imperial Highness
Joseph of Austria, who visited early this month. He
lodged humbly as the Count of Falkenstein in the
Hôtel de Tréville instead of going straight to Versailles to see the Queen his sister. He attended a*

240

lecture by Lavoisier at the Academy of Sciences and was much impressed by the new experiments on atmospheric air. He also went to see the paupers at La Salpêtrière and the prisoners at Bicêtre, which I thought quite uncalled for. And he inspected a school for the deaf and dumb, the first ever in the world, it appears, run by the Abbé de l'Epée. Mr Franklin later professed an interest in that and I consented to accompany him. He spoke of you with affection and declared that you would have had a great deal to say about what we saw, which I dare say is correct. He asked when you would be returning 'from the Loire' and I found myself unable to keep up the prevarication, hence his help in sending this letter. I am afraid that he was more diverted than shocked when I remarked that I have not the slightest idea whether I should be addressing it to Mademoiselle de Chercy, Madame de Luny or Madame Jacob. I ascertained that you were not married in Los Pasajes, but for all I know the captain united you on board ship. If not, and you remain unattached, I can only hope you will consent in the future to choose a husband in a more conventional manner.

It is nearly the end of May, and you left on the twentieth day of April: surely you must be safely on land now. Safe enough to begin putting yourselves in danger again, that is. I fear for you all.

Of course I see Madame de Billancourt regularly. I am afraid you must prepare yourself not to receive any letter from the daughter; she feels some resentment at your departure, which I have not been able to persuade away. The Marquise de La Fayette is well, and nearing her final month of pregnancy. The child Henriette is also well. They have received no word as yet from the marquis—nor I from you, of course. Besides social visits I frequent the opera a great deal. There is a fierce controversy here over the merits of Gluck and Piccini—the 'French' and Italian claques are busy shouting each other down.

I had every intention of cramming pages with

*information but I cannot: with every word I am
more weighed down by the thought of the dangers
you face. I cannot tell you how much I wish you and
your guardian had not gone. Everything is out of
joint whilst you are absent.*

*When your friends in Philadelphia pass you this,
believe it imbued with thoughts from Home, which
I hope is how you both view this house in the Rue
Jacob.*

> *God bless and keep you*
> *Your affectionate Aunt*

While Viviane was being invited to the more splendid
houses in the town, she also took time to explore the
vast market in High Street, where she found the stall-
keepers and their customers conversible and friendly.
From first light on the market days there was a throng
of people of every degree, and no one raised an
eyebrow at unaccompanied women who came there to
shop amongst the rest. In contrast to such places in
Paris, there was no uncomfortable bustle among the
stalls, no raucous shouting of wares, and everything
was conducted with the greatest tranquillity and order.

One day, after strolling the length of the massive
edifice, Viviane struck up a conversation with a
Quaker woman who then asked her home to take tea
with her. Meeting Mrs Redman's friends, Viviane was
deeply impressed by their staunch pacifism—several of
their husbands had been arrested and exiled to Virginia
because they refused to take the new oath of allegiance.
They did not believe that the United States should
claim independence, and they would not bear arms for
any cause, Republican or Loyalist. When Viviane
explained that she herself was in Philadelphia to
support La Fayette's company in their attempt to join
General Washington, Mrs Redman shook her head in
dismay. But her attitude did not diminish her courteous
hospitality, and she pressed Viviane to return the following week.

Then, at last, just when the absence of both La
Fayette and the Comte de Mirandol was beginning to

make her anxious, they all turned up on the same hot sunny day. The first she knew of it was in the cool of the evening, at a musical soirée. Mrs Christie had invited the noted Judge Peters, because she felt he would appreciate the wit and charms of her French guest, and also because she knew he could give clever, ready answers to the myriad questions that Mademoiselle de Chercy saved up to spring on her at the end of each crowded day.

The select gathering was duly assembled, when all at once the Comte de Mirandol was announced.

'Show him up!' cried Mrs Christie in satisfaction, casting a quick eye over her daughters, Polly and Georgiana, and concluding that he was about to see them at their best.

When he entered, however, he had eyes only for Mademoiselle de Chercy. But the company was far too curious to allow them to converse in private, so they had to go through their greetings and exchanges of news under the gaze of a dozen very curious onlookers. They managed well, the count with grave courtesy and his ward with her usual naturalness of manner and expression.

Introductions were made, and it was discovered that the judge and the count were acquainted.

'My dear Monsieur,' said Judge Peters in his slightly ironical drawl, 'your arrival is most opportune. Mademoiselle de Chercy has just begun to describe your latest ventures to us. Now we shall have them from the horse's mouth.'

The count replied at once, 'You wish to hear my purpose, or the Marquis de La Fayette's? My own can be told in a sentence: I have joined the Virginia Riflemen, and report for duty in three days.'

Mademoiselle de Chercy gave a quick exclamation, which was drowned by a question from one of the ladies: 'And this marquess—who is he, and what are his plans?'

He spoke to his ward rather than the questioner. 'They arrived in town today. All except two— Capitaine fell ill in Salisbury, and Du Rousseau de

Fayolle stayed behind to look after him. Our friend led the others to see the Congress this afternoon. They were not even admitted to the State House—they were met on the steps by a Mr Morris, and another man I don't know, a Mr Lovell, who speaks French.'

'You were with them?'

He shook his head. 'I ran into them later, quite by chance, at Clark's Inn, on the opposite side of the street. They all went there to drown their sorrows.'

'My word. What did my friend Morris say to them?' asked the judge.

'They were told to about turn and go straight back to France.'

'Oh no!' Viviane said.

'His Worship will tell you,' he glanced wryly in Judge Peters's direction, 'that the Continentals are beginning to think they could well dispense with French officers. Apparently the engineers that Deane sent a few months ago have proved quite useless, and Franklin has been asked to send more. It also appears that somebody called Fermoy recently disgraced himself at Fort Ticonderoga.'

The judge said soberly, 'It must have been a blow to you, Monsieur, to hear that Ticonderoga has been recaptured.'

The count nodded, then went on, 'Unluckily for our friends, there is a positive glut of ambitious Frenchmen clustering around the army, and they want no more of us.'

'What on earth are we to do?' Viviane said in despair.

'I joined them around the table in the tavern and we held a council of war. Don't worry, they began to look less glum once the wine had flowed for a while. There is still a lot they can do: write a memorandum to Congress, for instance, explaining the facts of the case.'

'Which are?' Judge Peters asked with interest.

'Only one of them—a gentleman named Kalb—is determined to get a command; the rest are breaking their necks to serve as volunteers. I told them they must emphasise that they have not come to be a drain on your coffers. La Fayette for one has such strong letters of recommendation that if he promises to serve without pay or command, I am convinced he will be accommodated in some way. As for the rest, I shall do what I can tomorrow through friends. I shall try to see Morris, too. I hope he and I can discuss the matter in a sensible manner and not in the street!'

Viviane said in a subdued voice, 'Poor Victor.'

He smiled at her. 'Our friend Jacob felt all the humiliation of their treatment and I don't blame him. But it would be absurd for them to come all this way and then give up at the first setback. So you are not to despair either.'

The judge said, 'If Monsieur de La Fayette has half the spirit of your charming ward, I think his best course might be to gain an introduction to General Washington. Courage and sincerity are strong recommendations in themselves.'

'You think it possible for the general to meet him?' the count said bluntly.

Judge Peters gave a subtle smile. 'I am sure he would much rather meet your countryman than General Howe! We shall see what can be arranged.'

The rest of the evening passed agreeably. Viviane was glad to introduce her new friends to her guardian, and even more pleased to see how captivated they were by him. Peggy Shippen, though scarcely sixteen, used all her flirtatious arts on him during supper, and looked jealous when he deserted her later to stand by the pianoforte and turn pages for Viviane.

There, in between pieces, they were at last able to talk. She learned that he had located all his Virginian friends, either at home or at the army camps. Then the Ogilvys at Chester had welcomed him eagerly and he had spent several days there.

'I am determined they shall meet you. You would like them, I am sure. They have three girls—young women, I should say, for they have grown mighty sophisticated since I saw them last—who declare they are wild to see you.' He glanced around Mrs Christie's opulent room, just managing to avoid Peggy Shippen's gaze as he did so. 'You are more than comfortable here, I see.'

'I must tell you, Monsieur, I never met a people like the Americans for hospitality. They have such warmth. I have been making comparisons with France, and I have decided that our welcome to strangers is very fine too, but for different reasons. In the best houses, like my aunt's, there is perfect consideration for everyone who steps across the threshold.'

'I agree. And Parisians are punctilious about introductions, and good conversation, and most delicate in their attentions to each guest.'

'Whereas what the Philadelphians offer, by contrast, is simple generosity. Do you know, I met a Quaker widow one day, who took me to her home on the friendliest impulse, and had me sitting there alongside her children, talking with her neighbours, as though she had known me all my life!'

'I can imagine it. I remember the first time I was invited to the Ogilvys'. It was a black Holy Eve; they pressed me to stay the night and celebrate Christmas with them the next morning, American-style. I declined at first.'

'Why? I am sure it was not because you were going to midnight mass—you refused to come with Aunt and me last year.'

He said levelly, 'Christmas is not my favourite time of the year.' Then his expression relaxed. 'But I consented in the end: you will find that prevailing against Constance Ogilvy is a hopeless task. I shall never forget the welcome. They have a gift for making guests feel protected and cherished, almost part of the family.'

The voice of Peggy Shippen's older sister, Betsy, reached them across the room. 'We are being discussed. My French is as full of holes as my Spanish lace, but I *know* we are being discussed.'

Viviane turned at once and smiled. 'We were talking of manners.' She paused, to keep them in suspense, then went on gravely, 'When I was a little girl my mother told me just how to behave when I eventually

246

went into society. She said, "In Paris, all you need is to be clever and obliging. And if you cannot be both, be clever."'

They all laughed, except her guardian. Then they looked at her uncertainly.

She continued, 'In America, I find you lean the other way. And people are much more than obliging: they are truly kind.'

Judge Peters applauded this remark, then said, 'Will the Comte de Mirandol be so *obliging* as to give us a song? Your niece has revealed that you are a great exponent.'

Her guardian looked at her, alarmed. 'What possessed you to tell them that? Who told you—?' He stopped in confusion.

'Madame de Billancourt,' Viviane lied promptly. 'There is a pile of music just there, behind you. And if you find the songs are set for tenor voice, you are not to cry off; I am perfectly capable of transposing the key.' He still looked reluctant, and she found herself saying with some feeling, 'You will not refuse me?'

As he turned away to look through the sheets of music, she wondered whether memories of singing with la Farrucci had made him hesitate. She hoped crossly that he was not going to stand beside her with his mind full of the Italian beauty he had left behind. Then she cheered up, for the crucial thing was that he *had* left her behind, on an instant's whim, which surely ruled out any sentimentalising now.

Most of the pieces in Polly Christie's collection were Italian love songs, so eventually he chose one that Viviane pronounced not too hard to accompany. They found his first note on the keyboard and she ran through a few bars to ascertain the key. When they began, to a hushed and expectant room, he took the lead as she had hoped and allowed her to send the music flowing deftly beneath. The beautiful melody was unhurried, with many sustained notes that suited the dark, warm quality of his voice. It was odd, but as he sang the first phrase, tears welled in her eyes and she had difficulty making out the score. For a while her playing was automatic, but then she regained control and they brought the song to a moving conclusion.

The applause was heartfelt and the company absolutely insisted on more. 'We can see you have practised together for years!' cried Mrs Christie.

He leaned over her to fold the music away. 'If they only knew. I cannot conceive how you managed that.'

'It is not so hard, as long as you take the initiative and let me muddle on in your wake. For your next, I think I saw "Le Rondine" there. At least I shall not have to sight-read—I played it for Buysson in Charles Town.'

'Did you now?'

They played on, the company responded with delight, and for a time it seemed so much like a sparkling evening in Paris that they were both able to forget that this was Philadelphia, and wartime, and in three days he would be gone to take up arms again.

Victor de Luny was in the depths of misery. The fortunes of the company in Philadelphia had been extremely mixed, and so far he felt he had suffered worst of all. The Marquis de La Fayette had been lucky enough not only to meet General Washington, but to be treated by him with the utmost kindness. He had been accepted into the Continental Army at the rank of major general and been granted Mauroy, Brice and Gimat as aides-de-camp. Victor, however, was unsuccessful in his application. Congress insisted it had no places for the rest of the volunteers, even Monsieur de Kalb, and had softened the blow only by offering to pay their passages back to France.

Thus it was that, on his last morning, Victor rode to the camp near Germantown to bid La Fayette goodbye. As it happened, he found the marquis about to accompany General Washington on an inspection of the troops. The general suggested he ride with them, and Victor accepted with conflicting feelings, for it would pain him to see the army he could not join, and he was ashamed of his poor English, which was not even half up to La Fayette's.

When he saw the ragged and ill-equipped state of the Pennsylvania Militia and the even worse state of the Continentals, he reflected that he should have been glad not to be sharing their fate, but he was still wretchedly disappointed. He had received a letter from his parents that morning which had moved him to tears. To think he had made his mother ill again with worry, left France with hardly a sou and endured a backbreaking journey, only to be cast off by the Patriots!

If La Fayette was as appalled as Victor by the state of the regiments they saw, he kept this to himself. When Washington said that he feared a gentleman from the French military must wonder to see soldiers in such condition, the young marquis replied: 'Sir, I have come not to teach but to learn.' The remark was well received.

As they emerged from a copse of sassafras trees into the encampment of the Riflemen, Victor spied the Comte de Mirandol at once in the first rank. His height and build were unmistakable; otherwise Victor would hardly have known him, for he wore the so-called uniform of the Riflemen—a long, fringed linen over-shirt with shoulder capes, a wide leather belt, buckskins, and pliant leather shoes, Indian-style. Most of the men had not bothered to fasten their long hair back, and the brims of their round black hats were turned up or down at whim on an untidy variety of angles. Some wore headgear made from raccoon fur, and with their tanned and unshaven faces they looked for all the world as if they had just come down from the backwoods after a hunt.

General Washington dismounted and spoke to them, and all gave him respectful replies through which their devotion plainly showed. He talked to the count and, when he learned his name, mentioned that he had heard of him through Benjamin Franklin, who had sent a letter of recommendation about him to John Hancock, the President of the Congress. He said he was surprised to see the count had not used his influence as a veteran and his friendship with men such as Franklin and Benedict Arnold to obtain a command.

The count smiled and said, 'I did not come here to sue to my friends, Sir, but to meet the enemy.'

The general was not going to let him slip into the background so easily, however, and asked him to join the group as they rode around the rest of the camp. He exchanged views with him about the northern campaigns of the past, and listened with attention to every comment he made. As soon as he could, the count reined back and came to talk to Victor, who at once told him he was obliged to return to France.

He frowned and said, 'Could you not join La Fayette as another aide-de-camp? There will not be much to do for a while, but the moment we face up to Howe the situation will change.'

Victor shook his head despondently, and they rode on together in silence. He looked ahead at General Washington, thinking that the destiny of so many men reposed in that tall, imposing man. With his somewhat grave face, the general was massively dignified. But Victor had already noticed that he was not distant; on the contrary, he seemed very alert to what people said to him and how they said it. He appeared to understand readily the true nature of things, including the calibre of those around him. He was loved by those who followed him, and adored by La Fayette; the strong affection between these two was already formed.

At the end of the inspection the count took leave of the rest and returned to his post. Victor saw him go with regret, thinking it would be for the last time. But after the general himself had ridden away, La Fayette took Victor to his quarters and told him he had been given permission to include him in his entourage. Overwhelmed, Victor thanked him fervently for pleading his case so well, but the marquis swore it was none of his doing. Days before he had used all the persuasion he could, and fancied that it was the count who had worked the miracle by speaking aside to General Washington.

That night Victor sat up late writing a letter to his parents, which was all the more urgent because the Marquis de Luny had threatened in his last to take ship for America himself and enforce his son's return. What could be more humiliating for the officer he now was, than to be wrenched from the glorious field of battle by his father?

... I can never thank the count enough. For a start, he would not let me. Second, we shall be on the move soon and I am not likely to see him, for I shall be on duty alongside my friends. I only hope I shall justify his confidence in me by giving a good account of myself in the coming battle.

The English have come south from New York under General Howe and are prowling in full force along the coast. It is a puzzle whether they will seek to land in the Delaware or in Chesapeake Bay. For us there are many choices, one of which is to defend Philadelphia itself. We must manoeuvre to meet the English from the best possible position. Whatever happens it will be soon. After waiting many long months I am eager for this trial: we shall show them what Frenchmen can do.

I should like to take my farewell of you in case this is my last letter, but I cannot find the words. You know what France and my family mean to me. My dearest wish is to prove worthy of you.

Your loving son
Victor

On 24 August the army marched on a grand parade through the streets of Philadelphia. It was a gesture of hope and defiance, a last chance to receive the acclamation of the Republicans and to demonstrate their determination before the Loyalists, a last contact with the city and Congress whose liberty they were about to defend. They marched in ranks twelve deep, relishing the friendly welcome from the men, the women's handkerchiefs waving from upper windows, the crowds of eager children who ran alongside. And most succeeded in suppressing the niggling idea that General Howe's troops might one day receive a similar welcome from this rich and complex city.

The soldiers' threadbare uniforms and motley equipment were disguised with fresh sprigs of greenery gathered from the woods as they came in. Viviane watched them from an upper window of the house on Chestnut Street as they marched westwards out of town. Seen from above, through the trees outside Mrs Christie's house, they looked like a badly pruned shrubbery in motion.

La Fayette and his aides rode near the front of the column, and she was thrilled by their handsome appearance. It was impossible to guess that this was the company whose horses had broken down on the way north, who had abandoned half their gear for lack of transport, who had been robbed by Americans on their journey and scorned by them when they arrived. Now they were dressed in new uniforms ordered and paid for by La Fayette, they were better mounted than most of the regular cavalry, and their bearing was such that no one could have known how little military experience they possessed amongst them.

She gazed at Victor de Luny and recalled the distant morning when he had come galloping to Mirandol on his hunter and hailed her as she leaned from the window, to tell her the news from America. The summer sun shone on his hair as he swept off his hat to wave it at the crowds. He did not see her; she wanted to cry out, but there was a great din from the street below and she knew she would not be heard. In less than a minute, the little company had passed by.

By contrast, her uncle found her before she even glimpsed him. All at once Polly Christie gave a cry and pointed: directly below was a tall man in buckskins, a rifle slung over his shoulder, looking up at Viviane, baring white teeth in a wide grin.

'Sister Anne, Sister Anne, what dost thee see?'

She caught her breath in surprise, then rallied and called, 'A veritable army of Bluebeards, Monsieur.'

He glanced swiftly behind him at the Riflemen filing

past, their moccasins making hardly a sound on the stone paving in the centre of the street, then said impatiently, 'Lord knows where we're off to; I'll try to ride back later—where will you be?'

The women had been invited that evening to the Shippens's house, on Second Street, but suddenly nothing seemed to matter more than seeing him in private. She would think up some excuse to stay behind. 'Here, all evening.'

'Fine. Catch.' Suddenly he hauled off a thick wreath of vine leaves hanging across his shoulders, swung it behind him and tossed it up to her. She leaned out at once and plunged her hand into the spinning circle of green. As he waved and loped away, laughing, she pulled it in over the windowsill. The plaited stems felt sinewy and strong in her hands, but the leaves were already wilted from the heat.

Much later, when she received him alone in the drawing room, he seemed a different man, all his gaiety gone. He consented to sit down, but did not look disposed to linger. He opened the leather pouch that hung with the powder horn from a strap across his chest, and took out a folded piece of paper.

'Addresses. The Ogilvys in Chester: if you have to leave Philadelphia by the south, go to them. If you are forced to go inland, I have friends in Lancaster who will readily receive you.'

'Inland? You really think we could be attacked from the Delaware?'

He shook his head. 'It will be some time before we know anything. The army goes southwest, but who can tell if that is the right direction to confront Howe? I wanted to be sure you had options.'

'Do you think a Frenchwoman would come to harm if the English were to take the city?'

'No. But they might make it difficult for you to leave. And we might well lose contact with you. I do not want that.'

'Rest assured, if there is any evacuation from

Philadelphia, I shall join it. But I cannot believe I am at risk. All I can think of is the dangers *you* face.'

He shrugged. 'The greatest risk at present is tedium. We must manoeuvre across country endlessly until the British make up their minds about where to land and how to attack. Don't waste time worrying yet; the worst of military operations is the waiting, and so our young friends will discover.' He paused a moment then said, 'Oh, Victor de Luny and the marquis send their fondest greetings.'

'They look well. Are they prepared?'

'As well as they can be. The marquis is in good heart, despite the news about the *Victoire*.'

She looked at him in suspense. 'What?'

'Captain and crew are safe, as far as we know, but she struck the bar leaving Charles Town and went to the bottom. So La Fayette has lost both cargo *and* ship. It's fortunate he's a rich man.'

The cold and controlled way he gave this awful news incensed her for a moment, and she got swiftly out of her chair and began to walk about the room. Then she allowed herself to see what the sudden return of his old reserve meant: quite simply, they must part, and he liked the necessity no more than she did.

He rose also, and she stopped in front of him. 'I don't know what to say.' Words filled her head none-theless. *What if I never see you again?* But it was unthinkable to pronounce them. 'I know what my aunt would say, however. God bless and keep you.'

He took her hand in both of his. It was the first time he had ever been less than articulate before her, the first time he could not match—overmatch—her in con-fident response. He said nothing at all, just folded her hand tightly in his as he leaned forward and pressed his lips to her forehead.

There was a moment when one of them might have spoken, as he stepped away, bowed deeply and looked at her for the last time before turning to leave. But Viviane's throat constricted and they both remained silent as he quitted the room.

14

FIRST BLOOD

On 11 September Washington's army was drawn up along an extensive front on the east bank of the Brandywine Creek, awaiting the enemy, who were moving steadily towards them from a town called Kennett Square. The Comte de Mirandol's company was attached to Major General Nathanael Greene's division positioned at the centre of the line at Chadd's Ford, where the first assault was expected. Victor de Luny and the other aides-de-camp were with the Marquis de La Fayette amongst General Washington's staff at headquarters, some distance north of Chadd's Ford.

The first messenger to come in reported that Colonel Maxwell's riflemen, who were on the English side of the ford, were under attack; everyone was convinced that this was Howe's main thrust. The troops on the right wing under Major General John Sullivan were concealed in the woods upriver and had not yet engaged; a report was received from a Major Speare that there were no British troops to be seen in that direction. Meanwhile the attack intensified downriver and the Pennsylvania Division under Brigadier General Anthony Wayne went into action.

Then a confusing incident occurred: a tall farmer came riding up at breakneck speed and flung himself from his horse, demanding to speak to General Washington. He said the English were marching through his land: they had crossed the north branch of the Brandywine in force, and must be circling to get behind the Americans' right wing. This Squire Cheyney was a stranger to Washington, though he swore that Wayne and everyone in the district knew him for a Patriot. But the general, doubtful about information that so flatly contradicted the intelligence brought by Major Speare, decided to wait for further reports. It was an unsettling situation, however, and in order to be doing something, La Fayette asked permission for himself and Victor de Luny to ride off and observe the action at the ford, which was granted.

The fighting at Brandywine Creek was the young men's first sight of a battle. Both banks of the creek were strewn with bodies and the air was filled with the crash of arms, shouting and smoke. It was impossible to tell which side had the upper hand. Most of Maxwell's men had been pushed back across the water, but the attackers were coming under fire from Proctor's cannon in the rear. The big guns did not play a major part in this battle, however, the brunt being borne by the infantry and the one company of cavalry, led by a courageous Pole, the Count Casimir Pulaski. The British advances were very disciplined; La Fayette noted that they fired volleys with levelled guns, while the fire from the Americans was aimed. He agreed with Victor that this made the latter more deadly, but he could not help seeing that the Americans did not hold formation as well as the British, and he was haunted by the thought that neither Continentals nor militia had yet learned to withstand a British bayonet charge. Contemplating all this, and looking down on the frightful mêlée in horror and confusion, Victor was quite ready to obey when La Fayette said they must return to headquarters.

They arrived in the midst of furious activity. A report from Sullivan had at last confirmed what poor Squire Cheyney had been repeating for an hour: a second column of English led by Cornwallis was about to fall upon the right wing from the rear.

Things happened very quickly. Nathanael Greene was given the order to withdraw his division from the creek and turn them against the new English attack, and Sullivan meanwhile tore his troops away from the oncoming flank of the English and tried to bring them around in an arc to meet Cornwallis head-on further east. General Washington raced on horseback with Greene through the countryside to intercept them, and La Fayette and the others followed, electrified by the general's unspoken fear that they would be too late to prevent the destruction of Sullivan's force.

It was then that Victor caught his only glimpse of the Comte de Mirandol. He was amongst Greene's division, keeping up a smart pace as he ran with a little group of Riflemen, who now looked even more like wild men of the mountains. Their faces were black with gunpowder—whilst in action they ripped open their cartridge papers with their teeth—and many had shirts cut to ribbons or were naked to the waist. The count yelled a greeting to La Fayette as they passed, and kept on running across a field of barley.

When the troops finally engaged with Cornwallis it was pandemonium. Arriving pell-mell as they did, none of the American companies manoeuvred properly into position and their officers had to kick, shove and bawl to get them into any semblance of order. La Fayette was horrified to witness how unprepared they were. As Reserve Captain at Metz he had had scores of men to command and their battle training had been impeccable. He almost wept as he watched the chaotic American line waver and fragment. 'Who drilled these men?' he shouted in anguish. Then he drove his horse towards a group of stragglers and harried them into formation.

It grew dark and everywhere the Americans were in retreat. La Fayette received a report that Wayne's troops had broken and were fleeing as Hessian mercenaries from the British side plunged across the ford and chased the Pennsylvanians up the banks of the creek. Despite Greene's support, Sullivan's men also began to give way. The woods were full of flying shadows as the infantry panicked and ran. Victor was still in the saddle; he, La Fayette and several others got long torches burning and rushed through the gloom trying to rally the men who were stumbling along the tracks towards them. Count Pulaski appeared, racing back and forth like a madman, cursing the fleeing infantry. La Fayette and his friends managed to block a bridge and turn soldiers back with torches thrust in their faces, and the young marquis pleaded with them to reform and face the enemy. Some responded and he dismounted and went amongst them, rallying and encouraging them. Into the depths of this dreadful muddle came the general's order for a full retreat. It was then that Gimat, still on horseback, looked down at La Fayette amongst the foot soldiers and turned pale.

'Monsieur le Marquis,' he said, 'you have a boot full of blood.'

La Fayette had been wounded in the thigh by a musket ball. It had passed through the flesh without touching the bone, but he was losing blood fast and his friends were desperate to get him to safety. Thus they joined the retreat and moved as best they could towards a place called Dilworthtown. Wayne's troops meanwhile were veering southward, their retreat covered by a fierce rearguard action fought by Greene's division, which cost the lives of many Riflemen.

The army fled all the way to Chester, and Victor's hair prickled on his scalp with the thought of Howe ordering his troops to pursue; fortunately he did not, or the withdrawal would have been a rout.

In Chester, medical orderlies soon found a surgeon to attend to General Washington's young protégé, and within an hour La Fayette's friends, who had all stayed with him, were relieved to know that the wound was cleaned and well cared for, and he had reasonably comfortable quarters and good attendance. It was pitch dark, but the whole town rang with the shouts of men, the grinding of iron-shod wheels on stone, the whinnying of restless horses, and hoarse cries from amongst the hundreds of wounded being constantly brought into the town. The whole place was awake, and so was Victor, despite his utter weariness and despondency. Unable to sleep alongside the others in the cramped room where La Fayette lay in pain, he walked dazedly out into the street. It was only after he had wandered for half an hour amongst the carts, horses and people thronging the thoroughfares that he remembered he had on his person the address of the Ogilvys, the Comte de Mirandol's friends.

He asked directions at an inn where the front

parlour was crowded with wounded soldiery, and then walked for a quarter of an hour to find the house, on the outskirts of town. As he went up a gravel drive through the park that surrounded it, he could see lamps lit on the ground floor and lanterns on either side of the huge front door. With luck he would find the count there, or at least news of him. He went up the broad flight of steps and under the portico.

When he knocked, the door was instantly opened by a liveried servant. Ignoring the man's inquiry, Victor looked beyond him, for he had seen a small figure come out into the hall and stand at the foot of a vast staircase. He felt rather than saw the tension in the still form and, hurriedly giving his name to the servant, he stepped past without waiting for an invitation and walked in. He found himself confronting a slight young woman, neatly dressed, who had a beautiful face and soft blue eyes. Awkward now, after his impulsive advance, he silently admired the smooth fair hair drawn back from her forehead, her steady gaze.

The servant was beginning to protest behind him, but the woman's voice was calm: 'Can I help you?'

'I am a friend of the Comte de Mirandol.'

'You are French! You ride with La Fayette? Come in, please.' She walked away, and he followed her. She led him to a well-furnished drawing room, explaining as she went, 'I am here by myself. My parents and my sisters have gone into town, to our factories and ware-houses. They are doing what they can for the wounded, and helping with shelter for the troops. Someone had to stay home, and as I am the youngest . . .' She faced him and held out her hand. 'I am Abigail Ogilvy.'

He took her fingers in his, gave a sketchy bow and staggered as he did so. 'You are worn out. Do sit down. Let me fetch you something.' She glided towards the bell pull, then stopped and said suddenly, 'Do you have word of Jules?' Once he registered whom she meant and shook his head in disappointment, she gave a quick sigh.

When the servants brought him bread and ale, and a cool damp cloth so he could wipe his face and hands, they talked, and he told her everything that had happened. It seemed to him that they spoke for hours. She offered to go back with him to La Fayette, to make sure he was well tended, or to have him moved to their house, but he told her the surgeon had recommended that the marquis rest where he was for the night, and they would all move on in the morning, taking him to Philadelphia for greater safety.

She urged Victor to lie down upstairs and sleep, but he protested—first, he could think of nothing more restful than talking the night hours away with her; second, he must keep her company until her family returned—at which she gave him a lovely smile. Shortly after this he fell silent, and when the others came home they found him slumped in the chair with his arm on the rest and his hand in hers, as she sat looking at his pale, sleeping face.

Next morning the Ogilvys tried to keep him with them after breakfast, but he was determined to check on La Fayette, his friends, the count, and his horse. He discovered that the others had found transport and were already prepared to take the road to Philadelphia, and the marquis, though in a great deal of pain, was able to travel. Victor was in a dilemma: none of them had heard anything of the count and no one had precise news of Greene's men. He could not imagine arriving in Philadelphia, coming face-to-face with Viviane, without being able to tell her whether her guardian was dead or alive. In the end, he decided that he would let the others go on, and if need be use the whole day to locate the count; they would travel slowly, so he could catch them up.

It was nearly three weeks since Viviane had promised her uncle that she would join any evacuation from Philadelphia. Congress was arranging for new quarters in Lancaster, and many a nervous citizen had headed for parts west and north, yet she stayed on. Despite the frightening rumours and conflicting bits of information she heard every day, it was still hard to believe in a close threat to the city. The English troopships, after being seen and counted off the coast, had eventually landed well south, at Head of Elk on Chesapeake Bay, the very day after Washington's parade through the city. The Patriot forces, which were constantly on the move through Pennsylvania, New Jersey and Maryland, sleeping in the open without even enough blankets to cover them by night, spending the days foraging, trying to arm and keep hold of their recruits, and making bullets from lead ripped off the roofs of Philadelphia mansions, would somehow manage to turn aside the English.

She learned nothing of her guardian at first. His mute farewell had prepared her to receive no messages, and she wrote none herself, for it was depressing to know how many of their letters were already wandering the country or on the high seas and might never reach their destinations in America or France. It was true that there was an express courier running twice a day between Philadelphia and Lancaster, beyond which other mail could conceivably go, but it would torment her to write and receive no answer. For once, she agreed with him that silence was the best course.

Then suddenly came his letter, and she felt a deep pang of regret that no word of hers had reached him in the wilderness where she constantly pictured him.

My dear Ward

Today is the seventh of September. Happy birthday. I should like you to know I remembered, as I always have, however little you believed I thought of you.

I have nothing like my gift of last year to offer. Unless you would like a sketch of the surroundings: a large gabled barn filled almost to the rafters with a golden mass of hay, picked out here and there with the sleeping form of a rifleman who unites in his person almost all the attractions of the farmer's pigs that are rooting about at the foot of the ladder.

Every time Washington is vouchsafed a new vision of General Howe, we are herded off in a new direction. We are camped along a branch of the Schuylkill

261

at present, and tomorrow we shall wade across yet
another stretch of river and lumber southward again.

Our host distils his own liquor, and the condition
of the riflemen I see about me can be attributed to
his talent with the local juniper. My handwriting
displays the same horizontal tendency. I should
probably not be writing at all. I would not, if I could
think of anything but you.

   Your devoted guardian
   JR de C de M

Soon after, reality struck. When the guns began at
Brandywine, the thunder rolled all the way into Philadelphia, and soon the rumours began to surge in after
it. Much of the news was conflicting, but just as darkness fell a horseman arrived with absolute confirmation
that the Patriot army was in flight. Few slept that night,
and at six o'clock next morning dispatches from Washington were read to Congress. By then the city was
mobilised to reinforce the forts along the Delaware and
the spiked barriers that stretched across the river
approaches, to prime the city artillery, to receive the
wounded from the countryside.

They streamed in, on horseback, on waggons and
farm carts, on stretchers, on foot. They were taken into
houses and church buildings, laid in rows in the yard
and gardens of the State House, and in the great rooms
of the Carpenters' Hall, where Viviane went with the
Wharton women and stayed all day to help. During
the terrible hours while she tended the men in the
crowded library upstairs she gained piece by piece the
news of her friends: that La Fayette had been injured
and was being brought into town, that the other young
Frenchmen were still with him, all alive, as far as her
informants knew. But no word of the Comte de
Mirandol.

In the evening she ran along Chestnut Street to Mrs
Christie's, eager for a message, scarcely daring to hope
for more. There was a single note: from her Quaker
friend, Mrs Redman, who made bold to ask Mademoiselle de Chercy for some urgent household supplies

that her hostess might be kind enough to part with. Viviane was unreasonably disappointed at first to see whom the letter was from; then she was surprised, for it was not hard to guess that, despite her principles, Mrs Redman must be looking after wounded men.

It was a cry for help that Viviane could not ignore. Persuading Mrs Christie to part with the linen, balms, tinctures and other items that were needed, she took a servant with her to carry them all, left a note of the High Street address where she was headed, and set out.

The soldiers that Mrs Redman had taken into her home were farming lads, from Massachusetts and New York. One, Thomas Keane, was the only son of a widow. He had joined the Continentals after they were chased from Bunker Hill; when Viviane expressed surprise that he should enlist at the very time when so many were deserting, he smiled painfully and said, 'No call to stay on the farm by then, Mamselle. The crops were trampled into the fields by Hessian boots and we didn't save a grain of seed for next harvest. So we walked off the land for a whiles. My mother is with some of our folks near Prince Town.'

She smiled at him. 'And now you are in the city of brotherly love.'

'I been here but once, on parade. Where did you say this house is?'

'In High Street, next to the market, not far from Bartram's store.'

'Ah, I spied that on the day we marched through. They had a window full of china. I have a notion to take my mother one of them pencilled Pennsylvania teapots one day. When we've cleared the English out and things are regular again.'

She was worried that talking would weaken him, for his shoulder wound had given him a fever; his blue eyes were too bright and his tow-coloured hair was damp with sweat. When she had made him as comfortable as she could, she went down to the kitchen, where Mrs Redman was preparing the family meal. Her three small children, round-eyed and rather fearful in the presence of this fine French lady in her

263

silk and lace, waited silently around the deal table, perched on wooden benches that just brought the chin of the smallest up to the level of the white, scrubbed surface.

Viviane sat on the end of one bench and smiled at the eldest, who gazed at her with a disapproving expression that gave him an old-fashioned look. It occurred to her that he might think the soldiers were in his mother's house because of her. She looked across at Sarah Redman, whose square composed face radiated calm reliability.

'Madame, I did not think it wise to give Mrs Christie the idea that the wounded men were here. I told her they lay in the yard of Bartram and Dundas.'

'First, thee'll call me Sarah, as promised. And my thanks for the precaution. Thy hostess's husband was a Tory until the day he died, and a great ally of the Friends; if she let fall this among troublemakers, I might be investigated.'

'By whom?'

'Our Meeting has been as clear as the Scripture on this matter for years,' Sarah said placidly, beginning to ladle soup into the children's bowls. 'Thee'll eat?'

When Viviane thanked her, she explained while she served the meal. In 1775 the Philadelphia Yearly Meeting had forbidden Quakers to take an oath of allegiance, bear arms or act in any way to support rebellion against the English sovereign, his laws and representatives in the Colonies. Since the Meeting's decision, more than three hundred Quakers accused of contravening it had been disowned by the Society. The powerful Friends commanded an obedience which the revolutionaries could only dream of, and in fact they formed the most coherent Loyalist body in Pennsylvania. Viviane knew that it was strict adherence to their edicts that had led to the arrest of the husbands of Sarah Redman's friends and their exile to Virginia. It astonished her to see this deeply religious woman go against her pacifism and risk being ostracised from her own community. But this was not the right time to ask her about it.

The meal over, the children were about to leave the table and prepare for bed. Before she went upstairs, the three-year-old plucked up the courage to ask Viviane a question. 'Art thee a fashion doll?'

The little girl's face held such wonder that Viviane could only smile, without having the least idea what to answer. Sarah reproved her daughter, and explained to Viviane that Philadelphia ladies kept abreast of fashions across the Atlantic by having dressed dolls sent over from Europe every season; the miniature models could be seen on the counters and in the windows of the best dressmakers.

Viviane looked again at Sarah Redman. She wore exactly the same clothing every day—a simple blue and yellow skirt, a plain bodice with a frill around the neck, and a linen apron. Her little girl might well believe that real women were clothed in this way, and anyone who resembled a figure in a shop window was somehow a doll!

She smiled at the child again. 'I am a visitor from another country; that is why I wear these clothes. Next time I come, I shall bring some pictures with me. Even our horses wear different things in France! I shall show you.' She rose from the table as Sarah began to usher the children from the room. 'Let me clear up while you put them to bed. Then I'll go upstairs and sit with the men until you come.'

Sarah nodded and left, and Viviane began to set the kitchen to rights and prepare to wash the utensils. Her mind slipped from the task to what haunted her in this otherwise peaceful house: the plight of the two young men. She and Sarah might be of use to Thomas Keane; but it seemed that the other, who should never have been moved from Chester, and had been stitched up again and abandoned by the surgeon the night before, was beyond their help.

She was washing the bowls when a knock came on the front door. Wiping her hands on a cloth, she hurried through a low entry hall: she found it an odd dwelling, for the kitchen and the parlour occupied the whole ground floor of the house, with the tiny hallway between them; because Sarah Redman never seemed to use the parlour, the kitchen was effectively the main room. She opened the door to Mrs Scattergood, a friend and neighbour. Something was preoccupying her, for when Viviane sat her down in the kitchen and offered to fetch Mrs Redman, she did not respond in her usual mild and courteous way. Instead she kept Viviane standing by the table and plied her with questions about who was in the house, and what she was doing there herself.

Viviane gave guarded replies, managing not to mention the wounded men or the supplies she had brought.

'I don't wonder to see *thee* here, a'course,' said Rebecca Scattergood.

'No,' Viviane said quietly. 'I have a great deal to learn from Mrs Redman.'

Rebecca had no time to digest this before Sarah appeared at Viviane's side, and bluntly took over the dialogue.

Yes, there were two injured men in the house. They had been left on stretchers outside her door for an hour while the cavalcade of wounded passed by; and when Thomas Keane had looked up and spoken to her, she had them brought inside. She hoped that if ever her own son should be lying wounded in a strange street, then some good wife would come to his aid. She could find no sentence in Scripture to tell her she had just done a wrong deed. And they were soldiers no more: Thomas was going back north when he could walk, and Ethan Herrold, as like as not, would never walk again.

Viviane excused herself at that point, turned, and went up the stairs. Behind her she heard Rebecca Scattergood say, though in a more subdued voice, that her friend chose strange times to consort with 'revolutionary Papists'.

Sarah Redman's reply was low but clear. 'If thee reprove my actions, Rebecca, I thank thee for giving me guidance. As for my guest's beliefs, dost thee forget this very city of ours was founded upon liberty of religion? If she asks me a question, my answer more often than not comes from Scripture.'

Faced with this new perspective, Rebecca Scattergood decided to take the matter no further. And if she refrained from censuring Sarah Redman for tending the sick soldiers, the other women in the community would follow her lead. They would be especially impressed when she told them of the Frenchwoman's humble admission about her lessons from the Bible. If Sarah Redman could persuade an idolatrous Roman to spurn Latin texts and hearken to the good news in plain English, what could they do but praise God for it?

Upstairs, Viviane helped Thomas Keane drink some water, then moistened a cloth to put across his brow. At the other side of the room, Ethan Herrold lay with his eyes closed, his breathing shallow and uneven, his thin face so pale that it scarcely stood out against the lime-washed wall. Thomas was not up to talking, and the silence in the room was full of suffering.

She stood for a while by the window, looking out. Dusk had fallen on the street, and the vehicles and figures hurrying by looked sinister as the shadows under the street lamps met and mingled and swept apart again. If only she had more to do, then she might be able to stifle this ache of waiting and wondering about her friends and her guardian. Sarah Redman's reference to Ethan Herrold echoed in her mind. *Like as not he will never walk again.* For a second, her matter-of-fact tone made Viviane recoil, as though from cruelty. But now, alone with the injured men, she was forced to face up to the cold truth of the statement, and to realise that it applied to countless others. La Fayette perhaps, and whom else?

Then her heart gave a leap as she recognised one of the hastening figures in the street. He must have gone to Mrs Christie's, obtained the address and come looking for her. She turned at once from the window, frantic to get downstairs in time: numbers were not marked on Philadelphia houses, and even the streets were not signposted—he might pass by unawares. Just at that moment Sarah entered, and Viviane quickly explained where she was going, took her candle and reassured her that she would not bring the gentleman indoors.

Hurrying downstairs, she put the candle on the floor in the hallway and flung open the door to find Victor de Luny on the step.

He had a dreadful look of anguish on his face, but her relief burst out: 'Thank God you are safe.'

He reached out and took both her hands. 'Vive, be prepared.'

She snatched them away and clasped them in front of her. 'La Fayette? Tell me he is alive.'

'He is not in danger. But—'

'No. Not here.' She kicked the candle out, stepped forward, shut the door behind her and set off up the street, walking so rapidly that Victor had to take several strides to catch up with her.

'You must listen to me.'

She took a shuddering breath. 'Yes, I suppose I must.' She walked even faster. She wanted to stop her ears, to rush away from him so that his words could not hurt her.

Then she turned and grasped his arm, bringing him to a halt. 'My dearest friend, forgive me. You come from a battle, and by some miracle you were spared. And I will not let you speak! Tell me quickly.'

'The Comte de Mirandol is missing.' A low sound escaped from her, but she kept her eyes fixed on his face, willing him to go on, to get it over. 'I stayed behind in Chester today to look for him. I searched everywhere. But there is no sign of him.'

Still with a hand on his arm, she began to walk on. In a voice she hardly recognised as her own, she said, 'Captured. Wounded. Dead. Which?'

'I talked to the Riflemen who were nearest to him at the end of the battle. He was with Greene's division, and they were in the rearguard action, so they fought right on into the dusk. The men I spoke to got separated from him finally, and moved back towards Dilworthtown with the rest. The Riflemen do not surrender. And I don't think . . . I believe at that point no one was taking prisoners.'

Viviane saw a church up ahead and pointed. 'Let us go in there. So: wounded?'

He said reluctantly, 'I'm afraid the last person to see him said his face was covered in blood. But he was still on his feet, firing from the cover of some hickory bushes on a knoll. There were five or six others with him. They are all reported missing.'

In silence they walked further up the street and entered the church. It was not one of their own, but it was welcoming, for there were candles lit so that people could pray. Viviane could not talk, just sat trembling beside him, while in a murmur he told her something of the battle. He mentioned his glimpse of the Comte de Mirandol, then hurried on to describe the retreat, his stay at the Ogilvys', and La Fayette's departure that morning. Viviane could not raise her head; she sat looking at the stone floor, clasping her hands in her lap.

'His company commander told me there is no report of the count among the dead or wounded. He says it is too soon to despair, and he would hate to lose him: the respect for him is such that the others would have followed him anywhere. He has given me his belongings, which are few enough. I have left them with the Ogilvys, and I shall arrange for them to be sent to you.'

'Was there nothing more you could do?'

'Of course. I went among the wounded. Vive, they are five hundred and more. Can you imagine?'

She reached out and pressed his wrist. 'Yes. I am sorry. Go on.'

'And the dead. They were laying them out in the fields. I got quite close to the Brandywine. Do you know, the British are so much at their ease that they have made camp, as comfortably as you please, and done all their washing? There was linen drying on the bushes, all along the bank. I felt I should go mad, just looking and thinking what it was like there yesterday.' He took another breath. 'I did not find his body.'

'What can we do?'

'Nothing. Wait.'

She looked at him then. 'Where do you go, back to La Fayette? Can I help? Shall I come with you?'

He shook his head. 'He is well looked after. You should go home to Mrs Christie's. You are as white as paper. Try to sleep tonight; tomorrow we shall have news. One way or the other.'

She shook her head and stood up, her body taut with purpose. 'Walk me back to Mrs Redman's, if you please. I shall be grateful if you will take a message to Chestnut Street: I am needed here and cannot leave.'

Victor sighed and got up. 'Is this wise?'

'I have no choice. I must be active, or I am lost.' Her mouth twisted as she said the last word, and with a huge effort she managed to shut a door in her mind—the one that opened on a line of soldiers' graves, gaping like raw wounds in the earth. There was no certainty. Only when the fatal message came would she reopen that door.

Much later, Viviane sat looking at the sleeping faces of the young men, faintly illumined by an oil lamp on the table near the window. Sarah was resting, while she herself had gone beyond tiredness into another realm. In a strangely detached way, she examined Ethan Herrold's features. With the bloom of health on his cheeks he would be handsome. If his mutilated body were whole, as it had been yesterday morning, he would be a fine, strong man. He looked her own age. She wondered whether he had a sweetheart, or a wife. If so, perhaps he was leaving children behind him. This life that was about to be cut off, had it been fulfilling? No one knew, for Tom had heard nothing about his companion except his name, and Ethan had not said a word since he had been carried into the quiet room. He might be on the run from misery; or he might have been on the brink of joy.

She thought of her guardian, and remembered what her Great-Aunt Honorine had once said, when she was trying to argue her into more tolerance towards him:

'He has had an unhappy life.' At the time she had dismissed this as a ridiculous exaggeration. She still had no way of judging how true it might be, but when she looked back on the year she had known him, one thing was certain: she had done nothing herself to improve his existence. On the contrary, resentment had set her against him. She had made his life troublesome, quarrelled on every point that touched her own affairs, done her best to destroy every possibility of harmony between them. Only after they had both left France did she realise that she and her aunt, though not even his blood relatives, represented the only family on earth that he wished to call his own. If their new understanding had lasted longer, perhaps she could have narrowed the abyss between them. But it would have needed a great effort on her part, for he had known rejection and practised restraint too long to try to bridge it himself.

If she had been a different person, would he ever have come back to America? Would he have risked death again in some muddy Pennsylvania field, or might he now be in France, making a new life without her interference? She had a vision of what her aunt would feel if she received news of his death. For it was sheer tragedy that a man so handsome, strong and clever should be cut off, without ever having known the happiness of a wife who loved him or children to follow him. She thought of all the men she knew, and realised she could not name his equal.

Tom shifted restlessly in his sleep, though he did not wake. But the movement roused Ethan, and he opened his eyes for the first time. His grey gaze was clouded; it was a while before he focused on her face. She was frightened, feeling how death stood in the room, and unable to imagine what she could say if this shattered man realised he was confronting the end.

But his first whispered question was just, 'Where am I?'

'In Mrs Redman's house, in Philadelphia. You are safe; we are looking after you.'

He stared at her for a long time, with the misty look that gave the impression of dreams passing behind his

271

eyes. Then he gave a slow smile. 'You talk mighty funny. But you're the purtiest woman I ever saw. Promise you'll stay.'

'I promise. You must let me help you: are you in pain anywhere?'

'No. Is it all right if I sleep? You won't go away?'

She shook her head, and he closed his eyes.

Minutes passed. She found she was holding her breath. She touched his hand, but his eyelids did not flicker. Unsure whether he was asleep or unconscious, she sat on, waiting.

She must have dropped into a doze eventually, for the knocking on the door downstairs made her start. She felt frightened again, the noise seemed so loud, but neither of the young men stirred, and there was no sound to indicate that Sarah was rising to answer the summons. Then suddenly she was wide awake. It must be Victor, with news.

She lit a small candle at the lamp and glided from the room. She darted down the stairs with the candle flickering, willing him not to knock again and wake the household. She crossed the little entry hall, put the candlestick on the floor, pulled back the bolts with shaking hands and wrenched open the door. She had one second to recognise the dark figure looming on the doorstep before a breeze blew the candle out. Then she screamed.

Her cry ripped through Jules like a knife. She took one step forward then stopped, her body rigid, one hand supporting her against the doorpost. Then she uttered a high-pitched moan like an animal in pain, and shuddered, and the sound came again as weird sobs shook her upper body, making him put his hands out to take her shoulders and then bend close and whisper in her ear, begging her to stop.

'Who? La Fayette?' he asked urgently.

One hand came up and grabbed the front of his shirt, her fingers digging into his chest as she gasped, trying to speak.

272

'I thought he was all right.' He had believed everyone at Chester when they gave a good account of the marquis. Which had provided the excuse he wanted, to go to Chestnut Street first and find La Fayette later. The Christies' servant, sullen at being woken, had given him her address but no news. 'Luny?'

She was not listening, so he put his fingers gently under her chin, tilting her face so that he could look straight into the golden eyes. But it was so dark that what he could see most clearly were the tears gleaming on her cheeks.

At last she managed to speak. 'You. I thought you were—'

As the meaning of her words hit him he lowered his hands. With her fingers still twisted in his shirt, she tugged him towards the doorway. Then she turned quickly and went through the hallway and he followed her into a kitchen, faintly lit by embers in an open-doored range.

'I must see you,' she said wildly. 'Light a candle, I have to see you.'

'Great God.' He could not keep his voice from shaking. 'What have they let you think? Hasn't anyone the sense to *wait*?'

He got no further, for she stopped him with a cry. 'Don't you dare speak to me about waiting! And how can you talk about *sense*?' She locked her fingers together and brought them to her lips. 'Where is the sense in all this?' She was not looking at him. Her shoulders were bent and her hands twisted, as though she were about to turn them against herself.

He did the only thing possible; he strode forward and put his arms around her. Firmly, paternally. He kept his voice very low: 'Stop. It's all right. Sit down, here.'

At that moment the Quaker woman stepped into the room, holding a candlestick high. She paused by the door, took in the scene, and gave him a long steady look as he stood there in the pale light. It was as though she saw through to his very bones. Slowly he transferred his hands to his ward's shoulders, then

273

repeated his command. She obeyed, subsiding onto the bench at the table and letting her head fall between her outstretched arms. He was not even sure that she was aware of the other woman.

He held the level gaze. 'My apologies. You will excuse my being here at such an hour. But I cannot leave her in this state. So if you will allow me . . .' He took a taper from above the fireplace, held it to the embers, then transferred the flame to a thick tallow candle in the middle of the table. When he drew a chair close, his ward stirred and sat up. Before taking the seat he raised his eyebrows at the still woman by the door. 'May I?'

She barely nodded, then said, 'Thee art welcome, for her sake.'

He sat down, knowing that he would never be welcome in her house, for this or any other reason.

She remained by the door and he concentrated on the face before him, the staring eyes, the irises clear as amber under a film of tears. She was fine-drawn, trembling, on the edge of exhaustion. God knew what she had seen and done over the last two days; whatever it was, she had had no sleep. He should never have let her stay in Philadelphia.

She spoke. 'Victor said you were missing.'

'Everyone has been extremely foolish. Including myself, if you tell me so. But look: there's not a scratch on me. When Jacob has a bit more experience under his cocked hat he will learn not to run about with the first story he hears after a battle.'

'You are not to criticise Victor to me. When everyone has suffered so much.' Her lips quivered and she could not go on.

He cursed, and the Quaker woman flinched. Viviane, however, remained with her eyes fixed on his, with such distress in them that he wanted to cover them with his hands. 'I've nothing against the young idiot, God help me. In fact, you'll be glad to hear he distinguished himself in the fight. They all did. La Fayette is already being cried up as a hero.'

'What *happened* to you?'

274

'I went off with a platoon and we brought back some prisoners. They broke off from the rest in the dark and we took the chance and chased them up into the hills. It was the devil of a nuisance to bring them back, but now they're locked up at Chester. They'll be exchanged for some of our boys—maybe tomorrow.' He looked deep into her eyes. She seemed calmer. 'It was worth it. I don't regret it, except for this. How could I predict that Jacob would come charging back here and—'

'He didn't, he searched and searched first. He asked the Ogilvys about you, everyone.'

He cursed again, but under his breath. 'I was going to contact them myself, but Washington sent for me. I never reported to the regiment either. As soon as he released me, I grabbed a horse and got here as fast as I could.'

'They said you were wounded.' She looked at him more closely and her eyes grew wide again. 'Your hair is all matted with blood!'

'Nonsense. How can you tell under the dirt? It was only a graze. I swear to you, there's not a thing wrong with me that a bath won't fix.' He changed the subject. 'La Fayette—have you seen him?'

'No, he is across town.' She told him the address.

'What are you doing here? Why are you not at Mrs Christie's?'

'I am helping Mrs Redman. There are two wounded men upstairs. I promised to stay with them.'

'God.' He said to the silent woman by the door, 'Look at her: she must rest. Have you a spare bed? Otherwise I shall take her to Chestnut Street.'

They both gazed at him with indignation; his ward because he was talking over her head, and Mrs Redman because he was treating her and her house without the slightest ceremony. Damn it, did they imagine he was about to go bowing, scraping and making polite conversation in the middle of a night like this?

She replied coolly, 'Mamselle de Chercy may sleep in my children's chamber. The bed is made up, and I am about to relieve her in the sick room.'

275

There was a pause. Then, despite their keen observer, he reached out and put a hand over the quivering one that was clenched on the deal table. 'I'll go now. But not until you tell me you will rest.'

'Shall I see you tomorrow?'

'Of course. Where will you be, Chestnut Street?'

'If I can be spared, I thought to visit La Fayette. All my dear friends, I have not granted them a moment. But it depends on ... one of the young men upstairs.'

'I see.' He did not, quite. But in this state he preferred not to. 'I shall meet you there at ten tomorrow. And we can discuss what happens next. You realise, don't you, that all your plans must change?'

'And yours?' She slid her hand from his fingers and rose to her feet.

'General Washington has just changed mine for me.' He rose too. 'I'll explain tomorrow.' He would take leave of her in this room, under the cool Puritan gaze. 'Don't come to the door. Go upstairs and rest. Good night, my dear.' He took her hand again, bowed, and kissed it. Then he released it and bowed again. 'Mrs Redman.'

'I shall see thee out.' She put her candlestick on the table and walked into the hallway. As he made himself turn away, he saw there were still tears in his ward's eyes.

She whispered, 'Tomorrow, then.'

He walked past the woman into the street without looking back, and she closed the door at once. There were two hollow thuds behind him as she shot the bolts home. His horse, tethered to a hitching post on the edge of the brick sidewalk, swung its head towards him in greeting. There was not much light to see by, and he fumbled as he unlooped the reins.

He was hit by a wave of exhaustion. He had always envied the way horses could sleep standing, and for the first time he realised how easy it might be, to sway against the beast like this, and rest his forehead against its warm neck, slip into the dreamless dark. But the moment he closed his eyes, one thought rushed in to fill his mind. She had wept for him.

His throat constricted painfully and his own tears welled. Appalled, he wound one fist in the horse's mane and pressed his face against it. Tense in every muscle, he stayed in that absurd posture for a while, fighting the first battle of the new day, then managed to mount. His vision was so blurred and his memory so confused that he took a moment or two to figure out which part of town he was in. Then he pulled the horse's head around in what he hoped was the right direction and rode off to find La Fayette.

15

PHILADELPHIA LOST

Next morning two of the city troop, the Philadelphia Light Horse, made an inspection of the households on High Street. Viviane was awake, neatly dressed and sitting in the sickroom when they got to the front door. Sarah let them have a look through the lower rooms, then accompanied them up the stairs. Viviane rose when the two men entered and greeted them softly, but the officer, though he sent the other man out, made no effort to move quietly or lower his voice when he spoke.

He had lists in his hand, and talked to Tom as he flicked through them, licking a pencil and making a quick note on two of the sheets.

'Very well,' he said loudly when the conversation was over. He glanced at Viviane and jerked a thumb towards the still form on the other side of the room. 'You vouch this is Ethan Herrold?'

'Yes. He is very ill. Can we speak outside?'

He seemed to take note of her for the first time. 'French, ain't you? Is your husband with the Continentals?'

'No. But my friends are. Please come with me.' She stepped past him and opened the door.

With a nod at Tom, who oddly enough looked cheered by this brusque visit, the officer followed her into the narrow corridor beyond. He folded the lists, put the pencil in a pocket of his short, dark brown coat and looked past her at Sarah, who was standing in the doorway of her children's room, a little frieze of heads peering around one side of her skirt. 'We're requisitioning. Linen and blankets. Kindly show the corporal your stores.'

'Such things were taken from me long since,' Sarah said in a low voice.

'Where are they, downstairs? Open all the cupboards, Corporal. Unless you're minded to aid him, ma'am?'

Sarah turned, told her wide-eyed children to stay in their room, and set off down the stairs after the corporal.

Viviane looked up at the officer's tanned, craggy face, which matched his rough voice so closely. 'What will you do for our wounded, Monsieur? No surgeon came to them yesterday.'

He shrugged. 'They are on the list.'

'What does that mean?'

He looked at her wearily. 'It means we know who they are and where they are. And their families have been informed.'

'How do you know their people will receive the message?'

'We don't. But if they want to come and fetch them they can.' He gave a wry smile. 'Though there's more going out of the city than in right now. Right across the Delaware into New Jersey. What are you doing here, may I ask?'

'Trying to be of help.'

The way she said this got through to him. He gave a small start and his dark eyes, which had begun to travel appreciatively over her form, hardened in surprise. He said nothing for a moment, then replied gruffly, 'You think we do not look after our own?'

She bit her lip, but replied nonetheless, 'You do not help them by taking things from this house. Mrs Redman uses the blankets of her children to cover these men. I know she has no more; I have slept here myself. Under a tablecloth.' Ignoring his slow smile, she went on earnestly, 'She is not rich. She has three children and no husband. Why not take from the merchants in this street, who have more to give?'

'Ma'am, we've been through this city again and again like a dose of salts. If the shopkeepers hereabouts have anything useful left, it's well hidden.'

She turned on her heel, went into the children's room where she kept her things, and pulled a bandbox out from under the bed. The children drew near, and gaped at the gold coins she counted into her hand. Then she returned to the officer and held them out on her palm,

'I think, when the merchants receive this, they will make some discoveries.'

He stammered, 'There's no call for that, ma'am.'

'I know you need tents, boots—so many things. There are Frenchmen in the army. You think I would not look after my own?' He was still nonplussed, so she took his broad hand, opened it and folded his fingers around the money.

They stood looking at each other for a moment, and she saw blood flush briefly along his cheekbones. Then he glanced towards the stairs, where the sound of doors closing came up from below.

He stood straight, brought the heels of his high-topped boots together and gave her a quick military bow. 'Thank you, ma'am, and good day.' He looked back at her before descending the stairs.

She turned and went into the sickroom.

When she arrived to visit La Fayette, they were all so overjoyed to see her that her spirits lifted on the instant. Her friend lay in a large room, surrounded by the aides. She told him, with a little laugh, that he was holding court like a monarch. He greeted her with his characteristic boyish smile and an outstretched hand. He was so pale that his freckles stood out like brown ink on parchment, but his voice was firm.

'His Majesty would leap to his feet if such a vision as you were to walk into the room. My apologies, dear Mademoiselle de Chercy, for this shameful posture.'

She took the chair that Gimat had just vacated and smiled down at him. 'You do not realise: I have become very used to sitting at bedsides in the last two days. And to making very pragmatic observations. Are you quite comfortable with that wig on?'

'Not quite. But one must keep up appearances.'

'You may do that very well if I comb your hair for you. Doctor Franklin wears no wig, so while you are in his city you need not either. Gimat, Brice, will you each put a hand under his shoulders?'

She gently took the wig away and Victor handed her

a comb. The marquis lay back again and looked up at her in bright-eyed amusement as she coaxed his thick red hair off his brow and behind his ears. She said, 'I am no coiffeuse, but it is astonishing how practical I have become since landing in America. I have not even found the need to engage a maid in Philadelphia— Mrs Christie's servants are quite skilful enough for my present standards. There: you will do perfectly.'

He smiled and closed his eyes for a moment and she looked around the room. 'Is it safe to stay on here? They say all the wounded who can travel will be evacuated in the next few days.'

'We're going to a place called Bethlehem,' Brice said. 'It is a Moravian town. The marquis will have expert care there, and they can accommodate all of us.'

The marquis opened his eyes. 'It was Washington's recommendation. So of course I shall follow it. And the sooner I can rejoin him after that, the better.'

'Moravian?'

'A religious settlement,' Victor said. He looked at her anxiously. 'Will you come with us?'

'It depends when you leave. I am helping to look after two of the wounded, and . . .' She found it impossible to say what would happen to Ethan Herrold, or repeat her pledge to him, especially in these circumstances. 'I have promised to stay in the house. Mrs Redman has three small children. She cannot cope on her own, and none of her friends will help her; she is a Quaker.'

'We go as soon as possible. The Comte de Mirandol is arranging things for us, and when he arrives we shall decide.' He had a sudden thought: 'I know! If Chester is safe, why not go there? It is scarcely any distance, and the Ogilvys would be glad to receive you. They have already told me so, in fact Mademoiselle Abigail Ogilvy has heard so much about you, she says it is quite impossible to credit it all until she sees you in person.'

Viviane was not quite sure that she wanted to meet this young lady on her own account, but she was disarmed by Victor's admiring, affectionate look as he waited for her reply, and by his eagerness for her to share his new acquaintance. He was proud of her, and it warmed her to know it. She was thankful that she had been brave before him when he brought last night's news. Her friends respected her: they were all in this together, at the same level. The only person who knew how she had lost control was her uncle.

'I shall make up my mind in the next few days.'

'Will there be anyone left in Philadelphia by then?' said Gimat.

'Certainly. My hostess Mrs Christie, for one. The Whartons, Judge Shippen and his family. None of them have any plans to abandon their great houses and leave their affairs to languish just because the future looks a little uncertain. This is their home.'

'*A little uncertain,*' the marquis murmured. 'I applaud your phraseology, Mademoiselle.'

'I have it from you. That is just how you write to your dear wife.'

'True!' Some of his animation came back. 'Did you know I have received a letter at last? Count Pulaski brought it to me from Paris. It is here.' He moved one hand slightly and she realised what the gesture meant: it was under his pillow.

Tears threatened; she hoped he would not see them. 'That is wonderful. How is she? It would have been written before . . .'

'Yes. Before her lying-in. So I know nothing of that, or whether we are parents of a new baby daughter or a son.' He smiled. 'But she was well and in good heart when she wrote. When I think of the dozens of letters I have sent her, and so far only one of hers has got through to me. I suppose most of mine are in the hands of King George!'

At that moment the door opened and the Comte de Mirandol walked in. Everyone greeted him warmly and he responded cordially to each, but Viviane could tell that he was most preoccupied with her. His first look on entering had been towards her where she sat by the bed, and the words he exchanged with the young men sounded mechanical, as though all his real attention were fixed on this one corner of the room.

She rose as he approached, and after making a quick bow he said at once, 'You are well? You look it.'

'Yes, thank you, Monsieur.'

So did he. There was no sign of fatigue: his face, with its strong lines and smooth skin, had its usual colour; and the black hair, tied neatly back, was clean and glossy. He had on a fresh shirt, a soft leather one this time, and someone had even polished the worn belt that caught it to his waist, and the sheaths that held the knife and tomahawk on each hip. She wondered momentarily who there might be at Vine Street to help him to this military readiness. And at the same time she was hit by the memory of the night before when he held her for a moment against the tattered, filthy shirt he had worn on the battlefield, and she felt his arms tight around her and the pulse in his throat beating against her forehead.

She thought he might remember too. Breathless, she found she had sat down again.

He turned from her, however, to speak to La Fayette, examining him from the foot of the bed. Eventually he said, 'We must not tire you. I have a map here. Are you up to seeing it, or shall we all decamp to the next room?'

'Show me,' the marquis said eagerly.

Viviane collected herself, rose and moved away so that they could gather around the bed and discuss the journey to Bethlehem. It became clear that her guardian had arranged for the party to be taken by water to Bristol within days, and thence on to Bethlehem, a distance of about twenty leagues, but he would not go with them himself. While they talked she realised what a difference he had made to the company, from the moment he walked into the room. La Fayette was their inspiration and, though not one of them needed to say it, the count was their strength. She was seeing him with new eyes; she valued that firm, unruffled resolve, and realised exactly what it meant to the young men— they could depend on him. And so could she.

Yet there was more: depths that none of the others could guess at. She recognised his strength, but she had also seen his calm reserve swept away in an instant by her scream in the dark; she remembered his voice shaking with emotion, his desperate plea for her to speak, to let him help her.

She turned away and pretended to look out a window as her neck and cheeks grew warm with a blush of confusion. In one sense, she was acutely ashamed: what a way to greet a man returning from action! A mature woman, full of joy that he had been spared, would have known how to receive him, how to welcome and cherish him, how to rescue his mind from the horrors he had just escaped. Would Honorine de Chercy have shrieked at him like a madwoman? Displayed such weakness of mind and spirit that *he* was obliged to comfort *her*? She doubted it. But still she could not regret that encounter in the middle of the night, for it had destroyed so many of the barriers between them. They were more vulnerable to each other from now on. Because they were closer.

Trying for more composure, she half turned to look at him once more. At this slight movement the green eyes flicked up to observe her. His gaze was intent and he did not smile. In a moment he returned to the matter in hand, and it was then that she realised with a jolt that they had finished deciding what the rest of the company were doing, and had begun to talk about his own departure. Somehow she had thought that he would be in the city for days, perhaps longer; the relief of knowing he was alive meant that it had not occurred to her to wonder why he was not with his regiment. She supposed she would have to accept it if he were about to return to duty but, absurdly, she had a wish to shelter him, just as she now recognised his wish to protect her.

He was saying, 'I leave in half an hour. Two of us go, given the importance of the dispatches. I have Washington's from Chester, and they're to hand me the others at the State House.'

He rose to his feet as Victor said, 'We wish you a safe passage, Monsieur. You have the advantage of knowing the territory.'

'And those at journey's end,' said Gimat. 'You have fought with Daniel Morgan, have you not?'

'Yes, though I have never met General Gates.'

'*Gates?*'

They all turned to look at her. Why had she not been listening? Gates was the commander of the northern armies, beyond New York, far up the Hudson. 'North! Is that where you go?'

'Yes.' He stepped towards her. 'There was no opportunity to tell you last night.'

She gazed at him, going cold inside. Just as things had altered between them, just as she had learned at last to value his support, he was taking it away. She could guess why: this swift ride with dispatches would take him in the direction of the only place in the world he really cared about—Canada.

Her dismay was so great that she could not keep it out of her voice. 'I wonder that you choose to do this now.'

'I am ordered to do it. By General Washington.'

He drew nearer and the others, guessing from her exclamation and his controlled tone that they would prefer the conversation to be private, began a discussion of their own. But it made her upset and uncomfortable, to be tackling this momentous subject within their hearing. Once again, she longed to talk to him alone. Yet he obviously felt differently, since he had made no attempt to manage anything of the kind. Perhaps he actually preferred to have this conversation in company.

Before she could say any more he spoke again. 'Nonetheless, I could not go without first making arrangements for you. There is a coach leaving for Chester tomorrow, with an escort. Friends have checked for me: I have every confidence you will be conveyed safely. I have booked a place for you.' He took an envelope out of his pocket. 'Here are the details, with a letter from me to James and Constance Ogilvy. You will be kindly received.'

She took the envelope without looking at it. She could scarcely credit the dispassionate way he was handing her these instructions. 'I thought I had made it clear I would choose my own time to leave.'

'But circumstances have rather caught up with you. I am sure this is your best course.'

'And if I would rather direct my own?'

As she looked up into his eyes she remembered suddenly how they had seemed in the dim kitchen before he embraced her—dark forest green. Now, as they widened in the light from the window, they were the colour of mountain snow water. He said, 'I am sure you have reasons. May I know them?'

'I have made a promise and I must stay to fulfil it.'

'To whom?'

'To . . .' she glanced towards La Fayette, and faltered. Her friend had closed his eyes in exhaustion, but that did not mean he was not listening. 'To someone at Mrs Redman's.'

'I see.'

She did not like the way he said this. He was making it very difficult for her to explain, but she had to try. 'You do not understand. Ever since I came to America I have been no more than an observer. Here, for the first time, I have a chance to help. That is why I do not want to leave, not yet. You do not understand what it is like when someone really needs you.'

His expression became harder. 'I understand two things: you refuse to accept my arrangements for your welfare, and you expect me to spend God knows how long in the north without having the slightest idea where you are or what you will do next.'

She gasped. 'But you said you were only carrying dispatches! Do you not return, at once?'

'No, I am to serve with Daniel Morgan's rifle corps.'

It was a blow. It was a worse blow that he said it without a flicker of emotion. She put a hand on the windowsill and looked out at the blank wall of a neighbouring house. He had no regrets about leaving. There was only one minor matter which he needed to clear away beforehand, and that was his duty to her.

She straightened and gave a tight and unconvincing smile. 'I apologise. It ill becomes me to interfere with your plans. I can see it would be much more convenient for you if I were pigeonholed in Chester.'

She did not meet his eye, so she could not see his expression, but his voice had an edge that she well remembered when he said, 'If you are pleased to be sarcastic on such an issue, there is nothing more I can say to you.'

She flared up. 'I am not being sarcastic, I leave that to you!' Then she looked at him in despair, knowing that he had no idea how much it hurt her to be returning to the old opposition, to be wielding the weapons she foolishly believed they had put aside for good. And now those weapons were sharper, capable of inflicting much keener pain. Before he could reply she took a deep breath and tried to soften her voice. 'But please, I do not want you to think I am not grateful.'

He grimaced. 'I do not seek your gratitude, Mademoiselle.'

What then, my obedience? But she did not say it. 'I am sorry to question your decision, but I am not yet ready to flee this city. I have grown very fond of Philadelphia; I feel as though I belong here, and I shall find it hard to leave. But of course I shall, if and when it becomes necessary. You have my word on that.'

She was trying to reassure him, but his face showed only that he was baffled and angry. Not with the cold fury she once used to inspire in him; instead there was a bitterness which she had never seen before, and which for a moment or two he could not conceal.

Then his expression closed completely and he turned to address the others. 'My time is up. I must be going. I wish you all a safe journey and the best of health until we meet again. I shall send word to you as often as I can, and hope to have good news of you in return.'

The young men were solemn as they said farewell. They heard nothing in his deep tones but the unspoken thought that they shared themselves—who knew when and where they might meet again? But to Viviane, watching him move amongst them to say goodbye, the mood of this leave-taking was unbearable. His dark frown, the veiled eyes and frosty profile told her that

287

he had withdrawn to a place more remote than ever, where no word or action of hers could reach him. When he stopped before her at the last his face did not change at all, except for the hard compression of his lips as he bowed over her hand, his fingers barely touching hers.

She murmured, quietly enough for the others not to hear, 'Is there nothing more we can say?'

'You have already made yourself quite clear, Mademoiselle. And I must go.' There was a fractional pause before he said quietly, 'God bless you.' Then he turned on his heel and left the room.

Faint with disbelief, Viviane leaned against the embrasure of the window. For some time she was paralysed by what had happened. This was a quarrel far more wounding than any of the others, and it had happened at the very worst time. It was as though she had cursed him before he turned to leave, perhaps for ever.

She came to her senses after a moment, to realise that all the young men were gazing at her in alarm. Next second she was running across the room. She wrenched open the door, darted into the corridor and flew down the main staircase. Her breath sobbed in her chest as she tore open the front door and rushed out onto the steps.

He was already in the saddle. When he turned and saw her, his hands tightened on the reins, so that the gelding tossed its head and did a little dance on the paving of the street. She darted forward, oblivious of what the horse was doing, but he brought it under control, and at the same time he bent and took her outstretched hand.

She cried, 'We cannot part like this!'

'No.' His grip was so hard it hurt. 'Forgive me. It's just . . . I cannot help being afraid for you.'

'I shall take care, believe me. But what about *you*?' Her voice broke.

He said in rough mockery, 'If you cry, Mademoiselle de Chercy, I shall not be able to leave. And they will shoot me for disobeying orders.'

Still holding his hand tight with both of hers, she

said breathlessly, 'They would not do that to a French-man, surely?'

'I should prefer not to find out.'

The impatient gelding plunged sideways and their fingers slipped apart. Terrified that he would ride off before they could mend things, Viviane said with firm clarity, 'I want never to quarrel with you again. And never to disappoint you again. When you return—when we rejoice at your return—you will not receive the kind of greeting I gave you this time. I swear it.'

Something happened in the green eyes that held hers so intently—a shift, a change, that was like a sudden movement in still water, hardly visible on the surface before it sank again into the shadowy depths.

He gathered the reins up and sat erect in the saddle. Taut-backed, with its neck arched, the gelding took a few quick steps backwards, widening the gap between them.

She saw rather than heard him say the word, 'Adieu,' and as she cried the same farewell after him, he wheeled the horse, to put it straight into a canter and then fast into a gallop. As he tore away from her down the wide, echoing street, the gelding's hooves beat on the stone paving like the rattle of distant gunfire.

Viviane returned to High Street with such a strong idea of her own selfishness that she dreaded she might have let Ethan Herrold down as well; but he was still alive, though weaker, and had not regained consciousness while she was out. So this was one promise she could keep.

An overworked, exhausted surgeon came to see both men in the afternoon. He was pleased with Tom's pro-gress but gave the women no false hope for Ethan. Viviane spent as much time as she could in the sick-room, allowing Sarah to carry on with her normal life, as normal as it could be in a city that was being deserted by the hour. The road outside was full of the constant grinding of wheels on stone as people and supplies were carried away. The prices at the market began to soar. And when friends came to see Sarah, all the talk was of when the English might ride in. Viviane never went downstairs when they called.

Next afternoon she was alone in the room with Ethan while Tom was testing his recuperative powers by talking with Sarah and the children in the kitchen. Viviane sat by the still figure in the bed, staring at the opposite wall, her mind going helplessly over the same ideas again and again. She thought of the man at her side, whose life was ebbing away because of a war that had begun with the blood spilt at Lexington, more than two years before. Even then, even after that first fatal salvo, might there not have been some way to prevent this war, to negotiate with King George's ministers, as Franklin had striven so hard to do in London? Where was the crucial point when American became willing to turn against American in order to throw off the British? For the wounds were going deeper: the devastation that had driven Tom and Ethan from their homes, the relentless dedication of men and equipment to the struggle, the occupation of cities—Franklin's home town of Boston, New York. In a few weeks, perhaps a few days, Philadelphia would be wrenched from the men who had paid such a price at Brandywine; yet thousands of their compatriots were preparing to line the streets again and cheer the English in. The pain, the waste, filled her thoughts and haunted her dreams.

There was a slight movement beside her and she turned her head. She gave a start: Ethan's eyes were fixed on her in a wide, unblinking stare. With no mists behind them this time, the light grey irises had an unearthly clarity. He had been examining her; for how long, she could not tell.

He moved his lips, but she could not hear a thing.

She leaned closer and smiled at him tenderly, ashamed of the alarm she had displayed, overwhelmed by how little she had been able to help him.

He still had the reflective look that must have come over his face as he was contemplating hers.

She caught the whisper. 'No regrets.'

She was close enough to feel his faint breath on her cheek, so the words touched her like a caress. Then he closed his eyes.

Since he could not see any longer, she had no reason—nor any power—to stop the tears when they gushed out. She remained bent over him, crying almost silently though her lips were parted, and with one hand she stroked the hair off his brow. He did not move, and she could not stop weeping. Her throat and chest ached and the tears ran down her cheeks and fell, dampening the coverlet.

After a time Tom came in and, when he saw her, and Ethan's face, he went back downstairs for Sarah. Viviane only moved when her friend came and wrapped her arms around her and gently drew her away. None of them knew at which moment Ethan had died, under the rain of tears.

In the last days of September an unpleasant northeast wind that brought almost constant showers induced a mild depression in Mrs Christie, who felt there was quite enough water surrounding Philadelphia without her having to put up with a thoroughly wet autumn. She kept indoors, planning the girls' winter wardrobes, but noted uneasily that the eternal drizzle seemed not the slightest discouragement to Mademoiselle de Chercy, who went out at least twice a day.

Mrs Christie had mixed feelings about her very popular guest. In normal circumstances she would have derived undiluted pleasure from seeing her create a sensation amongst the most sophisticated citizens of Philadelphia. But there were two matters of concern: her activities and her connections.

After she returned from the Quaker household those activities seemed innocuous enough at first. Her spirits were somewhat dimmed in the evenings and she rarely performed on the pianoforte, having for some reason lost her taste for music; but she remained conversible and captivating enough for all that. During her daytime calls, however, on which Polly and Georgiana often accompanied her, she had quite different things in view.

Apparently, soon after being admitted to a house, Mademoiselle de Chercy would fix the hostess with her most charming smile and say, 'I am requisitioning today.'

Taken aback, the lady would murmur a few words of polite inquiry, whereupon the demoiselle would draw a little notebook out of her reticule and consult her list.

Her request would go something like this: 'Now, I know you could not possibly part with the beautiful horse blankets they threw over your greys when last you visited Mrs Christie. But the rug on the seat, that is the kind of thing one so constantly replaces, I daresay you would be glad to pass it on. There again, perhaps I am reading you quite wrongly, and you are about to press something entirely different upon us. You need not lift a finger once you have told me, we can collect everything.'

By the time the lady realised her guest was in earnest, some commitment had usually escaped her lips and, true to the demoiselle's word, two respectful men from the city troop would be at the kitchen door on the following day, ready to load the household's donation into a cart.

'You have no notion how disarming she is,' Polly confided.

'I don't think *dis*arming is quite the word,' her mother said smartly. 'This is not an occupation suited to a lady of our family. You and Georgiana are not to go with her in future.'

'But the army is in such need,' Georgiana said. 'When Mademoiselle de Chercy describes what it must be like for them, shifting miserably about in the rain between the Delaware and the Schuylkill—'

'They must shift without us,' said Mrs Christie. 'It is far too late to be trying to rescue *that* situation. The truth is they cannot defend Philadelphia, and we must prepare ourselves to live in a city full of Englishmen. I should prefer you not to be associated with any extremists, girls. Mark my words, there will be arrests once we are occupied. No informers will be permitted the freedom of the town once Howe takes it over. Happily we know no gentlemen likely to suffer such a fate, and I am determined that in the event your father's Tory principles will be remembered.'

'Will you tell Mademoiselle de Chercy that you disapprove of what she is doing?'

'No, I shall not be so disobliging to a guest. I hope she will come to her senses and let this drop.'

This was by no means sure to happen, however, for all the demoiselle's connections threw her the other way. The greatest disappointment among them, Mrs Christie admitted to herself with a sigh, was the Comte de Mirandol. Who would have thought that such an impeccably turned-out nobleman, such a pattern of stern masculine beauty and fine manners, would have transformed himself so quickly into a leather-girt foot soldier? Into the kind of man who could exchange her drawing rooms and her daughters for swamps and skirmishes without even the appearance of regret, and whose only mark of attention to her family in the last few weeks had been to come hammering on her door at midnight after Washington's trouncing at Brandywine?

She had felt a pang, nonetheless, when the demoiselle mentioned that he had left town again; but she rallied soon afterwards. Tactically, her immediate plans were much easier to execute if he was no longer connected with her household.

The other problematic link was of course with the Marquis de La Fayette. He and his little corps of Frenchmen had much enlivened Philadelphia salons on their arrival and, since then, having got himself wounded and gone off to recuperate elsewhere, he was more talked of than ever. Polly and Georgiana took a hopelessly romantic view of him—much more so, in point of fact, than did the demoiselle, who had to caution them against mentioning her attendance on him before he left for Bethlehem.

It was vexing to find life so complicated all of a sudden, and Mrs Christie missed her husband in such a crisis. He had been a capable man who always smoothed away every one of her troubles. Oddly enough, she had never quite agreed with him politically, for unlike him she had an instinctive resentment of English exploitation of the colonies. She had been as indignant at the imposition of the first Stamp Act as any of the guests who had railed against it in her well-frequented salon. And when the Philadelphians prevented a repetition of the Boston Tea Party by sending the next cargo of tea back down the Delaware, she shared the glee of the people who massed at the quay and stopped the ship from unloading. Her husband, however, regarded such notions with calm amusement. His contention was that England could give the colonies much more than it took away. He would be happy, he said, to cease trading with the home country and give up allegiance to the Crown when someone proved to him that he would be the richer for it. None of the other merchants furnished any such proof, and when he died his large legacy to his wife and daughters served to substantiate his views. It was partly out of respect for his memory that she steered her daughters away from expressing republican sentiments in company, and determined to receive the English occupiers with dignity.

This did not stop her from shuddering in horror when the news of Paoli came in. Despite the armies' relative proximity to each other, there had been no pitched battle since Brandywine. However, there was always the possibility that Washington would order some flying assaults, and eventually a detachment of Americans under Brigadier General Anthony Wayne was sent against part of Howe's forces. They were taken by surprise at a place called Paoli and cut to ribbons. It was a massacre; those Americans who could not flee from the scene tried to surrender, but were all bayoneted by Hessian troops.

Mademoiselle de Chercy happened to be home next afternoon, and Mrs Christie found her alone in the principal drawing room, sitting by a window looking out on the street.

'My dear, you look shattered.' A horrible thought struck her. 'Your friend Monsieur Jacob was not with Wayne?'

'No, Madame. I knew none of the men who perished yesterday. But I feel as though I did.'

Mrs Christie said affectionately, 'You will forgive me if I mention it, but it is my considered opinion that Howe will be sending Cornwallis into Philadelphia very soon. Delightful though it has been to welcome you here, I should not dream of asking you to bear our burdens and remain in an occupied city.'

Mademoiselle de Chercy gave her a shrewd look that was almost instantly replaced by a melancholy smile. 'You are very good, Madame. In your kind home, I have become a Philadelphian. And for that very reason, I must make up my mind to leave.'

On 26 September Major General Lord Cornwallis marched part of the British army into Philadelphia. He and his commanders were unfamiliar with the city, so they were guided in by two Loyalists, Enoch Story and Phineas Bond Jnr. Headed by the light horse and a military band, they entered the city along Second Street, in good order. Cornwallis rode next, at the head of the main body of troops; then followed the artillery, the Hessians, and another band. At the rear, in colourful confirmation that they had come to stay, was a caravan of carts and waggons, some of them transporting Hessian women, and countless horses and livestock. The rain had cleared at last, and the spectacle took place under an almost cloudless sky. The exuberant populace that lined the thoroughfares were mainly women and children, though some of the 4000 or more men left in the city were amongst them. A large proportion of the crowds were Quakers.

Sarah Redman stayed home that day, however, and received a surprise visit from Viviane de Chercy.

'I had half a thought thee had left town already,' Sarah remarked.

'Without saying goodbye to you? No, even Lord

Cornwallis could not chase me away as easily as that.'

'Thee knows they will be rounding up the republicans soon and naming them to the English as spies?'

Viviane replied with a little laugh, 'Yes, the great wheel is turning right enough. To tell the truth, I intended to be gone before now. But when I was ready to leave Mrs Christie, the Shippen girls cried out upon me. They told me I promised to visit with them for at least a week before I left Philadelphia. They made me feel so guilty I have consented to stay.'

'So that is why thee came to me today,' Sarah nodded. 'For the Shippens live in Second Street, do they not? And at this moment are gathered at the casement waving to the soldiery?'

'I have no idea. I only know I am exactly where I wish to be today, redcoats or no redcoats.'

As usual the three children were with their mother, and Viviane looked down and smiled at them. She had been sorely tempted to buy the youngest a fashion doll as a farewell present; but she was not at all sure that the little girl would have been allowed to play with it. Nor had it been easy to think of a present for Sarah that would not offend her morals or her pride.

She had had no trouble finding something for Tom Keane when his mother and cousin came to fetch him. They had left gladly for Prince Town, in the back of the cart a wooden box containing a tea set of Pennsylvania pencilled ware. For Mrs Christie and her daughters, she had chosen lengths of luxurious silk which they could have made into dresses in the Paris fashions they admired.

Smiling, she held out the present she had finally hit upon for Sarah and her family. 'I do hope you will accept this book and read it to the children.'

Sarah took it from her hands, scanned the title, and a slight frown appeared between her fine, straight eyebrows. The author was Benjamin Franklin and the title was *A Child's Companion to Mischief*.

'It is not quite what you might think,' Viviane said swiftly. 'It is really a collection of cautionary tales. You will all laugh together over it, I promise you. Only glance at it, and you will see what I mean. You cannot object to Franklin—he calls himself a Friend, after all.'

'True,' Sarah said with the beginnings of a smile. 'And he is a member of at least two different Philadelphia congregations as well. As thee might say, he is hedging his bets.'

They laughed and embraced.

That day, Victor de Luny was in Worcester. La Fayette had appointed him to ride about the country and gather information, a task he enjoyed principally for the opportunities he took to visit the Ogilvys in Chester. But today he was to attend a council of war in a farmhouse at army headquarters. There he was allowed to observe but not speak, and it was graciously understood that he would take notes so that he could report back to the marquis.

During the discussions Victor was very much aware of Brigadier General Anthony Wayne, who sat in the corner near him. This was the commander whose men had been slaughtered at Paoli, yet his indifference to the meeting was so obvious that he permitted himself to read a novel throughout. Victor was close enough to note the author: Tobias Smollett.

To wrap up the arguments about strategy, General Washington finally proposed an attack on Howe's division of the British forces, which was occupying Germantown. When he asked the opinion of his commanders, ten out of the fifteen spoke against the plan. The general looked gravely at them all, as though challenging them to come up with something better. Then he turned towards Wayne.

'And what would you say to this, Brigadier General?'

Wayne clapped the book shut, slammed it against his knee and cried, 'Say? I'd say nothing! I'd fight, Sir, fight!'

When they did, Victor was with them, having volunteered to join the light horse led by Captain Allen McLane of Delaware.

They marched towards Germantown all through the

night of 3 October, the idea being to attack at dawn next day and take the English by surprise. Conway's brigade and McLane's light horse were the first to meet the English when they came upon the pickets at Mount Airy. It was sunrise, but a thick fog came down; battling their way through it, they managed to capture two field pieces. Then at Beggarstown about two hundred yards away, the light infantry, the very troops responsible for Paoli, woke up to them. Wayne's division came up at this point and moved straight into action, charging in with shouts of vengeance and rushing amongst the Hessians with fixed bayonets, giving no quarter.

The light horse continued the advance as part of Sullivan's force, moving in along Germantown Road. They were supposed to join up with a second wing led by Nathanael Greene, but visibility was atrocious: the fog had been made even more dense by smoke streaming in from the backlots of the town, where acres of stubble and buckwheat had caught fire. Thus some of the troops, after being on foot fourteen hours without food and water, now had to advance into battle through fields of flame. Meanwhile Greene's men were still nearly an hour away from the spot where they were supposed to complete the grand pincer movement that Washington had so carefully worked out.

Victor soon discovered how hard it was to take a town. As they crashed through streets towards the main British line in Market Square they had to tear down fences and make their advance building by building. When some of the enemy barricaded themselves into a big, commanding stone house in their way, one of the French officers insisted it should be bypassed. The general, however, took the advice of Knox, the Chief of Artillery, and scores of lives were lost trying to capture the place, including that of Washington's deputy adjutant-general, Lieutenant William Smith. When Smith went forward under a white flag to invite the surrender of the redcoats under siege, they shot him down a few yards from the door.

It was appallingly difficult to maintain bearings while separate centres of gunfire kept on developing. The fog caused the worst confusion: when some of Wayne's men on the outskirts saw figures up ahead that seemed to be firing on them, they exchanged shots for several minutes, until they realised they were shooting at Americans.

Victor was caught right in the middle when the English made a strong advance from a road called Schoolhouse Lane and forced their way between the Americans' two main corps. From the east the Virginians tried a push in towards the centre to aid them, but met with fierce resistance. They were exhausted: one of the commanders, leading his men along Mill Road, kept falling asleep in his saddle, right in the thick of the battle. When Greene's brigades were finally turned back at Lukens Mill, the whole of the 9th Virginia Regiment was taken prisoner.

Pulling out just in time from their hopeless position in the centre, the men of the light horse began to slip away. As he tore through the outskirts with his companions, Victor was chagrined to find that once again he was taking part in a full retreat. In open country, where they had to move through some rough terrain, the retreat became panic. If the English had not stopped several times to reform their lines, they might have crippled the American forces completely. The writer Tom Paine, who served under Sullivan like Victor, later remarked how lucky it was the British pursuers kept a 'civil distance' behind them.

By the time Victor reached camp again he calculated he had covered forty-five miles during their heart-breaking manoeuvres. And he still had to get back to Bethlehem and recount the whole wretched affair to La Fayette.

He found, however, that his friend had already heard some of the details, and was nowhere near as despondent as Victor himself.

'You must learn to see it tactically, as I do.'

Victor's only reply to this was a gloomy stare, at which the marquis had the grace to blush.

'My dear friend, you have borne the brunt while I have lain here taking my ease. But what I would not give to have been with you! Still, remember what Sullivan is saying.'

'Yes, I know. He calls our retreat "a flight from victory".'

'Precisely. As he points out, if all our columns had actually been able to come together at the same time, Washington's plan would have succeeded. And you and I would be having a very different conversation.'

'I'm sorry, La Fayette, I am no soldier yet, but I know a defeat when I am in one.'

'Nonetheless, you really cannot compare this with Brandywine. The damage is nowhere near as great and the consequences are not so dire. We failed to dislodge the British from Germantown, but they have not gained an acre more of strategic territory by beating us off.'

Victor rose. 'I congratulate you if you think this disaster encouraging. I find nothing in it to sustain me.'

La Fayette's eyes went flinty with irritation for a moment, then he said, 'Forgive me. After all you have sacrificed, I have no right to lie here and tell you not to be exhausted and ground down. I have not even granted you a moment to recover. When you are fully rested, you must take some leave. Why not visit your friends in Chester?'

He knew he was forgiven when a grateful smile spread across his friend's tired face.

16

THE SORTIE

Peggy Shippen was in the grand drawing room in the house on Second Street, decorating the lacquered top of an escritoire with little spatters of ink as she wrote out a list of names, her pen streaking across the sheet of paper.

'And Mr Robbins. There, I make it eighteen. Mama can be comfortable, for we have *not* invited *every* redcoat in the quarter—only twelve, in fact.'

Viviane looked up from her embroidery. She had never been fond of prinking out little bits of linen with flowers, but during her few days at the Shippens' she had found it a good excuse for holding her tongue. The judge was a genial host to their occupiers, but Viviane could not reconcile herself to making polite conversation with the officers who visited the house.

She said, 'Robbins, the gentleman who came the other evening?'

'Yes, he is still in town.'

Viviane had not enjoyed the attentions of this New York merchant. She said without much hope, 'Does he bring his wife?'

'No indeed. You don't realise how extraordinary you are, Mamselle—there is not one lady in a thousand who would undertake travels like yours! He has left his wife at home and come to seek opportunities here, while Philadelphia flies the Union Jack.' Peggy dusted sand over her paper and sprang up as her sister entered the room.

'Here is the list, and I have put Captain John André at the head, just for your benefit.'

Betsy gave her younger sister a quick glance, smiled in a slightly superior way and ran her eye down the page. 'Mama asked me to make sure it is a balanced group—if we are to be asked to their balls, the right gentlemen must feature.' Then she nodded and handed it back to Peggy. 'I believe it will do. Though I had as lief they were American officers; and I'm sure Mademoiselle de Chercy shares my thoughts.'

'Mamselle would like at least *one* to be French. Someone tall, with a black mane and a voice like a honey bear's, would you not?'

Peggy laughed slyly at Viviane but Betsy protested: 'You do jump to conclusions, sister mine. Just because a lady is admired does not mean she must care for one admirer more than another.' She smiled at Viviane. 'Apropos of tonight, I shall ask Mama to seat Mr Robbins further down the table from you. I saw the look you gave him the other evening and I could see he quite destroyed your appetite!'

'You are mistaken,' Viviane said swiftly, then paused at Betsy's confused look. 'I mean, as to my guardian. He certainly does not—' She stopped again, then said, 'Let your mother place Mr Robbins where she will. I should never presume to dictate to such a considerate hostess.'

As it happened, Robbins sat opposite her at supper and paid her constant attention. His idea of amusing gallantry was to tease her on the subject of the Frenchmen under Washington's command. He told a story about the general's assertion that American men were much taller than the French; to prove his point, Washington had had all the officers rise to their feet at once around his dinner table, and the French lost the competition.

Suppressing the urge to floor him with the example of Comte de Mirandol, Viviane instead said sweetly, 'The brain is a very heavy organ, Monsieur, which keeps my countrymen from growing tall. All we can conclude from the comparison is that American officers carry their brains in their legs.'

A portly English officer sitting next to Robbins joined heartily in the laughter. 'Is it an advantage, though, to be top-heavy with intelligence? Eh, Mamselle? What about your compatriot Coudray—it might have been his weighty head, now, that toppled him into the Delaware.'

'Coudray?' Robbins said, turning his fleshy face to his neighbour.

'The French engineer who was planning and super-
vising the fortifications on the river. He was drowned
out there, not long since.'

'We have not seen the last of the French engineers,
however.' The speaker was Captain John André, a
handsome, fair-haired Englishman who was already
a favourite with the Shippen women. 'I have been
making a survey of the river forts, and I hear there is
a Captain de Fleury due to join the Americans soon on
Mud Island.'

One of his superior officers gave him a level look
and he went on with his meal, leaving the remark
hanging in the air. Viviane did not wonder at the
officer's wish for caution, but she did not see what
informers for either side could possibly gain from the
knowledge that John André was drawing up maps and
reports on the Pennsylvania navy, or with the news
about Fleury.

Robbins fixed his keen grey eyes on her again. 'Have
you met either of these Frenchmen?'

'No,' she said truthfully. 'My friends are all in the
Continental Army.'

The hostess gave her a swift glance at this frank
statement but said nothing. The situation in Philadelphia under the new occupation was delicate and
confusing. In the first few days, parties of Loyalists had
roamed the streets, marking houses with chalk and
making citizens' arrests of supposed republicans, so
that the Walnut Street gaol was soon filled to over-
flowing. Much to Tory resentment, General Howe
ordered the release of these political prisoners and
restored order. Mistrust was rife; with Washington's
troops only fourteen miles inland at Whitemarsh,
patrols tried to keep surveillance of anyone leaving or
entering the city, but much information, of varying
usefulness, naturally leaked in and out of Philadelphia.

The portly officer said, 'I conclude it will be in your
interests, Mr Robbins, when our navy manages to lift
the chevaux-de-frise and give safe passage up the
Delaware?'

'Indeed. If that happens I shall sail down with the

303

first shipment from New York myself—I would miss no opportunity of seeing my good Philadelphian friends again.' He gave Viviane an insinuating smile.

After the meal he attached himself to her, quite unconcerned that his banter was not to her taste.

'Mamselle, you must be my engineer and explain to me these chevaux-de-frise that everyone talks of so fluently. I nod my head when anyone mentions 'em but I'm hazy about what makes 'em so formidable.'

'They are underwater barriers, Sir, that are laid across the shipping lane of the Delaware. They are made of heavy spikes of wood and metal. The English navy tries constantly to raise them so the ships can sail up the river. But they are attacked from this side by the Pennsylvania navy. And the chevaux-de-frise are protected also by the forts on the islands.'

'And it's French ingenuity that put 'em in place, eh? I hate to tell you so, Mamselle, but that won't be enough to halt the British. Galleys and fire ships cannot hold out for ever against warships. The forts will fall and the sea horses will be set loose and English frigates will soon be anchored off Philadelphia. So you'll be besieged by land *and* water, I fear.' He put his hand on the velvet seat of the sofa and leaned closer towards her: 'A bird in a velvet cage.'

She had no idea why, but it was even harder to put up with the persistent Mr Robbins this evening. She rose and looked around the room. Everyone else was occupied and she could not think of an excuse to abruptly join some other group and leave him sitting alone. She nodded to him, said, 'Excuse me, Sir, I shall just go and fetch my embroidery,' and glided out of the room.

He had so few manners that she knew he was quite likely to get up and follow her into the hall, so instead of heading across it for the stairs she darted down a corridor which led to the library and breakfast room. The library door was open; she went in and shut it behind her, then crossed the room, which was lit only by a fire, to an alcove where she sometimes came to read. There was a curtain, which she pulled across—it ought to be beyond even him to come looking for her, but she would remain out of sight for a few minutes at least.

There was no sound of pursuit, just a loud knock on the front door followed by urgent voices in the hall, then her part of the house fell silent again. She felt foolish, sitting in the dark alcove staring at the wall. She had made an unsophisticated retreat from a relatively harmless guest, but somehow she was too upset to stay and do battle with him. With this strange sense of defeat came the sudden realisation that she had made a huge mistake remaining in the city, despite the kindness of the Shippens. The sooner she found a way to leave, the better.

Then she stiffened: she could hear the library door opening. But it was not Robbins who entered, for at once she heard and recognised the voices of two men—John André and his superior.

'I want a quick word with you, Captain. Shut the door.'

André said as the door closed, 'About the message, Colonel?'

'Yes. We must act at once. And we have need of your reports: can you lay hands on them tonight?'

'Yes, Sir.'

'Good. You will leave here, collect them at once and bring them to headquarters. It's urgent: I believe we've a chance of blowing a hole in the river defences off Mud Island.'

'But that's where the Americans are strongest, Sir! And only their own pilots know the passages through the chevaux-de-frise.'

'Well, we've got our hands on a pilot, and he's turned coat. Not only that, we possess tonight's password for all American vessels that seek to pass by or land on Mud Island. We must seize the opportunity, for we'll never have another like it.'

'The navy will attack in force?'

'Not until tomorrow. Tonight, one vessel must prepare the way. A boat is to put out from the Jersey shore towing a chain of mines.'

'We have *mines*, Sir?'

'Low rafts, loaded with explosives. They should be invisible behind the boat in the dark. She'll signal the password by lantern to Fort Mifflin on Mud Island as she approaches, to avoid being fired on. Above the first frame she'll position a raft and light a slow fuse. Then on to the next. The rafts will all be timed to blow at once, at which point the boat will have to skip lively to go free.'

'It's a brave plan, Sir. But will the concussions go deep enough to damage the chevaux-de-frise?'

'What else can you suggest? There's no show of grappling them and hauling them out. It will be done at low tide, to give the best chance possible. If it destroys enough frames, our warships can be warped through at dawn. Your charts are vital—we have to know exactly where to place the charges.'

'Where am I to take them, Sir?'

'To Commodore Hamond. Then it's the navy's job to get a vessel across and up the Jersey shore and accomplish the manoeuvre in the dark. Dismissed, Captain. I'll make your excuses here and you'll report to me in fifteen minutes.'

In a moment both men had left the library. Viviane sat frozen, thinking it through. She could see no flaw in the plan. Cornwallis's headquarters were just along the road in Second Street itself. André could collect the charts in no time, attend the briefing and race south with an escort. If he met no Pennsylvania militia patrols on the way he would get through to the English gun batteries on the large tract of swampland known as Carpenter's Island, on the Pennsylvania shore directly opposite Fort Mifflin. From there he would be assisted to slip downriver to the English fleet, moored not far above Chester.

There was nothing she could do to stop him, nor anyone she could turn to with the information, for all the allies she knew and trusted were gone from the city.

Unable to stay still a second longer, she left the room, went quickly along the corridor, across the empty hall and up the stairs. As she reached her chamber, she heard below her the sound of the officer's voice as he took his leave. Colonel Bellamy, that was his name! It was important to remember every detail when she handed on the information.

And with this instinctive thought came the solution: where André went, so could she. Faster, and more directly—downriver, straight to the fort. The Pennsylvania navy commanded the city shores and all of the Delaware above Mud Island, so André could not take to the river until he was below it. But she might, if there was a boat to carry her. And she knew exactly where to look for one.

Viviane had had no difficulty threading her way through the back streets towards the southern end of town, but she ran out of luck once she neared her destination, which was the cluster of buildings around the old wharves at the mouth of Dock Creek. She rounded a corner one street from the shore and found herself face to face with two British soldiers of the night watch.

She stopped at once and pulled tightly around her the plain cloak she had lifted from the housekeeper's room at the Shippens'. Concealed underneath it were all the things she had decided to bring with her, wound tightly around her body.

The soldiers held no lantern, since in the main streets of this city they could rely on the public lighting. It was not bright here, however, as they had stopped between two street lanterns, and they had to lean close to examine her.

'What are you doing here?' the taller one demanded.

She curtseyed and made no effort to amend her French accent as she said, 'Good evening, M'sieur. My lady 'as sent me on an errand.'

'A maid? Alone at this time of night?' the other said, his eyes growing keener. 'Where are you off to?'

She raised her face. 'M'sieur, let me proceed, I beg of your kindness. I go to ze midwife. My lady . . .'

The taller soldier gazed at her with greater interest;

she might have a very rotund body under the voluminous cloak, but he found her face uncommonly beautiful. 'And who may your mistress be?'

'Mrs Wharton, Monsieur, of Fif' Street. Zey could spare only me to run for ze *accoucheuse*. Please let me go. It is of ze urgency.'

'Perhaps I could escort her, Sergeant?' the second soldier offered.

The other looked at him sternly while Viviane held her breath. It was obvious neither of them would be averse to abandoning the watch and accompanying her on her way. But at last the sergeant shook his head: the Whartons, who lived on Society Hill, would be unlikely to allow their expensive French maid ever to fraternise with the English rank and file. Pursuit tonight would be fruitless; besides, duty called.

'You may go. Tell your mistress we would not stand in your way on such an errand. Otherwise, consider yourself warned.'

She curtseyed again and passed by. The other gazed down at her and murmured, 'Our compliments to Mrs Wharton, Mamselle. When next I go by Fifth Street I shall inquire how she does.'

'Of course,' Viviane said breathlessly, and hurried on.

She could feel their gaze on her until she reached the dark collection of buildings at the end of the street and plunged into a side lane. She had been here before on a requisitioning excursion, to inspect some dry goods which were stored in one of the Willings' warehouses by the river. Mrs Willing had given her leave to choose a few sacks and arrange for them to be picked up by the Philadelphia Light Horse the next day. While she was there, word of her purpose reached the inhabitants of the back lane and she was touched to be given more gifts for the cause by some of the local householders.

One of them was a handsome black woman who handed her a roll of canvas through the carriage window as she left. 'We got no call for this no mo', Missy. Take it and welcome.'

A white woman not far off sneered at her, 'Since when do the likes of you care what happens to the Pennsylvania militia? We all know where your man is—down at Carpenter's Island working for the English!'

To Viviane's surprise, the only reaction to this jibe was a slow wink, directed at Viviane as the young woman stepped away from the vehicle. In a languid voice she murmured, 'He gone fishin again, that fo' sho'. Different kind of fish, is all.'

Since the English had taken over Philadelphia, many workmen had been tempted downriver to build the fortifications, especially those, like the woman's husband, whose livelihood had been taken away by the war. First the Continentals and then the English had commandeered all the vessels they could find, from both sides of the Delaware, so the commerce of fishing and river transport had been gradually suspended. Now scores of unemployed Philadelphia workmen were accepting the English offer of eight shillings a day to labour on the gun posts that were being constructed on the Pennsylvania shore of the river.

After the woman's ironical comment, however, Viviane had left with the strong impression that the absent husband was doing more than digging earthworks—he was mining for information as well, which he and others had found a way to pass on to the Patriots.

Even in the dark it was possible to make out the door from which the black woman had emerged that day. It was set in the windowless wall of a long wooden building, right on Dock Creek, which looked to be a boathouse or storehouse or both.

Her three quiet knocks were not answered. She repeated them a little more loudly, praying that she would not wake the neighbourhood. Inside a yard further down the lane a dog barked.

Next thing, however, the latch lifted, the door opened slightly and a face appeared in the gap; the whites gleamed in the woman's large eyes, which narrowed at once in disappointment and suspicion.

Viviane said softly, 'I am sorry to come at this hour. Forgive me. I met you not long ago—you gave me a tarpaulin for the Continentals. I have just got by the soldiers. May I come in and speak to you?'

'Yo' name, Missy?'

'Viviane de Chercy.'

Her face and form meant nothing to the woman, but somehow her name did: the door opened wider and at once she stepped inside. When it closed behind her she was standing in pitch darkness, but without a word the other began to move away, the floorboards creaking as she went. Viviane picked her way after her, across a wide floor in the direction of several large pale squares that began to form in the blackness: windows, looking out on the water. She did not dare speak, for it was obvious the woman was cautious about their voices reaching the ears of neighbours beyond the timber walls.

In the far corner was the head of a staircase that plunged steeply to ground level. As she felt her way down in the other's wake, Viviane suddenly saw a golden shaft of light spill across the foot of the stair, for a door had been opened onto a brightly lit room.

She paused in the doorway. The lodgings within consisted of a fair-sized kitchen with a wood range, and beyond it a space that was bedroom, storeroom and workroom in one. Viviane could see nets and rods hanging on the wall at one end, a workbench in the middle with the half-completed keel of a boat on top, and at the other end a couch covered in blankets. It was a warm, welcoming sight, and even the scents were inviting, for the delicious smell of fresh bread was creeping from the oven and Viviane caught the tang of new sawdust from the room beyond. The husband, it seemed, might not always be as far away as the neighbours reckoned.

She stepped in. 'Do you remember me? I came to fetch supplies from the Willings' factory not long ago.' The woman, who was standing by the table gazing at her, wrinkled her eyebrows and put one slender hand over her mouth. Realising why she was tempted to

310

laugh, Viviane said with a smile, 'I have not grown fat in the interval! I have all my things about me.' She opened her cloak. 'I must leave Philadelphia tonight.'

She watched the large brown eyes carefully and saw the amusement die. She waited.

'Missy.' It was a low voice, smooth as velvet. 'Mah name's Miriam.' She gestured: 'You safe to take off those things and set down. Why you come here?'

Viviane did as she was told, unwinding the layers of clothing, being careful not to dislodge the money and jewellery invisibly wrapped into the folds, and sat down at the table. Warmth from the stove reached her through the travelling dress she wore against the cold October night. She took a slow breath, trying for the calm that this dignified young woman had shown from the first.

'I need a boat. I must get down the river to Mud Island tonight. Can you help? Do you know where I might hire a boat? Or buy one?'

Miriam put her head on one side, considering. 'I might. If'n I knowed why.'

Viviane told her everything, since she had no choice but to trust her, and also because there was something indefinably comforting about her solemn, curious gaze. As she listened, Miriam sank down at the end of the table, tilted her chin and rested it on two bent fingers and her thumb, with the other two fingers pressing into the satiny skin under her cheekbone. Despite her ease of manner on the day they met, Viviane had rather expected her to be shy or confused at this visit, but the intent eyes were unwavering. Miriam was no slave or serving woman, and she presided over her kitchen with the same confidence as Sarah Redman.

Viviane finished by saying, 'I thought that if I could put a small boat out from the shore without being seen, I could row down to Mud Island. The tide is going out, is it not?' Miriam nodded. 'So the current will assist me. Then I can tell someone at the fort what the English are trying to do. There may be a Frenchman there, called Fleury. I'm sure I can get him to listen.'

Miriam shook her head, her eyes wide. 'You know

nothin about the rivuh, the sho's, the islands. Nothin like what mah man and me know.'

'I realise that. But maybe that doesn't matter. I may be challenged by a Pennsylvania ship on the way. Then I shan't need to land on the island at all—they can convey the message for me.'

'Where you goin' then?'

'I'll try to land below Mud Island and get through to Chester by land. I'm not coming back to Philadelphia. That's why I'm prepared to buy a boat—I can't promise the owner would ever see it again.'

Miriam shook her head again. Then she got up from the chair, took a cloth and opened the range door. She peered in for a moment, before using a flat wooden paddle to lift out two golden loaves of bread and slide them onto the pale, scrubbed tabletop. The rich aroma of the bread began to fill the room as she checked the fires on each side of the red-hot oven and clanked the iron doors shut on them. 'They'll keep.'

Then she stood looking at Viviane, the hand that held the oven cloth balanced lightly on her hip. 'Me and mah man, we got but one boat now and it ain't goin' out of mah sight.'

Viviane said, 'Won't you even consider selling it to me?'

'I'll go with you. I'll take this he' bread down to mah man, like I done befo'. On the way I'll take you to the fo't. Then we land downstream so you can get to Chestuh.'

Viviane rose. 'Would you really do that? But it's dangerous. I don't like to ask you.'

'Ain't no way you goin' alone, not in *mah* boat!' The voice was peremptory, but behind the large eyes was a glimmer of the ironical humour that Viviane had seen there before.

Mud Island was aptly named for two reasons: at high tide most of it except the fort at the southern end was underwater; and all of it could be flooded at will by opening the dykes built to protect Fort Mifflin, which had been erected in 1772 and had undergone very little improvement since. What usefulness it possessed was due to its original designer, an English captain named John Montresor, whose present task, as irony would have it, was to destroy his own handiwork, from the batteries on the Pennsylvania shore.

Fort Mifflin had been taken over by the American commander, Colonel Smith, and his staff the day after the English walked into Philadelphia. Its most secure line of defence was the zigzag freestone wall which had been built facing the river on the south side, and which also extended along most of the east side, though it ended upriver in an earth embankment and a deep ditch. Urgent work had begun on the rest of the perimeter, and now a palisade of pine logs fifteen inches thick, built along the north and west, completed the enclosure of the barracks, the officers' quarters to the south and the wooden blockhouses in three corners.

Miriam furnished these details as she rowed her shallow-bottomed river boat on a tricky course down the shores of the Delaware. They had slipped from the mouth of the creek like an otter from its lair, intent on their own stealthy movement, avoiding rock and shallow, treacherous eddy and dark shoal; unable, in that mute crisis, to worry about eyes that might follow them from the fringes of the city. As it was, on that black night no one saw or challenged them in their silent glide downstream.

Viviane did no rowing. From the moment Miriam unslung the skiff from its hiding place beneath the piles of the boatshed, she had spurned any assistance. When Viviane offered to take the oars for a while, she laughed, with a gurgle in the back of her throat that echoed the river itself. Once they were under way, however, Viviane, facing forward, her hood pulled well over her face, was placed to tell Miriam what the night and the water indicated beyond.

She became Miriam's eyes as the dark river revealed its swirling, shimmering expanses by the faint light of the stars; Miriam's whispered questions called forth her powers to describe and analyse, teaching her lessons about a river which she had never learnt in all her childhood wanderings by the Loire. As they skirted islands of reeds, promontories of slick water that bulged with hidden menace, she learned the Delaware in the way that a hand comes to know a smooth, sinewy body, lying still under the fingers, but ready to rise and respond, violently at one instant, languidly seductive at another, to each caress.

Where the current was swift, Miriam would stop rowing and lean forward on her oars. Viviane bent low also, to shrink the black silhouette they made on the water, and take the chance to speak softly with her companion.

The lights of the city had long dimmed behind them and, scanning the wide river across to the invisible New Jersey shore, they could make out no sign of any other vessels. Viviane guessed that Miriam did not wish to be questioned by the Pennsylvania navy; she and her man, Jake, wanted no relationship with any kind of authority. They had once been slaves in South Carolina, but when they were granted their freedom they moved north, looking for a new life. They had chosen Philadelphia. Jake began working on the river, and she took in laundry. With their savings they managed to buy the skiff and join the flotilla of transport vessels on the Delaware. Later they invested in a larger boat, which the Pennsylvania navy had requisitioned.

Viviane was going to ask why Jake had not joined the navy once his civilian career was cut short, but she refrained. She knew there were black men in the galleys, guard boats and fire ships on the Delaware, but she was not sure how well they were treated. Jake had chosen his work where he wanted it, downriver, and was accorded a certain independence by his English masters, who turned a blind eye when he slipped away at night to meet Miriam, unaware that he now and then made contact with the Pennsylvania militia and gave them the latest information about the batteries. The rendezvous for both assignations was a hut, hidden not far from a narrow creek south of the

English positions, which belonged to a Patriot farmer.

Viviane had stowed all her things in a sack Miriam had given her, and pushed them under the thwart where she sat. Under Miriam's were the two warm loaves, wrapped in a cloth and placed in an oilskin bag with other supplies for Jake.

'You figured right, did you but know. I was comin' down tonight anyways. Cain't hea' no cannon tonight, so the's no ships fightin' in midstream. We can move out soon and row down the far side of the island. Slip down that reach so I can set you down on the bank under the fo't where the's no palisade.'

'Do you think they will let us approach?'

'Better they don't see us till we land. But if'n you know the passwo'd, now ... Did you hea' it?'

'No,' Viviane whispered. 'Why, do you have a lantern?'

'Sho' have. But we cain't use it. If'n they fi' on us, lay in the bottom of the boat till it hits the bank. Then holluh out that name—what you say it was?'

Viviane told her.

François Louis de Fleury was sitting in the gloom playing Telemann. One dim candle on the opposite side of the room flickered above a few sheets of music, but the notes bubbled up out of memory, in a bright, fluent cascade strenuously directed towards calm.

It worked, of course, even here. The flute, which had travelled better than he, poured out the full, rounded notes like pearls over black velvet. When he swayed forward from the chair at the beginning of each run, he saw the candle wink at the ivory tip, beyond the active blur of his little finger. Seduced into a new complicity of light and rhythm, he mastered his energies to maintain the exact tempo of the piece, remembering, pleasingly, just where to take each covert breath, then failing to breathe at all for a while once it was over, sitting as still as the instrument on his knee, staring into the tiny haze of light on the other side of the room.

When the problems marched back into his head, he lined them up dispassionately and counted them off. The bank of the western ditch, which must be raised to protect the palisades; the main battery, suicidally exposed to ricochet and horizontal shot; the lack of a last-resort defence within the walls. There should be fraised work in a tide ditch to protect the battery; they needed mines and blinds to counter bombs and small shells; and the men he had seen today were so wretchedly provided for that they worked in the cold half naked.

Colonel Smith had been doing his damnedest without an engineer; now the colonel was aware how much better he could do once—if—the right supplies and men came in. He himself had arrived earlier than expected, so in principle he had a few spare days in which to register all the other lacunae of Fort Mifflin. Meanwhile Smith, whom he was thus assisting to look as intelligent as possible, could order in what was needed. He would add his own voice when the real work started. It was a matter of timing.

The knock on the door, when it came, was doubly impertinent: he had no official duties at present, and even if he had, any sentry should hesitate to rouse an officer in the small hours of a black and silent morning. The visitation could hardly be prompted by the sonata: in these anchoritic quarters they had assigned him, all it was likely to awaken were the rats.

He got to his feet, laid the flute on the chair and said penetratingly, '*Entrez.*'

The excuse, which the soldier gave with a tolerable admixture of apology, was hallucinatory: outside was a woman from Philadelphia who had just waded across the shoreline with a military escort, while her Negro companion waited in a rowboat under guard.

'And the colonel sends her to *me*?'

'Colonel Smith is asleep, Sir.'

'Then you may re-employ your talents and wake him.'

'Beg pardon, Sir, but the lady asked for you. By name, Sir.' Not by description? Hair yellow, eyes blue-grey, fortune undisclosed, some military credentials, last seen heading for a depopulated ruin on a mudbank . . .

'You desolate me. But since I appear to be awake, show her in.'

A cloaked form appeared in the doorway; he bowed and, as he straightened, she murmured his name. She threw back the hood.

The startling hazel eyes examined him ironically, but the voice conveyed no unjust pique as she said in French, 'Telemann has journeyed here with you, Monsieur? I confess that Mozart crosses every border with me.'

He stepped back, retrieved the flute and gestured for her to be seated. She looked around the room, observed that the only other place to sit was the truckle bed, and lowered herself gracefully onto the chair, the drab cloak parting to reveal fine brocade clasped around an exquisite figure. He rescued his gaze from discourtesy by transferring it to floor level and inflecting it with concern.

'Mademoiselle, you appear to have crossed the Styx in a sieve!'

She did not even glance at the caked shoes, the sodden hems of dress and cloak. 'My name is Viviane de Chercy. I came to Philadelphia with my uncle, the Comte de Mirandol, and the company of the Marquis de La Fayette. I have been in the city since the occupation and I have just learnt that tonight, at low tide, there will be an attempt by the English to destroy the chevaux-de-frise on this stretch of the Delaware, directly out there.' She pointed.

'Where you have just come from,' he said slowly.

'Indeed.' She told him, succinctly, what she had heard when she lingered in the alcove of the Shippens' mansion and eavesdropped on two English officers. Distracted by the image, he was almost sorry when she moved on to the rest, omitting only the name of the Negro woman who had assisted her.

When she finished he realised he was still holding the flute. Wondering briefly whether Mozart ever composed for the solo instrument, he laid it on the table by the candle and turned.

'Describe the proposed manoeuvre to me again, if you please.'

She did so, then looked at him steadily, the wide eyes, like gilded mirrors, each containing a candle flame. It appeared he owed her a sketch of the outcome.

'This is what I shall propose, Mademoiselle. When we spy any vessel approaching from the direction of New Jersey, even if it flashes the password, we shall send up a flare to observe it.'

'What if it is a Pennsylvania galley?'

'It will take the flare as a warning and withdraw.'

'You might expose them to fire!'

'But we shall also alert them to the possible presence of an enemy vessel.'

'I see. And if the flare shows you a boat towing mines—' there was a fractional hesitation, 'the fort will open fire?'

'Exactly.'

She swallowed. 'What are your chances of destroying the vessel?'

Given what he had seen today, precious few unless the target were a floating blockhouse. He answered the unspoken question: 'Mademoiselle, they must signal for safe passage before they are in position over the chevaux-de-frise. If they continue to approach, we shall aim *over* the vessel, at the rafts.'

The candles leaped in the depths of each mirror. 'So, they must either withdraw or see their weapons blown up before they are of use.'

'Precisely. I shall order the lookouts posted at once. Pray excuse me.'

When he came back into the room, she had risen. He said, 'Now, Mademoiselle, allow me to thank you for your information and your splendid courage. And to arrange some accommodation for you and your servant.'

'I should prefer your permission to leave.'

'To where?'

'My companion has promised to take me to a rendezvous further south. Then I shall make my way to an inn on the Chester road. By daylight I shall get some kind of transport to the town, where I have friends who expect me. There are no British troops in Chester at present, I believe?'

'No, but—'

'My companion must make this rendezvous tonight, otherwise she is in danger. Her movements, and those of the man she is meeting, must not be known to the English.'

'Two women, alone?'

'We have come unscathed thus far, Monsieur. And women may pass where a boatload of men could never go. If we are challenged, I shall lie in the bottom of the boat as though I am ill, and my companion will say she is taking me to my family along the shore.'

'You cannot go without protection.' He swung on his heel and went to the other end of the room, where the two bulky rolls of canvas in which he carried his effects were still flung out like a tinker's wares on the floor. But no tinker could have fashioned the piece of craftsmanship he brought back to her.

Unexpectedly, she took it from him at once, the better to admire the polished wood, the delicate incisions on the steel. If she noted the double D engraved on the barrel, she would be unlikely to guess that he was giving away a family heirloom; so he resisted the temptation to tell her the initials were those of a woman.

He watched her hands. 'You know how to use it.'

'The Comte de Mirandol taught me. After much persuasion. We were on board ship—he consented only because our target practice was over the side.'

He returned to his luggage and picked out the rest of the gear. 'You load it thus.' She watched him collectedly and nodded when it was done. 'The powder horn is in the bag also.' He handed it to her and she took it and the pistol, but then shook her head.

'This is precious. Of Spanish make, is it not?' When astonishment kept him silent, she continued, 'And you have far greater use for it than I.'

'Mademoiselle, if you will not accept it for yourself, consider it a gift between gentlemen. I have heard of the Comte de Mirandol, from men who hold him in the highest regard. When you meet him again, pray present this to him with my compliments.'

'You are very good, Monsieur.' Her eyes met his and he noted, with disproportionate regret, that their vivid glow was for the receiver of the weapon, not the giver.

'On the contrary, I am just one French volunteer paying tribute to another in a war that is not our own. To *two* others.' He bowed over her hand. When he raised his head he saw that the last golden smile was all for him.

Miriam seemed to have found the narrow creek by feel rather than sight, and now she propelled the skiff inland with a single oar, digging into the shallow bed and pushing the boat against the sluggish current of dead low tide. Bushes grew thick along the banks and occasionally the bare branches of trees arched overhead. There was no wind, and sounds reached the women clearly in the still air—the rustle of some night creature making its retreat under a nearby hedge, a dog barking in a distant farmyard and, still further off, the faint thudding of hooves.

The first shot, when it came, fell on their ears like a blow: a single detonation from a cannon upriver. Miriam plunged the oar into the sand and held onto it while they both stood up in the boat, which gently rocked as they watched the sky to the northeast. Suddenly a glow was visible: they could not see the flare itself, but its incandescence spread through the frigid air above the river like haze around a giant candle.

They waited, breathless, for half a minute, then Miriam motioned Viviane to sit down again. She had explained that the stealthy passage up the creek would not take long, but they would then have to skirt several fields by creeping through a wide copse of trees, before they reached the dense woods leading up into the hills, and the hut where she always met Jake. Speed was their greatest ally at this point. The stretch from the shore to the woods was the most exposed part of their journey, for an English mounted patrol might well pass by: they often made a silent sweep of the countryside at some distance from the batteries, varying their direction each time, to discourage forays into the area by the Pennsylvania militia.

Viviane listened intently in case the hoofbeats became audible again, but she failed to distinguish any before the second burst of fire began. The pounding woke the echoes along the wide river behind them, reverberating from shore to shore across the low islands and deep-running water. Intermittent bursts continued while Miriam found the spot to leave the boat, where it could be tugged up a slender tributary of the stream and lie under a clump of evergreens whose branches, tangled together over the ditch, provided complete concealment.

By the time the two women had hauled the skiff into position and taken their burdens further up the embankment, the crash of cannon fire upriver had ceased. There had been no massive explosions, so Viviane knew that the guns from the fort could not have hit the mines. She tried to visualise the enemy vessel turning to withdraw, towing its armoury back to the New Jersey shore. She tried not to visualise shattered bodies in the dark water.

As she followed Miriam quietly along the higher ground and then into the trees, there was the merest hint of more light in the sky. But it did not penetrate under the canopy of pines or show them the way through the scrubby underbrush. Miriam reached behind, took Viviane's hand, and with her soft, warm clasp guided her through the gloom.

To either side of the broad copse, fields of pasture were visible between the tree trunks. Viviane made out the black forms of cattle here and there, feeding peacefully. Once she caught sight of two riderless horses, their heads lifted, standing together by a rail fence on the other side of a paddock, and her fingers involuntarily clenched Miriam's.

Then, with not a breath of warning, a rider was upon them, looming between two massive trees on the other side of a kind of clearing. They reacted instinctively, darting at once into the low bushes on each side of the place of encounter.

He had been waiting motionless for their approach; now he urged the horse forward, and above the hollow sound of its hooves they heard a click and then made out the movement as he brought a long rifle to his cheek. The gap in the canopy above allowed the faintest of early morning light to drift down and outline his form as he spoke: he wore a dark cape over a red coat, and a black forage cap.

'Show yourself or I shoot.'

The well-trained horse responded to another signal and took a few sliding diagonal steps to prevent the soldier presenting a target himself. His loud voice was perfectly steady, however, and so was the rifle that pointed at the bush behind which Viviane crouched, her hands on the stony ground. Her thoughts raced: he believed he had surprised just one person; he was not really sure of that person's position.

She made a swift movement and he fired. The bullet whipped through the leaves and thudded into the ground behind the bushes further to her right, where she had just flung a stone.

He moved at once, sending the horse crashing through the foliage after it, then wheeled amongst the trees, cursing, while he reloaded the rifle.

She had perhaps fifteen seconds. Miriam, a few yards to her left, shifted position, as though she were about to make a run for it, then changed her mind and froze.

As the soldier executed another rapid turn through the trees, Viviane dug furiously in the sack beside her and, absurdly, began counting in her head. She found the small bag and opened it. The powder felt dry. Then the horseman re-entered the clearing. This time, as Viviane rose to her feet, unseen, she could distinguish him with electrifying clarity—the solid form, the sheen of boot and buckle, the pale profile laid avidly against the sleek butt of the rifle. Which was pointing straight at the place where Miriam was hidden.

Viviane fired.

The soldier pitched out of the saddle, the rifle flew from his hand, and the horse gave a great start, shuddered and then stood still. The man had fallen heavily on the other side. The two women rushed forward and reached him at once, but it was Miriam who bent close to examine him.

She raised her face to Viviane, her eyes gleaming. 'You got him in the shoulder.' She flung him onto his back. 'Winded him too.' The soldier's eyes flicked open but he could not move.

'Quick,' Viviane said, 'grab his rifle.'

As Miriam obeyed, Viviane swept up the horse's reins and mounted, tucking her skirts high. 'Throw me our things.' The soldier gasped and stirred. 'Now get up behind me.'

'I cain't ride!'

'You can now. Put one foot in the stirrup, here, and swing up, I've got you. And hold tight. They'll have heard the shots: they'll be here any second. Let's go.'

The soldier struggled into a sitting position and cried out as his horse, neatly side-stepping him, responded to Viviane's heels and lunged out of the clearing.

The charge through the pine plantation was painful. Dry twigs whipped at them, Miriam clung to Viviane with a convulsive grip that threatened to topple them both, and they stayed on only because the sure-footed horse managed not to stumble or to wipe them off against some overhanging branch. And all the while Viviane had in mind the vile idea that it knew its way so well because it had come through the copse already—towards them. Which meant that the hooves she now heard—distinct from, more concentrated and much fainter in sound than those of their own mount— were approaching from in front.

Then all at once they were out on open ground. Miriam twisted and gave a groan—two fields back, streaming out of the pines where they had left the redcoat, were five riders.

Viviane registered them without letting the horse slacken pace. There was a ditch ahead with a low hedge at the top; in a few strides they were over them both, with Miriam still precariously up behind. The cattle tracks on the other side, deep and fairly straight, led to a byre, flanked by the edge of a wood that was so dense it looked drawn in Indian ink against the subtle charcoal hues of the farmland.

The light was changing further: it was fractionally easier to see. It was easier to be seen. They had to reach the wood before the other riders cleared ditch and hedge and got them in their sights again.

The horse flew beneath them, its hooves drumming on the firm turf beside the cattle tracks, its strong neck and head pumping with a powerful rhythm. Viviane leaned low over its neck and Miriam, her hands around her waist, moulded herself to her back. Viviane twisted one hand in the flying mane and reached the other along the warm, glossy neck. She had never loved an animal so keenly.

Then they were in the trees and Viviane, panting, threw herself to the ground, pulled Miriam down after her and hissed, 'Run.'

Next, without a second to spare for a grateful word, she yanked the horse's head towards the lower ground within the margin of the trees and moved to its flank. As she hit it twice, sharply, with the pistol butt, tears leaped to her eyes. Without further prompting, it careered off through the trees, and she darted into cover and peered out.

Down the track she could just discern the ragged group of riders breast the rise. Then they wheeled and came straight for the wood. They could hear the fleeing horse, even if they had not yet seen it.

She shot up the slope after Miriam.

In the last quiet before dawn, before even the birds began to stir, the women sat in the dark on the wooden floor of the hut. They had hidden on sandy earth under the floorboards for a while, but the pursuit had died away; no one had come near the crown of the hill, and finally they let themselves into the tiny building to share some of the bread and provisions that Miriam had carried there for the absent Jake.

'You're sure he'll come? He doesn't have much time.'

'He'll come. If'n he don't, I can wait till tomorrow night. But you got to go now, so you can get to the tavern befo' light. You don't look so bad now you put on clean clothes.' She chuckled. 'You eve' goin' to be able to wea' that dress again? All that mud and dirt and hoss sweat!'

'I think I can get it clean: I had months of practice on the ship coming over.' She put her hand on the loaf as Miriam took the corner of the cloth to wrap it again. 'You make beautiful bread.'

'I use nothin but good flour, fine wheat, no mattuh how much it cost. Me and Jake, we got so sick of co'nbread we never touch it no mo'.'

'Is that what you ate down south?'

'Sho'. Nothin but co'n. Mash and buttermilk in the mo'nin, grits, and co'nbread in the evenin. Down at Polk Swamp, raisin' pawn.'

'Pawn?'

'Rice. These days, eve'y time I get sick of i'onin clothes, I recollect wo'kin to clea' that rice. Puttin' it in a dish and fannin' the trash out of it. Puttin' it back and throwin' in the co'n shucks—mo' co'n, you see! Couldn't get away from it!' She laughed so much she had trouble recommencing. 'You tea' those co'n shucks up in little strips and throw them in the pan. Then take that pestle and go back at it again. Make the rice pretty. Make it white. I used to do that mo' times than a little.' She knotted the cloth around the bread, saying in a different tone, 'You goin' home, aftuh you seen yo' friends?'

'I don't know. But I'll never go back to Philadelphia, not until it's free again. How shall I know you're safe?'

'Tell me yo' friends' direction and I'll send a message.'

'Thank you. And now you can give me *my* directions.'

Outside the hut they leaned against the rough wooden wall and Miriam pointed out the features of the landscape in the grey predawn light. The low hills into which they had ridden gave way in the south to gentler pastures and silvery water meadows down by the Delaware. Beyond another soft fold of the land, russet-brown with autumn trees, was Chester. Miriam's finger picked out the faded sails of a windmill on a knoll, which marked the vicinity of the roadside tavern. Viviane reckoned it could not be more than three miles away. She would reach it while the sun came up, walking along hedgerows filled with birdsong.

She put her arm through Miriam's. 'This country of yours, I hope you don't mind if I love it just a little.'

17

THE SUITOR BLESSED

For some reason that she could not explain to herself, Viviane had not expected to like the Ogilvys. Her guardian, one of the least effusive beings she knew, had sounded almost lyrical when describing Constance Ogilvy and her daughters, and Victor de Luny was deeply impressed with the youngest, Abigail; yet their praise set Viviane's teeth on edge. The Ogilvys sounded a cosy, united family, and she feared that on meeting them she would feel an outsider. They might make a royal fuss over the count and Victor, but they were male; as for females, the family already had enough of them and to spare. Yet half an hour in their company banished every misgiving, for they shared in abundance the quality she had come to value most in Americans—generosity that came from the heart.

James Ogilvy was a wealthy tobacco factor, who had built a mansion on the outskirts of Chester soon after his marriage to Constance, the only daughter of another powerful merchant in the town. Their style of living, in keeping with their large house with its pillared portico, and the green park surrounding it, was opulent and lavish; but it was neither the grand façade nor the richly liveried servants that struck Viviane when she arrived at the foot of the steps: it was the sight of Constance Ogilvy herself hurrying down them with hands outstretched towards her.

'I declare it is you; it is Mademoiselle de Chercy, is it not? I saw the gig from the balcony and I cried out to the girls, "I wager I know who that will be!" At last! And you are safe. And well?'

Still panting from her rush downstairs, scarcely allowing time for a conventional greeting before she gave directions for Viviane's small bundle of luggage to be brought in, she ushered her up towards the open front door. 'He will be so relieved! Your uncle, I mean. If only he were here to see you. But you must try to put up with us in the meantime. My daughters await you inside, in due form: they are for ever telling me it is unheard of to meet my guests on the steps, but when there is such a joyful reason, I think I am old enough to be excused for breaking the rules.'

Viviane looked quickly at her, diverted. Her round, smiling face and thick blonde hair, which had not a hint of grey, made her look no older than forty-five at most, and she was tripping up the steps like a woman of twenty.

'It is I who feel old today, Madame. Please excuse my clothes and my appearance, and I confess I am very tired.'

'Of course. My husband is from home, so you will not be interrogated about disasters Philadelphian. We shall not expect any news from you until you are thoroughly rested. Just do me the honour of meeting my daughters, then we shall whisk you upstairs.'

In fact Viviane fell into conversation very easily once she met the three young women, and almost forgot her weariness as they spoke.

Augusta, the eldest at twenty-three, was like her mother in the face, though tall and statuesque. She had her mother's quick perceptions also, coupled with a ready wit. She said how impatient they had been to meet her. 'Once we heard from Jules about his movements and yours, we expected you hourly.' Then, when Viviane could not help giving her a startled look, she said at once, 'Your uncle, I should say. But we were little girls when we first met him in Louisiana, and he allowed us to call him so then, so we still do. We claim all the privileges of childhood, whenever they suit us.'

'I see. And I call him "Monsieur", just as Monsieur Jacob calls his father.'

Abigail said in her quiet voice, 'Mademoiselle de Chercy, we are in the secret. Monsieur de Luny has told us his real name. And a great deal about his family and his home in the Loire.' Her blue eyes were lowered as she said shyly, 'It is very near Mirandol, I believe?'

Viviane nodded, wondering how many other details they might have been told. But surely neither her guardian nor Victor would mention the thwarted elopement, each having quite different reasons for silence on that subject.

May, the middle daughter, was the most animated and curious of them all. She inquired about the journey down from Philadelphia and Viviane simply told her that she had come by coach, without any disturbance or delay, and then in the gig from town. She had no intention of telling the Ogilvys about her night on the Delaware. She must never describe the meeting at Fort Mifflin and what happened on the shore, nor say anything about Miriam and Jake. The less she revealed, the safer all their mutual secrets would be.

May was satisfied with her answers and soon turned to questioning her at length about where she came from in France and what her home was like. May had dark wavy hair, and brown eyes that sparkled with interest as Viviane began to describe the valley of the Loire and the château. The others were equally fascinated, and instead of wanting to know everything about Paris, they were most eager for her to speak about Mirandol.

She realised why, quite quickly, for Constance Ogilvy mentioned that her guardian had sent them several letters from the Loire after his arrival at the château.

Glancing at her kindly, the older woman said, 'And of course he sent us a note from Charles Town when you landed—the first we knew that he had returned to America. I was happy to learn that your relations with him had become so cordial. It made us especially eager to welcome you both.'

Again Viviane repressed a start, and she could not help asking, in as nonchalant a tone as possible, 'He used to complain about how we got on?'

Constance smiled: 'By no means; I just detected in his letters the same restless spirit with which he went away, so I knew he had not settled down.'

Augusta said with a laugh, 'His letters are far too brief to leave room for either complaints or encomiums. With your uncle, one is always obliged to read between the lines.'

'Really? I have received so few myself, I could not say. They are brief, certainly. But not unfeeling. At least his last, which he wrote to me on my birthday . . .' Her voice trailed away, and she felt unexpected tears in her eyes.

May, not noticing, said at once, 'Oh, when was that, when is your birthday?'

But Constance Ogilvy rose and said, 'Mademoiselle de Chercy, let me show you to your room. It is quite up to you when you join us later. But I suspect all you want is to lay your head upon a pillow.'

She rang for a servant, and Viviane rose. There was compassion in all the young women's bright, attractive faces as she excused herself and followed Constance Ogilvy upstairs.

Next day she was sitting in the morning room with James Ogilvy, who had come to have a chat to her before he went into town. He was a tall, dark man, about ten years older than his wife, with a direct and pleasant manner.

'I should prefer to spend the morning here, Mademoiselle, but business is not easy in these times. While Philadelphia was free there was even a boom in some industries, but the war is likely to do little for me until we win it. After Brandywine my factories held more wounded men than goods. That was when we first met your friend, Monsieur de Luny.'

'Yes, he told me of your kind welcome.'

'Abigail's, in point of fact, for the rest of us were from home.' He paused, then said thoughtfully, 'It distresses me to think of the sacrifices that young man makes for our country. He has such an open, happy disposition. Brandywine cast him into the depths; and every future encounter, be it defeat or victory, will wreak the same havoc in him. He has no defences, beyond that unreflecting courage of his. It pained us very much to see him go back to the front.'

'Abigail tells me she has been giving him English lessons,' Viviane said. 'When he visits next time, I shall

330

scold him about his progress, and tell him he must stay in Chester longer if he expects to improve.'

He smiled and rose. 'Do so, Mademoiselle, with my blessing. A conspiracy of women is precisely what Monsieur de Luny requires just now. By the way, have you received the post yet? There is a letter for you from France.'

It was from Honorine de Chercy: brisk, informative, fond and full of unspoken pleas for her return. It had been written two months before, and gave Viviane a mournful feeling of dislocation.

Paris is unamusing just now; so many people are out of town for the summer; the streets are hot, dry and dusty, and the salons little better. There have been no upheavals in government—to be sure, Taboureau resigned some time ago, but it was hardly likely he would get on with Necker for long.

The situation in America is viewed with gloom at the moment. We go on the opposite swing of the pendulum from England, where news of the fall of Ticonderoga produced tremendous joy. Apparently King George burst into Queen Charlotte's dressing room crying, 'I have beat them! I have beat all the Americans!' The main sensation I felt on receiving this news was relief that your guardian is not in the north as before.

Adrienne de La Fayette and her little family continue well; please pass this on to the marquis when you see him.

Is there anything I can send for your comfort or your guardian's? I am sure he does not look after himself as he should: his valet told me he left his heaviest greatcoat in the Rue Richelieu. I do not like to think he may be committed to a northern campaign in the autumn. General John Burgoyne—a playwright, if you please, who would do better to stay scribbling at home like Beaumarchais—has been commanded to lead an army down from Canada to join up with the other English forces in New York. You see I am become as well-informed on matters

331

*American as you once were. It only increases my
anxiety to know there are two huge armies bearing
down upon the city where by now you and your
guardian must have arrived.*

Then Victor came, with all the news of Germantown.
He was so delighted to find her there, so transparently
glad to see Abigail, and so ready to throw himself into
the life of the Ogilvy household that it was days before
Viviane quite understood the distress that James Ogilvy
had guessed at. But one night, alone with herself and
Abigail in the music room, when everyone else had
withdrawn after an evening of duets and family parlour
games and laughter, he began to talk about the battle.
In a detached, undramatic way, with no lurid details,
he told them about the long, tense march through the
night, the gunfire in the smoke-filled woods, the way
the English had made a blockhouse out of a mansion
called Cliveden and filled the garden with bodies.

Neither of the young women knew whether to make
him stop or let him talk on, but when at last he began
to cry, and apologised, and she was afraid he would
escape from the room, Viviane rose, pressed his shoulder and left him to Abigail, who slid onto her knees in
front of him and looked silently up into his face.

Next day things went on as before and the young
people enjoyed one another's company unabated. By
now the two French and three Americans used Christian names amongst themselves, and Viviane had
almost got used to hearing the name 'Jules' pronounced
also. But it caused her a strange envy to hear it on the
lips of the Ogilvy daughters. Her sense of dislocation
continued, and she knew what caused it: whatever the
company or the entertainment, there was a void in
every room that only one person could fill. She had
quarrelled with him for so long that their short truce
in America seemed far too fleeting. She wanted to be
with him, so he could learn that all her resentments
had disappeared. For this alone, she had come to need
him, and it still caused her an obscure pain that he had
chosen this very time to depart.

She could not rest until he returned and she put things right between them. And she needed someone to whom she could confide the truth about how she had left Philadelphia. With great restraint, she had not said a word about it to Victor, but she knew that when her guardian arrived she would have a listener who could understand and comment justly on what she had done during that black night on the Delaware.

Then came a letter, over which the family jokingly protested, since there was none for them. James Ogilvy marvelled that her guardian had been so ingenious as to get a message through against such odds.

'Maybe he fell in with a scout or another man carrying dispatches. Whatever the case, he must have been mighty persuasive to push it all the way here. There now, go read it in peace.'

She took it into the garden and sat on a chilly stone bench against a maple, under a canopy of leaves that were beginning to put on their autumn scarlet. It was brief, certainly; and unlike the Ogilvys she found she did not have the canny knack of reading between all the lines.

My dearest Ward
I write this in enemy territory where we have the devil's own job to get through and where a letter would have no chance. I shall keep this until we reach camp, wherever that may be, and find a messenger to take it south.

You have no doubt heard this good news: on 19 September Gentleman Johnny Burgoyne received a smashing setback. He was on his way south to Albany to meet up with one army marching along the Iroquois Trail from the west (under Lieutenant Colonel St Leger) and another to be sent up the Hudson from New York by General Clinton. Well, St Leger was turned back at Fort Stanwix in a Continental victory, and Clinton seems to have made up his mind that with Howe gone to Pennsylvania he'll keep his own troops to defend New York. So dramatist Johnny (odd how this war attracts playwrights),

333

without hope of enlarging his troupe with reinforce-
ments, is resting between acts in a hastily fortified
position where the Continentals last brought him to
halt, near Saratoga on the Hudson.

I have just toasted you in whisky provided by a
young Stockbridge Indian who will come with us the
rest of the way—he has a taste for the excellent
spirits distilled in Vermont, and never travels
without a supply. After the toast he demanded that
I describe you. When I had finished cataloguing your
perfections (I left out the penchant for espionage you
displayed in Paris), he nodded approvingly and made
a sage remark which I cannot repeat to you. Never
fear, it was not improper. Only impossible, and so
would have no interest for you.

I have written you several notes on the way, but
this will probably be the only one to arrive—and,
coupled with my message before Brandywine, give
the impression that I only came to America for the
liquor. I am at the point where I should stop either
writing or drinking, or both, for we move before
dawn.

I cannot say adieu. I must see you again. So it is
au revoir, my dear.

Many times in the next few days, she unfolded and
reread this letter, though she never opened it in
company. She did not show it to the Ogilvys, for it
seemed, with all its oddity, so particularly *hers* that she
did not want to share it. She gave them the military
information, which was already generally known, and
mentioned that her guardian must have got safely
through to the northern camp. None of them knew
whether to find this consoling or not.

Snippets of news came now and then from Philadelphia. Lord Howe was now quartered in the Penn
house, the best mansion in the city, and social life fea-
tured little else but English officers. Balls were being
held, attended no doubt by John André and the
Shippen daughters. The information that came from
the Delaware was as usual: stalemate between the

Americans to the north of Fort Mifflin and the British to the south. The chevaux-de-frise were still in place, so she knew that the flare and the cannonade in the dark had done their work, and no English warships could yet pass the line.

She feared for Miriam, wondering whether she had been able to meet up with Jake and return home safely. Then, early on the day after her guardian's letter arrived, a parcel was delivered for her. She opened it in the breakfast room, perplexed by its shape and weight, and the others looked on curiously as she peeled back an oilskin and then a cloth wrapping, until the object appeared in all its solitary splendour.

It was a loaf of bread.

Dumbfounded, they all gazed at it in silence. Then Viviane began to laugh.

'Is there no note?' May said in puzzlement.

Viviane shook her head. 'I have a suspicion my correspondent can neither read nor write.'

'But whoever it is has conveyed the right message just the same?' James Ogilvy said shrewdly.

'Indeed, Sir. I cannot confide what the person has said, but I am very ready to share the gift. Would anyone like a piece?'

May, who hated other people to have secrets, pouted and declined, but Victor and Abigail laughingly agreed, and pronounced the bread superlative. Its soft, fragrant interior held no further messages—unlike the loaf that Viviane had shared with Miriam in the hut, and into which she had been able to insert a gold ring, before the other woman, unsuspecting, wrapped it up to eat later with Jake. She hoped he had not broken a tooth on it, or he might decide cornbread was the more acceptable fare after all.

Once again, Viviane had to suppress the temptation to tell Victor in private about the encounter at Fort Mifflin and its aftermath. It was the day before her friend's departure for the army, and she knew he dreaded the time when he would have to report back to La Fayette, and to Washington, who by now led a force that was growing smaller by the day through

335

desertion. She knew also why he did not want to go, and his reasons had nothing to do with the state of the Continentals. Watching him with Abigail was like seeing a different Victor, younger in his new vulnerability before a woman, older because of his sense of what might lie ahead for himself and the one he loved.

In the evening there came a moment when the others were in the upstairs salon and Viviane went out onto the balcony to look at the stars, which were bright in the clear, cold sky. Though she had a shawl around her, the frigid air made her shiver.

Victor came out and stood beside her, looking down into the still garden, and came to the point at once. 'Vive, I need your advice. You have come to know her so well: do you think I have any chance?'

'You mean, does she love you?' She smiled at him sidelong, keeping her voice low. 'That is something you must ask her yourself. But since you want my advice, I do not think you need hesitate.'

'No. I mean yes. But what I really mean is, do you think she would have me?'

She drew a quick breath and he looked at her in alarm, his brown eyes large and glistening in the half-light that slanted onto the balcony. The white pillar behind him threw his head into relief, with its mass of curls and the handsome, fine-boned face that had been dear to her since childhood.

He murmured, 'You think she might not be able to leave her parents, her home? I fear the same. I lie awake tormenting myself about it. What do I have to offer her? A title she will not care for, and a home on the other side of the ocean, cut off from everyone and everything she is used to.'

She put a hand on his sleeve. 'Do not try to think for her, you cannot know her heart. You will only find out by speaking. I should like to help you; I long for you to be happy. I would willingly speak to her myself if you wish, but would you not rather do that yourself?'

He leaned on the balcony, closer to her, and gazed out into the dark. 'Oh Vive,' he whispered. 'If only I had the courage!'

Then Viviane was aware of someone behind them. She took her hand from Victor's sleeve and turned, her skirts brushing against him as she did so, and looked into Abigail's pale face. It was impossible to tell how long she had been observing them, but Viviane could see that the blue eyes were full of pain and she was fighting for composure. Just as Victor swung round, she ran off down the balcony, ready to dart inside through the French doors that led into the bedrooms.

But they were all closed against the night air. When Viviane caught up with her at the far end, she was huddled up to the cold glass outside her own room, her fists rammed against the pane, her head bowed to conceal her face. Her fair hair and slender figure, reflected faintly in the window, made it look as though a ghostly young woman on the other side were struggling to get out.

Viviane put her hands on the resistant shoulders. 'Dear Abigail. He has pleaded with me to say something to you. But I told him to be brave and speak himself. Is there a chance for you both to be happy? Because if so, he will come to you now.'

Abigail drew back and faced her. Her expression was an almost comical mixture of disbelief and joy. She could only nod, but at once Viviane turned back and took a few steps away to meet Victor, who was striding towards them, his face set.

She only said, 'My dear friend—' and passed on, but the light that sprang into his eyes on the instant was enough to tell her what the outcome would be when they encountered each other in the darkness behind her.

She went back into the salon and joined the rest in a very dull conversation about Maryland and Pennsylvania weather; and when she saw how steadfastly Mr and Mrs Ogilvy managed to pretend there were no absentees from the room, she longed to tell her friend that his suit held some hope of being accepted by Abigail's parents, despite his being a Frenchman and a soldier.

Victor spoke, she was sure, but not to Constance and

337

James. He left the next day without confiding in Viviane, but the painful farewell, and Abigail's tears afterwards, convinced her that they had pledged themselves to each other. He promised to return in a week; by that time, she suspected, he would have discussed the issue with La Fayette so that he might be free of other obligations and able to offer formally for Abigail's hand.

That afternoon she was on the balcony once more, having dragged one of the chairs in her room out to catch the fading sun. She had told the others she was going to read, but instead she sat looking through the pillars over the trees in the park.

She had no name for this kind of unhappiness. She knew grief and loss well enough, and where to draw the strength to go on. But this was different, and it felt very much like remorse. Ever since Ethan Herrold had died and she had been unable to save him, her whole American adventure had been painted in darker colours. She had come here, where death stood at her side every day, and she could not get past the idea that, without her recklessness, her guardian would not be in America. His choices seemed all bound up with hers; in opposition or in concert, he and she were linked. He had gone away, but something told her that no distance could truly separate them, save for one cruel blade that, in her imagination, waited for him in the forests by the Hudson.

A carriage came up the gravel drive and stopped in the sweep below her. Visitors on business or social calls were frequent at the Ogilvys', and Viviane had schooled herself not to go to the window if she were in a room overlooking the steps, or to hang over the balcony when someone new arrived. This time she did not even rise from her seat, but stole a look through the marble balustrade. There was a gentleman in the carriage, but the arm and hand on the top of the door were not those of the man she waited for. She heard the newcomer admitted and opened her book, but was soon aware of quick footsteps through the bedchamber as Abigail appeared.

She looked up. Abigail's face was flushed, and the blue eyes held both happiness and trepidation. She was so overcome she could not speak for a moment.

Viviane rose, bewildered. 'Victor?'

Abigail shook her head. 'No, but it is someone you know! You would *never* guess, never!'

Viviane gave a cry and rushed from the room. Abigail called out something behind her but she did not listen. How could she have told herself it was not his hand; why had she not darted down the stairs at once, like this, as though a whirlwind were at her back?

The others were in the front drawing room, where a tall, formally dressed figure stood by the window, against the light. As she stepped quickly towards him he turned to greet her.

It was Victor's father, the Marquis de Luny.

18

SARATOGA

Jules caught up with the armies of the Northern Department at the vast camp which General Gates had established in a place called Bemis Heights. Five miles to the north, Burgoyne's forces had dug in and constructed a number of redoubts on the lands of a Quaker farmer named Freeman, and were anxiously waiting there for Clinton to lead reinforcements up from New York. Correctly guessing that these would not be forthcoming, a good number of his men elected to desert, and for a fortnight or so the Americans had been rounding them up in the woods while their Indian allies, venturing even closer, picked off the unwary around the edges of the camp.

General Gates had nearly ten thousand men—militia from New Hampshire and Vermont, five Continental brigades, the 4th New York Regiment, a light infantry battalion and the Continental Rifle Corps under Daniel Morgan. After delivering the dispatches to Gates's staff, Jules reported to Morgan, whom he had last seen at Quebec the year before. He was glad to serve under this tough frontiersman, whose genius in wooded terrain owed nothing to conventional military tactics. In the field, his marksmen signalled to one another by a turkey call, a kind of whistle that hunters used to attract game, and could stay invisible until the last few minutes of their advance.

Jules was keen to make contact with his friend Benedict Arnold but, true to his old habits of military discipline, he busied himself first at the Rifle Corps' position, where in fact he heard a great deal of news about Arnold anyway.

The last time Jules had seen his friend was when they lay side by side in a field hospital after the catastrophe at Quebec. Recovered from the leg wound he received there, Arnold was made brigadier general and continued to serve with brilliance in the north. Along with his great gifts of courage and ingenuity came the impatience he expressed when he thought his fellow commanders lacked imagination or decision. On being promoted to general he made no secret of the fact that he considered Philip Schuyler, commander of the Northern Department, an unworthy rival. After the victory at Fort Stanwix, in which Arnold played a conspicuously courageous part, his forces moved to join the other army and, just before he arrived, Congress replaced Schuyler with Horatio Gates. Jules was not astonished to hear that a new phase of rivalry had begun at once, for there was a mighty flare-up between Gates and Arnold over Freeman's Farm, Arnold coming off worse when the angry Gates relieved him of his command.

Meanwhile Arnold had heard of Jules's arrival, and next day summoned him to the quarters he shared with General Enoch Poor, which was a hut belonging to Neilson, the Patriot farmer whose land they occupied.

Jules sat on the narrow porch until late in the afternoon, talking with Arnold and looking out through the crowded encampment. Against a backdrop of thickly wooded hills they could see the pickets on the perimeter, the cannon pointing northward from the heights, and the contours of the fortifications built by Polish engineer and artilleryman Tadeusz Kosciusko. Within were tidy rows of weather-stained tents, fireplaces scooped out of the earth and bristling with blackened iron supports for can and cauldron, and boxes of ammunition that were at last piling up, ending the drastic shortage which had made a stalemate of the first battle over Freeman's Farm in September. Men moved amongst the tents carrying bales of hay, since hay was all most of them had to sleep on; and there were women too, the wives and camp followers of the Continentals and some local Patriots who were helping to feed the troops. Jules remembered what he had said to his ward months ago in Los Pasajes about the privations of war in this beleaguered country. He might yearn to know where she was and what she was doing, but it was better than thinking of how she would have fared yoked to Luny, trailing after Washington's wasted, ragged troops through the mud and slush of Pennsylvania.

The war had shocked and changed her, nonetheless. She had La Fayette and his French company to worry about, and no doubt many Americans besides, whom she would have met during her time at the Christies'. She had obviously grown close to some of them—intimate enough to tend them day and night in that ill-lit box of a house on High Street, long enough to reach the emotional state in which he had found her.

He remembered the words: 'You do not realise what it is like when someone really needs you.'

She was right there. His first love had been for a woman who did not, could not, need him. Since then, he had chosen lovers who, like Gina Farrucci, sought passion but not dependence. There had never been any promises and, though there might have been pain when they parted, they all proved as adept as he was at concealing it. Since his first, shattering encounter, there had been no tragedies, no ruination, no children.

He looked up when Arnold's broad form appeared in the doorway, holding a bottle in each hand. His friend said, 'Your choice: burgundy or Saint Emilion?'

'*Bon Dieu*, how do you manage it?' He thought for a moment. 'Whichever has travelled best—the Saint Emilion, I suppose.'

'Done,' Arnold said. 'I've two more on the mantelpiece in here. The bricks are just the right temperature when the fire has died. A delicate balance, but I have it figured.'

He left his man to open the bottle and joined Jules on the porch. Privately, Jules marvelled at how habitable he and Enoch Poor had made the little dwelling. The cot beds they slept on were folded against the wall during the day, which left just enough space in the room for a table and a couple of chairs before the fire; yet Arnold, as usual, demanded and relished his creature comforts.

The glasses appeared and Jules held his against the fading afternoon light to admire the mauve tint in the centre of the wine that gleamed like a soft rose caught in flames. 'Where did you come across this?'

'In the British baggage train at Stanwix. That will be the delicious satisfaction of crushing Gentleman Johnny: they say he travels with scores of waggons full of his own necessities. He has a fine taste in French wine—he lived a long time in your country at one stage.'

'I didn't know that.'

'Eloped with an earl's daughter and then had to slip across the Channel to escape his debts. Yes, I wouldn't mind tapping into his supplies.'

Jules looked sideways at him. In profile, with his thick mane of hair and the aggressive curve of the strong Roman nose, Arnold looked like a lion brooding on future prey.

His friend turned, caught his eye and frowned. 'You heard about Gates? Expects my men to take the field on *his* orders when all he's done in the last few years is manoeuvre paper across desks.'

'I heard. But if he's a fool, he won't be the first one that ever commanded an army.'

'Command? He doesn't know the meaning of the word. None of them do unless they've been close enough to stare down the barrel of this war. I sacrifice myself in the field—my fortune, my hide, my best years—and no one has the gratitude or the plain sense to build on what I've learnt. You wait: listening to that damned idiot is like going back to nursery school.'

'He's a career soldier, though. English army in the fifties, then the Virginia Militia.'

'But he's been nothing but an administrator for years. They overlooked him for Schuyler. And look at Schuyler! Gates can give me fourteen years, but he's got nothing on me in experience. The truth is he cannot stand to have a younger, abler man ride in here and show him up for the dusty old clerk that he is. That's why he's down on me. But damn him, what do I care? The event will tell.'

343

That event came on 7 October when Burgoyne, sick of watching his army diminish and his men suffer from lack of supplies and support, decided to risk an engagement by testing the American left flank. The Americans woke up to the fact that a reconnaissance force of 1500 men and eight cannon were moving southwest out of the English camp to Barber's Farm. At three in the afternoon they themselves moved in to attack, in separate columns led by Colonel Morgan and Generals Learned and Poor.

Ebenezer Learned faced the grenadiers, the artillery and most of the British main front across open ground; while Enoch Poor's Continentals concentrated on their left flank, some of it visible across a wheatfield and the rest deployed in the woods. Meanwhile the Riflemen swung well out under Daniel Morgan to take on the right wing, which was also partly concealed by trees. These enemy troops were commanded by a fine leader, Brigadier General Simon Fraser, who held them together through assault after assault.

The fighting was hot and bitter from the first but, despite the crash of arms around him and the constant vigilance needed to make use of cover and force the enemy from theirs, Jules was in an odd mood, unable to keep mind and body on the task. He scarcely knew the men who fired and fell around him. There had been no campfire councils as there had before Brandywine, and he himself felt strangely altered. This battle was arguably more important even than the first: they were here not just to prevent Burgoyne going south to join Clinton, but to thrust him back over the border. It was a battle not over farmland but over the whole of the Northern Department. Yet something was detaching him from it. Arnold's towering discontent, perhaps. Or the sensation he had had, while coming north, of dragging his feet. For the first time in his life he was not springing alert into battle; absurdly, he found it hard to believe he was here.

The conundrum could easily have been solved at this point by an enemy bullet, but the sound of Daniel Morgan's voice brought him out of his dangerous sense of dislocation. The colonel was determined to do

344

something about Simon Fraser, who was endlessly riding up and down through the English position, careless of exposure, directing and encouraging his men. Morgan pointed him out to Tim Murphy, an old Indian fighter, and Jules watched as Murphy chose his vantage point and steadied his long-barrelled rifle on the active horseman beyond the enemy lines. He fired once, and the brightly clad figure moved on. Twice, and he disappeared, only to flash into view in another spot. The third shot blew him out of the saddle.

As Fraser went down, Jules shuddered and something snapped in his mind. On the instant, the prospect before him sprang into brutal clarity and without hesitation he ran forward. They saw the way now; they had to take it.

Fraser had in fact been trying to manage a strategic withdrawal as his troops shrank back under the Rifle Corps' punishment. Once he was killed, their retreat through the woods became a nightmare, with the merciless Americans in pursuit. Across the other side of the battlefield, the British left flank was also being steadily beaten back, and it was at this moment that Benedict Arnold took the field.

Cursing Gates and acting flatly against orders, hatless and waving his sword like a maniac, he charged between the two flanks on a huge bay horse, and a great wave of Learned's men followed him, to crash against the Germans who were holding the centre of the British front. The mass of the enemy army rolled back and continued to roll, forced yard by yard along their own tracks to the redoubts on Freeman's Farm.

It was only an hour since the first shot, but Burgoyne had already lost four hundred officers and men, and his artillery. It was only an hour, but that taste of success lent a kind of frenzy to the Americans. Jules, running through the lines under the wild impetus he had received at Barber's, knew neither who he was with nor exactly where he was heading: the only way was forward, through other bodies.

Arnold led a column of men in a series of attacks on the Balcarres Redoubt. Knocked back repeatedly, he suddenly wheeled his horse and charged off between two lines of fire to join the attackers at the second, Breymann's, where the Germans who held it let off only one volley before losing their nerve. They mutinied, turned tail, and Breymann was killed, some said by his own men.

When Arnold and the others smashed their way into the fort, Jules was not far away from his friend. So he saw the moment when the big bay horse was killed under him and crushed him as it rolled. By the time Jules had fought his way to the spot, there were others around Arnold. His left leg had been shattered by a ball, and he cried out and fainted when they tried to move him. Then he revived, demanded his sword and refused to quit the battle, urging his comrades on from where he lay. When they had in their sights the young Prussian who had wounded him, he begged for the man's life.

Jules' surge of mad energy was over. Dazed, he stood looking down at Arnold, then realised that he was so white they would lose him unless they got him from the field. It was not hard to find helpers to lift him onto a makeshift stretcher and tie a torn shirt across the wound, whereupon he lost consciousness. Without a word, Jules handed his rifle to someone and prepared to walk beside the litter back to camp.

He took turns with the bearers, but spoke only once. 'He's maimed for life.'

Beaten, cornered, the British shrank back through their damaged position across a ravine and, as dusk fell, the American army halted its advance. Uneasy quiet fell over the ravaged farmland and the steep forested slopes, and messengers began to go swiftly back and forth in the half-light between the forward positions and the heights. Jules and the others made it to the hospital tents, and without a second thought the count took it upon himself to go and tell Gates that Arnold was in the surgeon's hands.

He had never seen Gates, and even after Arnold's description of him had no idea what to expect. It did not seem to matter; all that counted was delivering the message to his face.

The men on duty outside Gates's quarters were not especially keen for him to proceed inside, but he went in anyway. He heard a voice raised in anger as he approached, and when he pushed his way into the room he entered upon a remarkable scene. An enemy commander, Lieutenant General Francis Clarke, had been captured after being shot in the chest, then brought in and laid on the general's bed. Gates was standing at the foot of the bed railing at him, so incoherently that Jules made no attempt to catch the words—all his attention was riveted on Clarke, for it was obvious the man was dying.

With the last of his strength, Clarke was trying to make himself heard. 'Whatever you say, you have chosen a pitiful cause to fight for. Name me one justification for you to stand there and—'

'Hold your tongue, curse you. You're finished and so is Burgoyne. Must I listen to you whine because you've taken a beating?'

White-lipped, Clarke said, 'You're a traitor to the land that bred you, Sir.' Suddenly there was a spasm across his features and blood gushed from one side of his mouth. Then he gasped and went on, 'I took this ball in the chest, for my King. You deserve one in the neck. For treason.'

Gates began to shriek at him. He stood with his fists clenched, his tall body hunched, the veins standing out on his long neck, and a stream of curses poured from his lips, drowning the hoarse, defiant speech of the man in the bed, while the bystanders gazed at them both in horror.

It was too much: in one stride Jules had his left hand at Gates's throat, slamming him against the wall. As he gagged and struggled, Jules said into his face, 'Not one more word. Now out.'

With the other fist wound into the front of the general's coat, he hauled Gates towards the door, which one of the others immediately opened. Once in the corridor he forced him towards the back of the building and held him halfway to the floor, in the dark, one arm across his throat, the other hooked into position for a

347

killing thrust. The others would give him perhaps half a minute, no more. His revulsion was so great it was all he could do not to finish the movement and silence the man for good.

He spoke very close to his ear, knowing that, miraculously, no one was yet approaching from outside either. 'Thousands just fought for you today. And you scream obscenities at a man who is choking on his own blood. I came to tell you Arnold has fallen. If he dies, beware: someone may do the same for you.'

Then he dropped him and walked out. No one came out of the room or challenged him when he stepped outside. No one came running after him when he strode away from headquarters and walked blindly into the woods beyond. There was a kind of path, deep in fallen leaves, alongside which pale tree trunks gleamed here and there in the dark. He plunged on by instinct, stumbling now and then, his mind raging, his face whipped by bare branches where the underbrush grew thick.

A shot whined over his head and he dropped to a crouch, listening. It could have come from anywhere. He waited, panting, then forgot it. He remained there for a long time and slowly, as a little starlight filtered through, his surroundings swam into milky focus. He lifted his hands from the earth and looked at them. Dirt, leaves and bits of twig stuck to them—in the gloom it looked as though a malignant fungus were sprouting from his palms.

He brushed them against his knees and flexed them. They were stained and sticky, as though with blood.

He lifted his head and listened. No one. Just as well, since he had no rifle. Rising carefully, he checked his belt. For some reason the knife was gone, but he still had the weapon euphemistically known as a siege axe. He had seen it used for other things that day.

There was no call to return; there was no call to go anywhere. He stood with his head flung back and eyes closed, empty. There was a smell of rain in the air. After another long interval he heard a sudden, startled cry. But it sounded high up, like that of a bird disturbed on the roost. Unless he was being stalked by a German in a tree, he was in no danger of ambush.

It set him on the move again, however, and he found the way without difficulty, skirting headquarters silently under cover of the trees and then walking openly into camp. If anyone had recognised him at headquarters, Gates could bring a court martial—he was welcome.

Having reported in to the Rifle Corps, Jules asked permission to seek out Benedict Arnold. He found that the surgeon was with him and needed another assistant while they set and stitched up the shattered leg. He helped with the bloody, gut-wrenching task and, except for a few minutes during which he went outside to vomit, he was able to support his friend through the hour-long ordeal.

Much later, feeling sick again, he was sitting by the stretcher bed with his forehead resting on his crossed arms, when Arnold finally spoke.

'I suppose when this is over they'll be sending you south again.'

He lifted his head. 'No doubt.'

'And then?'

With an effort he sat straight and looked down at the white face beside him. 'And then nothing. I've had enough.'

Arnold's eyelids flickered but he did not comment.

Jules got slowly to his feet and said, 'Let me give you some water.'

'Thank you. But first.' Arnold lifted his chin and narrowed his eyes as though he had trouble seeing in the candlelight. 'Chercy, I want you to promise me something.'

Jules stiffened and stared at him. Having just made the worst confession of his life he was about to be saddled—in true, histrionic, Arnold fashion—with a dramatic last wish. He held his breath.

Arnold opened his broad right hand and held it, rock steady, an inch or two above the coverlet. 'Promise you'll go back to France and get that king of yours to move his damned ass.'

Jules closed his eyes momentarily, then stepped forward and grasped the offered hand.

During the night the British kept campfires burning while they drew back and took shelter within their last bastion, the Great Redoubt. The following night, after burying Simon Fraser inside the walls, they stole away towards the Hudson, leaving six hundred dead.

Jules moved out with the Rifle Corps as they manoeuvred in an arc around the British forces, to cut off access to the pontoon bridge across the river which had been Burgoyne's line of approach from the north. For the next week, under an almost constant downpour of cold rain, the remnants of the British forces melted away through the woods and Gates's army swelled with reinforcements. Each morning the mists hung about the Hudson like a shroud, but Jules felt the spirits of the Americans lift. Ignoring his contrary mood, they were eager for him to share the taste of victory, and it caused him grim amusement when someone reverently returned the Spanish rifle to his tent.

The American numbers grew until a cordon of nearly 20,000 men began to pull tight around the British, who were blocked from retreat by artillery on the bluffs above the river covering their slender lifeline of boats. Halting at Saratoga, Burgoyne skirted the dilapidated fort by the river and decided to place his troops along the hilltops overlooking the riverside farms. There he was offered surrender 'with the Honours of War'.

Saratoga on 17 October presented an eerie sight: long columns of men drawn up across the fields on the west bank of the Hudson, their heads bowed and their arms laid on the grass at their feet as Gates strode between them to receive Sir John Burgoyne's sword. The general made the graceful gesture of handing it back, but Burgoyne was not so gentlemanly in reply. Sneering, he called Gates a 'granny', an old midwife.

Gates looked down his long nose and said, 'You're right, Sir. Today I have delivered you of 5000 men.'

19

TURNING HOME

The news of Saratoga swept south like a wildfire, lighting up the towns along its way. La Fayette, mended and just about to rejoin Washington, celebrated at Bethlehem; the general speculated dryly about what King George was likely to be saying to his Queen about this turn of events; the men of the American armies looked at one another in joy and relief.

Chester, mindful of the British fleet on the Delaware, the shore batteries nearby and Howe and Cornwallis brooding in Philadelphia, allowed itself discreet rejoicing; while Viviane, after the first great surge of hope at the word of victory, waited for a different message from the north.

Victor was with her one afternoon as she took a restless walk about the Ogilvys' bare orchard. He said, 'What I would not give to be there when the story hits Versailles! I wrote to Coigny and Silas Deane the second I heard, but they are bound to find out long before my letter gets there.'

'Perhaps not, since the mail is so unreliable. Think of La Fayette, he has not a word from his wife since Pulaski arrived. And yet I have reams from my great-aunt, and even a letter from Mademoiselle de Billancourt.'

'Truly? I did not realise. Is she well?'

'Yes, and as teasing as ever; she has not changed a jot. She is still furious with me for leaving Paris and she never would have written if your father and my great-aunt had not taken her into their confidence about his voyage. But once she knew he was to see both you *and* me she could not resist writing. She inquires about you very particularly. In fact I suspect that recent events might make her just a little jealous.'

He looked quickly at her, decided she was joking, and his features resumed their usual happy expression. 'I wish everyone could be as fortunate as I. My father could scarcely have timed his arrival better.'

'What a surprise he got. There he was, all set to haul you from the field—'

'And he could not have found an officer in America more willing to obey him!'

'Although strictly speaking, it is Abigail whose wishes you follow.'

He smiled at her fondly. 'Of course. She told me she could never bear to be a soldier's wife.'

She stopped at the end of the path between two rows of peach trees and pulled a brown, curled leaf from a jutting twig. 'My guardian warned me once that the worst side of military operations is the waiting. Of course he was trying to spare me from thinking what you soldiers must face. But I am selfish enough to say that waiting *is* terrible.'

'Vive, I am sure if the news were bad we would have heard. The reports say that in all the weeks of fighting at Saratoga, the British lost 1000 men, but the Americans lost less than half that number.' He caught her outraged look and said quickly, 'Now don't fly out at me, I am not trying to reassure you with arithmetic. All I mean is that if there was anything to worry about, word would have reached us by now. If you have no message, it is because he is coming himself.'

She crushed the brittle leaf in her palm and let the fragments drift from her fingers as they turned to retrace their steps along the sandy path. 'What a quantity of letters you have written since we came here. Far more than I—our friends in Paris must be the best informed people on the globe.'

'And soon I shall be able to tell them every detail in person.' She looked at him sharply and he blushed. 'Yes. Viviane, I wanted you to be the first to know.'

He hesitated for so long after this shy beginning that she spoke for him. 'You are returning to France? With Abigail?' When he nodded, she stopped and smiled with delight. 'Your father and the Ogilvys have given their consent?' He nodded again, with a grin to match hers, and she laughed outright. 'Then speak to me, for heaven's sake! On what am I to congratulate you? I demand to know the marriage date, the church, your

voyage, dear Abigail's words when she accepted you—
everything.'

Once he found his voice, he was very willing to tell
her.

The Marquis de Luny, driven by a powerful combi-
nation of wrath and fatherly devotion, had decided
quite soon after Victor's departure to go to America
himself and bring back his errant son. He waited some
time, however, until his wife was well enough for him
to leave her: she was even more devastated than he at
losing Victor, and her health suffered as a consequence.
On reaching the United States, the marquis had no
trouble tracking Victor to Chester, and he arrived with
the unswerving intention of taking him back to France.
French law gave him total rights over his son, and he
considered he had brought that sovereign law with
him, even into the midst of revolution.

He had steeled himself for unpleasant arguments in
an atmosphere of autumn storms and gunsmoke, but
he found in Chester the opposite of everything he had
expected. His son was a cherished guest in a cultured
household where the female members spoke a delightful if heavily accented French. Having formed a chaste
attachment for the youngest daughter, Victor was con-
ducting his courtship on impeccable lines: he had
obtained release from his military duties; he had made
an approach in due form to the parents, and he had
been in the process of applying by letter to his own
when the marquis arrived. His intended was cultivated,
well educated, likeable and gratifyingly beautiful. To
be sure she was not nobly born but, as Victor neatly
pointed out, a republic could furnish no aristocrats, so
birth was beside the point. The Ogilvys' land was
negligible but their fortune was not—Mademoiselle
Abigail would be embarrassingly well provided for.

The single consideration that gave the marquis pause
was his poor wife. She had sped him on his way to
save their son from a hasty commitment and the terrors
of war, and he felt that if he brought him back married

he was fulfilling only half his mission. But as the days went by he grew not only fond of Abigail, but convinced that the marquise would feel the same when she met her. He could think of no other objection to the union—the Ogilvys, though not practising churchgoers, were Catholic, and the ceremony would be performed in their parish church. His son, blissfully in love and eager for his father's approval, had at the same time a new confidence and maturity that impressed the marquis. He was proud of him and impatient to return with him to France. He even caught himself imagining the faces of his neighbours in the Loire when they met the calm, elegant beauty from America who was the future Marquise de Luny—and he smiled as he anticipated their astonishment.

For the first few days the marquis stayed at the best tavern in Chester, but thereafter he was a guest at the Ogilvy mansion. Discussions were amicably concluded, the day of the wedding was set for early November, and it was hoped that the marquis and the young couple could at once go south to Annapolis and find a ship that would take them back to France before Christmas.

The time passed agreeably. Although James Ogilvy was the only one of the family who did not speak French, in fact the marquis enjoyed his company best, since Ogilvy was a member of the local hunt and frequently took father and son out riding to hounds. He was also a member of the Radnor Hunt, where his friend Alfred Hart was Master of Hounds, and it amused the marquis that Ogilvy was never so angry about the English occupation of Philadelphia as when the subject of this favourite club came up. It appeared that some of Cornwallis's gentlemen turned up to ride with them one frosty October morning; Alfred Hart expressed great enthusiasm, proposing that when once the Englishmen had donned fox tails the rest of the hunt would be happy to give them a sporting start. He concluded the heated altercation this caused by quietly trotting the hounds back to their kennels and resigning his mastership. In exchange for this anecdote, the marquis and Victor described classic fox chases along the shingle beds of the Loire and invited Ogilvy to join them at some future date, for they planned that the whole family should visit Luny when once Abigail was firmly established at the château.

The marquis was hoping that the Comte de Mirandol would arrive in time to swell the French contingent in the church on his son's wedding day. Being unfamiliar with the horrors of this particular war, he was the only one in the household who felt quite confident that the count had survived Saratoga. He several times tried to reassure Mademoiselle de Chercy on that point, but made little headway.

One evening as she sat at the pianoforte looking listlessly through some music, he leaned on the instrument to talk to her. 'Of all the gentlemen I have met, your uncle strikes me as best able to look after himself. Depend upon it, he will be here at any moment.'

'You are very kind, Monsieur.'

He looked down at her, sorry to see his once lively and rebellious neighbour so depressed. 'I can remember a time when you would have been very cheerful to know there were a few hundred leagues stretching between you two! I am intrigued to see such a *revolution* in your sentiments, Mademoiselle.'

The answer to his sly smile was a resentful glance. 'You are astonished to hear that I am afraid for him when he faces danger and death?'

'Heaven forbid,' the marquis said gruffly. 'That is not what I meant, and you know it.'

Contrite at once, she said in muted tones, 'You are right. I can scarcely believe how I treated him at Mirandol. You were a witness to my behaviour then: can you wonder that I worry now? What if it is too late for me ever to make it up to him?'

He brought a chair closer to the pianoforte and sat down, collecting his thoughts as he did so, for her sadness was much deeper than he had suspected. 'You must not take this tragic view. I assure you, whatever your conduct, your uncle thought of you then just as I did—as a charming and wilful young person, never as an enemy. Since that time, it seems to me that you have grown into a mature, right-thinking and resourceful woman. Your beauty is no disguise, Mademoiselle; I am afraid anyone of intelligence can see right through you at once, to the true heart beneath. And since your uncle is a very clever man, he must be in no more doubt about you than I am.'

After this complimentary speech, he was appalled to see tears gathering in his listener's eyes. 'My dear Mademoiselle,' he remonstrated, 'I never knew a woman to try my eloquence so. What must I do to bring a smile to those lips—abuse you?'

He gained his point at last, for she gave a little laugh and looked at him ruefully. 'Scold me instead, Monsieur, if you wish. I am sure I need it.'

'I should much rather have your consent to my latest plan. Would you like to travel back to France with us? We are quite sure of finding a vessel at Annapolis. The crowning achievement, of course, would be to persuade your uncle to accompany us too.'

Her eyes sparkled. 'If he comes—*when* he comes, will you promise me to try?'

He had no time to answer, for at that very moment there was a loud knock at the front door, and Mademoiselle de Chercy leaped to her feet. It was ten o'clock and no callers were expected. Her lips quivered and her eyes were fixed on the drawing room door as Constance Ogilvy glided through it and into the hall without waiting for the servants.

Viviane heard the count's deep tones in the hall, gasped and took a step away from the pianoforte. Then she stopped. She had promised him she would be composed when next they met, but she had not the slightest idea how to manage it.

The others all rose under the same impulse and the three sisters, without a thought for formality, swept out with an eager rustle of skirts and went through the door before her. She followed, with James Ogilvy, the marquis and Victor in her wake.

He was just inside the door, clad in neat civilian clothes, his head bent to Constance Ogilvy. Viviane heard him speak her name, then her hostess in quiet reply told him she was with them. He said something softly, then looked up and saw her. A long look passed between them. Somehow Viviane could not smile, but she knew that the relief flooding through her was clear and shining on her face. His own was inscrutable; he was holding himself in.

Constance Ogilvy said something else and he dragged his gaze away from Viviane to listen politely. Viviane suddenly saw in him the signs of extreme fatigue and a strange, febrile kind of tension. She had a frightening, quite physical insight into his state—it was as though something had knocked him to the ground, and he had only just struggled to his feet.

She felt the shock on the instant, and it took only seconds for her to cross the floor towards him, but in the interval many things seemed to happen. She remembered how she had sworn to receive him, and she also saw how inadequate she would be once again. For it was Constance Ogilvy who placed a hand on his wrist and looked anxiously into his face and said, 'You have taken no hurt?' And it was she who received serenely the reply that might have offended another inquirer: a curt shake of the head, a look of greater reserve, almost of resentment.

Then as Viviane came to his side he turned and the moment came when he placed his hands on the tips of her shoulders and she put her fingers on his, at either side of his neck, so that they could give once, twice, the kisses on the cheek that the others must imagine to be their habitual family greeting, and which they exchanged here for the very first time. Viviane felt a twinge of irony, for the gesture that would have seemed impossibly intimate to her only months before, now seemed too formal and much too fleeting. Her lips left his lean cheek, she withdrew her hands and brought her heels to the floor, and now she had only her voice and eyes to convey the fullness of her welcome after the long trial of his absence.

'Thank God you are safe.'

'Thank God you are here,' he said.

Then the others, who had held back for her sake, surged forward. The Ogilvy sisters had scarcely begun to voice their joy before the marquis heartily announced himself, and had the satisfaction of getting a genuine start of wonderment out of the Comte de Mirandol. James Ogilvy and Victor joined them, and as Viviane stood silently by his side she had the foolish feeling that he was a creature at bay within a circle of loud pursuers.

When the hubbub had died down somewhat, Constance Ogilvy's calm voice finally prevailed, asking him where his luggage was.

'At the tavern.'

'Which one? We shall send for it.'

'Thank you, but I shall be staying on at the Black Boar.'

'Nonsense. You are to lodge here, as always.'

He made an effort to smile. 'And you are very good, as always. But you have quite enough guests already.'

'James,' Constance said, turning to her husband, 'explain to our friend that he will stay with us.'

He was about to reply, but the count forestalled him. 'I should prefer town.'

Ogilvy, with a shrewd look at him, made no protest, exclaiming instead, 'Suffer the man to move at least a step beyond the front door! Make way there, everyone, and let him in.'

The count shook his head. 'I walked over just to see how you all do. I must go. But I shall be back tomorrow, with your leave.'

'Walked! You shall go back in the carriage, but not yet. You may not be up to jawing all night, but I never knew you to refuse my cognac. Join us in the library for one glass, and tomorrow the ladies may pester you for news to their hearts' content.'

Viviane would have been outraged at this instant separation of the sexes; but she could see that her guardian was in need of rescue. When he nodded to his host she detected relief in his eyes—he had been in the house only an instant, but already he was looking for an escape.

The Ogilvy daughters protested, but Victor helped by persuading them to go back to the salon, so only the three older men moved towards the library. As her guardian passed Viviane he gave her an apologetic look which the others could not see, and she managed to smile in return and say, 'Tomorrow then?'

'Of course. Goodnight, my dear.' He walked on and the door closed behind him.

She could not bear to traipse into the salon with the others. She went to her room instead and lay fully dressed on the bed with her chamber door open, straining to hear all the sounds from downstairs. If he emerged from the library and joined the company after all, she would descend at once. If he took his leave in the hall, she would dart along to the gallery above the stairs and catch a glimpse of him before he went out the door.

She lay in suspense for an hour, during which most of the household made their way upstairs to bed, then she heard James and Constance Ogilvy coming up also. He had gone, so quietly she had not even heard the carriage leave from below her window. Disappointment engulfed her and she rolled over to bury her face in the pillow. She had waited so long to make amends, but his return gave her no hope that she could do so. Without rising to get undressed, hardly gaining an atom of comfort from the knowledge that he was safe, she let her tears spill over at last.

When he returned after midday on the morrow she felt that nothing had improved. The others adapted better than she to the gaps in his conversation and his reticence, and they ignored, or pretended to ignore, the bleak look in his eyes. But for Viviane each of these was like a reproach, and the more she strove to understand what the campaign in the north had done to him, the less she felt able to help.

James Ogilvy said at one point, 'We were shocked to hear Arnold was wounded. What news did you have of him before you left; will he be all right?'

'I do not know.'

May, always the most curious of the sisters, said, 'I should love to hear what expression Gentleman Johnny wore as he handed over his sword at Saratoga.'

'I was too far off to see it.'

'You struck no trouble in the State of New York on the way back?'

'No.'

She saw he could not tolerate sitting about for long, and not even music relaxed him. It reminded her of the early days at Mirandol when he used to disappear whenever she began to play, though he had grown infinitely more polite to her since, and more patient. She longed to tell him about Fort Mifflin and the redcoat with the rifle, but she knew instinctively that to talk of such a subject to him at the moment would somehow cause him further injury. So they went for walks, usually in a group, across the park or into town. Once he accompanied the sisters and Victor and herself on a long ride through the countryside, during which he let everyone chatter on around him, exchanging stilted remarks with her about the landscape while all the time she knew he would have preferred silence and perhaps solitude.

She knew the Ogilvys were concerned. One morning as she entered the breakfast room she heard James say to Constance, 'He has been this way before. Remember the time he frightened the living daylights out of the maid by sleeping on the floor? Yet a few nights later he was in bed like a civilised being. If he prefers to be on his own, so be it. Let him work his own medicine.'

The change came slowly. She was more often alone with him during his visits now, for Augusta and May, with whom he was a favourite, were constantly being called away to help with preparations for the wedding; and although he and she never talked about anything but the most trivial daily affairs, she felt that he was becoming slightly more at ease.

The day before the wedding they sat together in the music room and she opened the pianoforte and played pieces that reminded her of other places and other

360

times—of Paris, and home. After half an hour she looked over at him, and for the first time something in his face said, *Come and talk to me.* So she did.

As she settled herself on a sofa opposite him, he asked a surprising question. 'What do you think is happening at Mirandol just now?'

She smiled. 'November: Albert will be clamouring to prune the vines and Feray will be arguing that it is far too early.'

'He is right, is he not?'

'Feray is *always* right. But Albert has an obsession with bonfires; all he ever wants to do is cut and burn.'

'Is he that beanpole of a man with the prominent teeth?'

'The very same.'

'Of course. Last October he was torching stubble with such a passion he finished up looking like a smoked eel,' the count recalled with a smile.

She thought for a moment. 'And Revers will be shaking his head over the bills for the harvest dance. At least, if he is anything like Jean Lubain he will—stewards never feel quite happy about the labourers eating and drinking as they do for one day of the year.'

She saw a flicker in his eyes as she mentioned Jean Lubain and waited to see whether he would give any other sign of remembering their fierce argument on his account. Then a thought struck her.

'Oh. That is, if there *was* a harvest dance this year.'

'I certainly hope so. I left instructions.'

'Oh good.' She took a breath. 'I must say, I approve of your replacement for Lubain. Revers sent me some very sensible letters to Paris and answered all of my queries most willingly.' She looked at him more closely and gave a little laugh. 'I suppose *that* was on your instructions too?'

He nodded and changed the subject. 'November is usually the time for cleaning out the mirror pond, is it not?'

'Yes, before the frozen months. Though we shall have no ice on it this year, surely. The worst cold seems to come every ten years, and we have had our bout this decade. You were not in France, so perhaps you did not hear about that ghastly winter, and the famine, and the riots, two years ago?'

'I heard something. Refresh my memory.'

'Bread became very scarce in Paris, and too dear to buy even if you could find it, and that was how the riots started. There were marches in the streets, and people from the countryside surged right into the town of Versailles. It was suggested that the King should leave and go to another of the royal palaces, but he stayed and tried to find a solution, though of course he did not address the crowd. I must say, I was more impressed with the solution that the Paris rioters found all by themselves: they stopped the carts that were supplying flour. You see, it was the unregulated cost of flour that was making the bakers put up the price of bread. So then the people bought it in the street for what they considered a fair price, and they insisted on paying their chosen price for it in the shops too.'

'I seem to remember Franklin telling me something about this, not long ago. How could that be?'

'Because I described it all to him myself. He was fascinated. He said how remarkable it was that desperate, starving people should have such a right sense of the problem. Instead of injuring the tradesmen, or taking their property or ruining their livelihood, they came up with the idea of a fair price and stuck to it. He shook his head when I told him about the rioters who were hanged as scapegoats. Do you know, one of them was an apprentice of sixteen, who joined the march on a whim and never touched so much as a crumb of bread?'

'And that is the city you want to go back to.'

She held his eye and said, 'I want to go *home*. But only if you do.'

'Home,' he said. She could not tell how the sentence might have finished in his head, for she got no further reply.

Much later, everyone else gathered in the same room, and the expectant atmosphere of the eve of the wedding seemed to touch even him. Viviane had been

362

playing the pianoforte and he had chosen his usual chair in the corner near her.

May, taking advantage of this more relaxed mood, was bold enough to call across to him, 'You realise you will be singing tonight? Someone has told us your secret.'

His eyes met Viviane's. 'I have no need to ask who, this time.' To the others he said, 'I am afraid I am out of practice.'

May said, 'We forgive you; you may practise now. We shall talk amongst ourselves until you are ready.'

He rose and approached the piano, and Viviane pointed out the songs piled on a table nearby. 'I have not prepared any pieces, but I am sure you will find something there.'

They looked through them together, and when he had decided on one she located the key as she had done in Philadelphia and they tried out a few lines, softly, while the others talked.

It was odd, but once again, as soon as she heard his dark, beautiful baritone, tears sprang to her eyes.

This time he noticed, and stopped. 'What is it?'

'Nothing.'

'Nothing, she says, flooding the keys.' He placed his forefinger on a teardrop that sparkled on the keyboard beside her wrist.

'I am not!' She quickly wiped her eyes, grateful that he had moved so that he stood with his back to the room, shielding her.

His hand was still before her. 'No more music until you tell me.'

She kept looking at the keyboard and struggled to tease out one thread from the complex emotions that enveloped her. 'It is hard to explain. Maybe I am homesick. It is just . . . whenever we do this, I remember Mirandol.'

'Why?' The hand was snatched away.

She looked up at his startled face. 'I don't know. But I have the strangest notion that nothing will ever be quite right again until we play and sing together at Mirandol.'

This jarred on him, so much so that he took a step away. He kept his eyes fixed on hers, with an expression of alarm which she could not fathom. 'What on earth gives you that idea?'

She said quietly, 'It is not an *idea*, it is a feeling. So do not expect me to be able to explain it.'

At that he seemed to come to himself and remember where they were and what they had been about to do. He tried a lighter tone. 'When a woman brings her feelings into an argument, I can do nothing but withdraw gracefully. Let us see if we can manage this song.'

'I was not aware of any argument, Monsieur.' She replaced her hands on the keys and composed her features, and without further comment they began the performance, to the full satisfaction of their audience.

When it was over and he was folding the music away, he looked down at her and murmured, 'So you think we should go home?'

Her hopes rose at once and she glanced up to catch his expression. 'Yes. What do you think?'

'Quite frankly, I do not know.'

'What do you *feel*, then?'

A confused look of bitterness and embarrassment crossed his face. After a moment he said somewhat harshly, 'My feelings, Mademoiselle, have never been part of any equation: mine or anyone else's.'

Undeterred, she lifted her chin. 'Is it not time you changed that situation?'

His expression did not alter and he said with an effort, 'I cannot see how.'

'Not yet,' she said sweetly. 'But I pray that, in time, you will.'

He seemed about to retort, then changed his mind and simply put down the music sheets and moved away to join the others. For a moment she stayed behind, looking at her hands resting in her lap. It seemed to her that, without getting upset herself, she had penetrated for once beyond his iron barriers of reserve. Not far, but it was a beginning.

Next morning they were together on the balcony above the park, looking out over the treetops towards the town and a glint of the Delaware beyond. It seemed a natural moment to tell him how she had escaped first from Philadelphia and then from the English.

She watched his face with some trepidation and he listened to her with horror, but with no comment on either her recklessness or her actions. As the account unfolded, he interrupted now and then, unable to keep silent; but his questions, though abrupt, were practical. She felt she had never tried him more; correspondingly, she had never seen him exert such control over his own reactions.

Oddly enough, once he knew every detail, the subject he returned to most often was Fleury. He questioned her minutely about his manner, his appearance and his conduct towards her. The second thing he could not get out of his head was the pistol that Fleury had given her, and how she had used it.

'Do you wish to see it?' He shuddered, but she went on lightly, 'He had heard of you, you know, and asked me to pass it on to you, with his compliments. Wait.'

Before he could stop her she went along the balcony to her room. She unwound the pistol from the bundle of clothes in which she had concealed it and brought it out to him. One elbow was leaning on the chair arm and his hand was over his eyes, but he looked up when she reappeared and took the weapon from her. The pale sunlight glanced along the barrel, picking out the intricate chasing in the steel.

He examined it, then sat looking at it for some time. 'I can't believe you used this.'

'I am very happy to surrender it to you. Do you approve of it?'

'Approve? It is handsome, certainly.'

'Handsome is as handsome does: it only got him in the shoulder.'

With a quick exclamation he rose and stepped to the balustrade, to stand with his back to her, looking out over the park.

At once she rose and joined him. 'If I speak ironically, Monsieur, to hide my feelings, then I am afraid I learned that from you!' She continued, banishing all flippancy from her voice, 'We have both suffered from this war—I but a little and you far, far more than I can know. But we are safe after all, and able to go home together. I rejoice at that; I hope you do too.'

He said quietly, 'I do.' When he turned to look at her there was no answering smile, but the unmistakable light of admiration in his eyes conveyed, at last, the balm she had needed since the moment she had fired the pistol, in fear and desperation, at the soldier by the Delaware.

The wedding of Victor de Luny and Abigail Ogilvy took place on a cold, bright November afternoon. The mass was celebrated by an imposing priest who reminded Viviane somewhat of George Washington, though she was reliably informed by May, before the service, that he did not have Washington's false teeth. At the beginning of the ceremony this kept leaping into her mind at inappropriate moments and she had to stifle a great wish to giggle. Fortunately she managed not to, for she would have offended everyone.

The faces on her side of the church were solemn. She guessed that the marquis felt acutely the absence of his wife on this momentous day in their son's life, and she resolved to spend many hours when she got back to Mirandol describing everything in great detail to the marquise—including the excellent set of teeth, if need be—for she suspected that none of the principal actors in the drama would be quite suited to that task once they got home. There was a plan to hold a grand celebration at Luny, however, and invite all the neighbourhood.

Her guardian too was very grave, and he avoided her eye for most of the service.

The bride and groom made a touching couple and she could not help smiling tenderly as she looked at them. Victor spoke his pledges with such an earnest look on his handsome features that a most surprising sense of loss gripped her for a fleeting moment. As the bride's gentle, low voice was heard in response Viviane looked involuntarily up at her guardian and he caught her eye and gave her a quick, self-conscious smile. It was a silent recognition of his kinship with her: they were both outsiders, witnesses to a joy that only the couple before them could share.

The festive dinner at the house afterwards included a few chosen friends, and other members of the family who had been at the church—three of Abigail's grandparents and some aunts, uncles and cousins. On the French side were Vrigny and Gimat, who had managed a dangerous ride down from the army encampment, bringing La Fayette's greeting with them. The marquis was with the army again, but could not leave it to join them so soon after his recovery. The speeches and toasts were punctuated by bursts of eager translation, embroidered sometimes by comments which then had to be translated in their turn, amidst much teasing and laughter. Victor was more voluble than ever, and proposed the best toast to his own marriage, describing it as 'the first great love affair between America and France'. His bride blushed absolutely crimson as everyone rose to give the response. After it, the Comte de Mirandol proposed: 'May this union signal the coming alliance between our two countries,' and once again the table rang with acclamation.

That evening the bride and groom went away to spend a few days in a hunting lodge in the woods not far off, and during this time the Ogilvys helped to conclude the arrangements for the Marquis de Luny, the Comte de Mirandol, Mademoiselle de Chercy and the young couple to take ship for France. Numerous messages and commands passed back and forth between Chester and Annapolis, accommodation was arranged at a comfortable inn there for the whole party, and coach bookings were confirmed.

The count had the duty of some correspondence and they saw a little less of him in the days before departure, but the exchange of letters brought welcome news: Benedict Arnold was making a steady if slow recovery.

The farewells at Chester affected Abigail so much that they were a league into the coach journey south before she stopped crying. Her new husband comforted her fondly and, when the marquis painted a seductive picture of what Luny would be like during her family's visit in the following year, her smiles at last broke through the tears. The other members of the party were less talkative, the count because he was worried about a recent message he had received from army head-quarters, and Mademoiselle de Chercy because she was worried about the count's preoccupation.

Everything went smoothly in Annapolis, however. Viviane visited Mrs Christie's relatives one day while the count went down to the docks and finalised the details of their voyage. They were to travel on a Portuguese vessel which was heading across the Atlantic with molasses to be sold in Nantes on the French coast. The ship, the *Nascimento*, had been inspected when it came through the blockade and up the bay, and the captain expected to be questioned somewhere on the voyage out, but he intended to state that the three Frenchmen he was carrying originated from the Sugar Islands. Victor would give his own name, while the count, whose own might conceivably be on British records after his years of service in America, would give another. Viviane suggested he announce himself as the Baron de Ronseul, but he did not receive this in the spirit of fun which she intended.

On the morning that they were to sail, a rider delivered a packet to the inn for the count while they were all in the breakfast room. Their baggage had already been taken down to the docks, and they were having a last cup of coffee before leaving. He opened the packet, slipped the larger letter into his pocket and handed two others across the table to Viviane.

'From La Fayette. He has addressed one to his wife; the other is for you.'

She unfolded the single sheet of paper, then looked up. 'Are you not going to read yours?'

'Too long. I shall stay behind and tackle it when you all go. Let me catch you up.'

'Very well.'

My dear Mademoiselle de Chercy

It is many weeks since I last had the pleasure of seeing you, and I should be delighted to greet you again on American soil; but our friendship and, even more, the solicitude you have always shown to my wife and family, render me doubly eager to bid you God speed back to France. I have welcomed with tender gratitude all the good news you have passed on about my dear wife: her letters have been so rare that I have received most of my information through you alone. Now I beg you as a further kind favour to take the letter I enclose and place it in her hands when you reach Paris.

You cannot conceive how envious I felt when I bade goodbye to Monsieur Jacob, knowing that he would soon embrace those closest to his heart and be welcomed into the comforts of home. He has before him happiness and harmony with his lovely wife, and the Comte de Mirandol has the good fortune to return in your delightful company.

You know us so well, I beg you to tell my dear wife that she is not to imagine us Frenchmen hardened and made solitary by this war. On the contrary, for me it only confirms the superiority of female society. I was brought up by my grandmother and aunts; as suitor to my darling fiancée I submitted cheerfully to the benevolent domination of her mother and sisters, and my cherished desire is to live henceforth surrounded by my wife and children. Women are my life; to exist apart from those dear ones is the worst, almost the only real hardship forced upon me by the American struggle.

But my task is not yet over and I must be steadfast. I rejoice for the Comte de Mirandol, however, who returns knowing that his has been abundantly fulfilled. I heard from some of his companions that he distinguished himself more than ever at the Battle

of Saratoga—they were awed by the fury and deter-
mination he showed in the front line. Yet when I
dared to bring this up in a recent letter to him I
received no word in reply. Please convey to him my
warmest regards, and accept on his behalf and your
own my heartfelt wishes for a safe voyage and joyful
return to France.

With the most tender affection and highest respect
I have the honour to be, my dear Mademoiselle, your
most obedient humble servant,
(The Mis de) La Fayette

The *Nascimento* was a handsome ship for a trader, and
the passengers' quarters were clean. Viviane took only
a quick glance at her cabin, however, and spent the
rest of the time on deck, scanning the foreshore while
she waited for the count.

She breathed deeply of the salty air, caught by a
surge of emotion that was made up of pain at leaving
her land of endeavour and the thrill of heading home-
ward. She longed for the count to arrive so that she
could share these ideas, for only he could really understand them. She thought of the last time he had left the
shores of the United States, forced by duty to travel
towards an empty homecoming. She believed that this
departure was different, and his emotions would
resemble hers: regret at leaving a land she had come to
love, mingled with the bright anticipation of what
awaited them at home—the loving arms of Madame
de Chercy, Paris and their friends, Franklin's eager
welcome, the warmth of Mirandol.

The Lunys all joined her at the rail and they talked
fitfully, watching the ship's company bustling around
them and keeping an eye out for the count.

It was only when the last goods were stowed and
the main gangplank taken up that Viviane became
impatient.

'Everything looks ready—we must be due to cast off!
Does he not realise? What can be keeping him?'

The marquis said, 'Depend upon it, we shall see him
at any moment.'

370

'You told me that last time.'

'And how right I was! Do you imagine he would take the risk of missing this voyage?' He looked at her closely as he said with a half-smile, 'I have been observing him of late and I would stake my life nothing is more precious to him than accompanying you back to France.'

Her hands gripped the rail as she turned from him to hide a disappointed frown. 'He has an odd way of demonstrating it.'

A quarter of an hour passed and her anxiety grew to a frenzy. 'He has been held up. We must warn the captain and instruct him to wait!'

'They can only delay so long,' Victor pointed out, 'for we must catch the tide.'

'Then I shall wait for him ashore. I am not going without him.'

'Heavens,' Abigail said in alarm, 'do please stay with us, Viviane. We cannot leave you behind!'

'Wait,' the marquis said. 'Look, there is a cab coming, at a great rate. Depend upon it, he is here.'

He was not. Instead a young man leaped from the cab and ran to the quayside, gazed up at the row of people along the ship's rail and brandished a letter high in one hand.

'Message for the Marquess of Loony! Ho there, gentleman by the name of Loony.'

The marquis signalled for him to be allowed aboard and he dashed up the narrow gangplank, bowed and received a coin in exchange for the paper he held. After he ran back down, the gangplank was taken up, the mooring ropes were cast off and the ship's company sprang into action. None of the party tried to stop these proceedings; from the moment the messenger had spoken Viviane was stunned into immobility. Breathless, she waited for the marquis to unseal the letter.

It was two lines long. Reading them quickly, the marquis considered for a split second and then said, 'I understand. He has been summoned by General Washington.'

'I don't believe it,' Viviane cried. 'How *can* he? Is there no more explanation than that?'

'Yes. This is for you.' Opening out the bottom of the sheet he lifted out another, folded and sealed like the first.

She snatched the letter and stood for a moment staring at all their anxious, sympathetic faces in outrage and despair. Then she turned on her heel and ran below decks, brushing roughly past people in her path, oblivious to the sudden movement of the ship, intent on reaching her cabin. There she slammed the door behind her, leaned on it and let out the exclamation that had beaten against her ribs all the way below. It was a moan of pain, as though the marquis had thrust at her not a letter but the point of a knife.

She stayed with her eyes closed, her back against the door. He would not come. He would not stride onto the ship and stop before her, embrace her, hold her close to him for one agonising second. Then all at once she remembered what had happened after Brandywine, and the truth burst upon her. She wanted him. She wanted him like that: his arms around her, his voice in her ear. She wanted the length of his body crushed against hers, the pulse in his throat beating against her forehead.

Trembling, she walked unsteadily to the bunk and sat staring at his letter in her hands. She wanted all of him, for the rest of her life. Nothing he nor anyone else might say could alter that. She belonged henceforth in his arms, and the yearning was so great that it blotted out everything around her in a kind of mist. Only the letter burned in the centre of her vision, like a white beacon. He would stay ashore, letting her take this voyage without him, offering her nothing but this cruel, luminous sign of their separation. Yet as the ship bore her away she could still hear his whisper from weeks ago, feel the grip of his hands, remember the taste and smell of him as he held her against him. He could not do this to her now, it was impossible.

My dearest Ward

You have leave to be more angry with me now than ever before. No words can express how much I regret this. General Washington has called for me and I go at once to meet him near Gloucester. I expect to get back to Annapolis in a week or so, and will take ship to follow you as soon as I can.

It is impossible for me to tell you what my feelings were on receiving the general's summons and realising I would not be travelling in your company. I do not expect you to believe me when I say that our journey to America together was one of the happiest episodes of my life, nor could you possibly understand how much I looked forward to the voyage home.

You will not easily forgive me for leaving instructions that this letter be delivered at the last moment before your ship sails. I might have taken leave of you in person before riding to Gloucester, but I am too afraid that I shall lack the fortitude if you are before me.

My only shred of comfort rests in the hope that you will understand my response to Washington. If that man requests my advice I cannot refuse it, since, who knows, it may be the last time he asks it of me.

There is another issue, which I have been too selfish to admit: you may pass more smoothly through the blockade without me, as we cannot be sure how rigorous the inspection of passengers may be, nor how much risk there is of the English knowing what my activities have been in the United States. Indeed, you would be best to destroy this letter.

I hate having to stay, I hate writing this to you, I cannot—must not—tell you what this parting does to me. I have made my apologies to the marquis and thanked him in advance for the services I am confident he will render you in my place.

I wish you a safe and pleasant journey, and if you have reproaches for me, cherish them until we meet again and I beg your forgiveness in person—that day cannot come too soon for

JR de C de M

She read it once, so rapidly she hardly took in the words, then crumpled it in her hands, in anger and misery. It was briefer than La Fayette's. And much less elegant. And there was no friendship in it.

Then she spread it out feverishly and read it again.

For an hour she kept it in her hand, sitting on the bunk or pacing the narrow cabin while she went over and over the one sheet of paper. And gradually, as the ship began to rock and tip on the waves of the Chesapeake, carrying her further away from the man who had written the lines on the page, she began to read between them.

Phrases seemed to glow at her in the light from the porthole. She heard his voice in them, the voice of recent months, devoid of severity, with tones that now held messages he had never meant her to hear. She began to look further back. To the last moment in Philadelphia, when a mysterious impulse surged up and was quenched behind his eyes, and his farewell was battered down, unheard, under his horse's hooves. And even earlier, on the day of Washington's parade through the city, when he had come to bid her goodbye and then had been unable, when the moment came, to speak the words of parting.

She put the letter down on the bunk and hunted through her baggage, flinging clothes and possessions out onto the floor of the cabin, until she found his other letters, one written before Brandywine, the other before Saratoga. Abigail knocked on her door during this search, and she called out quickly that she was all right, she was resting and did not wish to be disturbed. After a while the soft footfalls faded away.

She sat down with his letters and went through them all over again. Her eyes burned with reading them. Then she put them on the lap of her dress and slowly drew her forefinger over the surface of each one in turn. Three crumpled and creased sheets of paper crisscrossed with invisible writing were the only evidence she possessed that he loved her. And meanwhile he would have not a solitary clue, not a single word, to tell him that she loved him. Until he came home.

20

LOVE LETTERS

Viviane was at the opera. The work was *Orpheus and Eurydice*, which Gluck had rewritten in French three years before. For the debut in Paris, Gluck asked the singers to act, which was unheard of, so on Viviane's first night at the Palais-Royal for many months, she had the chance to observe how they coped with this new style. The celebrated Sophie Arnould sang Eurydice, and Viviane was moved by the way she interpreted the simple stage actions, drawing on a power that came directly from the music. It was almost too hard to bear when Orpheus found her in the Underworld but was not allowed to look at her or tell her he loved her. As she followed him slowly about the stage, pleading for an explanation, her face and voice were so full of anguish that Viviane was aching for Orpheus to embrace her, even though she would die on the instant. It was dreadful when she did, crumpling like a moth in a flame.

No one around Viviane paid the same attention to the work as she did, except for Madame de Chercy. When it was over, Viviane turned and said to her with a smile, 'How lucky I am to see this so out of season. How is it that we have operas at such a time?'

'There was a command performance for the Queen last week, so they decided to repeat it. I am glad you enjoyed it; I first saw this opera just after you left town, and I was so sorry then to think that you had missed it.'

The melancholy fondness in her glance melted Viviane, who leaned over and pressed her hand. 'I hope the count may see it when he comes back. If anything could convert him from Italian opera, this would be the piece.' Then the memory of his liaison with la Farrucci hit her and she sat back with a jolt.

Her aunt did not seem to have made this connection, however, for she replied at once, 'Do you know, hardly five minutes go by without your mentioning him? I cannot tell you how it rejoices me to hear it.'

Something about their conversation, or perhaps simply the fact that they were not talking about him, seemed to rouse the gentleman behind them, the Baron de Ronseul, who was sitting with Louise de Billancourt, her mother and his.

He leaned forward and said, 'I should be very curious to see the little la Farrucci as Eurydice; what would you say to that, Madame?'

Madame de Chercy inclined her head only slightly to say, 'She has returned to Venice, I believe. Meanwhile, Sophie Arnould has already made the role her own.'

Viviane, who pretended to be examining the stalls from their box, did not turn her head at all, though she could feel the baron's gaze on the side of her face. Louise tried to wrest his attention back by saying, 'I cannot get over this sudden penchant for the opera, Monsieur. We are used to glimpsing you here but twice a year.'

'You object to my company, Mademoiselle de Billancourt?' he said, remaining in the same posture as before, so that his voice, despite its smoothness, vibrated unpleasantly close to Viviane's ear.

'By no means, if you are about to set yourself up as an expert. In fact I shall depend upon you for advice from now on.'

'I should much rather have the benefit of *your* instruction, Mademoiselle. I am an amateur of many precious things, but an expert on nothing.' He said in more muted tones, 'As Mademoiselle de Chercy so tellingly pointed out the other day, my greatest fault—and heaven knows I have many to submit for her correction—is lack of seriousness. If only she knew how serious I am on a certain subject.'

Forced into utterance, Viviane said coolly, 'I do not recall saying anything of the sort, Monsieur. In fact I cannot even remember our conversation.'

'Then I am doubly reproached,' he said with a short sigh, 'for I remember every word. I foolishly made light of the hardships facing the American armies, and you rounded on me with such scorn that I could draw only one conclusion from it—you believe me to be heartless.'

The only retort to this was, *Yes, and unprincipled as well*. But she was not free to pronounce it, nor could she think up a frivolous reply for the occasion—she had lost the knack for Parisian cleverness and wondered sometimes whether she would ever get it back. So she simply let the remark hang in the air for a moment, then said to everyone in general, 'Perhaps we should be going. They are lowering the chandeliers.'

Everyone got up and began moving out of the box, but then Viviane realised that her awkward posture, twisted slightly away from Ronseul during the performance, had caused her left foot to go numb.

'Madame, wait a moment: I have pins and needles.'

She bent to rub her ankle, then looked up to find the ladies had left the box to stand in the corridor outside. They were joined at that moment by others, but not by the Baron de Ronseul, who had remained with her. He perched himself on a chair arm two seats away and looked at her solicitously.

'May I assist you?'

She ignored him and waited with averted eyes for the tingling in her foot to cease.

After a moment he said, 'I cannot wonder that you refuse to speak to me.'

His altered voice made her look up in surprise. 'That is nonsense, Monsieur. We do converse; what is more, you claim to recall my every word.'

'And each one confirms your opinion of me. As I said, I do not wonder at it. In the past the world has thought me unconscious of my own iniquities and, villain that I was, I encouraged the belief; but in truth they have always loomed large to me—in my worst moments they have even been a matter of pride. You see I use no disguises with you. Lately,' he overcame a slight hesitation in speech, 'the stains and blots on my life have begun to torment me.'

She said in amazement, 'Really, Monsieur, even if you were sincere, this is hardly the time and place—'

'But you are the person! Who else is there in Paris to say what they really think of me? Even your silence just now spoke more than anyone's reproaches ever could.' She rose, but he arrested her with his blue stare and said rapidly, 'Mademoiselle, I am aware that I address the person in Paris who conceives the very worst of me. I have reason to suspect that confidences have been made to you in the past concerning my most reprehensible actions. My soul is stripped bare before you. I cannot ask even for the unthinking courtesy you would extend towards a new acquaintance, much less your recognition or sympathy. I can only beg for your guidance.'

Before she had recovered from this outburst she managed to say, 'I am sorry, I am quite unqualified to give advice on anything that interests you.'

He shook his head, but seemed to come to himself a little, rising and stepping out of her way. 'I can understand that my seeking to reform myself is ludicrous to you. But I have no idea where else to look for compassion. For I *have* seen compassion in your eyes—never directed towards me, of course, but it is there when your thoughts turn to objects worthy of your pity.'

His voice was humble as he murmured these words, but Viviane suspected that it only sounded this way because he took care not to be heard by the ladies outside. At any moment Louise would dart inquisitively back into the box; it irritated Viviane to be put in such a position.

As she stepped forward she said quietly, 'If you seek reform, Monsieur, I can only say that your best guide will be your own conscience.' She would have added, *if you have one*, but a glance at his chastened expression as she glided by made her hold her tongue. He did not attempt to stop her leaving the box.

Her mind was busy with his astonishing behaviour all the way down the staircase. The whole approach was uncharacteristic, in matter and demeanour. If he was acting, she silently congratulated him: he had talents to rival what she had just seen on stage. If he was in earnest, it could only be in pursuit of her, yet why chase after her now? Before she had left Paris for America, he had actually taken care to avoid her, or at any rate to avoid her guardian, for there was a deep antagonism between the two men. No doubt he only felt safe to importune her now because her guardian was away.

At this thought she returned to her obsession—there was no chance of keeping her mind on anyone for long except Jules de Chercy de Mirandol. And everything conspired to centre her mind on him, foremost being the victory at Saratoga, word of which had reached Paris before her, on 6 December, turning opinion around and riveting attention on the United States. Franklin had been one of the first to welcome herself and Victor de Luny back and he had not only rejoiced that her uncle was soon to return but broadcast the news around town. Franklin had kept the secret of her trip to America, but there were plenty of other stories to make tongues busy. La Fayette's heroism, Victor's battle experiences and his American wife were the talk of the salons, and everyone was burning to hear of Saratoga from the Comte de Mirandol.

Added to this, Madame de Chercy loved to speak of him, especially now that her grand-niece could at last bring herself to discuss him without prejudice.

All the while Viviane's secret life prevailed over the everyday, as she lived and breathed the dream of being with him again. For it was a dream: the overpowering shock of knowing she loved him and the heady few hours when she thought he loved her had been followed by over a month at sea, where some of her warm confidence had been swept away. She wanted him, she lived for him, but that did not mean that she could have him.

The ache of separation had resumed, stronger than ever. It cost her a great deal just to act normally, to give the impression she had returned from a long summer stay in the Loire, to slip back into Paris and take up an existence that was meaningless as long as one man was absent.

She stood amongst the group in the foyer of the

theatre, indifferent to what went on around her, while Louise and the baron bought lottery tickets. Louise teased him that these were his real reason for attending the opera and he exchanged some laughing banter with her, but after she and her mother had gone he returned politely to Viviane's side and offered to wait with her and her great-aunt until their carriage made its way to the steps of the colonnade outside. Madame de Chercy, deep in conversation with his mother, assented graciously and walked on ahead, so Viviane was forced to take his arm as he carved a way for them through the crowd.

He murmured at once, 'Thank you, Mademoiselle, for listening to my confession tonight, and forgive me if it offended you in any way—I could not help myself. Your eyes and voice have pronounced me a villain; can I be blamed if it is to you that I turn to seek hope? Can I help it if I long to see the scorn that kindles in your glance give way to the awareness of how much I regret my past sins?'

They came out into the night air. Viviane shivered and withdrew her arm. 'Monsieur de Ronseul, your confession was improper, and to carry on in this vein is impudent. I have no power to help you, and of that you are well aware.'

He flinched and turned his face away, ostensibly looking for their carriage and his own amongst the throng, but no doubt working out his next ploy. She looked at him in profile; she was used to his pallor, but tonight against the changing shadows of the street his face looked quite bleached of colour. For a moment she could almost believe that she had wounded him.

When the Chercy carriage battled its way through to the edge of the colonnade he moved forward to hand Madame de Chercy in, then helped Viviane onto the step. Just before she entered, and while her aunt was settling herself inside, he said in a whisper, 'Mademoiselle, I cannot believe you will refuse your guidance. Henceforth you command me. Whatever your wishes, I shall follow them to the letter.'

Furious that he dared take his nonsense to this point,

almost within the hearing of her aunt and his mother, she hissed, 'I wish you never to speak of this again.'

He let go her hand, made her a profound bow and said, 'Thank you,' in a tone of the deepest mortification. She turned her eyes from his pale face as the carriage rolled away.

The next day Viviane was relieved, when Louise came to spend the afternoon at the Rue Jacob, that as a friend she had nothing to reproach herself with. Ronseul would not dare renew his attentions and Louise was welcome to dally pointlessly with him if she pleased.

They sat in their favourite spot on the first floor, on the gold brocade sofa by the window in the blue drawing room. The sofa was strewn with large oriental cushions that could be arranged to support them while they lounged and chatted and glanced over one outspread arm now and then to look through the tall panes and examine the traffic passing by in the street.

'What a shame Monsieur de Luny has gone down to the Loire. I do so like talking to him, despite his shameless betrayal of my dearest friend. I scolded him so much over it when we first met that he went quite red with embarrassment.'

'How cruel of you. No wonder he was keen to escape from Paris! He will be back in January, though. I am not sure whether he will bring Abigail or not, it is just a business visit.'

'It would be better if he did not. Oh, I know you adore her, but you have to admit she is a bit of a social liability. She has some French, I grant you, but the *accent*!'

'I am sorry to hear you say that. I spent a great deal of time on the voyage helping her with her French. Dear Victor is of no use, for he talks away to her just as rapidly as he does to the rest of the world. But she is settling down at Luny and will make progress, I am sure, for the marquise is so considerate and patient. I long to see them all there.'

Louise pouted. 'Do not tell me you are yearning for rustication, after having neglected us for the best part of a year. You will at least wait for your uncle to turn up?'

'Oh, Louise, that is *all* I wait for.'

This outburst brought a spark of curiosity to Louise's bright eyes. 'What, the double-dyed villain has changed his colours? Am I to understand you converse these days without drawing blood?'

Viviane looked down and pulled at a tassel on the velvet cushion under her elbow. One instinct when she came home had been to tell Louise everything, to unburden herself to at least one person. But the other, stronger feeling was that she must protect this hidden love, for she had absolutely no way of knowing whether it would ever be shared. So she replied, 'I am glad to say our relations are quite cordial. No one could have been more surprised than I when they began to improve. But there you are.'

Louise bounced lightly on the cushions as she gave a laugh: '*Won*derful! I always told you how deeply acceptable he would turn out to be. Thus I have leave to call him an angel after all.' She settled back with a satisfied sigh. 'Do not be surprised if I fling myself at him when he returns—I have a mind to make someone jealous.' Then she looked up, saw Viviane's face and laughed even longer. 'Oh, dearest, do not look at me like that. Have you lost the knack of telling when I am funning and when I am in earnest? You have been away far too long and it is exactly as I feared—the Americans do not have a sense of humour amongst them.'

'You are forgetting Doctor Franklin.'

'By no means: he is the exception that proves the rule, which is why he is here and not there.'

'He is here to lay siege to Versailles.'

'And he is doing so well: since your precious United States came up in the world he has been seen constantly, walking about the gardens with the Queen. They say she dotes on him. So, next step, perhaps an audience with His Majesty.'

'At last. I hope so.'

'Apropos of the Queen.' Louise moved closer and leaned towards her confidentially. 'Did you know her brother of Austria came to visit Paris while you were away?'

'Yes, my aunt wrote to me of it.'

'And do you know why he came? You would never guess: it was to advise her on how to make a father out of our Gracious Majesty.' She giggled. 'Apparently in the intimacy of the bedchamber the young couple did not go to work in quite the right way.' She caught Viviane's expression and said lightly, 'Oh, I know no details. This was all explained to me in secret with the greatest propriety, with delicacy even, which is surprising when one considers who furnished the explanation. In such circumstances I am too shy even to give you his initials.' Viviane was still frowning so she added teasingly, 'I assure you I have made no advances in coquetry since you went away, despite the tempting company.'

Viviane decided to change the subject. 'What are your plans for this week?'

'Have you forgotten? You promised to come with me to the Garenne so we can see the new leopards.'

'If you wish. By the way, I made a discovery about my uncle that may tarnish his glamour for you. Did you know he was once a menagerie keeper?'

Louise burst out laughing. 'Your sense of humour is coming back with a vengeance!' Her face grew sober again. 'And I promised Maman to go to church this Sunday, I cannot think why.'

'We shall be there too. My aunt always likes to go on the Sunday before Christmas.'

'Oh good, I am content. I shall pray for snow, and sleigh rides in the Bois.'

And I shall pray for no winter storms in the north Atlantic, and a safe journey home.

Before this, however, a letter arrived. Viviane was at home alone on Saturday morning when a special messenger brought it to the Rue Jacob. When she caught sight of the white square of paper on the major-domo's

383

salver as he walked into the salon, she sprang to her feet and rushed forward, startling him. He handed it to her with a bow and she could not wait for him to leave the room before scanning it quickly and preparing to tear it open. But she registered just in time that it was not addressed by the hand she now knew so well, in every vigorous trait.

The disappointment was so crushing that she sat down for a while without even glancing at the paper in her fingers. Then at last she unfolded it.

Mademoiselle

You have forbidden me to speak, but I thank God that you did not forbid me to write. Would you prohibit everything that holds me to life? I dare not describe to you how my heart contracted at your words, nor the agony caused by the memory of how you said them. But you also accuse me. You cannot in all justice forbid me to plead my case. After that, if you will, may silence fall between us.

You call my speech impudent—*literally, shameless. Yet I expressed nothing but the shame and disgust that overwhelm me when I look back on my life. And in hours of painful contemplation I cannot recall a word, phrase or inference in that speech which deserves the epithet* improper.

I beg you to tell me what crime I commit in daring to look to you as my guide. Can you have so hard a heart that you refuse the message of hope that might raise my spirit from its prostration? Dare I say that I believe your mercy to be greater than any cruelty you may seek to show?

If you had a cold rectitude, a marble virtue, you would not be receiving this letter. But your goodness has a fiery quality which has drawn my crippled soul towards you whether you will it or no. I have seen the warmth of your feelings, I know that you have felt their impulse. When I allude to your flight from Paris in April, I do so with the assurance that I have never breathed a word of what I guessed to a living soul; and I mention it only to explain my idea of you

384

as a woman whose strength is proven and entire. Society, if it divined the motive for your journey South and West, might censure you. I, on the other hand, honour a virtue that has withstood trials and endured. Your secret, like everything connected with you, is sacred to me.

You may ask yourself why I write. I answer, first, because you are more obdurate than any jury to which I might address myself, and I have need of your judgement. Second—but I fear that very judgement too much to confess the other, irresistible impulse that compels me.

Low as I have crept in your estimation, I stand even lower in my own. I shall comply with your wishes, and not a word shall pass my lips in your presence without your permission. It is in your power never to hear my voice again if this earnest supplication stirs that animosity in you that has so pierced my soul. I beg only five words: 'I have read your letter.' To any other man this sentence would be an empty formula; to me it would lend the strength to live another day of a miserable existence.

I am eternally
The humblest of your servants
Alain de Ronseul

She read it through and sat looking at it in horror. For him to write to her at all was an effrontery, but what he said turned her cold. She had no regard for the author of the letter which might cloud her reception of it—this was blackmail. He was counting on her tolerating him from now on, for she could not avoid him, refuse to speak to him, forbid him to communicate, unless she was prepared to let him tell the whole of Paris that she had eloped to America. A tale which would be embroidered, she had no doubt, with intriguing speculations about what she might have been up to there since April.

For a while she distracted herself by wondering how he had come to guess the truth. But it was hopeless, there were too many friends who might have let fall a crucial remark in his hearing. Abigail perhaps, all unknowing, might have made a revealing reference while struggling with a French conversation. Victor might have let slip her name in one of his voluble flights. Franklin might have allowed himself a mysterious comment about her that Ronseul's sharp mind had interpreted with deadly accuracy. It was out of the question that Louise could have spoken to him about it, for her friend had sworn to keep all Viviane's secrets and prided herself on her loyalty.

She read the worst paragraph again and the insinuating phrase *the warmth of your feelings* leaped out at her. It did not matter how he knew that she had eloped to join Victor; the disaster was that he did know it, and would tell the world unless she stopped him. It would be a catastrophe. The damage to Victor and his new wife would be cruel, for he would be made to look a rogue and she ridiculous. It would destroy the friendship with Victor for ever; they had kept Abigail from the slightest suspicion of what had tempted Viviane to Spain and Victor's wife thought of them only as friends since childhood. Even that was enough to cause a shade of jealousy that would always be in the air between them. This revelation would erect an impassable barrier.

The damage to herself was incalculable. She closed her eyes and bit her lip as she allowed herself to imagine her guardian coming home to the eager enthusiasm of Paris society. She had a vision of them crowding around him, full of avid curiosity about his exploits and dying to see his face when he learned that his ward's elopement and her amorous intrigues in America were the talk of the city. He would be assailed with ribald questions, thinly veiled under a polite air of concern. He would be invited to explain away her actions, forced into half-truths and prevarication, which would be met by amused disbelief.

Most tormenting of all was her fear of what he would do if he found out that the scandal had been spread by Ronseul. She wanted no battles on her behalf; after all they had gone through, she could not contemplate this worst of endings.

She spent a sleepless night and went to Saint-Germain on Sunday without having hit upon any solution to her problem. She shrank from discussing it with Madame de Chercy: her aunt had endured enough trials, and Viviane could not bear to destroy the happiness which she had rediscovered lately, and which only awaited the arrival of the count to be complete. She could not possibly talk to Louise and she could never embarrass poor Victor by writing to ask his advice. She must act alone.

When they reached Saint-Germain they discovered that the Billancourts were already there, seated in a crowded part of the church. Madame de Chercy was disappointed that they must take a seat far away from them, but Viviane was relieved.

Before they moved into the nave they stopped to look at the beautifully carved crèche that was always brought out and decorated for the Christmas season. Viviane looked at the little child Jesus in the manger and could not help thinking of Adrienne de La Fayette and her new daughter, Anastasie—the two members of her friend's family who awaited him in Paris. Their first daughter, Henriette, had died from a sudden illness before her own return. It hurt her to realise that as yet her friend might not know he had lost his beloved child. And he might not even have heard about the birth of the baby Anastasie, although it had happened so long ago, on 1 July.

Madame de Chercy leaned towards her. 'My dearest child, you are crying. Whatever is the matter?'

'I am sorry, Madame, I could not help thinking of Henriette de La Fayette. How cruel it is for her mother and father.'

'Indeed. Let us say a prayer for them.' Honorine de Chercy looked moved as they walked down the aisle to their seats.

When Viviane knelt and closed her eyes, images came back of her visits to the Rue du Faubourg Saint-Honoré in April, after the marquis had left for Bordeaux. Adrienne de La Fayette liked to keep her daughter by her, and Viviane had often sat with her on the floor, playing with a wooden Noah's ark full of animals which was the little girl's favourite toy. Henriette had caught something of the anxiety that gripped everyone in the house at the time, and sometimes asked Viviane, very earnestly, where her Papa was. Viviane always told her that he had gone hunting in a forest, and played hunting scenes with the carved animals to amuse her.

She was touched very deeply by what had happened to La Fayette and his family. When she had visited Adrienne, on her first day back, and had put his letter into her hands, they had talked for hours. Amongst other painful details she had learned that, directly after Brandywine, the English newspapers had been the first to publish articles about the marquis's part in the battle, some of them wildly inaccurate and nearly all placing him at death's door. It was by the greatest luck that the truth reached Adrienne de La Fayette at the same time, in one of her husband's own letters, or the house in the Rue du Faubourg Saint-Honoré would have been a tragic place indeed.

Viviane was scarcely aware of her surroundings for a long time, but halfway through the service she happened to glance along the row opposite and her heart nearly stopped. The Baron de Ronseul was only yards away, his fair head turned her way and his eyes intent. He was simply dressed and wore no wig, and this somehow had the effect of making him look less self-confident and more vulnerable. He nodded to her nervously when she caught his eye, but she looked away at once in consternation. She knew perfectly well, from Louise's letters the year before, that he never attended church for the purpose of worship. He had found out where she would be today, and turned up to judge the effect of his letter.

It was foolish of him: he would have done better to surprise her in the square afterwards for, by the time the congregation left, her mind was made up. It was torture enough waiting for her guardian as it was, and she could not bear to think of him returning to find her own reputation at its lowest ebb. She must hold

Ronseul off but not antagonise him. Once her guardian was home, it would surely be possible to end the contact somehow.

Standing about on the paving stones afterwards while her aunt spoke to friends, and Louise was talking gaily about their visit to the Garenne, Viviane was concerned that there would, after all, be no opportunity to tackle the baron. Yet if she could not speak to him, she ran the risks of either receiving yet another compromising letter or hearing her story on everyone's lips the next day.

He was as adept as usual, however. He simply waited until most of the group had gone, including the Billancourt ladies, then approached while Madame de Chercy was free and said, 'I have a question on the mass that I am confident Mademoiselle de Chercy can answer for me. I have my missal here: may I beg her counsel for a moment?'

Honorine de Chercy looked at him in surprise but nodded her assent, and next thing Viviane found herself drawn a little apart to a spot 'where the light was better', to be shown a page in the book. She had made no protest about joining him and had rather expected this to prompt a return of his usual arrogance, but he was too careful for that. In fact he stood beside her in absolute silence, with an earnest look that at length reminded her of his absurd promise not to utter a word to her. Drawing herself up, she took the offered initiative.

'Monsieur, I have read your letter.' A flash of triumph appeared in the blue eyes, which she saw and quenched. 'I have read it and understood it perfectly. You force a reply from me with the threat of advertising what you see as a past indiscretion of my own.'

His eyes widened. 'You accuse me of coercion? You would add another reproach to those you have thrown at me? If I did not already worship you as an angel, my dear Mademoiselle, I might dare to say that thought is unchristian.'

'Monsieur, I desire neither your denials nor your compliments, for none of them is sincere.'

She was worried that this was pushing him too far, but to her surprise he looked if anything more downcast than ever. After a short struggle with himself he said, 'You are unjust, but I cannot blame you. All I can do is repeat my plea for guidance.'

She took a breath. 'Very well. If such is your wish, I do have a suggestion: that you apply to my aunt's confessor, Father Berny, and begin a course of religious instruction. He is a priest of this church.'

It was risky to call his bluff quite so thoroughly and she watched him with secret trepidation. But after a start of surprise he murmured, 'Thank you. You have no idea what this means to me; it is far kinder than I deserve.'

Out of the corner of her eye Viviane could see her aunt looking their way; he closed the book that he was still holding between them, stepped back and made a bow, saying, 'Henceforth I should like you to hear of me only things that merit your approval. I must not hope for more. I must not *say* more. God bless you, Mademoiselle.'

He turned and walked away before she could be sure of reading his expression.

Viviane's most steadfast, secret hope had been that the count would be home by Christmas. It seemed almost impossible, for it depended on his being lucky enough to have as swift a voyage to France as she had enjoyed herself, but still she yearned for him to come in time.

When he did not, and there was no letter either, she was so miserable that by Christmas Eve she began to think she could not bear to attend midnight mass with her aunt. This would have disappointed Madame de Chercy terribly, however, for the memory was fresh in both their minds of the count's refusal to accompany them the year before. It would be doubly dreary for her aunt if she were forced to go alone and contemplate the gap in her circle on this night that placed such a loving light on the family.

So Viviane went, but during mass she was depressed

further by solemn thoughts. She realised now that in a reserved and unassuming way, the count had tried to stand in the place of a parent. Duty had called him to protect her, watch out for her, think about her future. If over time his emotions had become fonder towards her, what hope did she have that he would ever admit to them? She suspected that there were occasions when he had had to force himself not to declare his feelings, but if that were so, he had always succeeded. It occurred to her that his withdrawal from the voyage home was just such an occasion, and that he had used the summons from Washington as a plausible excuse not to be near her for weeks in the close confines of the ship. Not to share almost every waking moment with her, to talk, to hear her voice, with the same thrill as she would have listened to his.

There was no way of being sure about any of this until he arrived, and the longer he stayed away the greater grew her fear that he would never come at all. Superstitiously, she looked around the grand soaring church for a sign somewhere that might give her hope. She did not find one. The crowd in the nave, the rich colours of clothing and vestments in the bright candle-light, the comforting words of the blessing, raised Madame de Chercy's spirits, but for Viviane they were in such contrast to her mood that they hurt.

In this state it jarred her to the bones to be suddenly confronted by the Baron de Ronseul as they left the church. He was impeccably dressed and bewigged, his handsome features wore a more open expression than usual and his eyes gleamed when they met hers, which made Viviane sure he had lain in wait. He stepped forward and exchanged Christmas greetings with Madame de Chercy the moment she drew abreast of him, and received a benevolent response. But Viviane could not be so tolerant. With her heart aching for one man, she was not going to smile and utter platitudes to another. She did not listen to his eager opening, barely nodded in reply, and her indignation swept her onward to where the carriage waited.

Madame de Chercy had to almost run to catch her

up. 'Mademoiselle, is this suitable behaviour for tonight of all nights? The baron is scarcely a favourite with me, but at least I acknowledge his presence!'

'Excuse me, Madame, but I treat him as he deserves.'

'You may well think so, but he does not. I have never seen a man so taken aback; I actually thought for a moment he would burst into tears. It was thoughtless, my dear—you cut him to the quick.'

'He will recover.' She turned to her aunt before they entered the carriage and laid her hands on her shoulders. 'Let us not say a word more about him. There is only one man I want to talk about tonight. Embrace me, and tell me he will come home.'

Honorine de Chercy's reply was to kiss her and put her arms around her shoulders. 'Depend upon it, we shall see him soon.'

Another letter arrived the next day. This time Madame de Chercy was at home, and it was she who took it off the salver. Seeing Viviane's expression she said with a swift shake of the head, 'I am sorry, my dear, it is not from your uncle. I do not recognise the hand, but it is addressed to you. A Christmas wish from one of your friends, no doubt.'

She handed it over and left the room. Viviane's heart sank, fearing more impertinence from Ronseul, but when she looked at the inscription she did not recognise the writing. With some curiosity, she unsealed it and began to read.

Mademoiselle
Forgive the desperation that makes me address this in a disguised hand and send it by another servant. I cannot bear you not to open it.

By your behaviour last night you repudiated every good intention I have expressed. You denied the first impulse that made me apply to you, and indicated that I must pursue the Christian path without your help. Having stripped that hope away, you leave me no alternative but to confess to the second, powerful

392

reason that renders me speechless when I am near you and makes my hand shake thus when I write.

Mademoiselle, I love you, with the greatest passion that a man can feel. This attachment has wound itself into the core of my being, and will be extinguished only with my own destruction.

When I first realised what influence you had on my heart, I withdrew from your company in alarm. I knew my past had sullied me in your eyes and I feared for my own happiness if I yielded to the exquisite pleasure of seeing you again. But chance drove me to your side: a succession of invitations threw me in your way, and I had not the fortitude to deny myself a single meeting. And in the meaningless intervals that succeeded I lived for you alone.

You have been wont to condemn my actions, but in this case, Mademoiselle, I did not act, I suffered. The more enmeshed I became, the less strength I had of mind and body. Then I reached a point where I felt that by applying to you I might find some way to cauterise the pain of loving you without hope. I thought that if you unequivocally spurned me I might learn to stifle my obsession. Not so. When you first advised me to seek instruction, I felt a rush of joy. But the blood drained from my heart when you walked past me last night. I have put myself in your hands, I am no longer responsible: it is you who decide my fate.

I did wrong to speak to you, and you were right to castigate me for doing so. I should have continued my cherished plan, which was to so improve and reform that eventually I would gather the courage to address you as a suitor. But I must confess to another base impulse—jealousy. I saw you surrounded by eligible gentlemen, all entranced like myself by your beauty and accomplishments. I knew that time was required to alter the fixed dislike that made you shun me; I feared more and more that that time would not be granted me, however earnest were my efforts to rise in your estimation. My outpourings at the opera came from an overcharged heart that

*could bear no more. You will say this proves me
impatient, and I can only reply that love is impatient
and impetuous, or it is not love at all.*

*I do not know where to turn. I will not meet you
in society. Unable to hide my emotions, I would
incur your displeasure, which I cannot face. But
neither can I live utterly cut off from you. Mademoiselle, I beg you to reply to this letter, even if it
is to upbraid me as you have done already. Meanwhile the world hears nothing of you from my lips
but the deepest reverence.*

*Your abject servant
Alain de Ronseul*

She was trembling. To receive this, when she longed
for another letter entirely, stretched her endurance to
breaking point. The language did not conceal his aims:
he had stopped asking for public recognition and was
after a secret correspondence. When he had compromised her sufficiently, the next step would be to
demand meetings in private.

She forced herself to read it again. He said nothing
about having applied to Father Berny, an item so insignificant to him that he had not even bothered to lie
about it. She wondered whether, after insulting her
intelligence and propriety like this, he would continue
to flirt with Louise in front of her; but it seemed likely
that he was in earnest about at least one thing: she
would not have to speak to him again. She sighed. It
gave her some respite, for even a practised libertine like
Ronseul would scarcely expect her to be panting to
reply to his latest effusion. She would wait a week,
neither bothering about him nor mentioning this to
Louise, and see what solution she could find at the end
of it.

She went upstairs to her bedchamber, unlocked the
desk and put the letter into a drawer with his first. But
after she had turned the key, she sat down and thought
again. What if, during the delay, his stamina failed him
and he broadcast her story anyway? Panic took over
for a moment, then she put her head in her hands and

considered him again. It occurred to her suddenly that there was a rivalry and hatred here that went beyond his professed love. She was his ostensible target, but what if the real one were her guardian himself? Ronseul already had it in his power to make the count's return to Paris highly embarrassing. But dishonouring his ward was a greater blow by far, and if he thought he could deal it, he would surely be prepared to hold his hand on the other issue.

At this point, Mathilde knocked and entered. This was the very young woman whom she had dragged all the way to Los Pasajes and then abandoned to the wrath of Madame de Chercy, but despite these trials Mathilde had been prepared to return to the Rue Jacob and remain in Madame de Chercy's service until Viviane came home. In response to which she received warm and considerate treatment from her young mistress and they had become quite endeared to each other.

It was not usual, therefore, for Mathilde to have to conceal any of her feelings before Viviane, and this time she stepped quickly into the room in such a glow of emotion that she did not even notice her distress.

Viviane looked at her in amazement, for she was standing a yard away, opening and closing her mouth without uttering a sound, her eyes shining with urgency, her body quivering with an excitement that made her bounce up and down so that the heels of her little satin slippers beat a soft rhythm on the floor.

Viviane leaped to her feet and at the same instant there was a commotion in the lower regions of the house. She heard her aunt calling her in a high, breathless voice that sounded as though she were rushing along the landing.

'Is it he? Is it?' She almost shrieked the question at Mathilde; then, without waiting another second for an answer, she was out in the corridor.

Madame de Chercy was ahead of her but could not move as fast. With shameless haste Viviane dashed to the head of the stairs and looked down past her hurrying form.

He stood at the foot gazing up, a smile on his face that recalled at once a sunny day in Philadelphia, when he had thrown his wreath of greenery to her in a parody of the knight bestowing his token on his lady, his eyes alive with hilarious mockery and also with something else that flashed at her now as she whirled around the newel post at the top and plunged down the stairs towards him.

21

EXPOSURES

Viviane hurtled down the staircase, almost toppling her aunt, who stumbled, drew back and laid a hand on her bosom with a gasp.

She had intended to stop before him, to submit to the decorous, familial embrace they had first exchanged at Chester. But on the last stair but one she tripped.

He laughed, put out his arms and she fell into them.

It happened so fast that to keep his balance he half turned with her, lifting her off the stair. For one lightning second her chest was on his and her lips touched his cheek. She could smell the morning soap on his skin. He might have walked from the next street to see her rather than returning from weeks of travel.

Then he set her on her feet but kept his hands tightly gripped around her upper arms. 'Let me look at you.'

She gazed deep into the green eyes. 'I am well. I shall be well for ever.' But she had no idea what she was saying. The fingers of one hand were hooked through the wide buttonhole on one side of his coat and she wanted to tug him towards her, to restore the touch she ached for. 'I have waited so long.'

'Never again.'

Then Madame de Chercy was with them, and at once he put out a hand to her, drew her in and kissed her cheek, and all three dissolved into a vast embrace. Locked close within one of his arms, Viviane pressed her face into his shoulder and heard, close to her ear, her aunt's broken exclamations as she clung to him. Then Madame de Chercy began to cry, and at this he loosened his hold and bent his head to look fondly into her face. 'Dear Madame.'

Her aunt stepped back and said in a shaky voice, 'I don't think I shall ever get over how you left, without warning. With scarcely a word. *That* is what made it so hard.'

He glanced from her to Viviane and put his palm

over her fingers that were still wound into his coat. 'I knew I should meet with reproaches.'

Then he startled them both by falling to his knees before them. His hand still held Viviane's and with the other he clasped Madame de Chercy's. When he raised his eyes there was laughter in them, under a sheen of tears.

The servants by now had all gathered irresistibly in the hall, but he ignored the astonished faces around him and gazed up at the two women. 'Forgive me, I beg you. I have never done anything right in my life. But pardon me, and I am a new man.'

Madame de Chercy gave something between a laugh and a sob. 'Nephew, get up, for heaven's sake. This is ridiculous.'

'Only if I have your forgiveness.' He was speaking to Viviane. She felt the vibrant pressure of his hand on hers as he said the words.

She whispered, 'Nothing that you do could ever injure me. I know that.'

Madame de Chercy dried her eyes and said with a passable return of her old briskness, 'You are forgiven, Monsieur, and have leave to rise.' When he did so, she would have steered him at once into the drawing room, but he glanced at the crowd around them and the servants took this cue to come forward and give him their welcome.

He had a quick word and a smile for each, and when he came to Mathilde it broadened to a grin. 'When I last saw you, I am afraid I was roaring like a trooper. Dare I ask pardon for *that*?'

Mathilde was pink with embarrassment. 'Monsieur, I have followed instructions and forgot it altogether. And you have always been the most generous master, absent or no. We are that glad to see you home, Monsieur.'

Madame de Chercy could not wait to shepherd him into the drawing room, to ply him with refreshments and questions about his journey, to sit and drink in the sight of him—fresh, healthy, unscathed, unwearied by weeks at sea and the coach journey across the rough roads of France, which he seemed to have taken at breakneck speed.

To speak to him at all, Viviane was constantly forced to interrupt her aunt, but every time his eyes met hers she found it hard to recall what had been burning on her tongue the second before. Even while speaking to her aunt, he could not help often looking her way. So much was going on behind the green eyes that she could not interpret all of it, but she knew he had been overwhelmed by her greeting and he had no desire to go anywhere or do anything but be in this room. Nonetheless her mind faltered, even as he sat and smiled at her. He was here, but he was not yet hers. And the longer this first meeting went on, the more she could feel the old existence softly closing in around them again.

One of her earliest questions was about Mathilde. 'I do not understand, she spoke as though you employed her.'

'Mademoiselle,' her aunt said for him, 'your uncle has paid Mathilde's wages since the day you set foot in this house.'

She stared at him. 'I owe you so much. How can I ever thank you for all these hidden favours?'

'You do so now.'

Her heart soared: surely he meant that it was enough for him simply to be with her? But if this was his message, it passed quite unnoticed by her aunt, who continued talking almost in her old comfortable way, altered only by the joy that sprang into her eyes now and then and was answered by a bright glance from his own.

Her aunt said, 'You will find your household waiting impatiently for you. We have made sure everything is in readiness.'

'Thank you, that is too kind.' He turned to Viviane. 'I said in my letter from Haddonfield that you were not to trouble over that.'

'Your *letter*? I have had not a word!'

'No? My luck, as usual. I saw La Fayette there, quite recovered. This will thrill you: he has been given a

399

command at last. He has a Virginia regiment of 3000 men, whom he can drill all through the winter to his heart's content. They are already better shod and clothed than ever before in their lives, thanks to his bottomless bank account.'

'I am pleased for him.' Behind her smile was the dark knowledge of the news her friend would one day receive from his wife.

The penetrating green eyes saw every nuance of expression in hers. 'What is it?'

Knowing how reluctant Viviane would be to pronounce the words, Madame de Chercy said gently, 'I am afraid a great deal has happened to the marquis's family while he has been away. His second daughter was born in July, and she is healthy. But they have lost their first, Henriette. She passed away not long ago.'

'My God.' Appalled, he gazed at Madame de Chercy for a moment, then looked across at Viviane. 'You were fond of her. This is very hard.' His tender glance changed and he looked away. 'It will shatter him. When I think what distance and war does to people.' He thought for a moment, then said, 'The Lord knows how they will be able to end it. Washington has come close to despair. When Philadelphia went, I believe he thought it would be fatal.'

Viviane said hesitantly, 'I told Doctor Franklin how the English took the city, but he said, "Let us say rather that Philadelphia has taken Howe."' He looked up and gave a half-smile, so she continued, 'To be sure, it is a place that offers ample entertainment to keep an army occupied. Let us hope that they linger there well into spring and are less threat to Washington in consequence.'

'Amen to that. They've got naval company now as well. You'll be sorry to hear the English smashed their way up the Delaware last month and the forts have fallen.'

'I did not know. So the chevaux-de-frise were finally broached.'

'It's a wonder they held out so long. It's partly due to your efforts that they did.'

'I don't suppose you know the casualties at Fort Mifflin? Capitaine de Fleury?'

'He soldiers on. He's a good man, I hear.' Then he said, 'And how is Franklin?'

'Transformed, since Saratoga. He has got through to Versailles, though he has been granted no audience yet. Last time I saw him he told me a secret: in July a preliminary agreement was signed, promising a treaty. If the King honours it, there may even be a breakthrough in the new year.'

He closed his eyes. 'Thank Christ. And we never thought to see the day.'

Viviane gave a sudden cry and the others both looked at her in alarm. 'It is *Christmas Day*! I dreamed that you would come back at Christmas, and here you are.' She rose, ran across the room, put her hand on his where it lay on the arm of the chair, and bent to kiss his cheek again. 'May the blessings of the season be yours.'

He gave a soft, startled laugh, and when she straightened she could hardly see him as she looked down and tried to catch his expression.

'If you cry, Mademoiselle de Chercy, you will be the undoing of us all. And I object to having tears streaming down my face when I call for the presents I have brought home.'

'Your luggage!' cried Madame de Chercy in her turn. 'I did not even instruct anyone to bring it in.'

The major-domo, who had clearly been hovering in the hall, popped his head into the doorway at this point and announced that the count's effects had been deposited in the blue room as always.

When Viviane returned to her seat they all looked at one another and laughed.

Jules stayed three days at the Rue Jacob then persuaded himself to move back to the Rue Richelieu. It was a time of unaltered bliss. He and his ward went everywhere together: to see Franklin, to comfort Madame de La Fayette as best they could, to bring salonnières

401

like the Marquise du Deffand up to date with the American War.

He was sought after to an extent he would have found irritating at any other time, but somehow he sailed through the engagements without having to think twice about the myriad questions, some of them bordering on the cretinous, which society saw fit to pose. He was fêted, and he noted cynically that the gently born women paid him more attention than before he went away. He was courteous to them all, and even consented to take his ward's friends driving in the Bois de Boulogne when he would have much preferred to take her alone.

One day when he conveyed Mademoiselle de Billancourt with them, they passed a carriage going the other way and he saw the Baron de Ronseul again for the first time. Neither vehicle stopped, but they were moving slowly enough for Jules to see the expression on the baron's face as he recognised them. A look of deep chagrin instantly marred the baron's features and he gave them no greeting. Jules observed both his companions and saw a satisfied smile creep over Mademoiselle de Billancourt's face, while his ward remained quite expressionless and did not meet his eye. The Billancourt's dangerous dalliance with Ronseul was obviously still going on, and his ward liked it as little as she had before she went away.

It took him a while to get her talking openly again, but he managed it before the drive was over and he felt the familiar warmth steal into his chest as she smiled back at him. He was under a spell that he could not break. But she could, at any moment: she bound him with a gossamer web that could be ripped apart by one twist of her fingers. It was a constant marvel to him that the gesture was not made.

At times like these he believed for a few ecstatic seconds that he might be able to take his place beside her in the role that had always been denied him. But to do so would mean revealing the truth, and with that thought his familiar pain returned. How could he justify breaking the silence of twenty years, when

he had no idea how it might alter him in her eyes—
and worse, when he knew exactly what it would do to
her image of her mother? For as long as he carried out
the duties of guardian given him in Robert de Chercy's
will, he honoured the two people he had wronged long
ago. Out of respect for their memory, he had been able
to continue referring to Viviane de Chercy as his niece.
And though he had never been able to lodge that
phrase in his own mind, he had managed despite everything to think of her as his ward. At last, incredibly,
she had allowed him to offer her his protection; he had
no right to ask for more. And if in some mad moment
he did, he must lay all the secrets of the past before her
clear scrutiny. He owed her nothing less.

Viviane was at the opera again, and in a state of intolerable tension. The last week had been the most
confusing time of her life. She had expected that every
moment she spent with her guardian after his return
would contain unmixed joy; but love and desire over-
took her so strongly that sometimes she could scarcely
speak to him, and when she could not be with him, or
others interrupted their meetings, it threw her into an
agony she had never experienced in all the long weeks
of his absence.

She was useless at home or in society because she
could not stop thinking about him, as though by filling
her mind with his image she could will him to do the
same with hers. She could not bear to go out and talk
to other people, because while she was concentrating
on him less, she had the superstitious idea that he
might escape from her altogether, break free from the
clinging power of her thoughts.

Apart from him, she had no energy, no desire for
company. Sometimes on her way upstairs she would
lean against the banister rail, stopped short by a
longing that was like the onset of illness. She wanted
to faint, to lose consciousness, to escape this weird
suffering for an instant.

Then it would be time to see him again, and she

would spend hours getting ready, worrying over her clothes, working at her appearance, afraid that she would look too young, too staid, too bold, too elegant, overdecorated, too eager, too stiff ... When they met she felt she was behaving as unnaturally as a nervous young woman at her first ball. Everything she said sounded wrong, nothing he said could satisfy her longing. She did not want to talk, she wanted to be alone with him, to touch him, look into his eyes.

She was appallingly unsure, however, whether being alone with her held the same luminous importance for him. When others interrupted their conversations, she could not detect in him the anger and dismay that at once silenced her. Now, just at the time when she had believed they were close at last, she began to fear she did not know him at all.

The evening at the opera had taken on enormous significance in her mind. Of all things, music had the greatest power to draw them together. The deep emotions that drove him and that he so rarely allowed her to see were closest to the surface when she played to him at home, and it had become one of her fantasies that he would come to her as she sat at the pianoforte, kneel beside her, take her in his arms.

She went to see another performance of *Orpheus* trembling with anticipation, and was instantly disappointed. When their party entered the box, Madame de Brissac, who had issued the invitation, asked her to sit in the first pair of seats and then plumped herself down beside her. The count sat behind, speaking little, and hardly ever to Viviane, and she found herself staring blindly at the stage, deaf to the music, tense, straining to hear the slightest sound from him.

For she learned, the moment she sat down, that the diva who was to sing Eurydice was Gina Farrucci. It would be the first time he had heard her perform since the days of their liaison, and Viviane was racked with tormenting questions. She wondered whether he was glad not to be sitting in the front row, so he could see la Farrucci without being seen and have perfect freedom to admire her charms as he had done for the months he knew her. During the performance others chatted softly around them but he was silent, and she imagined him enthralled, recaptured by art and the artist.

At the end of the first act he excused himself and disappeared. She feared the worst: he had gone backstage, entranced all over again by la Farrucci, hoping that her former regard would win him entry to her dressing room. She was so desperate that she had a frantic urge to escape and go home, but the party with her were very merry and there was no prospect of escape—she had come with Madame de Brissac and could only leave with her.

The next act began, and conversation continued almost unabated. Though the orchestra was good, no one was impressed with the singer playing Orpheus, and Eurydice was not yet due to reappear. Eventually all but Madame de Brissac drifted away from the box in response to other friends, then she grew restless too, and decided to visit the loge next door.

'I shall be gone only a few minutes—the viscountess has just beckoned me, and we have something to say to each other. You will not mind for such a short while?'

Viviane shook her head, praying that she would go quickly. Everything had become intolerable. The beautiful music, the soft lights, the murmur from the audience, the brilliance of the clothes and jewels in the theatre, all oppressed her. Tears came, and although she kept her eyes towards the stage she could not see or hear the opera. She could only feel her own misery.

Then a hand closed over hers. She turned and found her guardian sitting beside her. When their eyes met, she saw that his expression was open and tender. Did he know what she felt, or did he think the music had moved her?

He began to take away his hand, but she tightened her fingers. A question sprang into his eyes but he did not speak. He had believed her under the spell of the music; now he was not so sure. But he left her his hand.

Under one impulse, they looked down at the stage. He was leaning towards her and did not draw back. He was so near she could feel the warmth of his skin; she would only have had to turn her head for her lips to brush his cheek. At the edge of her gaze the flash of his silk collar, caught between the dark coat that sat smoothly across his square shoulders and the golden tone of his tanned face, burned like white fire. She felt the nearness of his body all down her side—she was in two halves, one hot, the other shivering. His hand was warm over hers and she felt its pressure; he was waiting for her to speak, but she could not without saying, 'I love you.'

The place was a blur, but the music intensified and ran through her veins so strongly that she lived rather than heard it, and more overpowering than the music was the sensation of his hand around hers. The tears dried on her cheeks and she did not speak until he turned to her again. Still looking at the stage, afraid that the tenderness in his eyes would be gone when she raised hers, she said, 'Where have you been?'

'In the loge opposite, didn't you notice? Then I saw you crying.'

'I always cry in this opera.'

'Is that all?'

She looked up then, and was overwhelmed, as though he were gazing into her soul. The glow from the stage below lit up the green of his eyes, but the expanded pupils and the thick, black lashes made them dark and soft.

She whispered, 'I was lonely.'

'Why? Because you were alone in a box for two minutes?' When she did not speak he answered himself. 'No.' His lips compressed slightly. 'Someone is making you unhappy.'

She nodded.

'Tell me.'

'I cannot.' She wanted his hand in hers, she wanted him close, she did not dare say anything that might drive him away.

Then there were voices outside the box. He held her

eyes. 'I wish you would confide in me. Your happiness means more to me than anything on earth.'

It was all she could do not to close the warm, pulsating distance between them and press her lips to his. She could not speak.

At any moment the others would surge back into the box. He drew a quick breath and said deeply, 'I came tonight to be with you. I had no idea about the opera, the singers, who else would be here. They mean nothing. You are my life.'

There was a burst of voices around them and all the others returned. He released her and sat back, but she was still drowning in his gaze. She whispered, 'Will you come to me tomorrow?'

He rose, bowed, and took her hand again in both of his, bringing it to his lips in a swift gesture that sent a shiver through her body. He just said, 'Tomorrow,' and after a last look into her eyes walked out of the box, leaving the rest of the company staring after him.

At the breakfast table next morning two messages were delivered, one for Madame de Chercy and the other for Viviane. Her aunt sat gazing at the page in her hand for some time, then lowered her *pince-nez* and gave Viviane a long, contemplative look.

'Your guardian has invited himself to dinner today, at three. This is in his usual enigmatic style, but he does mention something about wanting to ask my advice. Have you any idea what that may refer to, Mademoiselle?'

Viviane felt herself blushing as she met the inquisitive, kindly gaze. 'I . . . I think we should wait and see, Madame.'

Her aunt put both letter and *pince-nez* on the table. 'Perhaps. And what does Mademoiselle de Billancourt have to say?'

'She invites me there this morning. I should like to go, unless you have other plans. I need an occupation.'

'By all means, my dear. But do not be late returning, it would be disobliging to your uncle.' The innocent tone in which this was said did not fool Viviane and she rose, blushing more fiercely than before, and escaped quickly from the room.

When she had been an hour or so at Louise's, however, she began to feel that she might have been better to languish at home until he came. There was an awkwardness between her and her friend, for which she partly blamed herself: as long as she did not confess to Louise about the baron's pursuit, she felt as though she were deceiving her. Louise also had a tendency to make teasing remarks about the count, who was now a grand favourite, and she was always pestering Viviane to bring him with her to supper, and speaking of him on the slightest of occasions. Today she went even further.

'Do you know, I have fallen for your guardian so catastrophically that I am thinking of changing allegiances? I have not thought of A de R in a whole day.'

They were in the music room and Viviane was sitting beside Louise's harp, idly running a forefinger across the strings. She stopped and looked up at this comment, and there was no disguising her reaction.

Louise's eyes widened. 'What, I am not to joke about him? Have you thought, dearest, that I may soon not be able to laugh about him at all? And you are not to tell me he is too old for me: angels are ageless.'

This could not go any further. 'Louise—' her lips quivered and she stopped. 'Louise, I am in love with him.'

The effect on her friend was so sudden that she got to her feet. An expression of the utmost dismay crossed Louise's face, followed almost instantly by jealous anger. Speechless, she paced the carpet in the middle of the floor in a hasty circle, then came to a stop before Viviane, her hands on her waist.

'You are not serious. This is unthinkable.'

'I love him. And I think he loves me.'

'*Jésu*, what am I to *say* to you?' Then she knelt quickly down at Viviane's feet, looking up imploringly. 'I must persuade you out of this. Please hear me, for the sake of our friendship.'

She was so much in earnest that Viviane was moved.

'I know you care about me. But say what you like, I love him for good.'

Louise put her hands over her face and said determinedly through her fingers, 'Let me try; let me at least try, rather than—' She took a breath and began again in a strangled tone, 'You can hardly deny that he is old enough to be your father.' Viviane would have protested at this abrupt reversal, but Louise rushed on, 'I shudder to say this, but heaven knows, there may be young women and men in America today who by rights ought to bear his name. Do you see anything in his past behaviour to rule this out?' Though Viviane looked at her with indignation, Louise went on, 'Do you expect him to marry you? My dear, he is not a marrying man. He has never courted even one lady of good birth. It would take a talented woman indeed to trap him into matrimony. I am not saying it could not be done, but are you the one to do it?'

Viviane gasped. 'I can scarcely believe you would speak of him like this. And to me.'

'Like *what*? I am trying to make you see the truth before you expose yourself. He is neither a domestic nor a constant man. He has spent most of his life cut off from family and society, and will go adventuring again whenever it suits him. How many more rides in the Bois do you expect to enjoy with a man who prefers the ends of the earth over Paris?'

Viviane rose. 'I thought it would be hard to confide in you, but I did not think it would hurt like this. It is best if I go home.'

To her consternation, Louise did not get up, but instead leaned right forward, put her forehead on the floor and said in a tragic voice, 'Then I must tell you. I owe it to my best of friends.'

'What?'

Louise got to her feet, her face solemn. 'Please wait. I have something to show you. Promise me you will stay here until I get back.'

Viviane sat down when Louise ran from the room. It was a lonely moment. She felt as though she were on a promontory, looking over an unknown ocean.

There were storms on the way, but she had no notion from where they might come; there was only a deep sense of foreboding.

Louise returned quite soon, with papers in her hand, but she did not open them at once. Instead she sat on a chair facing Viviane and said, 'My dear friend, when you contemplate spending your life with this man and putting your happiness in his hands, then I must speak. Cast your mind back: remember how much antagonism you felt towards him yourself, before you went to America. Forgive me when I say that when I knew you might be travelling with him alone, I could not help expressing doubts to my mother. I expected her to reassure me, but I could never have predicted how. She told me that she was convinced he would never take advantage of you. She said he would protect you, that he had the strongest reason in the world to do so. I did not understand her—and it was then that she told me, in confidence, of letters that were written to her by your great-aunt while she was staying with you both at Mirandol.'

'What on earth are you trying to tell me? Of course my great-aunt wrote well of him, she has always stood up for him, even against my worst criticisms.'

Louise looked down at the papers in her lap. 'Your great-aunt wrote these to my mother just after the count returned to Mirandol. You know how long and detailed her letters always are. They also reveal things about the distant past, about the time before your mother and father were married. Should I lay them bare, or would it be better if you never read them? Oh, my poor Viviane—but it would be a crime if I did not show them to you. You think of this man as your guardian, your uncle . . . but he came to Mirandol as a stranger, and brought into it sorrow and division— read the letters and see!—and he is neither your uncle nor deserves the name of guardian, which implies kindness and protection. If you want to know who he is, read these.'

Viviane sat back and ignored the outstretched papers. 'They were sent in confidence, to your mother.

If you are so intent on my reading them, at least tell me why.'

Her eyes round, Louise said with awful clarity, 'What can one say of a man who profits by a brother's absence to make love to that brother's future wife? Who leaves when the mischief is done, never to return or acknowledge what he has committed? What else can one conjecture, knowing that the bridal couple were married a week after Christmas, and that their baby, *though born on the seventh of September*, was yet healthy and well formed and suffered not from being born "early"?'

Viviane looked at her aghast. The words came at her like bludgeons, so heavy that she could not register all the damage they caused.

After a moment of silence Louise went on, 'How could you have suspected the truth, when neither your father nor your mother ever discussed it with any member of the family? Indeed, the secret was so well kept that of all the Chercy clan I believe only your great-aunt observed what was going on, and even she seems to have grasped only half the story.

'Read the letters and see if I am wrong. Never, never tell your aunt about this, and give them back to me directly, so I can replace them in Maman's desk.' She rose and went towards the door. 'I shall make sure you are not disturbed.' She hesitated, looking at Viviane dolefully, then said, 'If only I had never seen these letters, but I think I was guided. You have a right to know about the man you wish to call "husband", and to discover whether in fact he should be known as the nearest relation you have on earth.'

Viviane was in her bedchamber, dressed in one of her new gowns and elegantly coiffed, waiting to go down to dinner. She was seated before the mirror, staring into it with blank eyes that had so worried Mathilde that she had made the mistake of asking a puzzled question, and had been ordered from the room.

Everything hurt. It was as though Louise had taken

a portrait of her parents and ripped it up before her eyes, then thrown it in her face. After reading the letters, she had left them by the harp and walked straight out of the Billancourts' without seeing anyone.

Her aunt had been in another part of the house when she had got back to the Rue Jacob, and she had gone directly up to her room. She had walked the floor, unable to keep still, gripped from time to time by a hateful impulse to run to her aunt and confront her with what she had done by writing those long, descriptive, diabolical pages to Madame de Billancourt. And to hurl at her the vile implications they contained.

But she could not bring herself to do it, to sully her own lips with the words. For it was obvious that her great-aunt had not questioned—had never even rationally considered—the facts of her parentage. And if Viviane challenged Honorine de Chercy with her own letters, she would have to admit having read them herself, and also betray the indiscretion of Louise and her mother.

Every now and then she would halt in the middle of the room, crippled by pain, as the memory of one passage or another tore its way through her. Scenes from his arrival at Mirandol were mingled with images from the Christmas before her parents married. His visit to her mother's grave, on the very first day. Violette de Chercy at the piano, as he leaned on it and sang words that only the pair of them really understood. *I am jealous of my own mother*. The sleigh, his gift, falling to pieces in the stable at Mirandol. *Am I in love with my own father?* His white face as the ring was slipped onto her mother's finger at Christmas. *The sapphire ring that I sold, the blue of her eyes*. And hardest of all, his tears, as he learned how her mother had died.

At half past two a servant was sent by Madame de Chercy to ask her if she would be coming down before dinner. She said no. She almost said she was ill—for she was—and would not be going down at all. But she could not stay in her bedchamber for the rest of her meaningless life. There was one more ordeal to come and she must gather the courage to get through it.

Soon she would see him. Soon he would speak. Of what? Which truth was he about to unveil, of all the secrets that he held so closely within himself? There was a bitter taste in her mouth as she remembered his letters to her and the constructions she had so fondly built on them. Empty. What could she deduce from his behaviour to her since they sailed for America: love? If so, what if that love was *paternal*? A tenderness he had developed for her without being able to prevent it, an instinctive attachment he could not deny to his only child, even though he had left Robert de Chercy to bring her up and claim her as his own. A love without passion or longing, utterly unequal to hers for him. A love that now condemned her to hell.

The summons came and she went down. He rose when she entered the drawing room and gave her a look that to her new perception seemed troubled and nervous. She forced herself to accept the touch of his hand, to say a few words.

Almost at once he said, 'Are you quite well?' When she did not answer he turned on Madame de Chercy. 'You have not persuaded her down here while she is indisposed?'

Her aunt looked concerned. 'My dear, Mathilde told me you did not look quite the thing, which was why I inquired before. Are you sure—?'

Viviane said in a low voice, 'Kindly cease discussing my health. I am perfectly fit to join you.'

Dinner was announced at that moment, and after a second's hesitation they all walked in without further comment.

Then followed an hour of agony, during which Viviane could scarcely speak, swallow or hold up her head. He was very perturbed by her manner and visibly disappointed that he could not draw her into conversation. Meanwhile she stole glances at him and tormented herself trying to discern in his handsome features any resemblance to her own. She failed, but then she did not greatly take after Violette or Robert de Chercy either, so looks would not do for a guide.

After supper he asked her to play but she refused, sharply. By then she was exhausted. She hated him, for his dalliance with her mother, his deception of Robert de Chercy, the callous way he left them both and never came back, his unfeeling entry into her own life, the lack of trust between them from the moment of his arrival. She hated him because he might be her father. And all the time he was there within reach; she could have put out a hand and touched him, a word from her could have revived his tenderness.

Eventually Honorine de Chercy announced that she was retiring, and asked Viviane to entertain the count on her own. In the old days of their opposition, leaving them alone had been part of her campaign to get them over their difficulties. The irony of such a ploy at such a time hit Viviane with a force that drove her to her feet when her aunt left the room.

He took a step towards her. 'You are going? Do not let me keep you, if you are not yourself.'

'*Not myself.*' She said it too softly for him to understand. Then she closed the door and walked back into the room. She was facing him, but could not bring herself to speak.

He looked at her in confusion. 'I have never seen you like this. If you are not ill, then something else is wrong. Have I offended you in some way?'

She gave a sudden exclamation and half turned from him.

'I beg you to tell me. Speak, give me an answer, let me make amends. I would do anything for you.'

Viviane turned back to him. He looked at her with such supplication that for an instant she wanted to throw herself into his arms and tell him everything, as though he were her saviour and not the author of all her sorrows.

She managed to say, very slowly, 'That may be, but when we first met it was certainly not the case. I am sure you recall your conduct when you first came home—that is, to Mirandol.'

He gazed at her in bafflement. 'I do. It would be false to claim I could ever make amends for that; I know

414

I hurt you then. And you know how much I regret it.'

'If you want me to explain my feelings, you must bear with a little more of the past. I remember, when you came to the château, your disregard for me seemed to extend even to the memory of my parents. I never saw you visit their graves, though they lie close by our chapel.' This hit home: he flinched and went pale. 'You never spoke of my father, until I did so myself. And not a syllable have you said about my mother, except in the worst argument you and I have ever had.'

He cut her short. 'I see. And you are determined to argue with me tonight, all over again. But I will never argue with you on that subject. It is better if I leave.'

He made for the bellpull to summon a servant, but she prevented him by saying, 'I talk about my father and mother, and at once you want to escape. Did you dislike them so much?'

That touched him so nearly it brought him to a halt. He said with his back half turned to her, 'You do not know what you are talking about. You are also lacking in respect, to them and to me.'

She said in a harsh, challenging way that did not fit the words, 'So you loved them?'

He faced her then, with a new expression in his eyes that she thought was apprehension, and it pierced her to think how close they might be to a confession. He said quickly, 'What is this? What are you after?' And when she did not answer, after a time he said very low, 'Yes, I loved them. I hope you are satisfied. Am I permitted to leave?'

'Not yet. I have another question that I might have asked these last months, if I had not been a stupid innocent, kept in the dark all my life about the most intimate family details.'

She said these words in the hardest tone she could muster, but there was a pain in her chest that intensified at his reaction, for he gave a start, and looked at her in suspense and said not a word. She continued, 'You are the only person living who can tell me whether Robert de Chercy was my father.'

He sat down abruptly as though she had struck him,

and looked at her with horror. He forced the words out. 'How can you say this? How can you even think it?'

'I must. I know more about my family now than I did yesterday. They say it is a wise man who knows his own child. But I have a right to hear the truth from you.'

'What do you believe?' Then he put a hand over his eyes. 'God no, don't say it. I don't understand. How could you possibly—?'

She looked at him in anguish. He did not deny it. He sat there sickened and appalled, but he did not deny it. He was accused—he knew he was accused, though she had not said it—of fathering a child on his brother's wife, but his mind shied away from that and he fastened instead on the mystery of how she came to condemn him.

He said through his teeth, 'Who has put this in your mind? Or is it something from a warped imagination—is your old hatred of me so deep that you—?' He could not finish, or look at her, and he got up and moved away.

She could not let him think she had made up such a charge out of her own resentments, and in a rush she told him about the letters. He caught the facts as quickly as he had taken the first thrust of her condemnation. He started when he heard her great-aunt's name, gazed at her in disbelief when she mentioned the construction Louise de Billancourt had put on her letters then, as she came to a stop, his revulsion turned to anger.

'You think your vile question deserves an answer? When it was hatched in the mind of a prurient little schemer who throws herself at every man in reach? It is time you gave up her company, if this is to be a pattern of your future dealings. Though you loathe me, that does not give you the right to fabricate these calumnies. I cannot bear to speak to you.' His voice failed him and he turned away from her with a grimace. At last he managed to say, 'You shall have your answer. I never want to see you again.'

Then he was gone.

22

NEGOTIATING FOR FRANKLIN

Jules went straight to his house in the Rue Richelieu. Too sick to make it up the stairs, he walked into the salon and sat slumped in a chair. When his anxious servants came in he dismissed them and told them to shut the door.

He closed his eyes and the whole afternoon exploded at him as though shot from the mouth of a cannon. Absurd details burst in his mind. Red. She had worn a red dress. He had never seen her in that colour before: the colour of rage, of accusation. He recalled Honorine's kind eyes and her concern for the family: warm, confiding, solicitous, damning.

His mind traced its way back along a burning path. She would never have read the letters if he had not said he would speak. He would never have said anything at the opera if he had not heard the name of Ronseul coupled with hers the previous afternoon. Though it had been no more than a murmur between strangers in the corner of a drawing room, which ceased the moment he entered without him finding out what it meant, his loathing of the baron and anxiety for her had driven him to take the greatest risk of his life: he would explain his claim to protect her and at last have things clear between them.

He thought of her face, groaned, and tried to push the image away. The door of the salon opened and his major-domo walked quietly in and stood by his chair, about to utter some paltry excuse so that he could wheedle out of him what was wrong.

'Excuse me, Maître, but the valet found something on your chamber floor while you were out. He was going to put it back in the box with the rest, but he found it was locked.'

Jules gave him a dazed look. 'What?'

'It is a ring, Maître. I thought it best to give it to you, considering its value.'

The man held it out on his palm. It was the sapphire, which he had bought back from the jeweller with the rest of her pieces, months ago. He had taken it out and looked at it in the morning, assailed by memories, by dread, by impossible desire.

He put his hands over his face. 'Get out.'

After a moment he heard the slightest click on the tabletop at his side as the major-domo deposited the ring, then footfalls and the soft closing of the door.

He must go upstairs. Open another box. Take the last step back along the burning path. It would hurt, but not as much as having lost her for ever.

Next morning, two messages from the Comte de Mirandol were delivered to Madame de Chercy's in the Rue Jacob. Having read hers, Madame de Chercy looked across the breakfast table and said, 'I have just received three lines from your guardian, telling me that he leaves Paris today to spend an indefinite period at Mirandol. He barely sends his compliments.' She looked at the packet in front of Viviane. 'Yours looks more substantial. Are you prepared to tell me what it may contain, Mademoiselle?'

Viviane shook her head.

'Then read it in peace, and I hope it sheds some light. He has made you miserable, that is obvious. But until either of you vouchsafes an explanation, I shall leave you to deal with each other as best you may.'

Madame de Chercy rose and left the room with dignity. Viviane sat staring at his handwriting on the packet for a long time. This was her answer. Her eyes were sore, her whole body ached, but she must force herself to accept it.

There were two letters. One was on a fresh sheet and written in his hand. The other letter, enclosed within it, consisted of two discoloured pieces of paper, folded but with no name on the outside. She spread out the single sheet first.

Mademoiselle

Have the goodness to read this, then I shall trouble you no more. You hold me in abhorrence, and for this you have your reasons; but one, which you alluded to yesterday, is false. If your accusation touched only me, I might be able to remain silent, but it touches another, whose memory should be a beacon in your life, and who loved you. Whatever you may think of me, I cannot allow you to spend another day imagining evil of your mother.

I am thus determined to do what nothing else on earth could make me do: show another being the enclosed letter. You will see that it is faded and creased. That is because I carried it on my person for years. I eventually locked it away; in time I should perhaps have destroyed it, for it was written by a dying woman, whose confidences, offered in weakness and pain, must be held sacred by the one to whom she sends them and are not for the judgement of others.

You have formed your monstrous idea of my actions by reading letters never intended for your eye, which honour should have forbidden you to open, and which have brought you much distress. I urge you now to read a document which may itself do some violence to your feelings. If so, you must suffer this without reproaching me, for I show it to you with the utmost reluctance. Nor will I allow it to make you think less of the woman who brought you into the world. She has every right to your respect and devotion, just as while living she never forfeited those of your father.

I received this letter eight years ago. Less than a week later I received another telling me of your mother's death. I did not reply to the first. I have often wished that it had never been written, and just as often have been on the point of destroying it. If I ever dreamed that another person had seen it, I would have felt like destroying myself. Read it, Mademoiselle. I shall never discuss it with you, and for the rest of your life I charge you to keep as silent on these matters as I myself have for twenty years.

With shaking hands, she unfolded the second letter.

My dear friend
They tell me I am ill, but do not say how ill—yet
their eyes hint that I shall soon lose what strength I
have, and thus be unable to pen this in secret. If I
have waited a lifetime before writing to you, no
doubt I should keep my resolution. But tonight the
past comes to me vividly, and I cannot deny the
foolish woman I once was and the young man you
were. If you have changed as much as I, you may be
indifferent to this letter. I hope for your sake you
are.

Yes, I am changed. Since the day I married I have
been blessed with the knowledge that I can make
another person happy. And then our daughter
arrived, to set the seal on our joy. I have been lucky
in Robert, luckier still in having his sweet child to
love, and most fortunate in this life I have led with
two people whom I adore.

You do not know how much I wish this were true
for you as well. But when Robert gives me your
letters and I scan those measured lines, where you
tell us so much about what you do and so little about
yourself, I cannot read peace or contentment there,
nor anything of the heart I know you to possess and
which you conceal from us both.

Forgive me. This is why I write, to beg you to
forgive the thoughtless creature I once was. Yet I
have no excuses. From the time I met you at Mir-
andol I would not allow myself to think, only to feel.
To deny here what I did feel would be to blaspheme
against love. You were always more aware of our
dilemma than I, you were tormented by it once
Robert arrived, but I refused to face it. I rejected any
idea of the future. I lived only for the moment, and
I wanted you there. I could not conceive of your
absence; it already hurt when you were away for a
day—I would not imagine life without you.

I surrendered myself to events and to the choices
made by others. And you never understood such

blindness. I remember that day in the snow, when you tried to tell me how terribly we might hurt Robert, and I refused to listen. I even protested at how innocent you and I were, that no one could point a finger at our conduct, that we had hardly touched. And you kissed me fiercely, for the first and only time, and pushed me away. And I remember that you begged me to make the choice—to break Robert's heart or set you free—and when I wept and would not answer you looked towards the house where everyone was so merry inside, and said, 'You have already chosen.'

And then I let you walk away. I could not call you back: I was paralysed with misery. Wherever I turned I would cause pain or scandal. I had the power to hurt Robert, the count who already treated me as a daughter, my family. I wanted an answer to fall from heaven; and then I saw how selflessly Robert loved me. In the end I could not bring myself to go back on my word to him.

Before God, by the tenets of the church, I have been a loyal fiancée and a faithful wife. No stain attaches to your conduct or mine, and my thoughts and heart have long been turned towards my husband with devotion. But I cannot go to my grave without asking you to forgive a wrong that I once did to you and Robert, even though not a word has passed his lips on the subject. I have the guilt of putting a distance between brothers who love each other.

I do not expect a reply to this letter. I deserve to have this ache in my heart and to feel these tears fall. I have always been blessed with greater happiness in life than I have earned, and this should be my solace. In this solemn moment I pray that if you need solace too it will be given to you, and if I have caused you pain, that pain is long over. This first and only letter to you I send with love.

Violette de Chercy

Viviane took the letters upstairs to her chamber. By the time she got there she was crying, not with the wrenching sobs that had kept her from sleep the night before, but with helpless tears: for herself, for him and for her mother. Last night, when she knew everything was over between them, it was grief that prostrated her, for she loved him and she had driven him away. And she had wept for the loss of her illusions about her parents: she had worshipped her mother and adored her father, as though they were creatures without fault. It had hurt abominably to find out that they were human, capable of failing others and themselves.

Now jealousy of her mother dissolved when she received this glimpse of a woman approaching death, and read the loving words that referred to herself. Adoration for her generous, devoted father came back redoubled, along with self-reproach for having thought for one second that he might not be truly hers.

And at last, too late, she understood the man she loved. His passions, his self-mastery, his loneliness. She might have been the one woman in his life to respond freely and completely to him, but he believed that her love, which had opened amidst such storms and hardships that it had scarcely had a chance to flower, had twisted already into hatred.

Concealing any surprise they might have felt, Jules's household had set to with the packing and more than half completed it by midday. It was beyond him to go traipsing around Paris saying goodbye to his now numerous acquaintance, and he employed a clerk from his Paris agent to come by and copy out notes which he signed and addressed himself: *Regret that I am unable to take my leave before going down to the country, etc. etc.* He was just directing one to Benjamin Franklin when the old man himself was announced, whereupon he screwed the paper up, threw it in the fireplace and, leaving the clerk at his business, strode out of the library towards the salon.

Franklin had the look of having arrived in haste but, when he saw Jules, the quick greeting he had been about to make died on his lips. 'My friend, are you all right?'

'Passable. Do not concern yourself. Sit down, and pray forgive the chaos, I am off today for the Loire.'

'Oh.' Franklin took a seat, looking deeply disappointed.

Jules paused on his way to the door and raised an eyebrow at him. 'You have problems? Anything a glass of burgundy would fix?'

'No.' Franklin shook his head. 'That is, call for the wine by all means, Chercy. And if you can spare the time to listen, I am eager—desperate, rather—to seek your help on something.'

'I have all the time in the world,' Jules said caustically. He spoke the order and came back into the room, taking a chair opposite Franklin. 'Fire away.'

'Is Victor de Luny in town?'

'I do not know, but he is expected. Shall I send to find out?'

'In a moment. Let me tell you what he has done first. The fact is he has put us in an almighty coil by writing a series of damned idiotic letters back from America.'

'To whom?'

'Silas Deane. Let me explain: this morning I received a visit from a stranger claiming to be the messenger for an English agent who has intercepted five of Luny's letters, written during the campaigns in Maryland, New Jersey and Pennsylvania.'

'Stormont sent him?'

'No, Lord Stormont knows nothing about them. The agent is out to exploit this purely for himself; if I were to complain of him to the English embassy, it would be my word against a shadow.'

'Can a few letters from America do any harm? Stormont's men must have got their hands on hundreds by now.'

'Yes, and I wish them joy of them, for some of our correspondents are the dullest dogs. But my visitor has given me good cause for alarm. He let me have one of them, the mildest, or so he claimed.' He handed it across, and Jules ran his eye down it as Franklin carried

423

on irresistibly, 'I have never read anything more virulent or ill-judged. De Luny was obviously drunk with the idea of rebelling against everything monarchy stands for, French or English. His strictures on his own government make *my* hair stand on end; the reaction they would get from even the meanest member of the administration does not bear contemplating.'

Jules remarked, 'He does not confine himself to generalities, does he?'

'Read on. There is a telling attack on the "blunders" and "inconsistencies" of your Sovereign Majesty Louis XVI, a scathing indictment of the war office—'

'"Ill-informed and destructive of France's honour".'

'And worst of all, an outcry against the members of the ministry who opposed La Fayette's departure to the United States. Amongst other things he refers to the Duc de Broglie as a "coward". And this apparently is the least inflammatory letter!'

'Well,' said Jules, looking up, 'what does the agent want?'

'My dear Count, we are threatened with the release of all the other letters to the press. You see what a blow it would be. Here we are on the verge of persuading France to enter the war with us, and all at once we are faced with a disastrous embarrassment to His Majesty's government. La Fayette for the moment stands in the light of a hero, even to the ministry which opposed his going: but when they read these letters, written by one of his own aides, aggrandising the marquis and vilifying the Duc d'Ayen and the ministers of the King, they will turn on him in fury. Imagine the outrage at court if they read this kind of thing in the English press: a denigration of French policy penned by a stripling who claims to know more about the American conflict and foreign affairs than they do!'

'You are right. No one at Versailles will stand for being pilloried before England. And the King would hate being made to look as though he were badgered into the alliance by hotheads like Luny.'

'These letters will be a diplomatic catastrophe. They are bound to hold up our negotiations, just when everything was going well.' Franklin shook his head. 'At worst, they may stop France from ever entering the war.'

'I take your point. So what is the price?'

'They will hand the originals to us and keep them out of the hands of Lord Stormont for 5000 livres.'

'*Bon Dieu!* When do they want the money?'

Franklin looked embarrassed. 'I can raise it within a week, but the extortionist wants it in cash tonight. I suspect the haste is to prevent our mounting a protest or investigation.'

'Just a minute,' Jules said. 'Have you no clue where this demand comes from?'

Franklin shrugged. 'Naturally I had the messenger followed when he left the house, but the devil eluded my man. I cannot guess which of the English agents is masterminding this disgraceful bargain, but whoever he is, he has the upper hand.'

'What guarantee do we have that copies of the letters are not already on their way to London?'

Franklin said, 'They would have no impact unless the English could verify them. Stormont is a confounded nuisance, but he is a gentleman: he would never sanction a release of documents like these unless the originals could be produced. Which is why I need them to be given over to me and not him.'

'Very well. I take it you would like me to advance you the 5000?'

'Thank you, Chercy,' Franklin said, 'you are the truest friend we have. I shall give whatever guarantees you propose on behalf of Congress. I am convinced we must do this.'

'I wish I were so sure. How do we know there are only four more letters?'

'*Only?*' Franklin burst out. 'Would to God he had never written a line of such damaging rubbish! Look at it: his prose is a gift, all in his own brand of English, larded with the strongest epithets he could find in the lexicon. Every word has the most ghastly ring of authenticity.'

He paused for breath and Jules said, 'I agree, the

newspapers would have a field day. I should like to ask the author about the letters, just the same—I have a mind to go to the de Luny town house and see if he is there.'

Franklin put his head in his hands. 'Heaven knows, I am loth to line some villainous clerk's pockets over this, but I cannot take the responsibility of calling his bluff and telling him to publish if he chooses. We have come too far in our relationship with the ministry, and the United States desperately needs this alliance. It is my dilemma, though, not yours; if you cannot help us, my dear Count, no explanations are required.'

'To business.' Jules said, drawing his chair closer. 'When and where do I hand it over?'

Franklin looked up. 'I did not intend dragging you in that far. I shall do it myself.'

'And meet with whom? We have no idea who is behind this. What if it is a larger scheme, an attempt to compromise you? I have vast doubts about it. There is something even more wrong than what we see on the surface. I cannot work it out. But you must not go, not with negotiations at this point in Versailles. Just tell me when and where.'

Franklin took a paper and his spectacles out of his pocket, put the spectacles on and looked piercingly over them at Jules. 'After all you have sacrificed for us, I do not like asking you to do this.'

'Monsieur le Docteur, it is my money and I will hand it over. Take it or leave it.'

At two o'clock Mathilde was sent up to Viviane's room with the message that Monsieur Victor de Luny awaited her downstairs, alone.

Her heart sank. She had been looking forward to finding out how Abigail enjoyed life at the château and how his family did, as soon as he returned to Paris, but now she hardly felt fit to walk two steps, let alone spend half an hour listening to all his good news

Then suddenly she caught her breath. *Alone.* Did this mean he had something difficult to discuss? The

426

dilemma of Ronseul, which she had given no consideration for days, surged back into her mind. It was a week since the baron had demanded a written reply and she had not granted him one—what if he had started the rumour of the elopement? She went cold at the thought of Victor receiving such a welcome to the capital.

She asked Mathilde to tell the footman she was at home to Monsieur de Luny. Then she made a vain effort to improve her appearance and went downstairs.

When he turned from the fireplace as she entered, his face confirmed her fears: he looked nervous and overwrought. Her own looks shocked him, however, so he was the first to speak, ignoring the formalities as usual.

'Vive, you look terrible.'

'Thank you. You have something to tell me. What is wrong?'

'Don't you know? You have not seen your guardian?'

She winced and managed to say, 'Not today. Why?' With a jolt, she imagined what would happen if the name of Ronseul had come up as the source of the story. She steeled herself to hear the worst.

'He has just been to call on me, and a rough quarter of an hour I had of it.' He shuddered. 'I'm ashamed to tell you this, but I must, for I need your help. I'm sorry, let us sit down.'

Unable to say another word, she took a chair and looked at him with dread.

'You must warn him. He is a hundred times more likely to listen to you than me, so please lose no time in getting hold of him before he leaves Paris.'

She said in panic, 'Warn him? Against whom?'

'Let me explain.' He grimaced, then said in a strained voice, 'A crisis has blown up. It's all my fault. There is a secret agent who has letters from me to Silas Deane, and he is threatening to publish them in the press unless Franklin buys them back. I wish I had never written them. At any rate, Franklin and your uncle both judge that they would ruin America's credit with France if they got out.'

Viviane let out her breath, then took another and said, 'So this is nothing to do with—? It is just about these letters?'

'*Just?* It is the greatest calamity, and all my doing, and your guardian has lectured me over it until I have a headache!' He gave her an anxious glance. 'You are not obliged to do anything about it, of course. But there is something I think he should know, and you are the one to tell him, because I very much doubt if he ever wants to see my face again.'

Viviane looked down at her hands. She could not refuse her help point-blank, but he did not know that he asked the impossible.

After this short silence he went on, 'He is to hand over 5000 livres to the agent tonight, at a villa just out of town, on the road to Montmartre. I know it well, you pass it on the way to a cabaret called the Epée de Bois. He is supposed to go unarmed, but he will take weapons in his carriage. He has only to go to the door of the villa, and there he will exchange the money for my four letters, and be allowed to leave in safety. The name of the place meant something to me vaguely at the time, but I was in such a state I made no effort to recollect. When I did, I came straight here. I know the owner.'

'Who?'

'The Baron de Ronseul.' She started, but he went on, 'It always stands empty and he never uses it—his family bought it as a country house, but he dislikes the country and he despises hunting so he has no reason to go there. On the face of it, it might seem a nice deserted spot for a secret agent to arrange a rendezvous.'

'But you think there is more to it?'

'Exactly. For a start, Ronseul openly scorns the American cause, and he takes a perverse pleasure in inviting the English diplomats to his suppers—Lord Stormont himself went once. The agent could be using the lodge with Ronseul's knowledge.'

'Or the baron could be involved! Think: to whom did Franklin apply the moment he got into this difficulty? My guardian. And to anyone with the slightest knowledge of how the American cause fares in Paris, this would be a logical step. What if Ronseul has guessed that it will be he who goes to the villa?'

Victor nodded. 'The baron hates him. He looks daggers at the mere mention of the name Mirandol. He might plan to twist things so that your guardian can be named as a conspirator with the English.'

'Or he has something even more vicious in mind.' Her hands were clenched in her lap. 'When is the rendezvous?'

'At seven.'

'Can you not warn him yourself?'

'I told you, the last thing he wants is to listen to *me*! I have never seen him in that mood; to be quite frank I was glad when he left. You are the one to tell him, he will weigh every word you say.'

'I'm afraid my influence with him is not what you think,' she said miserably.

'Nonsense, surely you realise he worships you? Vive, if he does not love you like the very devil, then I am an Englishman.'

She got up from her chair and walked away to hide her expression, then paced up and down on the carpet in the centre of the room. She could not go to his house and face him; it hurt abominably just to think of the look in his eyes the night before. But there was another way.

'Can you sketch a map for me, and write in the name of the villa?'

'Of course, if you like.' He went to the desk in the corner and leaned over it, the pen scratching on the paper. 'It is Les Rosiers and the name is carved into one of the stone gateposts. Warn him the place is Ronseul's and the greatest danger may attach to the meeting. Tell him I shall go with him if he is prepared ever to speak to me again.'

'Will you be at home this evening, if I need to contact you?'

'Depend on me.' He gave her a self-conscious smile as he bowed quickly over her hand.

She looked into his eyes and smiled back. 'Tell me, are you and Abigail happy at Luny?'

'We could not be more so.'

'There is something I have been meaning to say to you, but we are so rarely alone. All those letters I once wrote you, I trust you have destroyed them? I shall burn yours, too. Though I regret having to do it.'

He stepped back and a dark flush appeared along his cheekbones.

'You do not ask why, but I shall tell you anyway.' She said gently, 'Dear Toto, despite my former ideas on the subject, you and I were never meant to be husband and wife, and I am heartily glad I learned that in time, if a little after you! But there are two of your many qualities which shine in your letters whenever I look at them—your courage and your generosity. Bless you for those, and accept my fondest wishes: may you be happy for ever, just as you and your dear wife deserve to be.'

The villa Les Rosiers was not hard to find; the only difficulty was persuading a cab driver to make the lengthy expedition out into the countryside along the Montmartre road in the dusk, and then wait in darkness until she were ready to go back to Paris. Though the evening was bitterly cold, the air was still and there had been no rain for days, so the well-kept road was passable. Viviane could see the threat of snow in the sky on this frigid first day of the year, but it did not fall.

No one knew where she was: Victor had left the Rue Jacob with the impression that she was about to approach the Comte de Mirandol, and later on she had been able to slip out of the house without telling Madame de Chercy. She had been cool and distant with her aunt ever since the morning at Louise's, so this sudden absence would cause further disappointment rather than alarm.

If the Baron de Ronseul were not at Les Rosiers, she would turn back to Paris at once, intercept the count on the way and at least warn him of the connection, if he were prepared to listen. She shrank from that confrontation even more than she dreaded tackling Ronseul alone. If the baron were there, she had no clear idea how he would greet her. She was about to find out.

It was six o'clock when she descended from the cab at the gateway of the villa and waved the driver on, telling him to stop just around the next bend, where she could make out overhanging trees.

The villa was built very close to the road, with only a few yards of gravel separating its tall gateway from three semicircular stone steps that led up to the front entrance. There was no lantern by the door, and at first she feared that there were no lights anywhere; but as she crossed the uneven gravel in the gloom she could see into both the large windows that flanked the steps, and she thought she discerned, in the furthest region of the house, a faint glow of candlelight. She braced herself: she had taken a risk by coming an hour early, but it looked as though there might be at least one person there to receive her.

It was not pleasant, standing alone in fitful moonlight, knocking at the door of an unknown dwelling. It was terrifying when the door opened at once, about a foot, and the tall figure of a dark-clad man instantly pressed itself to the gap. She managed not to scream, but her gasp woke the echoes, and she recoiled with a jump which nearly sent her back down the steps.

Then, to her consternation, the moment the gleaming eyes on the other side had summed her up, the door began to close again.

'Stop! Is the Baron de Ronseul in residence?'

There was a pause, then the door crept back to its former position. The voice inside sounded cavernous. 'You are alone?'

'Yes.'

'Wait.'

He was about to disappear again and close the door when she cried sharply, 'I shall wait *in*side, if you please!'

Another hesitation, then the door opened fully and she stepped into a cold, musty vestibule, quite unlit except for the candle the servant was holding in one hand. With the other he pushed the door shut and shot one of the bolts, which was squeaky with rust.

He did not look like a household servant; the dress, build and demeanour suggested some outdoor, physical occupation. He had no manners either, for without another word he was about to turn away and walk off to wherever his superiors were lurking.

'Just a moment! Is Monsieur de Ronseul on the premises?'

He stopped and half turned. 'Yes.'

She took an unsteady breath. 'Then kindly announce that a lady is here to see him. And you will oblige me by leaving a light. I am not going to stand about in the dark.'

He was thrown into confusion by this and stared around the dim vestibule, which had numerous sconces but not another candle, as if expecting someone else to come running out with a candlestick.

She sighed. 'Divide that candle—without letting it go out, if you please—and leave half with me.'

There was no need. A flare of light was advancing towards them from the back part of the house, for someone had taken up a whole candelabra and was walking swiftly with it, no doubt trailing wax along the invisible floors behind him.

'What the devil is going on?'

Viviane instantly recognised the peremptory voice: it was the Baron de Ronseul's. But he had no such fore-warning of her, and when he strode into the vestibule and saw her he came to a stop with such a jolt that one of the candles he was holding jumped loose, fell and hissed on the wooden floor, and he set the candelabra down with a crash.

He was stunned. Caught by the light so close to his white face, the blue eyes blazed like jewels. 'Mademoiselle.' Astonishment made the voice almost expressionless. Then he rounded on the man, who had dropped his own light, moved to the foot of the staircase and looked rather as though he were about to retreat to the upper floor. 'What were you doing inside? Get out and keep watch. Report to Maurois, don't bother me again.'

The man quickly unbolted the door and escaped. The baron bent, picked up the two stray candles, relit them and placed them in the sconces on each side of the door. Then he turned to look at her.

'My dear Mademoiselle de Chercy, a thousand pardons for such a welcome, to such a poor dwelling. If I had only known ... If I had ever dreamt ...' He stopped. Perplexity still overwhelmed him. Finally he said, 'You are here *alone*?'

She nodded.

Looking acutely self-conscious, he said hesitantly, 'To what do I owe the honour of this visit?'

Viviane was frozen, by the bitter chill of the dark, empty house and by a sudden paralysis: despite the fact that Ronseul's disarray handed her the advantage for a moment, she could think of nothing to say.

When she still did not speak, his expression altered and he said, 'Of course, how foolish of me: perhaps you do not see me of your own choice. Are you here ... at someone else's suggestion?'

Again she shook her head and he looked at her dubiously, making no move to usher her further into the house, but clearly unwilling for her to leave. This was exactly the kind of situation he must relish when he had been pursuing a woman as ardently as he had chased after her, and she expected to glimpse triumph in his eyes—but so far she had not seen it. Caution prevailed.

'May I ask, then, how you knew I was here?'

At last she found her tongue. 'I inquired of your household in the Rue du Faubourg Saint-Honoré, Monsieur, and obtained the direction.'

He said something under his breath. It sounded like: 'The devil you did.' Then his expression changed.

'You are shivering! What am I thinking of?' He took up the candelabra. 'Allow me to walk ahead of you and show the way. This place is barely habitable. It shames me to offer you so little comfort. But there is a room through here where at least you will be warm. Come this way, I beg you.'

She followed him out of the vestibule and through a large room, where all she could make out in the shadows to each side were the pale forms of pieces of furniture with dust sheets over them. A smell of mould hung in the chilly air.

Then he opened the door on what was obviously the breakfast room of the villa, for through the tall glass doors, only half obscured by drapes, she could just make out the paving of a broad terrace which no doubt led out to gardens beyond. As she walked in she was relieved to find it was in total contrast to the rest of the house: generous candlelight made it cheerful, the covers had been taken off the comfortable seating, a bright fire roared in the grate, the big table had been laid for supper, and on a lower table in front of the hearth was a large dish of dried fruit and biscuits, an opened bottle and a glass of wine, in which the flames maintained a fine ruby glow.

The baron's servants must have taken a great deal of trouble to look after him while he waited for the rendezvous, but they were not nearby, for she could hear no movement in the rest of the house.

He gestured towards a chair that was away from the door but not too near the fire. Seeing that the closest seating was at a respectable distance from it, she sat down, pulling off her gloves, loosening her fur pelisse but not removing it. Without missing a single movement of hers, he went to stand by the fireplace, where he had obviously been sitting in a high-backed chair. There he remained, looking at her with an appreciation which was steady but not impolite.

Despite his scrutiny she did not speak. She had rehearsed opening phrases throughout the whole drive but now found them all inadequate, for this encounter was too improper, too unfamiliar and much too dangerous for her to work out how to address him.

At last he said, 'May I offer you some refreshment?' She shook her head, then decided the direct approach would have to do. 'Monsieur de Ronseul, you must be wondering at this visit. I am here in dependence on your goodwill, which you once expressed to me most warmly. You told me you would consider my wishes: allow me to put one to you now. I should consider it a favour if you would let me have the letters Monsieur Victor de Luny wrote to Silas Deane from America.'

One of his earlier questions had revealed that he more than half suspected why she was there, but this did not prevent a grimace of chagrin crossing his face. He recovered quickly, however, giving a low laugh. 'This is frankness unparalleled even from you, Mademoiselle.' He sat down in his chair and glanced into the fire, his face overspread with a glow from the flames that made him look as though he were blushing. After a long pause he said, 'At the risk of offending you, may I point out a distinction? It is true, painfully true, that your wishes, your desires and your attitude towards me have held sovereign power with me for a long time. But not all my considerations are bound up with you, and if I claimed that they were, I would destroy whatever vestige of respect you may have for me as a man.' He looked up. 'It is not my purpose or my inclination, Mademoiselle, to give you those letters.'

She went to speak, but he forestalled her. 'Will you *frankly* tell me on whose behalf you make this request?'

'No one knows that I am applying to you. I make it myself, for the good of the United States.'

His eyes widened at the confession that she was here without anyone else's knowledge, then flicked to the clock on the mantelpiece, which showed that it was only minutes after six. He sat back and went on coolly, 'Let me make this quite clear: I have no interest in the good, or indeed the existence, of the United States. I am not a republican and I do not believe America should be a republic. The bargain over these letters was set up with my consent, but before I had time to think it through. Now that they are in my possession, I am not even sure that I wish to hand them over to anyone.'

'You want them to be released to the press? Why do such damage to a cause you care nothing about?'

He said impatiently, 'I abominate the form of government the Americans are trying to found. Let me elaborate. In France, in all the countries of Europe, government is undertaken by gentlemen, who are bred precisely to do that—to rule. Tradition and our systems ensure that the able members of the great families rise to power, prompted by their education, their upbringing, their sense of duty. Rogues and idlers like myself, meanwhile, attend to their own affairs and are overlooked, or discouraged from any interference in the way the country is run.'

He reached out to pour more wine into his glass and Viviane was so taken aback at hearing such a speech from him that she held her tongue. 'In America they are bent on destroying the traditions they inherited from the English monarchy. In future they will have no provision of talented men brought up to exercise government. All a man will need to give him a place in power is a large enough parcel of votes from an ignorant and capricious populace. In America, Mademoiselle, it is the rogues and idlers from the lower ranks who will rise up from the mire in which they are bred, and they will reign supreme, for there will be nothing to stand in their way. The consequences for that misguided country do not bear thinking of.'

She could not hold back any longer. 'I entirely disagree. America is led today by men of courage and principle.'

'Perhaps. Not for long. As soon as their ill-judged systems are in place, the downhill slide into mediocrity and ruin will begin.'

'Even now they are planning for their future. It will be founded on example and education.'

'Which they will not achieve.'

'The finest example is already there: in men like Washington and Franklin.'

He sneered as she named Franklin, but said, 'Washington serves his country as a war leader and the old man as a diplomat. America will be soon be borne on weaker shoulders.'

'You grossly underrate what is happening across the Atlantic.'

'And you, Mademoiselle, despite your first-hand experience, see it through rose-tinted glass.' Then he shrugged and said quietly, 'I am afraid all we can do is agree to differ: on this, as on everything else.'

Silence fell, then she started: at the edge of her vision there was movement behind the panes of the doors, as a bulky figure walked by on the paving outside.

He noticed and got to his feet at once; then, after a keen look out the window at his shadowy servant, drew the drapes right across with an irritated twitch of the faded velvet.

When he turned to her again she decided on one last try. 'I wonder if you would at least allow me to see the letters?'

He gazed down at her for a moment, then said, 'It hurts me to refuse you anything, Mademoiselle. Certainly you may.' Without moving from where he stood, he put a hand into the breast of his waistcoat and drew them out. 'If you care to look at the outpourings of a fool.'

She stiffened. 'You may dislike him, but you may not insult him to me.'

He took a chair by its gilded back, swung it close beside hers and sat down, placing the letters softly in her lap without touching her. 'I am jealous of him, for undeniably good reason, as indeed I am jealous of everyone who is close to you—even your guardian, though I know there is no love lost between him and you. The only friend of yours I do not detest is Mademoiselle de Billancourt, and that is because she talks to me of you.'

She shrank away a little, trying to disguise the movement by looking down at the letters, which had fallen open on her dress. She could see them clearly without even picking them up: they were scrawled in black ink, in Victor's round, familiar hand.

He said ironically, 'I need not ask whether you are

capable of recognising the gentleman's handwriting!'

He was too close for her to try to rip the pages to pieces or throw them past him into the fire. He was too near for her to be able to think very clearly, but two things were obvious: he was lying in wait with a pair of brutal-looking servants, and the bargain over these letters was less important to him than what he might decide to do when the meeting took place.

He was also too close for her to forget his extravagant claims to worship and serve her in whatever she commanded. How far could she push her influence over him, to avert the danger ahead? She raised her eyes to find his blue gaze caressing her. He put out one hand to take hers, so smoothly that she was able to quell the instinct to snatch it away. He contemplated it as he gently spread her fingers out one by one.

He said, almost in a whisper, 'The only favour you have ever granted me. Do I dare tell you how momentous it seems?' She held his gaze but could not force herself to speak. 'Do I dare hope that, though you came here for the letters, you came also with some pity for me in your heart?'

She read a message in the intent eyes: he had reached the point where he might reconsider the terms of the bargain. She had only to indicate that she understood. Her lips quivered, she drew a breath, then her throat constricted. She could not speak, but she left her hand in his.

At this an extraordinary tremor ran over his features. He said hastily, 'You really think me such a monster?' He dropped her hand, rose and went over to the fireplace, where he leaned for a moment looking into the grate.

Speechless, she stared at him. He turned and examined her face, then with a short laugh said, 'I have been at enormous pains to explain myself, Mademoiselle, but with all your sweet innocence, you will be the last woman in Paris ever to understand me!'

Then he glanced up at the clock and Viviane quickly gathered the letters into her hands, under her gloves. If he saw the movement out of the corner of his eye, he ignored it. Instead he looked at her again and said in a smooth, conversational voice, 'You are well aware that I have always organised my life around exactly what pleased me at any given moment. It astounds me that my philosophy is not shared by more people, and it has never caused me shame—until recently. But in the midst of the satisfactions that life has afforded me, Mademoiselle, I have sometimes been conscious of a lack. It seemed to me that there was something missing, something I desired but could not name. Not being an original thinker, on the occasions when this sense of privation struck me I was inclined to call it goodness, or truth, or virtue. But these are all poor words to describe what I looked for. Father Berny in his pious way refers to it as the mercy of God.'

She burst out, 'You are seeing Father Berny?'

He bowed. 'Since before Christmas. I was eager to tell you this on Holy Eve, but you punished me for my presumption.'

She said involuntarily, 'I never—'

He overrode her. 'Unfortunately the Father's phrases have no currency with me. The nearest I can get to a description of my search is to say I was looking for meaning. Inadequate, but it must do. And still I could not find it. Now, it would doubtless be very much more to my credit if I could claim I once learned it at my mother's knee. Or from my preceptor. Or in conference with devouts such as Father Berny. But I did not find it in any of those circumstances. In all my life I have clearly perceived it in only one unique presence. When I found it—and here my character fatally exposes itself again—it was in the person of a woman. I found it in you, Mademoiselle.'

There was no reply to this, so after looking at her for a moment with melancholy amusement, he went on, 'I found it exactly where I would also find the least trust and the most contempt. Yet I could not prevent myself from confiding in one or two close friends, merely for the relief of pronouncing your name. Nor could I help approaching you. And you shrank back. Even now, after all my efforts to conquer your

439

mistrust, even when you come to me tonight with that touching air of sacrifice, you still shrink from me.'

She looked at him in helpless confusion, unable to guess whether this was all lies, or whether, for the first time, he was allowing her a glimpse into his mind. Hot and uncomfortable, she shifted a little in her chair; the room was stifling and she felt prickles of heat under the fur around her neck. She looked into the pale eyes and read there exactly what was going to happen next. He had confirmed his indifference to anything but his own desires, he had candidly acknowledged that he repelled her, and he knew she was not with him now for the pleasure of his company. Nonetheless, he was about to cross the room with that wry, self-pitying smile on his face, sit down beside her and take her hand again.

She braced herself. 'Monsieur—'

Then it was over. With a wrenching grind of hinges and timber, the door beside her was flung open, to crash back against the wall.

In the doorway stood the Comte de Mirandol.

23

ALLIANCES

The door was thick and Jules had discerned nothing from behind it but the murmur of a man's voice. The knowledge that there must be at least two people in the room, however, had dictated the speed with which he opened it.

He took everything in with one glance and his heart gave a great thump, then faltered. *She* was here, in a chair just to the left of him, twisted slightly to gaze at him, appalled. And the man sent to meet him was Ronseul, who stood unarmed by the fireplace with one hand gripping the mantel, frozen in shock.

He lashed out at her: 'What are you doing here?'

She rose, pale, unsteady and tormentingly beautiful in the rosy light from the fire. 'I have Victor's letters.'

'How?' It was out before he even thought, and she took it like a blow. Beyond her, he saw the baron flinch.

Before she could answer he took three steps forward to stand beside her, close enough to sense her trembling. With his eyes still on Ronseul he said to her, 'Get out and leave him to me.'

'You do not understand,' she said, very low.

He said to Ronseul, 'What is she doing here?'

By now the baron, facing the inevitable conclusion that his henchmen were not about to come rushing in to rescue him, had managed to regain something of his usual poise. He dropped his hand from the mantel and rested it on the back of the chair at his side, prolonging the pause until Jules, straining for control, could hear the blood rushing in his ears.

At last the baron said, 'Mademoiselle de Chercy did me the honour of coming to see me this evening with a request.' Another pause, during which a mocking light came into the pale blue eyes. 'She asked me to relinquish those letters.'

'And?'

441

The baron raised his eyebrows. 'We were discussing the issue when you graced us with your presence.'

He looked down at her, to find she was gazing at Ronseul in suspense. More harshly than before, he said, 'Leave us.'

She put a hand on his arm and raised her face. He kept his eyes on the baron while she spoke in a soft but vehement voice that thrilled through him.

'I love you. Nothing in our past, nothing tonight or tomorrow can change that. I love you. And you love me. Look at me.'

He turned, gazed into the golden eyes and everything else grew dim. He could not utter the next question.

The baron's cold, bitter voice cut through the haze in his mind. 'Before you add insult to injury, you are to understand that Mademoiselle de Chercy has never deserved, nor ever known, anything from me but the deepest respect.'

She ignored him. She held Jules' eyes as she said again, in a firm voice that this time roused the still room, 'I love you. If you love me, come with me now.'

He looked over at Ronseul in time to see the effect of her words. A spasm crossed the white face and the baron shivered and stood staring at her until she followed Jules' gaze and looked at him too. The baron had a curious hunger in his eyes, but all he did was bow to her deeply and say with white lips, 'Adieu, Mademoiselle.'

None of them in that moment gave a thought to the letters.

Before he could change his mind, Jules took Viviane's wrist and, turning her with him, walked out the door. Neither of them looked back as he hurried her through the dark room beyond, the candles by the front door beckoning them on. He heard no movement behind them but his skin crawled with the thought of Ronseul changing his mind and seizing a pistol from somewhere: he was a hopeless shot, but the range was child's play. He looked back before they went outside: the luminous doorway at the end of the house was empty.

She did not speak until he had pulled the front door to behind them. 'Where are his servants?'

'No matter.' Jules's coachman had brought the vehicle to the gate as ordered and was sitting keen-eyed in the night with a rifle across his knees. Jules went forward and opened the door himself, then held out his hand to her. 'Get in.'

'I came in a cab. It is waiting further on, that way.'

'In you go. Boyer! Drive on, I'll follow. Where is it, under the trees?'

She paused with one foot on the steps. 'Yes. What will you—?'

'I'll pay the man off and get him to catch you up. You must not linger here.'

She got in, turned to face him and he shut the half door, clasping one of her hands hard in his before he turned and ran into the dark.

The carriage swung forward with a jolt and Viviane collapsed onto a seat, dropping her gloves and the letters on the floor. By the time she had picked them up and put them in one of the pockets at the side, the carriage was going at a smart trot. Very soon, however, she caught the sound at some distance of other hooves drumming on the road, and before long the cab was directly behind them. The coachman drew rein and, as the carriage slowed, she saw the running figure outside and leaned over to undo the catch of the door.

He leaped in, closed it and sat down quickly opposite her, breathing fast. After a moment he put his hands to his waist under the coat and unbuckled a long sheath knife, which he laid in the corner of the cushioned seat. Catching her horrified glance he said curtly, 'It was not needed.'

'What did you do to them then?'

'They'll live.'

As the carriage swayed and then began to roll more smoothly again, moving up to a cautious pace on the ill-lit road, she examined his face by the honey-coloured glow of the two interior oil lamps. His expression was restrained, his lips compressed, and there was a terrible trace of the way he had looked on the day of her accusation.

She burst out, 'Can you forgive me?'

His eyes filled with dread. 'For what?'

'For misjudging you.'

He sat back, confused, and digested this. Then he said in deep, earnest tones, 'I could forgive you anything. Except concealment. It has been the ruin of my life; it must not taint yours.'

She said at once, 'You may ask any question of me.'

Still with a look of fearful uncertainty he replied, 'Then will you tell me how you came to be with him tonight?'

'Victor rushed over to see me and told me about the rendezvous. After you left him, he remembered whose villa it was. He wanted me to warn you, and I told him I would.'

He said painfully, 'But you never came. Why not?'

She cried, 'Because I shuddered to think how you would receive me, after what I had done to you. I could not bear to imagine how you would look at me.'

He fell on his knees in front of her. 'Like this?' His eyes were wide on hers and she saw his love rise and surge in the green depths, unquenched, undeniable.

'No,' she whispered.

Then he closed his arms around her waist and kissed her, his weight forcing her back breathless against the cushions, his lips crushed to hers; and in instant response she clasped her hands behind his head and pressed him to her, her fingers tangled in his hair.

He released her mouth. 'I love you.' He kissed her forehead, her cheek, and said again into her ear, 'I love you,' his warm breath on her skin, his arms still tight around her body. He pressed his lips to her neck and when he kissed the place above her heart she gasped. Then he bent over with his face buried in her lap, his voice half muffled as he said, 'Tell me to stop. This cannot be.'

'*Why not?*' She tugged at him, both hands at his temples, trying to raise his face. He brought his fingers up to grab both her wrists, then sat back a little to look at her.

'My heart, I do not deserve you.'

'Monsieur.' She found it very hard to keep her voice

from shaking, but she succeeded momentarily. 'You once told me that I should wait until I knew what love was, until I found the man I could truly love. I have found him. I have chosen you.'

He brought her hands to his lips and closed his eyes. 'You don't know how vile it will be. You will be censured. You are my niece!'

Her hands twisted and she held his face between them. 'Not by blood.'

He opened his eyes. 'We shall be shunned. What will you do if all Paris is against you?'

'I shall go with you to Mirandol.'

The carriage swayed over a rough part of the road and he let go one of her hands to rest his on the seat. It brought his face closer and irresistibly she leaned forward and caught his lips with hers, snatching another kiss that ended as the vehicle rocked again. Next moment he was beside her, sweeping her into his arms once more. She clung to him, her hands digging into the cloth of his coat. With her mouth against his temple she said, 'I am yours.'

He kissed her again, long and hard. 'How can I let you go?'

'Never.' She wrapped her arms around him and pinned him to the seat with her slight weight across his chest, her forehead against the base of his neck. 'This is where I belong.' He tightened his arms and she sighed. 'When did you know? Was it when you came to me after Brandywine?'

He gave a low laugh that reverberated through her head and chest. 'A little before that.'

'When?' He did not answer and she could feel the pulse against her forehead quicken. She drew her head back and stared into the sea-green eyes.

He shook his head. 'One day I shall tell you. Not now.'

She was satisfied: it was the day of the parade in Philadelphia, when he had been unable to say goodbye.

With lingering, tender kisses she traced the contours of his face, rediscovering with closed eyes the features she had looked at with such longing ever since he came

445

home. 'It was in Annapolis that I began to suspect you. From your letters.'

He put one hand to her cheek. 'Great God, how could you guess? If only you knew how hard those letters were to write. If I had penned one sincere syllable, you would have taken fright.'

'I began to read between the lines. But it was not easy. And you were cruel, not coming back to France with me.'

He groaned and shook his head. 'I yearned to come back, and dreaded it. I imagined having to watch you fall in love, marry, never knowing.' He held her face between his hands, then ran them down her neck and onto her shoulders, bare under the opened fur pelisse. He murmured, 'I told myself your youth and beauty should be bestowed on a better partner than me. But it was no use, the only way out was for someone to put a bullet through me in the next showdown. I should have been glad of that except for never seeing you again.'

She wrapped her arms around his neck and pressed her cheek to his. On a dry sob she said, 'No! You are not to say these things! You are never to go anywhere, ever again, without me.'

He lifted her so that she was sitting across him and folded her even closer. He whispered into her hair, 'It is so hard to believe. We fought for so long, and every time it hurt like hell. You hated me too long to love me now.'

She shook her her violently. 'I shall love you for ever. It's too late, you cannot change that.'

With his hands on her upper arms he gently detached her grip a little so he could look into her face. 'I told myself I was coming back to Paris only to care for you as I had before, to protect you. I was determined to keep that resolution. But on the afternoon before the opera I heard someone say Ronseul's name along with yours. I was as jealous as Lucifer at once, and afraid for you. When I saw you that night I could not hold back.'

She traced the shape of his mouth with a fingertip.

446

'While you were away, he began to pay me too much attention. I held him off, without the least problem. All I lived and waited for was you.'

He caught the finger and kissed it, then said with hesitation, 'So, tonight . . . you hoped he would give you the letters, just like that?'

'I could not tell. He claimed that I had some influence over him, but of course he is such a liar. I had to see him before you did, I was so frightened of what he might do when you got there.'

He pulled her to him again. 'My dear heart! Thank God I came before time.'

She clung to him, her face in the hollow of his shoulder. 'I hate to give such a man the benefit of the doubt, but I do not think he would have harmed me.'

'He is in love with you. What kind of reassurance is *that*?'

Surprised, she tried to pull back, but he strengthened his grip. She said, 'Nonsense.'

He made a short sound, deep in his throat, but did not argue. After a while, he said through his teeth, 'God forgive me, I cannot let you go.'

She managed to pull back then and, gazing deep into his eyes, she said again, 'I love you.'

He drew in a husky breath, their lips met with redoubled force, then as his warm hands tightened around her waist she felt a wave of longing that threw her against him, and her mouth opened on his in a long kiss that sealed her surrender and his.

Towards the end of January, Madame de Chercy paid one of her regular visits to Madame de Billancourt. She did not take Viviane, for her grand-niece had not set foot in the Billancourts' home since the new year, and if they ever met in society the two young ladies remained on opposite sides of the room and avoided every chance to converse. The older women had coped with this situation by simply not referring to it; their friendship continued with its usual warmth and they shared their ideas on every other topic.

'How do the preparations for the wedding go?' Madame de Billancourt asked as they sat in the salon near the fire and as far as possible from the window, where snowflakes whirled softly against the panes.

'There is little to be done, since they want it kept so simple. Father Berny will marry them, and the only witnesses will be myself, Victor de Luny and his wife, Mr Silas Deane and Doctor Franklin.'

'And afterwards?

'The guests dine with us at the Rue Jacob, he and she will go to the Rue Richelieu until the next day, then they set off for Mirandol. The grander celebration by far is to be at the château; most of their planning has gone into that! I shall miss them, but they have invited me to visit them in the spring; in fact they have insisted that I spend every spring and summer at Mirandol. We shall see.'

'How can you contemplate that dreadful journey again? But you are so brave. I cannot conceive of marching into an inn—a lone gentlewoman—and commanding a meal, much less clean quarters. I never believe they know what it is to air bedding; I used to take my own sheets everywhere. Thank heaven I do not stir from Saint-Germain these days, the very prospect exhausts me.'

Honorine smiled. 'I must own I long for the change of season and another stay at Mirandol. It will give me the greatest pleasure to see the place joyful again. As for my nephew and Viviane, they are so happy they almost frighten me. They cannot do anything by halves; they used to be each other's torment, now they scarcely spend a moment apart. They smile at me pityingly when I suggest even the slightest moderation.'

Marie-Claire said generously, 'It is pleasing for them, to see how society has come round. Now that the first surprise is over, everyone has begun saying they predicted this match from the very beginning.'

'Yes, though fortunately no one seems to suspect they travelled together in America.' She decided the time had come to bring up a touchy topic. 'And it is no thanks to *some* that it is not generally known.'

Marie-Claire avoided her eye by looking into the fire and Honorine went on, 'My niece has told me that a certain gentleman knew all the facts: the correspondence with Victor de Luny, her disgraceful elopement, her visit to the United States. His knowledge was too complete, my dear Marie-Claire, to have been obtained from anyone except your daughter. It was this realisation, and other betrayals I can only guess at, that have caused their rupture.'

Marie-Claire stiffened and sat straight. 'As to that, you need have no fear that my daughter wishes to speak *of* or *to* her ever again. Her words to me were: "Viviane de Chercy has imposed on my friendship long enough."' At Honorine's movement of indignation she hastened on, 'I have her leave to give you her other news. Prepare yourself to be surprised. And before you are tempted to exclaim, rest assured that Billancourt and I are *more* than happy about it.'

Honorine looked at her in puzzlement. 'Tell me.'

'The Baron de Ronseul spoke and was accepted yesterday.' In the face of Honorine's mute astonishment Marie-Claire was able to continue more firmly, 'You know how long his acquaintance with my daughter has been, but apparently he had almost despaired of winning her affections and gaining her hand. Now that she has relented, he has very charmingly admitted to me how constantly he preferred Louise above all the females who have sought to attach him.'

'Marie-Claire, Louise cannot seriously believe that happiness lies before her with such a husband!'

Her friend snapped back, 'On the contrary, she told me this morning that he paid her the greatest compliment: he vowed that no other woman understands him as she does.' After a short silence she said in a quieter tone, 'My husband is more than satisfied with what the baron offers; indeed, few parents would be disappointed with such prospects. Monsieur de Ronseul pressed for her hand with the utmost energy. Billancourt and I cannot but succumb to a plea made with such generous ardour.'

About to speak her horror again, Honorine held her

449

tongue. Marie-Claire would never be able to discuss Jules and Viviane without a trace of the deep rancour that her daughter felt, whilst she herself could not open her mouth about the Baron de Ronseul without the certainty of being disobliging.

She finally said no more than, 'And when do you celebrate the nuptials?'

'On 8 February, two days after your nephew's.'

Honorine put out her hand. 'My dear Marie-Claire, there are a few things that have occasionally disturbed our friendship, but one issue we have never differed on—we both seek happiness for our families. Let us agree never to quarrel over what is best for them. I promise to listen to you whenever you confide in me, without reservation. Have I your promise in return?'

Marie-Claire pressed her hand gratefully. 'My dear friend, the young people henceforth have their own lives to lead. Let us enjoy each other's company all the more for that.'

On 5 February 1778, Viviane de Chercy received a final letter from the Comte de Mirandol.

My life
It is the eve of our wedding. I must write what you will not allow me to say when we are together. When I try to voice my doubts, you answer me with a divine smile, but still I do not believe. I have loved you, and you have loathed me, too long for this to be possible.

I was already trying not to fall in love with you before we left from Los Pasajes. After that, the only person I wanted to be with was you, and whenever I was I had to censor every utterance. During the times we were forced apart it got to the point where I could hardly bear even to speak to anyone else. Remember the last time I saw you in Philadelphia? On the journey to the Hudson I said scarcely a word to my companions. And when I did I revealed too much. I described you once to an Indian ally and he considered for a moment and said, 'This is the woman for you.'

It was like a blow on a raw wound. I growled at him, 'But I am not the right man for her.'

He held my eye and said calmly, 'That is for her to say.'

I love you, but I must not ruin your life. The whole of Paris pretends to approve our match, yet half of it surely thinks you insane to consent. I never cared about society before, but where else shall we hear the voice of reason? Speak to someone, ask advice, discuss this, even with your former friend Mademoiselle de Billancourt—there you will find warnings enough against me, if her recent behaviour is any indication.

It would kill me if you refused me now. But it is for you to say.

JR de C de M

Viviane awaited him that day with desperate impatience. He had promised to arrive at midday and when he was not there by a quarter after twelve she was tormented by the idea that he delayed because he was afraid of her response. She was so restless she disturbed her great-aunt, so she made herself wait upstairs.

The sound of a carriage in the courtyard, then his dark tones in the hall, sent her running to the top of the staircase.

Honorine de Chercy was at the foot, smiling upward. 'You may precede me, my dear. I shall not risk being bowled over a second time.'

With a stifled laugh, Viviane hurried down and arrived panting in the doorway of the salon. He was by the window; he turned and smiled.

With a firm step she walked across the room, straight into his arms, and kissed him. He made a quick sound against her lips, then hugged her to him with all his strength.

Set back on her feet again, she said, 'That is my answer to your letter. *Part* of my answer. The rest will take a lifetime.'

There was a movement beside them; she turned and blushed to see Benjamin Franklin. He stood a little distance away, a whimsical smile on his face.

'I take it my friend's letters have undergone a vast improvement. I recall, Madame,' he said aside to her great-aunt, who had entered behind them, 'that I once arrived in this very room to find you had been weeping over one of his missives from New Jersey.'

'Indeed, Doctor. And you cheered me up with your nonsense. You said how much you looked forward to hearing his conversation again, for it could not be worse than the appalling results his letters produced!'

Viviane smiled at Franklin and he said to her, 'Would that any writing of mine could call forth a response like yours. Instead I have an apology to make, in person.'

The count, who had kept his arm around her waist, said gently, 'Monsieur le Docteur has something to tell us.'

Franklin began. 'My dear Mademoiselle, allow me to express my deepest regrets. Mr Deane and I will not be free from official business in time to attend your wedding at Saint-Germain tomorrow.'

He must have seen the disappointment on her face but he allowed himself a tremulous smile as he went on, 'Only the most extraordinary event could keep us so occupied: tomorrow is the day on which his Majesty King Louis XVI signs an alliance between France and the United States of America.'

Viviane gave a cry, and delight shone at once in the old man's eyes. 'Yes. It is the greatest gift we commissioners could offer our country. Everything we have all worked for has come to pass: tomorrow the United States will stand stronger in the eyes of the world, together with France, and England must expect to bow before us.'

Viviane stepped forward and kissed him on both cheeks. 'With such an excuse, of course we forgive you for being absent tomorrow. Imagine how La Fayette will receive this news!'

'I have written to him already. He is at Valley Forge in Pennsylvania, in winter camp.'

Madame de Chercy shook her head and exclaimed, 'If only he were *here*. If only he had never gone!'

Franklin said with conviction, 'Madame, his influence on the course of the war has been incalculable. It is not too much to say that its first effect is the alliance we shall sign tomorrow. He has rallied attention across Europe and raised unprecedented support within France. Without him, the knowledge that hundreds of Frenchmen were risking their lives for Liberty in America might have meant little at Versailles; with him, the struggle has become publicly canvassed, acknowledged and finally upheld by the might of France.' He turned to the count. 'How can we ever thank him? How can we ever repay true friends like yourselves?'

'Monsieur le Docteur,' said the kind voice of Madame de Chercy, 'you are crying.'

She put a hand on his sleeve and his closed over it as he contrived to smile. 'And I congratulate myself, for tears are supremely appropriate to weddings. Tomorrow's day of union will be the proudest of my life.'

The count's arms came around Viviane from behind. 'And the happiest of mine.' The tremor in his voice told her that just then he was coping with as much joy as he could bear, so she saved for the morrow her promises of all their bliss to come.

HISTORICAL NOTE

Marie-Joseph-Paul-Yves-Roch-Gilbert du Motier, Marquis de La Fayette

Readers who are curious about La Fayette will be glad to learn that he weathered the winter of 1777–8 at Valley Forge cheerfully and earned the title of 'the soldier's friend'.

He continued to serve with distinction as Major General in the Continental army, commanding a Virginia regiment of light infantry. The French navy joined forces with the Americans under Admiral the Comte d'Estaing in July 1778, and in January 1779 La Fayette sailed for France to encourage greater French support. He returned the following year, when the Comte de Rochambeau brought the first French expeditionary force to America.

La Fayette was a valuable liaison between the Continentals and their French allies. He commanded the Continental army in Virginia and again distinguished himself at the Battle of Yorktown in 1781. When Independence was ratified at last in 1783, he returned to France.

La Fayette took his seat in the estates-general at Versailles in May 1789. The day after the fall of the Bastille in July, he was chosen as commander of the new bourgeois militia of Paris. In the early years of the French Revolution he was a trusted and respected leader: he spoke in the National Assembly on behalf of a bill to abolish titles of nobility and, after it was passed, never again used his own title. With Rochambeau he commanded the French armies as they fought off invasion by the European monarchies, but he ran into conflict with the new government during the Terror and in later years refused to support the imperial ambitions of Napoléon Bonaparte.

In 1805 Thomas Jefferson, then the American President, offered La Fayette the governorship of Louisiana, which he declined. In 1824–5 he made a triumphal return visit to his adopted country, where many honours were bestowed on him and vast crowds came to greet him. In the late 1820s he again took up public office in France and commanded the National Guard.

Gilbert and Adrienne de La Fayette had further children and a long, close marriage. He died in Paris in 1834, worshipped as a hero in France and America and revered as 'the man of two worlds'.

Born in New Zealand, Cheryl Sawyer spent several years studying and teaching in France. The experience inspired her to write her first historical novel, *La Créole*, and *Rebel*. Cheryl became fascinated by the Americans' epic struggle to forge their own nation while spending time in the hills of upper New York State some years ago. She now lives in Sydney where she divides her time between reviewing opera and classical music, and writing historical fiction. Her first short story, 'Asphodel', won the iRR's 'Write for the HeaRRt' Competition, awarded by iReadRomance of North America, the largest club for romance readers in the world. Cheryl's previous works include children's books and a translation of the *Journals of Jean-François-Marie de Surville*.

LA CRÉOLE
Cheryl Sawyer

From the exotic shores of Martinique to the dazzling
Court of Versailles, a strong and passionate woman
risks everything for freedom.

In the glittering world of 18th-century Paris, an exquisitely
beautiful and darkly mysterious Italian aristocrat who speaks
French like a native, matches wits with the intellectuals of
the day and gambles like a man, has the city at her feet.

But the celebrated Marchesina Di Novi has a secret that
would destroy her. Beneath the glamorous mask of an Italian
socialite is a runaway Créole slave from Martinique who has
sworn an oath to destroy her Master and free her people.
Now she is gambling with her life to win a fortune and her
freedom.

On the brink of victory, she falls passionately in love with a
man who by race, birth and rank is her enemy—the intriguing and handsome Guy, Marquis de Richemont. But she is
forced to enter into a deadly alliance with the scheming
Gervaise de Morgon, who threatens to destroy them both.

Against the bloody backdrop of the Seven Years War, La
Créole at last confonts her ruthless Master, her past—and
her future.

BANTAM BOOKS
ISBN: 073380 1765

THE LADY AND THE UNICORN
Isolde Martyn

In the grand tradition of Sharon Penman and Barbara
Erskine, *The Lady and the Unicorn* weaves medieval
fact and fantasy into an unforgettable tale of power,
passion and intrigue.

In 1470 the Wars of the Roses threatens to tear England
apart. Overnight a man can find himself set against his
brother or unable to trust the woman in his arms.

For Margery, the beautiful and spirited ward of Warwick
the Kingmaker, freedom is the only prize worth fighting for.
Disgraced after the philandering Edward IV seduced her, she
is determined no man will ever decide her fate again.

But the King has already set in train a deadly game of cat-
and-mouse that will pit Margery against his enemies and the
ambitious man who wants her. When he offers Margery an
irrestible challenge—to act as his secret courier to France and
help prevent the inevitable bloodbath the Lancastrians are
plotting—she is more than willing to risk her life to save her
family and win her freedom.

Caught up in a web of political intrigue and a dangerous
attraction to a man she should despise, Margery's mission
becomes a race against time to outwit her enemies and save
the crown.

BANTAM BOOKS
ISBN: 073380 199 4